A
Covert Affair

Also by Susan Mann

THE LIBRARIAN AND THE SPY

Published by Kensington Publishing Corporation

A
Covert Affair

SUSAN MANN

ZEBRA BOOKS
KENSINGTON PUBLISHING CORP.
http://www.kensingtonbooks.com

ZEBRA BOOKS are published by

Kensington Publishing Corp.
119 West 40th Street
New York, NY 10018

All Kensington titles, imprints, and distributed lines are available at special quantity discounts for bulk purchases for sales promotion, premiums, fund-raising, educational, or institutional use.

Special book excerpts or customized printings can also be created to fit specific needs. For details, write or phone the office of the Kensington Sales Manager: Attn.: Sales Department. Kensington Publishing Corp., 119 West 40th Street, New York, NY 10018. Phone: 1-800-221-2647.

Zebra and the Z logo Reg. U.S. Pat. & TM Off.

First Printing: September 2017
ISBN-13: 978-1-4201-4331-7
ISBN-10: 1-4201-4331-X

eISBN-13: 978-1-4201-4334-8
eISBN-10: 1-4201-4334-4

10 9 8 7 6 5 4 3 2 1

Printed in the United States of America

To Stanley Wolpert, Professor Emeritus,
UCLA Department of History,
whose History of India course
made a lasting impression

ACKNOWLEDGMENTS

I'm blessed to be surrounded by wonderful people on this grand adventure of mine. First and foremost, I'm grateful for the love and support of my husband, Ken, our daughter, Sarah, my parents, and my brothers and their families. Thank you to my marvelous agent, Rena Rossner of the Deborah Harris Agency, for her dedication and hard work on my behalf. My editor, Esi Sogah, is insightful, patient, and brilliant. It's my privilege to work with her and the entire Kensington Publishing team. Thank you to Ken and Russ for reading and speaking into the early drafts of this story. To my lunch companions, Lisa and Rebecca, thank you for listening when I go on and on about life, librarians, and spies. Added thanks to Rebecca for sharing her social media savvy with me. Friends, both face-to-face and Internet, you are the best. Finally, this long-ago history major would like to thank UCLA Professor Stanley Wolpert for bringing the History of India to life.

Chapter One

"Don't move," a voice said from directly behind her.

The library book nearly jumped from Quinn Ellington's hand. Standing alone in the stacks, she'd been so absorbed in its pages she hadn't perceived her stalker's movements. While she chided herself for being caught unawares, she was pacified by the knowledge that had she not immediately recognized the voice, its owner would be doubled over and gasping for air after receiving an elbow to the gut.

Two arms slid around her waist and held her tight. She smiled and said, "Now, why would I do a stupid thing like that?"

Chills raced through her when James Anderson kissed her neck and then straightened. "Ready to go?"

"Almost." She spun around, gripped his tie, and tugged him into a lingering kiss. She went nearly cross-eyed when she pulled back and looked at him nose to nose. "Now I'm ready."

He pinned her against the metal shelf with his body and gave her a kiss that had her knees buckling. He lifted his head and gave her a lopsided smile. "Me too."

Once assured her legs wouldn't give out from under her, she pushed away from the shelves and led him through the stacks to her desk. She set the book down and slipped on the jacket of her pantsuit. She couldn't wear jeans to work anymore, something she greatly lamented. It was one of the trade-offs when she accepted her grandfather's offer to work for the CIA.

James peered down at the book. "*Women of the OSS*. What are you working on?"

"I'd tell you—"

"But then you'd have to kill me. I know," James finished. "I'm pretty sure you can tell me without getting in trouble."

"Yes, yes, you're right, Mr. I Have a Security Clearance and You Don't," she teased. "For the record, I'm working on something pretty cool. One of the recruiters who visits college campuses is preparing a presentation that highlights some of the women who worked in intelligence in the past. She asked me to find some interesting stories."

"It won't be long before you're one of those women with interesting stories."

"We'll see. It'll be a while, since I haven't . . ." She was going to say, "Since I haven't trained at the Farm yet," but stopped. Other than the head librarian, none of her library coworkers knew the plan for her to become a covert operative. Only a handful of people within the agency did.

James nodded. "No matter what happens in the future, you already have one good story under your belt."

"That's true."

On their way out, Quinn stopped by her boss's office and knocked lightly on the door. At the muffled "Come in," she pushed it open and poked her head through the gap.

Linda Sullivan looked up from her computer. "Hello, Quinn. What can I do for you?" Six weeks before, Linda had told Quinn the information they collected, maintained, and provided to agency directorates was vital to national security and the safety of Americans around the world. By the time she left Linda's office that first day, Quinn was ready to do anything asked of her.

"I wanted to remind you I'll be away from the library for an hour or so," Quinn said.

"Thanks for checking in. You have an escort?"

"James Anderson." Without her clearance, she wasn't free to walk unaccompanied around CIA headquarters.

"Excellent. I'll see you when you get back."

"Yes, ma'am." Quinn pulled her head back and gently shut the door.

Quinn and James left the library and, after a short elevator ride, walked down a long corridor to their destination. They stepped into a front office and were met by a young man behind a desk. "Ms. Ellington, Mr. Anderson. Go on in. He's expecting you."

"Thank you," Quinn said.

Supervising Officer Aldous Meyers, her and James's Clandestine Services boss, glanced up from scribbling notes in a file. "Thank you, James."

"Yes, sir." He gave Quinn an encouraging smile before he stepped out and closed the door.

Meyers indicated a chair in front of his desk. "Have a seat."

Quinn sat as directed and waited. The acid roiling in her stomach was about to burn a hole in its lining.

He dropped his pen, folded his hands in front of him, and looked at Quinn with a penetrating gaze. "I hear from your instructors you're doing well in your unclassified training."

She resisted the urge to slump in relief. "That's good to know. Thank you."

"So well, in fact, I want to see you in action. I have a minor op for you this afternoon."

"Oh, okay." She paused. "Yes, sir."

"You sound hesitant," Meyers said. "Is there a problem?"

"No, sir. It's just that I thought we weren't allowed to run ops on US soil."

Meyers's lips twitched. "Yes, that's true. I've already cleared this with the appropriate domestic authorities."

"Of course." She could kick herself for questioning him.

He picked up a folder and handed it to her. "Your task is to follow this man."

She flipped it open. The man pictured appeared to be around sixty years of age. His hair was gray, as were his eyes and bushy beard. With his thick-rimmed, black glasses, he was rather monochromatic.

"His name is Karl Bondarenko, a Ukrainian weapons engineer. Our intel indicates he's developed an honest-to-God death ray and is in DC today to meet with a potential buyer. We need to know who that buyer is. All we need you to do is follow him and take pictures of whomever he meets with. Once we get photos of a face or two, other officers will take it from there."

"That doesn't sound too difficult. Follow him and take pictures." She studied the photo. "Will he have the weapon with him?"

"We believe the meet is only to discuss a deal, not deliver a product. If he does have a working prototype, he most likely has it stashed somewhere."

"What if he does have it with him and hands it off to the buyer? What do I do?"

"Operatives in the field can't call in every time they're faced with a decision."

That wasn't a helpful answer. While she was excited to be given the opportunity to stretch her fledgling operative wings, she was also keenly aware how important it was to not screw up. If Bondarenko's weapon fell into the wrong hands, lives would certainly be at stake. The sudden weight of responsibility felt heavy on her shoulders.

"Any other questions?" he asked.

"Where is he now?"

"He's registered at the Elegance Hotel in Georgetown. You'll start there. Also, do not discuss your task with anyone. Good luck." He extended his hand.

She gave him the file and left.

James rose from his chair in the outer office and gave her a questioning look. "Everything okay?"

"Yeah, it's fine. Can you escort me back to the library and then out of the building? I have an errand to run."

"Sure." He opened the door for her, and as they walked toward the elevators, James asked, "Is it something I can help you with?"

"No, thanks. I got it."

"Are you sure? I don't have much going on today. I can go with you." He pressed the button to summon an elevator.

The doors slid open. "That's nice of you, but like I said, I got it." They stepped on and rode in silence.

Back at the library, James waited by the front desk while Quinn popped into Linda's office to tell her she had something she had to take care of and would be out for the rest of the day. Then she snagged her bag and was out the door again.

They arrived at the building's exit security checkpoint. James stopped her just before she was to go through. "Come on, Quinn. Tell me what's going on."

Why was he being so pushy? "I can't. Let it go, okay?"

"You know how I worry about you." His face hung like a scolded puppy's.

Her aggravation with him dropped away and her tone softened. "I know you do, but it's no big deal."

"Can you at least tell me if you can still go to dinner with me tonight?"

She rose up on her tiptoes and kissed his cheek. "I'm not

sure how long this will take. I'll call you later and let you know. I promise."

"Fine," he said, still sounding wounded.

She turned, went through security, and exited the building. As she strode to her truck, she turned James's odd behavior over in her mind. Her grumbled conclusion was "Men are weird."

Chapter Two

Nervous excitement swirled inside Quinn as she sat in the lobby of the Elegance Hotel with a Brick Cobalt spy novel open in her hands. Of course at that moment, she wasn't actually reading it. It worked as a great prop while she kept watch for Bondarenko. It paid to always carry a paperback in her purse.

Adrenaline surged through her when the fancy brass elevator doors glided open, revealing Bondarenko like a prize on a TV game show.

Her head stayed bent over her book while her eyes tracked her quarry. Bondarenko, briefcase in hand, exited the elevator and walked across the lobby and out the door.

As her training dictated, Quinn didn't immediately jump up and follow him. She stayed in her chair and watched him through the window. He turned right and started up the sidewalk.

Careful not to appear too obvious, Quinn deliberately placed her bookmark between the pages, closed the book, and returned it to her purse. Then she slipped on her sunglasses and ambled out onto the sidewalk.

Bondarenko was half a block ahead. At the next corner, he made a right.

A few seconds later, Quinn rounded the corner and exhaled a relieved breath when she spotted him. She remained a respectable distance behind him and hoped she blended in with her fellow pedestrians enjoying the warm, early May sunshine.

The Ukrainian crossed to the other side of the street and entered a pub.

Quinn did the same.

The tavern brimmed with historic charm. It was one of those cramped spaces with wood everywhere. Tiffany-style lamps hung from the ceiling and cast circles of light on the bar and tables. Natural light streaming in from the window that fronted the pub helped brighten the room.

Only a handful of patrons sat scattered throughout the place, so Quinn had no trouble spotting Bondarenko. He sat alone at one of the tables near the bar. She meandered through the maze of tables and chairs and took a seat on one of the wooden barstools. From her vantage point, she could keep an eye on Bondarenko's table in the mirror behind the bar.

She ordered a Coke from the bartender and took out her phone, ready to snap pictures when Bondarenko's contact arrived.

A few minutes later, a man slid onto the stool next to Quinn. She cringed when he turned to her and said, "So, do you come here often?"

She glanced at him and gave him a polite smile. Easily twenty years older than her, his mustache was as cheesy as his pickup line. The cocky, smarmy vibe he gave off made her skin crawl.

Hoping to discourage any attempt at conversation, she

looked back down at her phone to convey disinterest. In a bored voice, she answered, "My first time."

"Oh, a virgin," he said, laughing at his own joke.

Ugh. *What a colossal douche.* Her teeth were clenched so tight her jaw began to ache.

Bondarenko stood and made his way toward the men's room. As he did, he brushed past her in the tight space between her and the chair behind. Quinn picked up her glass and sipped her Coke, not only to hide her face from the man she was following but to swallow down the venom she itched to spew at the ass next to her.

Smarmy Douche Canoe swiveled toward her and leaned in as she set her drink down. "You know, sweetheart, if you're new in town, I can show you around." The stale alcohol on his breath made her nose wrinkle as she tilted away from him. "I can show you a really good time."

The muscles in her face twitched while indignation flared hot in her chest. It was all she could do not to slap the smug bastard's mug with such force his knocked-out teeth would shoot across the room and embed in the wall.

She gulped down more Coke and glanced into the mirror. Bondarenko's table remained empty. "No, thanks. I have my boyfriend for that."

"I bet your boyfriend can't show you as good a time as I can."

So help me, if he touches me I'm gonna break his arm. Without looking at him, she said, "Not interested."

"Aw, don't be like that," he pouted.

She couldn't take it anymore. Unless she got away from Smarmy Douche Canoe, she was going to haul off and deck the guy. Not wanting to call attention to herself, she decided escape was her best option. She grabbed her purse and fled to the ladies' room.

In the end, it worked out well. She took up a position at

the restroom door. Peering through the crack, she kept watch for Bondarenko's exit from the men's room.

Another few minutes passed and the Ukrainian still hadn't emerged. He was either suffering from some serious intestinal distress—maybe he'd downed some dubious oysters and was paying for it—or something had happened. Worry began to gnaw at her middle.

When a man exited the men's room, she popped out from behind the door. "My uncle has been in there a while. Is he okay? Black glasses? Bushy gray beard?"

"Sorry," he answered and hiked his thumb at the door behind him. "There was no one else in there."

Tingling alarm buzzed through her. "It's empty?"

"Yeah. Sorry." The man turned and walked away.

Quinn pushed open the door, leaned in, and scanned the bathroom. Unless Bondarenko was standing on the toilet in the stall so she couldn't see his feet, it was as the man said. Empty.

Her mind flooded with questions as panic rose. How did he get past her without her noticing? Had she been so distracted by Smarmy Douche Canoe she didn't see Bondarenko leave? Why did he leave before the meet? Maybe the meet had already happened and he simply came to the pub for a drink. The worst question imaginable hit her: What if he was on his way to the meet now and she'd lost him?

Silently berating herself as the worst spy ever, she slalomed through the tables and hurried out of the pub. Stopping just outside, she scanned the sidewalk to her left and right. There was no sign of him.

"Dammit," she spat and thrust her hands through her hair in frustration. She was screwed.

She stood rooted to the sidewalk, trying to decide what her next move was. Her stomach dropped. She didn't have one.

The incessant electronic burbling of a cell phone caused her irritation to spike. "Answer the damn phone," she growled and glanced at the people occupying the outdoor tables. Not one made any movement to answer a phone.

She pushed aside her annoyance and threw back her shoulders. She knew what she had to do. The op was bigger than her pride. She'd call Meyers, confess she'd lost Bondarenko, and fall on her sword. Wanting some privacy, she spun on her heel and marched off in the direction of her truck.

"What the hell?" she muttered when she still heard that damned ringing phone. Was someone following her? She stopped, pretended to look in a shop window, and peeked to the side to see who stopped, too. No one. Everyone filed past. And still the phone rang.

The answer dropped on her like a ton of bricks. She rifled through her purse and found a cheap prepaid cell phone tucked in the outside pocket. She took a deep, calming breath and flipped it open. "Yes?"

A voice changer distorted the words. "The wire transfer has been received. Proceed to the southernmost bench in the playground area of Montrose Park. You will be given further instructions as to the location of the prototype."

The call ended. Quinn lowered the phone and stared at it in absolute bewilderment.

"Holy crap," she mumbled when the pieces fell into place. "The meet happened. With me." Bondarenko must have believed Quinn had been at the pub on behalf of the weapon's buyer and had slipped the phone in her purse on his way to the men's room. She'd lost Bondarenko but now was on the trail of the actual prototype instead.

No way would she call Meyers now. She still had a chance to turn her initial failure into a success if she secured

the weapon. Keeping it from the bad guys was surely a top
priority, even if the op hadn't gone exactly as planned.

She stuffed the burner in her bag and hurried to her
truck.

At the park, she walked to the playground and sat on
the appropriate bench. While she waited, she alternated between surveying the area and watching little ones climb on
the play equipment.

No one approached. No one called. Nothing happened.

A thought struck. What if her "further instructions" were
already there? Bending forward, she ran her fingers along
the underside of the bench.

A quiet yelp of victory bubbled up when her fingertips
touched what felt like an envelope. She peeled it from the
seat and withdrew a piece of paper with a couple dozen
Cyrillic characters written on it.

Using the Ukrainian keyboard on her phone, she
painstakingly hunted and pecked for each character. She felt
a real sense of achievement when all the words were in
recognizable English. Her triumph was short-lived, however,
when the words were, "Organic Dog Treats Bella Moose."

Her brow furrowed in confusion. What did dog treats
have to do with the location of a weapon prototype? Was it
another code to crack?

Applying Occam's Razor, she figured the obvious thing
should be her next step. A quick Internet search informed
her there was indeed a product called "Bella Moose's Organic Dog Treats." A picture of a smiling golden retriever
was featured prominently on the website. She knew she was
on to something when she noted a pet supply shop only a
couple of blocks away stocked them.

Tenacity was one of the things that made Quinn an excep-
tional research librarian. Once she was on the trail, she
wouldn't give up until she found the answer. That same

thrill of the hunt buzzed through her as she hoofed it to the store.

The door chimed when she entered. She headed straight for the treats and scanned the shelves. It only took a moment before she spotted the smiling golden retriever on the front of each bag.

As discreetly as possible, she nudged the bags around, searching for any kind of clue. When she came up empty, she feathered her fingertips under the shelf. Nothing.

She took one of the bags and skimmed the information on the back. It assured her the treats were "so tail-waggin' flavorful, your dog will wish she has opposable thumbs so she can open the bag herself." Quinn breathed a quiet laugh when she thought of her grandparents' dog, Pot Roast. His response to a bag coming between him and his treats would be "Bag? What bag?"

A quick glance at the list of ingredients had her admitting to herself that if she were ever hungry enough, she wouldn't be opposed to eating a treat or two. She read nothing relevant to her quest, however.

Working under the assumption someone was watching and her purchase of the treats would be a signal to approach and hand off the prototype, she took the bag and queued up in the checkout line. No matter what happened next, Pot Roast would be the beneficiary of her trip to the pet store.

As she waited, she idly wondered if she could cajole Rasputin, her brown tabby cat, to try one. She smiled when she pictured the look of utter contempt and betrayal he would certainly give her.

She paid for the treats. When the cashier handed her the receipt and her change, it came with a second piece of paper. Schooling her features, she clutched it all in her hand and hurried outside.

Written on the paper were two sets of numbers separated

by a comma. Both sets consisted of two digits, a decimal point, and then six more digits. Whenever she saw numbers like that, her mind automatically went to the Dewey Decimal Classification system. But Dewey numbers always had three digits to the left of the decimal. When she noted a minus sign in front of one of the sets of numbers, she discarded the idea completely.

When all else fails, search the Internet, she thought, and typed the numbers into the search box. A map popped up with a red dot indicating a café only a few blocks from where she stood. She doubted it was a coincidence that the restaurant was on the same block as the Embassy of Ukraine. Feeling like she was back on the scent, she power-walked to her truck and drove toward the café.

The parking gods smiled on her that afternoon. She pulled into a spot near the entrance to the pedestrian-only alley where the restaurant was located and checked the map again. She was practically inside the red dot. She hopped out of her truck and walked down the narrow lane of red and gray bricks until she came to a patio with a number of outdoor tables. At one of them, three men sat enjoying coffee and dessert.

As she neared them, the English bulldog lying under the table stood and lumbered toward her. His stubby tail wiggled with excitement. Quinn squatted down and rubbed the sides of his massive, wrinkled head with both hands. The dog received her greeting with happy, snuffling noises and then stuffed his face in her purse.

Baffled and annoyed, she looked up at the oldest of the three men and said, "Grandpa, you sent me on some elaborate wild goose chase to pick up dog treats for Pot Roast?" She scowled at Bondarenko, who sat grinning at her. "What the hell is he doing here?"

"Settle down, angel," her grandfather said evenly. "Have a seat and we'll explain."

Still frowning, she sat in the empty chair. Pot Roast flopped down next to her, dropped his head on her foot, and released a low, mournful sigh.

She arched an eyebrow at James, directly across the table from her. *"Et tu, Brute?"*

He lifted a shoulder and shot her a disarming smile.

"I take it there's no Ukrainian death ray," she said to Bondarenko.

"Nope. There's no Ukrainian death ray," he said, removing his glasses.

She sat up ramrod straight in surprise. She knew that voice. "Ben?"

Off came the wig and beard, revealing her friend, fellow librarian, and CIA covert operative, Ben Hadley. She'd met him when she and James rescued him from arms dealer Roderick Fitzhugh during their mission in England. She kissed his cheek in greeting. "It's great to see you. It's been a while." She settled back in her chair. "Now spill your guts or I'll rip them out."

Ben laughed. "I like how you're always so demure. You're a regular shrinking violet."

She smirked in spite of herself. "Yeah, because being shy and reserved would have worked so well growing up with five older brothers."

"Our Quinn has always been a bit of a spitfire," her grandfather said. The blue eyes behind his glasses gleamed with pride. Less than three months before, Quinn had received the shock of a lifetime when her grandfather revealed to her he'd been a spy for the CIA for most of his life. Not only that, but he and the agency had been watching her, waiting for the time when they could recruit her to become a covert operative. "Now, before you melt us with your death ray glare, you should know this was a training exercise."

"To train me to fail? I lost Ben completely at the pub."

"Yes, and that was the plan all along," Grandpa said. "This wasn't about your abilities to follow a mark or decipher clues. The object of this lesson was to teach you that even the simplest, most straightforward assignments can go sideways very quickly."

"*My* only task was to shake you," Ben said. "No matter how long it took."

"Well, it didn't take long," she said dejectedly.

"Don't be hard on yourself." He scrubbed his hands over his cheeks and smoothed his hair. "I've been trained to give people the slip, just like you will be."

"So the creep at the bar. Was he in on it, too?" she asked. "Did you send him in to hit on me to distract me?"

James bolted up. Fists clenched, he growled, "A creep hit on you?" He glared at Ben. "That was *not* part of the plan."

"Easy there, tiger. I had nothing to do with it. I just used it to my advantage. I slipped away when he had Quinn sidetracked."

Nostrils flaring, James looked like he could spit nails. "You didn't stay to make sure she was okay?"

Ben gave James an indulgent look and said patiently, "Quinn didn't need my help. She looked like she was about to ram her hand down the guy's throat and rip out his gizzard."

Quinn shrugged. "He's not wrong."

Mollified, James sat back in his chair.

Her grandfather chuckled and said, "She's a spitfire, all right." He sobered and added, "And no, angel, you did not fail. You're here."

"Yeah, but only after you gave me a call on that burner phone."

"It showed your willingness to continue despite the setback," Grandpa answered. "What would you have done if the phone call hadn't come?"

"I was about to call Meyers and tell him I'd lost Bondarenko."

"Because the importance of the op outweighed your failure," he said in a gentle voice.

"Yeah." She lowered her gaze and stared at the chocolate cake crumbs scattered across James's dessert plate.

"And that's why you succeeded."

Her eyes slid to Grandpa's face. He beamed at her with approval. "You put the op ahead of your ego. The rest was to give you some practice on keeping your task a secret and working alone. And as a side benefit, picking up some of Pot Roast's favorite treats."

"Speaking of treats." Quinn took the bag from her purse and opened it. A beefy aroma wafted up. Pot Roast snatched one of the soft morsels from her fingers and gobbled it down.

Using her grandfather's napkin, she wiped the dog slobber off her hand and asked James, "Is that why you kept needling me when you escorted me out of the building? You were testing me?"

"Mm-hmm. And you didn't give up a thing," he replied. If it was possible, he seemed more proud of her than even her grandfather.

Quinn looked into the face of each man in turn and then announced, "Well, since it turns out I didn't screw up as much as I thought I did, I think I deserve a piece of chocolate cake."

"Yes, you do," James said emphatically and looked to flag a waiter.

"How's it going in the library?" Ben asked.

"So far so good," she answered and went on to tell him about her Women of the CIA project.

"Speaking of libraries, that reminds me," Grandpa said. He reached into the pocket of his jacket hanging off the back of his chair and withdrew an envelope. "A good friend of mine at the Indian embassy sent me an invitation to the black tie opening of an exhibition of rare Indian manuscripts at the Library of Congress." He removed the engraved invitation from the envelope and held it up. "I thought the two of you would like to go. Shall I tell him you'll be attending in my place?"

"You and Grandma don't want to go?"

He shook his head. "We have swing dance class that night."

Quinn smiled. Her grandparents were adorable.

"Thanks for the invitation," Ben said with a roguish grin, "but this librarian will step aside and let James go with Quinn."

"That's big of you, dude," James said dryly. He turned to Quinn. "I'm game. I have a new appreciation for manuscripts, and I've never been to the Library of Congress."

She goggled at him. "You've never been to the—? I went the first week I was here."

Her visit had been akin to a religious experience. It wasn't just the beauty of the building, with its magnificent statues, busts, mosaics, and murals. Or the almost incomprehensible number of books, films, photographs, and so on the library held in its collections. It was that it influenced every library in the country, from the massive library systems in large cities to the tiniest branch libraries in small towns across America. It was a touchstone.

Her next question came with an accompanying smirk. "How are we even friends?"

"Because I have a cool car," he replied with a cheeky smile. It was true. His dark gray Lotus Elise was extremely cool. He looked like James Bond in it.

Returning his attention to Quinn's grandpa, James asked, "When is the exhibition? I hope it's before I leave for Moscow."

Quinn's stomach clenched when James uttered the word "Moscow." He would be returning to the same post he'd left six months ago in pursuit of information regarding a stash of hidden weapons. It was during that covert op that James and Quinn met and fell in love. Other than a six-week stretch before she moved to Virginia, she and James had been together ever since. And now he was going to leave.

"It's a week from tomorrow night."

"Perfect. I don't leave for another two weeks. You want to go, Quinn?"

Narrowing her eyes at her grandfather, she asked, "This isn't another one of your throw-Quinn-in-the-deep-end training sessions, is it?"

Grandpa huffed a laugh and shook his head. "You're so suspicious. And no, it's not. Rest assured it's completely on the up-and-up."

Already bubbling with excitement, she said, "In that case, we accept."

Chapter Three

Quinn was seconds from ripping off her shoe and flinging it at the fluorescent light above. She was already in a foul mood after having to endure yet another polygraph that morning. And now the unrelenting buzz coming from above worked her last nerve. The specter of James's departure the next week didn't help her mood, either.

She closed her eyes and focused on her breathing. Several more hours of work faced her, as well as the party at the Library of Congress she and James were to attend that evening. There was a part of her that wanted to change into her sweats when she got home, sit on the couch, and sulk.

That urge was exactly why she needed to get her roiling emotions under control. She wanted their final week together to be amazing. Her stewing in her apartment would be the opposite of amazing. She needed an attitude adjustment before the reception, and fast.

At the word "reception," she groaned and rubbed her fingertips against her temples. Her best friend and former coworker at the public library Quinn used to work at, Nicole Park, and her boyfriend, Brian, had become engaged on Valentine's Day. And as one of Nicole's bridesmaids, Quinn received daily wedding-related emails. Yesterday she'd asked Quinn's opinion on traditional wedding cakes versus cupcakes tiered to *look* like traditional wedding cakes. Quinn didn't really have an opinion but knew she needed to form one. When it came to Nicole's wedding, "I don't know" was not an acceptable answer. At least she had some time to think about it since she couldn't respond until she left headquarters. For security reasons, personal phones were prohibited inside the building. She could go outside, but that meant finding someone to escort her out, and that was a hassle. Banging her forehead on her desk seemed to be the only viable option.

"Excuse me, Quinn?" she heard in a soft voice.

Quinn opened her eyes and saw Patricia Jaworski standing next to her desk. Small and unassuming, Patricia looked like the last person on the planet who would work for the most famous spy agency in the world—which was probably the point. Quinn had learned quickly that Patricia was a top-notch librarian with the amazing ability to find anything, especially old agency white papers.

"Hey, Patricia," Quinn said. "What can I do for you?"

"There's someone up front who'd like to speak with you."

Quinn's first thought was of James, but there was no reason for him not to come find her at her desk like he always did. Maybe it was the recruiter she'd been doing research for. Quinn stood and said, "Lay on, Macduff."

Patricia smiled and raised her chin. "'And damned be him that first cries, "Hold, enough!"'"

"Well done," Quinn said. "Now I know who to come to for all my Shakespeare needs." It felt good to smile for the first time all day.

"If you're interested, maybe we could go to the Shakespeare Festival they put on at William and Mary during the summer. It's only a couple of hours south of here," Patricia said.

"Sure. That sounds like fun." William & Mary wasn't far from Camp Peary. Maybe she could get a weekend off if she was at the Farm training by then.

"Great." When they turned a corner and Quinn saw the back of a man with a medium build and brown hair, Patricia peeled off and said, "See you."

"Yeah, see you," she replied slowly, distracted by the thirtyish-year-old man who spun around at Quinn's approach. She'd never seen him before and had no idea how he came to ask for her by name.

He extended his hand in greeting. "Hi, Quinn. Cooper Santos."

As she shook his hand, her gaze flicked to his badge. He worked in the Directorate of Science and Technology. "It's nice to meet you, Cooper." With her librarian smile firmly in place, she asked, "How can I help you?"

He adjusted his wire-rimmed glasses and shifted from one foot to the other. "A team of us will be leaving on an assignment to Istanbul soon. I'm hoping you can do some research for me before we go."

"I'm happy to help in any way I can. I have to warn you, though, I'm only cleared to do unclassified work at the moment."

Cooper glanced down at the photo ID clipped to the waistband of Quinn's slacks. The blue strip across the bottom informed everyone in the building of her "unsecure" status. "Not an issue. We'll be doing some wining and dining while we're there, so I was hoping you could pull together a list of five-star restaurants and hot nightclubs for me."

"I can do that," Quinn answered. "For the nightclubs, are you interested in swanky and upscale, youthful desperation, or Caligula's bachelor party?"

Cooper laughed, flashing her a brilliant smile. "As tempting as Caligula's bachelor party might be, let's stick to swanky and upscale."

"Swanky and upscale it is. By when do you need this information?"

"The day after tomorrow should be fine."

"I'll get right on it."

Quinn expected him to turn and leave. Instead, he licked his lips and shoved his hands into his front pockets. "I was wondering if you'd like to have dinner with me sometime."

Her eyebrows shot up. She didn't see that coming. "Oh. Um," she stammered. She'd never been in a situation like this before. "That's really nice of you to ask, but I can't. I have a boyfriend."

Cooper's shoulders sagged. "Oh. Okay. Lucky guy." His head cocked to one side when he said, "I'm curious. If you don't mind me asking, does he work here at the agency? Did I miss asking you out before him by much? I mean, I had to ask around to find out who you are, and it took some time."

Oh. Wow. "Yes, he works for the agency, but we were together before I started working here."

"Ah. Cool. That makes me feel a little better. Which office does he work for?"

She clasped her hands in front of her. "It's not my place to say. You'd have to ask him."

"And I have the feeling you wouldn't tell me his name if I did." She kept her features neutral as Cooper considered her for a moment. "Tell you what. If the boyfriend works for Clandestine Services, I'll come by here every so often and see how things are going."

"Why would you do that?"

"If he isn't already stationed out of the country for some significant amount of time, he will be at some point. You'll stay here in the US . . ." He shrugged. "Long-distance relationships like that never survive."

Indignation flared at his suggestion. Not wanting to give Cooper the satisfaction of knowing James really was with Clandestine Services, she answered with a curt, "Not a problem." The rock lodged in the pit of her stomach belied her words.

"Fair enough," he said and dipped his head. "I guess I'll leave you to your work." His dark brown eyes looked directly into her blue ones. "And if things go south with the boyfriend, let me know."

"They won't," she said with more confidence than she felt. The conversation needed to be over. "I'll get that list to you as soon as possible."

"Thanks." He pulled open the door and walked out into the corridor.

Quinn stared at the door as it shut, feeling more jumpy and unsettled than ever.

Patricia came around the corner and stood next to Quinn. "Don't listen to him," said Patricia, who apparently had more than a little bit of spy in her. "I'm sure you and James will be fine."

"I'm sure we will." Still, Quinn asked, "You've heard of long-distance relationships working, right?"

There was a pregnant pause while Patricia's thumb ran nervously over the cover of the book she held. "Well, no. But as Shakespeare says, 'Love is not love which alters when it alteration finds, or bends with the remover to remove.'" She looked at Quinn with an encouraging smile. "Your circumstances might change, but love 'is an ever-fixed mark, that looks on tempests and is never shaken.'"

Quinn gave Patricia a grateful smile. "I love that. Thank you. Can I come talk to you when my morale needs boosting?"

"Of course. I've got a million of them."

"Good, because I have the feeling I'm gonna need them all."

Chapter Four

Rasputin sat on the bathroom counter of Quinn's apartment and watched as Quinn tipped her head to one side and pushed the back of her faux sapphire earring onto the post. She repeated the action on the other side and then adjusted the eagle pendant around her neck.

Jewelry deployed, she turned her back to the mirror and checked her dress. It was a simple but elegant sapphire blue that hugged her curves to her waist, then cascaded over her hips and ended just above the knee. She heaved a sigh in relief and said to the cat, "I don't look too bad." Rasputin meowed his agreement.

She switched off the light and left the bathroom. Rasputin jumped off the counter and landed with a soft thump. As she put her belongings in her new silver purse, she tried to keep the encounter with Cooper Santos from getting to her. But he'd poked her with a pointy stick, and as often as she recited the words of the Shakespearean sonnet, she still felt rattled.

A knock on her door interrupted her musings. Her breath caught when she opened it and found James standing there, looking diabolically handsome in a black tuxedo with shiny satin lapels, a crisp white shirt, and black bow tie. A lock of his wavy, dark blond hair fell across the center of his forehead.

From the other side of the threshold, James stared at her, stunned and unblinking. After a moment, he shook himself from his stupor and said, "Wow. You look . . . beautiful. Incredible. Wow."

Quinn stepped back to let him in. "And you look unbelievably hand—" The word ended abruptly when he took her in his arms and crushed his mouth to hers. It felt like a thousand volts of electricity shot through her.

"I guess I should wear dresses more often," she said when the kiss broke.

He waggled his eyebrows and kissed her again before releasing her and closing the door. "Only if you want to. I know you don't like wearing them." His gaze traveled over her from head to toe, an admiring smile on his face. "Kudos on picking that one out."

She breathed a quiet laugh. "I had help. This really nice salesclerk swooped in and helped me wade through the racks to find this one. You wouldn't believe the number of dresses covered with sequins, giant bows, and rhinestones." She shuddered. "I am *not* a rhinestone kind of girl."

"I think you would look awesome in some flashy bling. Either way, you look fantastic."

Quinn smiled her thanks and said, "So do you."

As if on cue, Rasputin chose that moment to greet James by rubbing his side against James's shins. The cat walked away with his tail up, pleased with the layer of hair he deposited on the black trousers.

Without a word, Quinn went to the counter, picked up the lint roller, and handed it to James. As she watched him lift his foot and roll the adhesive over the bottom of his pant leg, Quinn fought the emotions unexpectedly welling up.

James lowered his foot, and the second he looked at her, his expression morphed from amusement to concern. "Quinn, what is it?"

She swallowed hard and forced a smile. "Nothing. I'm fine. We should get going."

His light blue eyes scrutinized her face. "No, you're not fine. I'm not only trained to read body language, I know you well enough to know when something's bothering you."

Crap. She was powerless to stop the tears prickling at her eyes. "It's starting to hit me that we'll only be together for another week."

He wrapped her in his arms and pulled her close. "I know it'll be hard, but we'll make it work."

"We will?" She searched his face. "You want to do the long-distance thing?"

"Of course. Why wouldn't we?" He frowned, clearly puzzled by her question.

"I talked to someone in the library today who said long-distance relationships between officers stationed overseas and their significant others staying in the US always crash and burn."

James's eyes flashed with pique. "Who said that?"

"A guy from DS and T named Cooper Santos."

He broke their embrace and crossed the room. "I don't know him. When did you talk to him?"

"Today. He came into the library to ask me to do some research."

"And he just happened to mention long-distance relationships."

"Well, after he asked me out."

James tensed and growled, "He asked you out?"

"Yeah. I turned him down, of course. I told him I have a boyfriend. He wanted to know if you worked for the agency.

I said you did, but that's all. He asked which office, but I didn't say," she said, her words tumbling out in a torrent. "He said, 'Well, if he works for Clandestine Services' and then volunteered the long-distance dating stuff.'"

"If he works for DS and T, he has no idea what the hell he's talking about."

"He said he was just saying what he's noticed." She paused before asking, "Have you ever tried the long-distance thing, other than those few weeks when I was in LA and you were here?"

"No."

She wafted her hands through the air. "Then you don't know if it will work either."

"I do know, because I love you more than I've loved anyone." Blue fire blazed in his eyes. "Ever."

The significance of his statement caused her to take a literal step back. She knew James loved her. He had told her many times before. But he had also been secretly in love with a previous partner, and her death two years before during an op gone wrong had left him devastated. Did he really mean to say he loved Quinn more than Claire?

Quinn swallowed at the sudden thickness in her throat and croaked, "Ever?"

He crossed the room in three strides, took her in his arms, and gave her a toe-curling kiss. Goose bumps prickled when his lips drifted down her neck. "Yeah. Ever," he mumbled against her skin.

Her head tipped to the side. "I've never loved anyone as much as I love you. It's not even close."

She felt his smile against her throat. "I know the long-distance thing won't be easy." He lifted his head and looked into her eyes. His fingers laced at the small of her back ensured she wasn't going anywhere. "But we can make it work. My going back to Moscow isn't going to change the way I feel about you. And it's not like I'll be gone forever. It's only for a year. And I've already gotten permission to come home in August so I can go with you to Nicole and Brian's wedding. So really, I'll only be gone for three months before we'll see each other again."

"Whoa, slow down. Who said anything about you being my plus one?" She didn't even try to stop the smirk.

He pulled a face. "Are you kidding? How many obscenities—English *and* Korean—do you think Nicole would hurl at you if I wasn't your date for her wedding?"

"All of them," Quinn deadpanned.

"Are you willing to risk the wrath of a mildly unstable bride?"

"Nope. Not even a little. You are now officially my plus one."

"Good." He narrowed his eyes and asked, "So you're on board?"

She nodded. "Mm-hmm. I'll be in love with you whether you're in Virginia or Moscow or anywhere in between."

He lowered his head and kissed her. His hands seemed to burn through the back of her dress as she raked her fingers through his hair. He moaned and kissed her deeper. A thrill shuddered through her when he gently caught her lower lip between his teeth.

A moment later, James raised his head and croaked, "I think we'd better get going to this shindig. It's time to go show you off."

Her racing pulse began to slow. "In that case, I'd better go check my makeup." She wiped at the lipstick smeared on his lips with her thumb. "It's tempting to leave this here so everyone will know you're with me."

"Marking me as your territory?"

"Basically, yeah. You got a problem with that?"

"Nope. Not even a little."

On his shoulder, she spied a hair of hers threaded through the fabric of his jacket like a long, blond ribbon. She went to pick it off but changed her mind. She'd leave her mark on him after all.

Chapter Five

James and Quinn sat in the line of cars waiting to turn right from Independence Avenue onto First Street. Over the tops of the trees ahead, Quinn could see the upper part of the illuminated Capitol Dome. She was still getting used to living near the nation's capital. Every time she saw any of the iconic buildings and monuments, she suffered a serious case of goose bumps. And now she was about to attend a swanky party inside the Thomas Jefferson Building, the most famous of the three that contained the Library of Congress. She could hardly believe this was her life.

James turned the Lotus onto First Street and stopped at the entrance to the carriage lane in front of the building. He put the window down and held up the invitation for the US Capitol Police officer to see.

"Names?" the guard asked.

"James Anderson and Quinn Ellington."

The officer tapped at the screen of his tablet and then bent over to peer into the car. "Quincy?"

She leaned toward the open window so he could get a better look at her face. "That's me."

He glanced down at the tablet and back at her. "Enjoy the party." He stepped back and waved them through.

James pulled forward a few yards and came to a stop again. "Three of your brothers share names with Library of Congress buildings. Do you, George, and Monroe feel left out?" Quinn and her five older brothers were named, in order, after the first six US presidents.

"I do. Unfortunately, John Quincy Adams was a real slacker, library-wise, so he didn't get anything named after him. George and Monroe probably don't even know there's more than one building." She gazed out the window and up at the building's impressive stone edifice. "John, Tom, and Madison wouldn't know either, for that matter. They're not library nerds like me."

After a couple more minutes of creeping along the lane, they reached the entrance to the building. James handed the Lotus off to the valet and then gave their names to an officer stationed at the door.

They made it inside the building only to face the gauntlet of security. At least Quinn did. James flashed his ID and was waved through. While her bag was scanned as she passed through a metal detector, he waited for her on the other side with his hands in his pockets and a smug look on his face.

Having successfully passed through the crucible, she snagged her purse and hooked her hand around James's proffered elbow. "Show-off." She smiled when he laughed, the sound echoing around them as they climbed a set of marble stairs.

They reached the top of the steps and entered the Great Hall. Seeing it for a second time did not diminish her awe. Ornate white marble pillars and archways surrounded them. Two grand staircases led to the second floor. Looking straight up, she admired the colorful images and geometric designs painted across the arches of the ceiling.

The sea of black tuxedos was just a backdrop to the rich,

vibrant colors of the women's clothing. The dresses were beautiful, of course. But it was the *saris*, the yards of flowing silk in greens, purples, reds, blues, and oranges, that captured her attention.

Quinn bumped her shoulder against James as they wound their way through the crowd. "Don't get any ideas about ditching me for one of these completely gorgeous women."

"Don't worry. I'll be leaving with the completely gorgeous woman I came with."

She rose up on her tiptoes and kissed his cheek. "Flattery will get you everywhere, Mr. Anderson."

He smiled and covered her hand at his elbow with his. "With all these tuxes around, should I give you the same warning?"

She made a noise at the back of her throat. "You couldn't get rid of me if you tried."

James chuckled and snagged two flutes of champagne from a tray carried by a red-coated server. He handed one glass to her before lifting his to his lips. As he sipped, she noticed him scan the room. She knew he wasn't appreciating its beauty. He was assessing for threats, locating exits, calculating risks, reading faces. It was something he did every time he entered a room.

His gaze settled on something at one corner. From behind her champagne glass, she turned slightly to follow his line of sight.

A soldier stood at attention under the archway next to the base of the staircase leading up. He wore a crisp, dark green uniform with a red, yellow, and pink striped sash encircling his waist. A red turban, white gloves, and black boots with white spats rounded out the ensemble. With his thick black beard and eyes that never stopped moving, he was both elegant and intimidating.

Quinn spun in place and spotted three other men dressed the same way stationed in the other three corners of the Great Hall. "Indian Army?" she asked. She noted the impressive rows of medals on each of their chests.

"Looks that way." Threat assessment completed, he cocked his head and asked, "Would you like to schmooze amongst the glitterati or go find the exhibition and check out the manuscripts?"

"Do you even know me at all?"

He laughed, slipped his arm around her waist, and hugged her to his side. "Manuscripts it is."

They finished their champagne and placed the empty glasses on a passing tray. James's hand rested at the small of her back as they zigzagged through the crowd toward one of the staircases. Sitar and drum music played by two men sitting cross-legged on a dais drifted up with them as they climbed the steps.

On the mezzanine, Quinn stood between two sets of double marble pillars and looked up at the colorful stained glass ceiling. "This is incredible."

After a moment, she took his hand and led him to the area overlooking the Main Reading Room. A large round desk stood at the center. Three rows of wooden desks surrounded it in concentric circles.

"Check out the dome," James said. His voice was filled with the same awe she felt. A mural of twelve seated figures rimmed the round skylight at its center. The rest was covered in intricately patterned designs of glowing gold.

"This place is just amazing," Quinn said. They turned and started for the hall where the exhibition was installed. "I could come here every day for weeks and not see everything. And that's not even counting if they let me in the book stacks."

"They'd never be able to flush you out. I can hear the

librarians now. 'We don't know where she hides exactly, but we put food out every night, and in the morning, it's gone.'"

She laughed. "So in a month or two, I emerge from the shadows, all pasty-skinned and wild-eyed?"

"Yeah. Like Gollum."

"Hey!" She smacked him lightly on the arm with her evening bag. "I wouldn't look that bad . . . I have better hair."

"You have better everything," he said, waggling his eyebrows at her.

She snickered as, hand in hand, they followed the signs until they reached the exhibition. Barely inside the room, Quinn came to a complete stop. "James," she breathed. "Look at all these manuscripts. I don't know where to start."

Before he could utter a sound, she pulled him toward the display case with the fewest number of people clustered around it.

An ancient-looking book lay open under protective glass. "It's breathtaking," she said, gazing at the luminous illustration painted on one of the fragile pages.

"The colors are amazing, especially the dude with the blue skin and four arms," James replied.

"And the border around him and the mustachioed guy he's talking to is exquisite." Amorphous blue and gold beds of violet, yellow, and red flowers encircled the figures at the center of the painted page. Quinn read the information on the plaque alongside the open book. "This is a scene from the Bhagavad Gita. The blue guy is Krishna and he's talking to Prince Arjuna, who is having doubts about facing his family and friends on the battlefield." She glanced at the handwritten script on the facing page. "I'll have to take their word for it. The plaque says it's written in Sanskrit."

"Yeah, because if it was written in Hindi, you could totally read it."

"Totally."

They moved to another display case. "Okay, I wasn't expecting anything like that," James said.

A dozen pieces of flat wood akin to big tongue depressors were strung together like a book with a thin strip of leather. Quinn leaned in and squinted at the exquisitely fine etchings.

"It's part of the *Kama Sutra* written on palm leaves," he said and bent to get a closer look. "With illustrations, I see, although the pieces seem to be strategically placed so we can't see the, ah . . ." He stopped and tipped his head to one side. "Techniques."

She glanced at him side-eyed. "I'm sure the parents of the kids that will come through here will appreciate the curator's discretion."

"I'm sure." With a devious glint in his eye, he said, "I bet you're flexible enough to—"

Her elbow poked into his ribs, stopping him midsentence. "Watch it."

"What? I'm just saying."

"We'll have to find out sometime, won't we?"

A growl rumbled up and he slid his arms around her from behind. They stayed like that for a moment until he squeezed her and kissed the side of her head. "Maybe we should keep moving before we end up in serious trouble."

Her head dropped back on his shoulder. "That's probably wise." She hooked her hands behind his neck and brought his head down. Her lips brushed his ear when she said in a husky tone, "FYI, there's an English version online. No illustrations, though."

"That's no good. You know I only read books with pictures." When her laughter subsided, he said, "Tell me. You know about this online version because . . ."

"Because I'm a librarian and I know all things."

"This is true." He pecked her cheek before releasing her.

The juxtaposition between the two manuscripts displayed in the same case was striking. While the palm leaves had an earthy quality, the open book was more refined, its pages featuring an intricately painted scene with opulently dressed men astride exquisitely adorned warhorses.

"Do you find yourself searching for hidden clues when you look at that page?" Quinn asked. During their op in London, they'd discovered clues regarding a number of Soviet nuclear missiles hidden in the illustrations of a manuscript.

James huffed a quiet laugh. "I do. I was just wondering if those three elephants had some deeper meaning."

"So was I," she said. "This is a volume of the *Padshahnama*. It tells the history of the seventeenth-century Mughal emperor Shah Jahan's reign. This shows one of his commanders capturing a fort."

"Love and war in the same display case," James said.

"Shah Jahan was this warrior emperor, but when his beloved wife died, he had the Taj Mahal built for her as a tomb and monument."

"That's definitely an impressive gesture."

"She deserved it. She died while giving birth to their fourteenth child."

James's eyes widened. "Fourteen? She absolutely deserved it." After glancing down at the information card accompanying the manuscript, he said, "It talks about Shah Jahan having the Taj Mahal built, but it doesn't mention his wife or fourteen kids. Where'd you get that?"

She waved her upturned hands through the air. "Again. It's like you don't know me at all."

"Apologies, O Great One," he said, and dipped his head in a solemn bow. "I now know there is no limit to your super power of recalling bits of trivia."

"You're forgiven," she said and gave him a quick kiss.

He smiled his thanks and moved on to the next display case. "Quinn, come here. Check this out."

She joined him and began examining the manuscript. A voice behind her asked, "Are you Quinn Ellington?"

She spun around and faced an elderly Indian man with a beard as white as snow. He wore a tuxedo and a meticulously wrapped light blue turban.

"I am," she said, giving him a cautious smile. James tensed beside her.

His smile was as warm as his eyes. "Forgive me for sneaking up on you. My name is Darvesh Singh," he said in a beautifully lilting Indian accent. "I am a friend of Chester Ellington. It is I who sent him the invitation to attend this gathering tonight. He informed me his librarian granddaughter named Quinn would be coming in his place. I heard this young man use the name, and I wondered if you are she."

She relaxed and her smile turned genuine. "You're right. I'm Chester's Quinn."

His smile brightened. "Chester mentioned you would enjoy the exhibition more than anyone else in Washington. Most people have come through here and given the items no more than a cursory glance. Given the amount of time you have spent here already, I believe he was correct."

"We're enjoying examining these beautiful manuscripts very much," Quinn said. "I'm grateful my grandfather let us come here tonight in his place."

"I am sure it was his pleasure." Mr. Singh turned his attention to James and offered a handshake. "You must be James. Chester mentioned you were Quinn's beau."

Quinn smiled to herself. "Beau" was exactly the word her grandfather would use.

"I am. Happily so." James relaxed and shook the other

man's hand. "It's nice to meet you. How long have you known Mr. Ellington?"

"For many, many years. He used to come see me in India when we both worked in the import/export business." His head wobbled from side to side. "He would import, I would export."

Her grandpa's cover when he was an active operative had been an importer/exporter. She wondered if Mr. Singh had truly been in the same line of work as her grandfather.

"Do you still work in that business?" Quinn asked.

"No, I am connected to the Indian embassy here in Washington now."

It was sounding more and more like Mr. Singh and her grandfather had taken similar retirement paths.

"I've noticed the items on display have come from all over India," Quinn said. "It must have taken a lot of coordination to get so many valuable manuscripts together in one place. Were you involved with that?"

"I was, yes. The librarians and curators here at the Library of Congress have been so gracious and helpful. Of course, none of this would have been possible without the championing of the exhibition by our ambassador. He and those of us at the embassy worked diligently to coordinate it all." Mr. Singh looked at a tall man bending over a display case across the room. "And there he is now. Your Excellency." The man straightened and looked their way. Mr. Singh waved him over.

As the ambassador approached, Quinn made a quick assessment. He was almost the same height as James, and his hair was equal parts black and gray. She guessed him to be in his mid to late fifties. His smile was pleasant, if not slightly forced. The word that popped into her head was "aloof."

"Your Excellency, may I introduce you to Miss Quinn

Ellington and Mr. James Anderson. Miss Ellington, Mr. Anderson, this is His Excellency, Madhav Sharma, the Ambassador of India to the United States."

"Miss Ellington, Mr. Anderson," the ambassador said. His accent sounded more British than Indian. "I am pleased to meet you."

"It's an honor, Your Excellency," Quinn said as she shook his hand. Not versed in protocol when addressing an ambassador, she decided to take the safest course and follow Mr. Singh's lead. She hoped she hadn't committed a diplomatic faux pas that would incite an international incident.

As the ambassador greeted James, Mr. Singh said, "I was just mentioning, Your Excellency, how integral your support was in bringing these magnificent manuscripts to the United States."

"I felt it important not only as a touchstone for those of Indian descent who live here, but to expose people of all backgrounds to the art and literature of our diverse culture."

"It must have taken a lot of work," Quinn said.

"And a lot of security," James added. Four Indian soldiers dressed identically to the men downstairs stood at attention in the four corners of the exhibition hall.

"It is necessary to have our most elite soldiers to guard these items. Most are irreplaceable," Ambassador Sharma said.

"Sikh soldiers have been a vital part of the Indian Army for many years. They are valiant and fierce warriors." Mr. Singh's voice was laced with pride. "It was my honor to suggest they protect these precious bits of our heritage."

"Are you enjoying the exhibit?" Ambassador Sharma asked.

Quinn nodded. "Very much. The detail and artistry of the manuscripts are breathtaking. And the different media people have used to write on is quite creative. The palm leaves, for instance."

"Being able to effectively use the resources around us is an important skill. Necessity is the mother of invention, as they say," the ambassador said.

"I certainly agree." Quinn had been known to use library supplies for something other than their specified purposes on more than one occasion.

"If you will excuse me, I have other guests to greet," Ambassador Sharma said. "It was a pleasure to meet you. Enjoy the rest of your evening."

"Thank you. I'm sure we will," James said.

Quinn nodded and added, "Thank you for bringing these manuscripts here. It is an honor to see them in person."

"You are quite welcome." With that, the ambassador dipped his head and joined another group at the other end of the room.

James and Quinn spent another half hour looking at the rest of the manuscripts. When they rejoined the reception in the Great Hall, Mr. Singh hurried over to them. "Come with me, please. There are a couple of people I would like you to meet."

They dutifully followed him, snaking around clusters of guests until they reached two women standing together. Both were dressed in exquisite *saris*. The younger of the two was the most beautiful woman Quinn had ever seen.

Quinn instinctively took James's hand and laced her fingers with his.

Mr. Singh said, "Mrs. Sharma, Miss Sharma, I would like to introduce you to Quinn Ellington and James Anderson. Quinn and James, this is Mrs. Sonia Sharma, the wife of the ambassador, and their daughter, Kavita."

After a round of greetings and handshakes, Mr. Singh

said to Quinn and James, "I thought you might enjoy chatting with someone your own age. Kavita went to Georgetown Law School and recently passed the bar. She works at one of the most prestigious firms here in Washington."

Kavita shot Mr. Singh a look equal parts affection and exasperation. "I apologize for Darvesh's enthusiastic bragging. He acts as if getting a job as a lawyer in this city is an unparalleled accomplishment."

Kavita's witty reply immediately won Quinn over. "Don't sell yourself short," she said. "My oldest brother is a lawyer. Getting through law school and passing the bar is no small feat."

"I must admit I'm glad to be past that bit of it."

"I hear it's not much easier as a newly minted lawyer," James said. "Don't they expect associates to bill more hours than there are in a week?"

"They do," Kavita answered with a laugh. "Making sure I reach my minimum hours keeps me out of trouble. What do you do, James?"

"I'm a government wonk, like almost everyone else around here."

Kavita nodded. "And you, Quinn?"

"I'm a librarian."

"Do you work here at the Library of Congress?" Mrs. Sharma asked.

"No, so coming here tonight has been a real treat."

"A place of pilgrimage for every librarian, I'm sure," Kavita said with a smile.

"It is."

"Of all the manuscripts here, which was your favorite?" Mrs. Sharma asked.

"What a great question," Quinn said, her nose wrinkling

in thought. "Each one is stunning in its own way. But I'd have to say—"

"GRENADE!"

A brilliant light flashed and an earsplitting bang reverberated through the Great Hall.

Chapter Six

Quinn lay flat on the cold marble floor and did a quick inventory of her body. She felt no stabbing pain and could move all of her arms, legs, fingers, and toes. Her relief was short-lived when she realized she was blind and deaf. Heart pounding with fear, she prayed her current afflictions wouldn't be permanent.

She remained there, stricken, until the darkness in her vision started to slowly lighten. Her panic subsided further when her hearing began to return. Sound was muffled, like wads of cotton were stuffed in her ears. Still, it was something.

When she could make out the dark outlines of the stained glass windows in the ceiling, she tried to lever up on an elbow. The room immediately spun and she fell back.

She was vaguely aware of commotion around her but was unable to make out words or determine what was going on.

Her mind was a swirling jumble until a single name pushed through the haze.

James.

Terror ripped through her. Was he okay? She rolled onto

her side and struggled to prop herself up. Relief flooded her when she saw him upright.

He helped her sit. His face was riddled with worry when he shouted, "Are you okay?"

Ears still ringing, she read his lips more than heard his words. She gave him a thumbs-up. "You?" she yelled.

He nodded and surveyed the room, his jaw set with determination. Eyes on her again, he slid the pistol from his ankle holster and slipped it into her purse. "I'm going to check things out," he said loudly. "You stay here and make sure Mrs. Sharma and Kavita are okay. Copy?"

"Copy." Her shouted voice sounded tinny, which was an improvement.

He cradled her face with a hand and then scrambled to his feet. He stood still for a few seconds to regain his equilibrium before starting toward the staircase that led to the exhibition hall.

Watching James carefully pick his way along gave Quinn a chance to assess the scene. It looked like a war zone. The floor was strewn with people. US Capitol Police swarmed the room.

Kavita pushed herself up.

"Are you all right?" Quinn asked.

"What?" Kavita shook her head and pointed at her ears.

Quinn shouted her question again.

Kavita nodded and brushed back the hair that had fallen across her face.

Quinn's blood ran cold when she saw a still-unconscious Mrs. Sharma. A small pool of blood puddled around her head. Quinn slid over, grabbed her wrist, and checked for a pulse. "Thank God," she murmured at the throbbing under her fingers.

"Mummy!" Kavita cried.

"She's alive," Quinn said. "Looks like she hit her head on the floor when she fell."

Quinn stood and fought the dizziness. Once stable, she shouted at a policewoman, "Officer! The ambassador's wife needs medical attention!"

"Paramedics are on their way!" she called back.

"Sonia!" Mr. Singh cried. He checked her pulse and examined the serious gash on the back of her head. "We need to stop the bleeding." He reached up and unwound his turban, revealing the white kerchief covering his hair. Mr. Singh bunched up the long strip of material and said, "Quinn, lift her head."

Quinn knelt and did as she was told.

"Gently," Mr. Singh said under his breath as he pushed the material between Mrs. Sharma's head and the hard floor.

Quinn slowly lowered the head onto the makeshift pillow and applied an end of the turban to the wound.

Eyes brimming with tears, Kavita took her mother's hand. "What happened? Why would someone do something like this?"

Mr. Singh looked around. "I believe someone set off a stun grenade. They're meant to incapacitate, not kill." He frowned. "We can be thankful for that."

Quinn agreed. She didn't even want to think about the damage a fragmentation grenade would have wrought.

"As for why," Mr. Singh continued, "I cannot say."

Mrs. Sharma's eyelids fluttered and a weak groan escaped.

Kavita patted her mother's hand and said, "*Amma*, I'm here. It's time to wake up."

Quinn spotted James walking toward them. His somber expression told her the news wasn't good. His gaze sharpened when it fell on Mrs. Sharma. He stopped a few feet away and crooked his index finger at Quinn.

"Here, let me take over so you can go speak with James," Mr. Singh said.

His hand replaced hers, now covered with warm, sticky blood.

"Sitrep," James said when she reached him.

"Mrs. Sharma cut her head when she fell. She's starting to wake up. Paramedics are on their way. You?"

"Some of the manuscripts are gone. The locks on the cases were shot open." James took her hand and they walked over to the policeman in charge. James flashed his ID and said, "I'm a federal officer. Are all the exits secure?"

"Yes, and backup is incoming, so you can step off," he replied brusquely. "We've got this under control."

So much for interagency cooperation, Quinn thought. James didn't move, so she didn't either. She asked James, "Do you think whoever took the manuscripts might be hiding in the building?"

"They must be. Police were stationed at all the doors. How else could they get out?"

Quinn's gaze landed on one of the exits that led downstairs. It reminded her of a sign she'd noticed when they arrived. "There's a tunnel that goes from here to the Capitol building across the street. Maybe they took that."

The policeman shook his head. "Officers securing all the tunnels from here radioed in right after the flash bangs went off."

"Wait," James said. "All the tunnels? There's more than one?"

"On the east side of this building there's one that runs over to Adams. A second tees off from it and goes south to Madison."

"Have the guards in those buildings checked in?" James asked.

The man scowled and said peevishly, "Look, buddy. I

don't know who you and Nancy Drew here are, and I don't care. I already told you everything is secure. Now, step away so I can do my job."

Quinn's ire flared. "We're just trying to help. And you'd be lucky to have Nancy Drew—"

James pulled her toward the staircase that led to the ground floor. "As much as I'd enjoy watching you tear him a new one, we need to keep moving."

"What a tool," she said, still fuming as they raced down the steps.

The policeman's report was accurate. A cadre of guards blocked access to the Capitol tunnel.

James glanced around. "We came in on the west side of Jefferson. Officer Attitude said the entrance to the other tunnels is on the east side." With her hand still in his, they started in that direction. They walked past the library gift shop and through the visitor center. Their pace quickened when they entered a long hallway at the far end of the room.

The sound of Quinn's heels echoed around them until they arrived at the east entrance. Victims littered the floor, groaning and disoriented.

James slid his Sig Sauer from his hip holster. "They set off another flash bang."

"And went out those doors," Quinn said, pointing.

"Maybe, maybe not. Depends on their escape plan. If they thought there would be too many people outside this exit, they might have used the tunnel to either Adams or Madison. Have a car or van waiting at a less populated location. That's what I'd do."

Quinn huffed a breath. "Who are 'they'?"

"I don't know. But I assume the tunnel entrance is downstairs, so that's where we need to go."

They found the stairs, bounded down a level, and entered a dimly lit corridor with wires, cables, and conduits running along the ceiling. A sign attached to a wall pointed them toward the entrance to the tunnel.

They hurried past a cart full of cleaning supplies and stopped at the end of the corridor. One tunnel went straight while a second ran to the right.

"I'll go to the Adams Building," James said. "Will you be okay going south toward Madison?"

"I will." She slung the strap of her purse over her head and across her chest, then slipped off her heels and kicked them away. They slid across the floor and came to rest against the wall. She took out the Glock James had put in her bag, checked the magazine, and slapped it back in place. "Ready."

She turned and took one step.

James grabbed her wrist and tugged her arm. She spun around and crashed into him like a dancer doing the tango. He kissed her possessively and growled, "No heroics."

"I promise," she said and held his piercing gaze. "You be safe, too."

He kissed her again. "I will."

She gave him one last blistering kiss and then headed down the tunnel. She jogged with both hands on the Glock, ready to raise and fire if warranted. Even with no one else around, she stayed on the pedestrian side of the tunnel. No reason to crash into a rogue book truck.

As she ran, she noted how nothing seemed amiss. There were no marks on the white walls, no sounds other than her bare feet slapping against the cold concrete floor. No helpful clues had been dropped, telling her she was on the right track.

She approached the entrance to the Madison Building and dropped her pace to a walk. It became a stealthy creep as she crossed the threshold into the building.

Her senses on high alert and her weapon ready, she quieted her breathing and snuck along the corridor until she reached an intersection. She stopped, pressed her back against the wall, and peeked around the corner. Finding it clear, she spun out and sprinted across the gap.

A door flew open and a man burst into the hall.

She screamed.

Chapter Seven

The man whipped out a pistol, pointed it at Quinn and roared, "Drop your weapon! Drop your weapon!"

"Holy crap!" she shouted, her heart jackhammering against her sternum. "Don't shoot!" The second she realized he wore a US Capitol Police uniform, her hands shot up.

"Drop your weapon!" The veins in his neck popped out like thick ropes.

"Doing it now." She kept her empty hand up while she bent forward and set the Glock on the floor.

"Kick it away!"

She straightened, kept both hands up, and pushed the Glock away with her foot. "Easy! I'm with the federal government."

He scowled. "I need to see some ID, lady." At least he wasn't yelling anymore.

"No problem. It's in my purse. Is it okay if I open it?" She kept her tone even and unthreatening.

"Yeah, slowly. Don't do anything stupid."

"Don't worry." Hands trembling from the adrenaline coursing through her, she opened her purse with great care and removed her wallet.

"Toss it here," he demanded. "No funny stuff."

She battled the urge to roll her eyes. Like she'd fire it at him when he had a gun trained on her. "I put mine down," she said, eyeing his pistol. "Can you holster yours, please? My boyfriend would be furious if you shoot me."

"I don't give a rat's fuzzy ass if your boyfriend is mad at me."

You would if you knew he was a CIA covert operative who knew forty-two different ways of maiming you with a set of chopsticks, she thought. Not wanting to rile him any further, she answered with a simple, "Fair enough. Just asking you to not point that at me anymore."

She remained motionless as he considered her with a squint. When he returned his firearm to his holster, she returned to breathing.

Now that she wasn't afraid he'd accidentally put a bullet in her, she tossed him the wallet. While he scrutinized her identification, she studied him. He was an African American in his mid-thirties, around six feet tall and only slightly overweight. He sported a thin mustache and a yellow gold wedding band. The name badge on his chest read S. Green.

"It says here you do work for the government, but you're just a librarian," he said.

Her teeth ground at the words "just a librarian."

"What's a librarian doing with a gun?"

"I make sure people pay their overdue fines," she said before she could stop herself.

His head jerked up and he burst out laughing. "You librarians are real hard-asses, aren't you?"

She smiled, caught the wallet when he tossed it back, and returned it to her purse.

His gaze dropped to her hand. Jutting his chin at her, he asked, "Where'd the blood come from?"

"You heard about what's happening over at the Jefferson Building?"

"Yeah. Sounds like a real cluster."

"It's pretty chaotic." She lifted her blood stained hand. "I was a guest at the reception. The ambassador's wife got a gash on her head. I was trying to stop the bleeding."

He nodded and rubbed a hand over his closely cropped hair. "They told me to stay down here and watch this end of the tunnel."

"Have you seen or heard anything?"

"That's a negative. You're the only person that's come over here. Chatter on the radio says the guys upstairs haven't seen anything either."

She pointed at the Glock on the floor and raised her eyebrows in question. He nodded and waved a hand.

She picked it up. "I'm going to head back, then."

"If you don't want to call too much attention to yourself, I suggest you wash your hands first."

She looked at the dried blood. "Good call. Be right back."

She went into the nearby ladies' room and headed straight for the sink. Water tinged with red swirled down the drain. It took two rounds of soap before her hands were clean again.

As she dried them with a paper towel, she glanced at her reflection in the mirror. By some miracle, blood hadn't stained her dress. After tonight, though, she was pretty sure she'd rather bury it in her parents' backyard than wear it again.

She threw the paper towel in the trash, grabbed the Glock, and exited the bathroom.

Officer Green stood at the junction between the building and the tunnel. As she passed him, she said, "Hold down the fort."

"Copy that," he said and threw her a salute. "Gun-toting,

barefoot librarian. When I tell them about you, they're never going to believe me."

"Tell them I wore my hair in a bun. Then they'll believe you," she said over her shoulder.

His deep, booming laughter trailed behind her as she trotted away.

She was the first to return to where she and James had split off. Rather than wait around for him, she decided to find him at Adams.

She'd only traveled a short distance when she spotted James jogging toward her.

"I got nothing," she said when they met. She turned around and matched James's pace. "You?"

"It looks like the bad guys got away via the Adams Building. The two guards over there were unconscious."

Back where they started, Quinn found her shoes and slipped them on. They stowed their weapons, went up a level, and retraced their steps to the main entrance. They hung back and assessed the situation. Light from emergency vehicles parked in the driveway flashed across the faces of responders still rushing about.

"It looks like every agency in Washington is here," James said. "FBI, Homeland Security, Capitol Police, Metro fire, paramedics."

"Do we join them and add to the alphabet soup?"

He shook his head. "It's one thing to flash an ID to a guy like Officer Attitude in a fluid situation and say we're federal officers. It's another to have to give statements to the police and be vague about who we work for. Not answering directly tends to raise red flags. Our only debrief should be at headquarters."

"We need to sneak out."

"Yeah. The problem is all of the exits are blocked, and

even if we did get out, we don't know where my car is. God knows where the valet parked it."

Quinn peered around James toward the exit. She caught sight of Kavita walking alongside a gurney carrying Mrs. Sharma with a white bandage wrapped around her head. It relieved her to see Mrs. Sharma was fully awake as paramedics wheeled her out the door.

"If we can get out of this building, we can figure something out from there," Quinn said.

"Take the Metro or something." From his tone, Quinn could tell he was already mulling over their options. "We can't go out Adams. It's probably already crawling with agents since it was the escape route."

Quinn smiled. "I've got us covered. Come on."

She led him down the stairs again and half walked, half ran to the Madison Building.

At the entrance, Quinn raised her voice and said, "Officer Green. The gun-toting librarian is back."

He came around the corner and smiled. "Hey! Didn't expect to see you again so soon." He regarded James. "Is this the boyfriend?"

"Mm-hmm."

"Look, man. I'm sorry I pointed a gun at her."

"What?" James yelped and rounded on her. "He pointed a gun at you? When were you going to tell me about that?"

"Later, when things settled down." She put a hand on his arm. "It's okay. I was armed. He was just doing his job."

James expelled a breath in exasperation and stared up at the ceiling.

"Found yourself a real live wire, haven't you?" the officer said, chuckling.

"You have no idea." James was clearly trying to hold back a laugh.

"Anyway," Quinn said pointedly to get the conversation

on track again. "James is a resident at George Washington University Hospital. His attending just called and needs him there right away. We've already given the police our statements, but they aren't letting anyone go yet." She put a hand on her hip. "I mean, James told the old man we're stuck in this mess, but the guy's a real hard-ass." Her bangs bounced when she blew out a breath in frustration. "And James is *still* in the doghouse for when we went to Virginia Beach for the weekend and had the *gall* to turn off his phone so we could have some alone time."

James slipped his arm around her waist and kissed her head. "I'd do it again, sweetie. That weekend was magic." To Officer Green, he said, "But yeah, I really need to get to the hospital or my ass will be in a sling."

"Well, since you've already given your statements and she's a Fed anyway, I don't see why not. It's not like either of you are smuggling rare manuscripts out or anything. I'll escort you."

Quinn battled the smile twitching on her lips. She and James actually had snuck a manuscript out of a library once. "That'd be great. Thank you so much. We appreciate it."

"No problem."

Officer Green led them up a flight of stairs and through the lobby. Glimpses of the interior of the building had Quinn making a mental note to visit it in the near future.

At the exit, they each shook Officer Green's hand and gave him their thanks. "Come back and see me sometime."

"We will," Quinn said. "I promise."

They walked out into the cool night air. "Of course, I'll have to be Dr. Anderson if we ever visit Officer Green again," James said when they were a sufficient distance from the building. He draped an arm over her shoulders. "Are you sure you haven't finished your training yet? You're quite the accomplished liar."

"Only when it's government sanctioned. And I learned from the best, Mr. *Lockwood*," she said, referring to the alias James had used when they first met.

"Touché."

They joined the crowd of onlookers watching the activities across the street at the Jefferson Building. Above them, a helicopter circled with a searchlight shining down. "Should we try the 'Dr. Anderson needs to get to the hospital' line on the valet?" she asked.

He frowned and shook his head. "I don't think it will work. Those valets are so far down the food chain they wouldn't make a decision like that without checking with the police first. We'd be right back to where we started."

"So we need a good reason for them to not check with the police." She thought for a moment. A scene from *Trigger Pull*, a novel from her favorite spy series, sprang to mind. "I have an idea, but I have to go it alone."

"No way," he stated flatly. "You've already had a gun pointed at you once tonight. You're not going anywhere without me."

She pulled him away from the crowd. "No guns, I promise. I'm just going to talk. If it doesn't work, I'll walk away. No harm, no foul."

James remained silent for a moment and then heaved a resigned sigh. "I'll be here when you get back." He took the valet stub from his pocket and held it out.

She smiled and snatched the ticket from his fingers. "You'd better be." She bounced on her toes and kissed him. "I love you." Saying those words always sent a chill up her spine.

His smile lit up his face despite the trepidation lurking in his eyes. "I love you, too."

She pecked his lips once more before spinning around and zigzagging through the emergency vehicles and TV news vans clogging the street. Near the entrance of the carriage lane, she stopped, hid in the shadows of a tree, and scoped out the area.

The valet stand had moved from right in front of the library entrance to closer to where she currently stood. That was good. The farther it was from the authorities, the better.

Still in the shadows, she reapplied her lipstick, ran her fingers through her hair to give her an appropriately tousled look, and slipped off her shoes. She headed for the valet stand, circling around so that it appeared she had just left the building. No one paid her any attention.

With her shoes dangling from two fingers, she sauntered up to the twentyish-year-old guy in a red jacket and black pants—a different valet than the one they'd left the car with—and held out the parking stub. She lowered the register of her voice in hopes of sounding sultry. "Be a doll and bring my car around, please."

"I'm sorry, miss, but I'm not authorized to release any cars right now."

Her lower lip stuck out in a pout. "I just want to go home. I swear I didn't have anything to do with all that craziness in there."

"I wish I could help you, but until the police give me the go-ahead, I can't."

She glanced over her shoulder. Facing forward again, she stepped closer. "Here's the thing. I don't want to talk to the police 'cause I was sorta paid to be here tonight."

His eyes nearly popped out of his head.

"Oh, no! I don't do anything illegal. I'm an escort. It's all on the up-and-up. I was hired to come to this party tonight by a *librarian*." She said the word as if it was the lamest thing ever. "It turns out he's a really sweet guy. He's just kind of a nerd."

"Yeah, that makes sense. You're way too hot for a librarian."

She wanted to smack him with her purse for that crack. Instead, she winked and cooed, "The thing is, if the police run my name, my priors will pop up. I'm completely innocent and those convictions were based on some unfortunate misunderstandings. They'll come to the wrong conclusion about what I was doing here tonight." She invaded his personal bubble and settled a hand on his arm. "You can see my problem."

Equal parts awe and uncertainty overtook his face.

She could tell he was beginning to waver. Hoping to push him over the edge, she lifted her hands, her shoes still dangling, and slowly spun around. "I mean, I obviously didn't take anything. Where would I hide it?"

Completing her revolution, she lowered her chin and held his gobsmacked, unblinking gaze.

He shook himself from his stupor and peered over his shoulder toward the cluster of police officers not far away. He leaned in and said conspiratorially, "I can't bring you the car 'cause I can't leave my post. You'll have to go to it."

"That's okay," she said and gave him a coy smile. "I can walk."

He swallowed, blinked a couple of times, and took the ticket from her. As he searched the box filled with keys on hooks, he asked, "Which car is yours?"

"The dark gray Lotus."

His jaw dropped and stared at her. "The Lotus is yours?"

"What can I say? I'm good at my job," she purred.

The valet gulped, unhooked the keys from the panel, and held them out. He pointed back toward where James waited. "It's, um, it's right over there on First Street." There was a serious croak in his voice.

With two fingers, Quinn slid out the twenty-dollar bill she'd stuck between her bra and boob earlier and slipped it under the lapel of his jacket. "Thanks, sweetie." She plucked the keys from his hand and chucked him under the chin with her finger. "See ya." She turned and sauntered away, adding extra sway to her hips for fun.

When she reached the street, she slid her shoes back on but kept her pace nonchalant as she crossed to the other side.

James stood on the sidewalk, his eyes glued on her from the moment she came into view.

She smirked when they grew wider the closer she came. Stopping in front of him, she dangled the keys from her index finger and asked, "Do you want to drive, or should I?"

Chapter Eight

James set a mug of steaming tea on the conference table in front of Quinn. She breathed in the pungent aroma of bergamot and gave him a tired smile. "Thanks."

"You're welcome," he replied and slid into the leather chair next to hers. "We can both use some more caffeine after our short night last night."

After locating the Lotus, she and James had driven to headquarters, arriving around midnight. By the time their debriefings had finished and they were back at her apartment, it was 2:30.

Three hours later, Quinn's ringing cell phone woke her from a sleep like the dead. It took every ounce of control not to hurl it against the wall. As satisfying as it would have been, she answered and was summoned, as was James, to an early-morning meeting at Langley.

She glanced up at the clock. The meeting was to start at seven, and that was in three minutes. So far, she and James were the only attendees.

"I dreamt you and I were spending the weekend together in Virginia Beach," James said before taking a sip of coffee. "It really *was* magic."

"Yeah? Now we have to go there someday."

"I'm in," he said with a smile.

Her lewd response died on her lips when the conference room door swung open.

Quinn and James rose to their feet and watched the rest of the meeting attendees file in.

Deputy Director of the National Clandestine Service Diane Marchelli led the way. Aldous Meyers, a woman Quinn didn't recognize, and a younger man with a laptop under his arm followed the deputy director. Her grandfather brought up the rear and closed the door behind him.

Quinn's grandfather headed for the open seat next to Quinn while Deputy Director Marchelli, Meyers, and the unknown woman took their places on the other side of the table.

As they all settled in their seats, the guy with the laptop immediately set to work plugging cables into his computer. When the giant flatscreen monitor attached to the wall flickered on, Quinn wanted to lean over and quip to James her disappointment there wouldn't be 3-D holograms projecting up from the center of the table. The sober mood of the room made it clear she should keep her snarky comment to herself.

Deputy Director Marchelli, a woman who exuded authority, clasped her hands and set them on the table. "As you are all well aware, an incident occurred last night during a reception in the Jefferson Building of the Library of Congress. Coincidentally, James Anderson and Quinn Ellington were in attendance." She made eye contact with them when she spoke their names. "They have been debriefed, and their accounts have been critical to our understanding of the overall narrative. However, due to the effects the stun grenades had on them, important pieces of the story were understandably missing from their reports. We have obtained various closed-circuit security feeds that fill in those gaps."

She looked to the guy manning the computer. "Kevin, if you will."

Kevin furiously tapped at his keyboard. Video recorded from a camera above the Great Hall and looking down on the partygoers began to play.

"This recording begins approximately two minutes before the commencement of the incident," the deputy director said.

Quinn rested her elbows on the chair's armrests and leaned forward. The view was from above the staircase she and James had used to go up to the exhibition hall. She spotted James and herself talking with Darvesh Singh, Mrs. Sharma, and Kavita. She also saw the ambassador speaking with the two musicians seated on the platform.

As if reading her mind, Deputy Director Marchelli said, "Please note Ambassador Sharma's location."

A moment later, everyone in the room looked up at the same time. That was the moment someone had shouted, "Grenade."

A sudden, silent flash turned the screen white, like the frames of a nuclear bomb test film from the 1950s. The camera, like the human eyes in the Great Hall, had been momentarily blinded. When the images reappeared on the screen—at first washed out and then slowly sharpening—every guest was laid out on the floor.

"Kevin, pause, please," Deputy Director Marchelli said. The images on the screen froze. "As you can see, everyone in the room was incapacitated by the concussive effects of the flash bang."

An eerie tingling crawled across Quinn's skin when she spotted herself, James, the Sharmas, and Darvesh Singh collapsed on the floor.

"The question is"—Deputy Director Marchelli paused

until everyone's attention was riveted on her—"where is Ambassador Sharma?"

Quinn's eyes snapped back to the place where the ambassador had been standing. The deputy director was right. He wasn't on the floor as expected. "Maybe the guards did that Secret Service thing and hustled him away," Quinn ventured.

"You've come to the most logical conclusion," Marchelli said, nodding at Quinn. "However, the problem with that scenario is—"

"The guards would have been incapacitated, too," James and the deputy director said at the same time.

It felt as if a rock lodged in Quinn's chest. She didn't like where this was going. From the serious expressions on the faces of those sitting around the table, she wasn't alone.

Marchelli looked at Kevin. "If you could go back to where it started, please."

"Yes, ma'am," he said and tapped at the keys.

"As you watch this time, pay close attention to the upper right corner of the screen," Marchelli said.

Quinn stared at the spot on the monitor. To her surprise, the Sikh guard stationed in that corner of the room slipped away from his post and disappeared through an archway in the staircase. A half minute later, a small canister flew through the air from that same archway. She already knew what happened next. She stayed quiet, but her eyebrows knit together in confusion. Had the guard tossed the flash bang into the room?

"The other angle, please, Kevin," Marchelli said.

Images of the Great Hall recorded from a camera mounted on the opposite side of the room as the first appeared. As on the other side, two Sikh guards stood sentry in their corners. The guard stationed at the bottom of the staircase—the one Quinn and James had passed when they went to the second level—stepped through the closest archway and out of sight. A few seconds later, a stun grenade could be seen soaring through the air and into the crowd. Seconds later, the screen went white. Kevin paused the recording.

James shifted in his seat. "There was a second flash bang."

"Yes," Marchelli said. "From the time stamps of when they were deployed, they went off nearly simultaneously. Given the size and cavernous quality of the room, the soldiers must have felt it necessary to use two to ensure everyone was affected."

"Affect everyone except those who set them off by protecting themselves beforehand," Meyers added.

"You believe some, if not all of the soldiers were some-how involved?" James asked.

Deputy Director Marchelli didn't answer. She only nodded at Kevin, who then resumed playing the recording. She continued her narration of the scene once the effects on the camera had passed. "From this angle, you can see that the guard who did not leave the room was as debilitated as everyone else. The same can be said for the guard on the other side of the room."

After a few more seconds passed, US Capitol Police flooded into the room from all directions. There was a lot of pointing and running around and talking on radios. In the pandemonium, no one seemed to notice when two Sikh sol-diers hurried down the staircase and walked straight for the doorway that led to the downstairs steps.

At the same time James's entire body seemed to tense, Quinn sucked in a sharp intake of air.

She immediately recognized those two men. They had

been guarding the manuscripts. They left the scene with rucksacks strapped to their backs.

"It appears you both have come to some kind of conclusion," Deputy Director Marchelli said. "Care to share?"

James spoke first. "Some of the manuscripts had been removed by the time I got to the exhibition hall. It looks like those two guards snuck them out in their backpacks."

"Why would they do that?" Quinn asked.

The deputy director pursed her lips. "A video the Indian embassy received a few hours ago will shed some light on that. Kevin?"

A man in his forties appeared on the screen. With dark, piercing eyes, he stared at the camera with a gaze so fierce he appeared to be trying to melt it. His long black beard— one that looked to have never been trimmed his entire life—was in stark contrast to his crisp white tunic. His turban was royal blue, and the bandolier of bullets slung over his shoulder and across his chest gave him the air of an Old West gunslinger.

"I speak for the Falcon, who has decreed that it is time we Sikhs act," he said in English that bore no hint of an accent. The intensity in his tone was only surpassed by his intimidating glare. "We demand you, the government of India, allow us to establish our sovereign homeland of Khalistan. We have been ignored for too long. Our patience is at an end."

Quinn frowned and squinted at the man on the screen. She had no idea what he was talking about. When he held up what was clearly a very old book, her eyebrows shot up her forehead. It wasn't much of a stretch to guess it was one of the stolen manuscripts.

"Over thirty years ago, you stole irreplaceable treasures of our religion and heritage. Now you taste the same bitter tears we have wept for decades, tears that come from the pain of precious artifacts of faith being ripped away."

James turned to Quinn and gave her a puzzled look. She shrugged and made an I-have-no-idea-what-he's-talking-about face in response.

"The Falcon is aware that there will be those in the government who do not see any value in these rare and precious items. To them, these are simply worthless scribblings on old, crumbling paper." The man set the book down and brought into view the *Kama Sutra* James and Quinn had been teasing about only a few hours before. "Or palm leaves. In case they do not feel the issue warrants their attention, we have taken a further step we believe will motivate them to act."

The camera's view widened to show a disheveled Ambassador Sharma sitting on a chair. His tuxedo jacket and tie were gone. His white dress shirt was wrinkled and smudged with dirt and black grease. The man had most likely spent some time in the trunk of a car. From the way the ambassador sat with both hands behind him, Quinn surmised they were bound together. Ambassador Sharma stared at the camera with stoic defiance.

"Oh boy," Quinn whispered to herself.

"The fullness of Khalistan cannot be reached until every book and precious object you stole from the Sikh Reference Library three decades ago is returned to the Sikh people."

Quinn bolted forward when he mentioned the Sikh Reference Library. She didn't know what that was, but now she had an inkling as to why she'd been summoned to this meeting.

"When you have met our demands, the establishment of Khalistan and the items of our heritage returned, this man will be released, along with your priceless manuscripts.

Until then, he is our prisoner. Know that this is only the beginning. Very soon, acts of death and destruction will rain down until our demands are met." A malevolent shadow settled over his face, and his voice turned hard and cold. "Act quickly. As I have said, our patience is at an end." With that, the screen went black.

Chapter Nine

A bleak silence hung over the room.

"I'm sure you have a million questions," Deputy Director Marchelli said eventually. "I've asked Sadie Morales from our Office of Near Eastern and South Asian Analysis to give you some historical context that should help you understand his demands."

With a fingertip, Sadie pushed her glasses up the bridge of her nose and cleared her throat. "Thank you, Deputy Director." Sadie stood and Kevin handed her a small remote control. "As I'm sure you already know, the man on the video is a Sikh. Sikhism is a monotheistic religion that began in the Punjab in the fifteenth century. It is the fifth largest organized religion in the world."

She clicked the remote, and a map of India appeared on the screen. A section in the northern part of the country was highlighted in green. "Most Sikhs in India live in the state of Punjab. Primarily agrarian, it's known as India's breadbasket." She touched the remote again bringing up a different map. "The *state* of Punjab, by the way, should not be confused with the *region* known as *the* Punjab. The Punjab, which means 'five rivers,' covers an area that includes parts of both Pakistan and India.

"While Sikhs make up the majority in Punjab, they comprise only two percent of the total population of India. Some Sikhs feel they are not treated fairly by the Hindu majority in the central government and have for years fought for greater autonomy. The most extreme is the call for a sovereign Sikh nation carved out of India called Khalistan."

"Where does the name Khalistan come from?" James asked.

"It's derived from the word *khalsa*, which means 'pure,'" Sadie answered. "Those who have chosen to go through a ceremonial initiation called *amrit*, basically a Sikh version of baptism, are members of the community called the Khalsa."

"There's a great deal we could say about the religion itself," Marchelli said. "I've asked Sadie to focus on the issues raised in the video."

"Right," Sadie said. "The man in the recording is referring to the events surrounding a military incursion called Operation Blue Star. In June of 1984, the Indian Army stormed the Golden Temple complex, the holiest shrine in Sikhism, to apprehend a radical and his men who were holed up there."

A satellite image of a large square pool surrounded by a wide walkway and buildings appeared.

Quinn's eye was immediately drawn to a building at the dead center of the pool and the bridge across the water leading to it.

"Located in Amritsar, Sikhism's holiest city, the complex consists of a number of buildings. The holiest is the Harmandir Sahib, or Golden Temple itself."

As Sadie spoke, a picture of a blocky, rectangular building surrounded by water appeared on the monitor. Its gold-covered walls and domes gleamed in the sun. She pressed the remote button again.

"The targeted radical's name was Jarnail Singh Bhindranwale." A photograph of a man in nearly the same attire as the man in the video filled the screen, complete with cartridge belt across his chest. His intense stare made him look more than a little intimidating.

"He was what you could call a Sikh fundamentalist. In the late 1970s, he was an itinerant preacher. He traveled from village to village in Punjab, exhorting Sikhs to turn away from alcohol, drugs, and tobacco and return to the path of pure Sikhism. He was a charismatic firebrand, and what he preached resonated with a lot of young, disaffected Sikhs. He had a substantial following."

"Preaching clean living doesn't seem so bad," Quinn said.

"His preaching wasn't the problem. The problem was he was a radical who didn't play nice with others. He and his posse murdered his political and religious enemies. He had a literal hit list."

"That's not good at all," James said softly.

"In the early 1980s, Bhindranwale and his men were implicated in several of these assassinations. They eventually holed up in the Golden Temple complex to avoid arrest. During this time, the unrest in Punjab continued. Eventually, Prime Minister Indira Gandhi imposed President's Rule and sent in paramilitary police to roust out men all over Punjab sympathetic to Bhindranwale. Bhindranwale responded by directing his accomplices there to target Hindus, who he said were the Sikhs' oppressors. For example, there was an incident where a bus was hijacked. The Hindus were separated out from the Sikhs and shot."

The acid in Quinn's stomach churned. "Why didn't someone inside the Golden Temple arrest Bhindranwale?" she asked. "I can't believe all Sikhs approved of what he was doing."

"You're right. They didn't. But he was popular with a lot

of people, and for a while, no one had the political will to do it. And Mrs. Gandhi didn't want to invade a holy religious shrine. Even so, he turned the complex into a fortress."

Sadie brought up a picture of a brilliantly white five-story building topped with a golden dome. Each level was fronted with arched terraces. It was stately and impressive.

"This is the Akal Takht, the second most sacred building within the complex. Just as the Harmandir Sahib is the seat of spiritual authority for the Khalsa, the Akal Takht is the seat of temporal authority. Bhindranwale and company took refuge inside the Akal Takht, fortifying it with machine guns and semiautomatic rifles."

"He was hunkered down and ready for a fight," James said.

"He was. And he got it." Sadie's lips pressed in a thin line. "With the lawlessness ravaging the entire region, Mrs. Gandhi had no choice but to finally act. That action was Operation Blue Star. Starting June first, 1984, there were skirmishes in and around the complex. June fifth, the final battle was waged between the Indian Army and Bhindranwale and his men. Eventually, tanks rolled in and bombarded the Akal Takht." Sadie pressed the remote again. "It was heavily damaged."

"Wow," Quinn said quietly as she gazed at the photo that took the place of the previous one. It was also of the Akal Takht, but it was nothing like the gleaming white building pictured before. A huge, gaping hole had been blown in the upper story just below the dome. Black scorch marks scarred the façade above a number of windows, evidence the inside of the building had been on fire. Rubble was piled in heaps at the foot of the building. If not for its architecture, it could have been mistaken for one of the thousands of bombed-out buildings in Europe at the end of World War II.

"If Bhindranwale was inside that building, I have a hard time believing he survived," Quinn said.

"He didn't," Sadie answered.

Quinn sat up straighter. "What about the Sikh Reference Library the man on the video mentioned? You haven't said anything about that."

Sadie nodded as she looked down at her notes. "The brunt of the offensive was over by the afternoon of the sixth, and Operation Blue Star was wrapped up by the tenth. The position of the Indian government is the Sikh Reference Library located within the Golden Temple compound burned during the army's initial offensive." A picture of a row of burnt bookcases, their shelves warped and buckled, filled the screen.

"Did it catch on fire because a shell hit it or something?" Quinn asked.

"The Indian government white paper on Operation Blue Star states extremists inside the library building were lighting homemade grenades with matchsticks. Conclusions can be drawn from that statement."

"That sounds pretty straightforward," James said.

"It is, except a senior officer present at the time said snipers shot at a general and his men from inside the library building on June sixth, when it had already supposedly burned. He said the resulting firefight ignited the library."

"Two contradictory stories of how and when the fire started," Quinn said.

"Yes. To add more mystery, a Sikh official said he saw the library intact on June seventh. Now Sikhs allege the army removed all the books, including rare Sikh manuscripts, from the library before it burned."

"Do they have any evidence of that?" Quinn asked.

"Take a close look at this photo," Sadie said, pointing to the blackened bookcases.

Goose bumps rose on Quinn's skin when she figured it out. "There's nothing on the shelves. No ash, no burned book spines or covers. There should be some kind of residue left over if books burned."

"Precisely. Statements from a couple of government officials also support this allegation. A number of years ago, one said a handful of library office files were given back, this after everything purportedly burned. And a different official later said the army no longer had any of the materials that had been taken."

"And despite these contradictory statements from its own members, the government maintains the library burned?" Quinn's grandfather asked.

Sadie nodded. "The position is those officials misspoke."

"It's all starting to make sense," James said. "The guy in the video and the Falcon, whoever that is, believe the army lied about the library burning and instead took the books away. They think the government is still lying, actually has the books, and so kidnapped the ambassador to force it to give them back."

"That's a dangerous plan since it's unclear exactly what happened to the library," Quinn said. "They obviously take the disposition of the books very personally."

"It's a serious grievance for the Sikhs," Sadie replied. "It's perceived as the central government continuing to disrespect them. In their minds, as long as the books are held back, it proves they don't care about the Sikhs."

"And that bitterness propels them to fight for self-rule," James said.

Quinn looked at James and nodded. Turning to Sadie, she said, "Do you think it will work? Will the government give the books back? Maybe as a show of good faith, it could help get Ambassador Sharma released. It might be all the guy in the video and the Falcon get. I can't believe the central government would ever give in on Khalistan."

"No, they won't. But that's never stopped some Sikhs from trying. As for the books, the Indian government maintains they have nothing to return," Sadie said.

James rubbed his hand across his cheek in thought. "This has been very interesting, but I'm not sure what this has to do with us. Not just Quinn and me, but the agency. The FBI will take point in tracking down the ambassador and the stolen manuscripts. And Homeland will be keeping an eye on airports and borders in case they try to smuggle Sharma out of the country."

Sadie sat down when Deputy Director Marchelli spoke again. "You are correct. DHS is focusing on the Canadian border since there is a significant population of Sikhs there. They're also in the process of running facial recognition to determine the identity of the man in the video. And the Bureau is already analyzing it for clues as to where it was recorded, and examining the evidence from the Jefferson Building."

"Can they trace back to the computer that sent the video?" Quinn asked.

Marchelli shook her head. "It was burned onto a DVD and left on a counter in a men's room inside the embassy. They're checking embassy security footage, but it's been understandably chaotic due to the ambassador's kidnapping. It will be difficult, if not impossible, to nail down who left it there and when. And yes, the State Department is also involved, working with the embassy here and the Indian government in New Delhi."

"Looks like all the bases are covered," James said.

"Not quite," Marchelli said. "There's one more thing."

Chapter Ten

"Mrs. Sharma and her daughter have been apprised of Ambassador Sharma's abduction and have viewed the recording of demands," Deputy Director Marchelli said. "I was told the moment the video finished, both immediately asked specifically for your help, Quinn."

Quinn's head snapped up. "Me?"

The deputy director's lips pulled up in a small smile. "I believe their exact request to the Bureau was for 'Quinn and James, the gun-wielding librarian and her heavily armed escort.'"

Kavita must have noticed when James slipped his Glock in Quinn's purse, Quinn surmised. "I only told them I was a librarian. They can't possibly know who I work for. I never even said I worked for the government, let alone the agency."

"Don't worry," the deputy director said. "They don't know you work for us. Miss Sharma mentioned James had said he was a 'government wonk.' She also noticed how you both immediately became involved in the on-site investigation. I think that led her to conclude you are more than a librarian." She looked at James. "And a wonk. The Bureau contacted various agencies to track you two down. The request found its way to us."

"How exactly are we to assist them, ma'am?" James asked.

"You can well imagine their utmost concern is to secure the release of the ambassador. As we've already discussed, various agencies are already diligently working to find his location, free him, and apprehend his kidnappers. While that's in the works, the Sharmas have requested that Quinn, working under the assumption the library's books were indeed taken and not burned, try and track them down. As was mentioned earlier, they hope if they are returned as an act of good faith, they can negotiate the ambassador's release."

Quinn cocked her head. "I'm not sure how any research I do will turn up anything more than what's already known."

"If you remained here in the States, yes," the deputy director said. "You and James are going to India."

Quinn's jaw dropped.

Deputy Director Marchelli signaled to Kevin and Sadie. They began gathering their things while she closed her folder. "Supervising Officer Meyers will brief you on the details of your assignment."

"Um, ma'am? As I'm sure you're aware, I haven't been trained at the Farm yet. I've only done language acquisition, weapons, surveillance. Things like that." Quinn glanced at Meyers and back to the deputy director. "If you need a librarian, why not send Ben Hadley? I understand Mrs. Sharma and Kavita asked for James and me, but Ben's a better fit. He's a librarian and a fully trained operative. I don't even have my clearance yet."

"Oh, yes. That reminds me." She reached into her jacket pocket, pulled out an ID badge, and tossed it across the table. It slid to a stop in front of Quinn. "You have a briefing with security in an hour."

Quinn looked at the badge. A red strip replaced the blue

one that had previously declared her pariah status. Cages must have been rattled.

"And while yes, you're correct that Ben Hadley has the appropriate training and experience to handle this assignment," the deputy director continued, "had we thought he was a better fit, he would be here regardless of the request from the Sharmas. Let's just say you are much less likely to engender distrust from anyone you'll interact with."

In other words, no one would suspect a young, female librarian poking around and asking questions was doing so under the auspices of the US government. Apparently, the agency believed that couldn't be said of Ben. "Yes, ma'am," Quinn said.

"Finally, as for your unfinished training, we believe the Fitzhugh op has provided you with more than adequate experience to draw upon. You and James made an excellent team. We're confident you will again."

"Thank you, Deputy Director. I'm sure we will," James said and rubbed the back of his neck with a hand. "One thing. I'm scheduled to leave for Moscow next week."

"Moscow has to wait. The current situation takes top priority." The deputy director's eyes shifted back and forth between Quinn and James. "Any further questions?"

Quinn stared at her, stunned and overwhelmed. She wanted to ask how she was supposed to find an entire library that had been missing, presumed burned, for over thirty years. And even if the books did still exist, they could be anywhere on the entire subcontinent of India. Or the world, for that matter. Despite her seemingly impossible task, she gritted her teeth and reeled in her misgivings. She would answer the call. The ambassador's life hung in the balance, and it was her duty to do whatever she could to help save him. She shook her head and said, "No, ma'am."

"Excellent." Deputy Director Marchelli picked up her

folder, turned on a heel, and strode out the door. Kevin and Sadie followed in her wake.

Quinn turned her attention to Meyers. "The Riordans are going to India," he said, referring to the cover name of the married couple Quinn and James had used in London the previous December. Meyers pushed two passports across the table.

Quinn picked up the one in front of her and flipped through the pages. The UK stamp told her it was the same passport. The identical stamp on James's would only add to the authenticity of their cover. Not that anyone had questioned them as a couple, especially given their current relationship status. What surprised her was the visa with "Republic of India" emblazoned across the top already attached to one of the pages. Talk about expedited.

"You two leave this evening for New Delhi. From there, you'll fly to Amritsar and meet up with Ravi Bhatia, our operative in Punjab. He works for a solar energy company as an engineer while watching for any Pakistani influences attempting to destabilize the area."

"Is that a possibility in this?" James asked. "That the Pakistanis are involved somehow?"

"At this point, we're not ruling anything out. Your primary task, James, is to ascertain if there is a Punjabi connection to the Falcon, whoever he is, and what happened last night. You'll work with Ravi on that. You work for an American investment company looking to expand into India. You've looked up your college friend, Ravi, and are investigating potential investment in the company he works for."

"Yes, sir."

"Quinn, you're once again a UCLA research librarian. You jumped at the chance to accompany James to Amritsar to see the Golden Temple. The Sikh Reference Library inside the complex has been rebuilt, so you'll start your investigation there."

"You don't want me starting in New Delhi, since the Sikhs believe the central government still has the library books?"

"No. You'd drown in a sea of red tape. Start in Amritsar where it all began, and follow the trail from there."

"Yes, sir." One thing immediately jumped out at her as a potential problem. "I'm afraid my high school Spanish won't be much help in India."

"Many people speak English. If there are any issues, Ravi speaks both Punjabi and Hindi." Meyers waited a beat before asking, "Any other questions?"

"What do I tell Linda Sullivan?" Quinn asked. She swallowed a groan when she remembered she still had to research nightclubs in Istanbul for Cooper Santos.

"She'll be informed that you've been temporarily reassigned," Meyers said.

Quinn knew Linda wouldn't ask any further questions, which was a refreshing change from her former boss, Virginia Harris, library director. When Quinn had returned to the library from her impromptu mission with James to London, Virginia had given her the third degree every day for two weeks. Given the chance, the woman would have tied Quinn to the rack and gleefully cranked it to eleven to get Quinn to spill. Thankfully, uncomfortable desk chairs were the only torture devices housed inside the Westside Library. Virginia finally gave up when it became clear that Quinn's response was ever only going to be "I'm sorry, Virginia. Client confidentiality." Quinn and Nicole had enjoyed watching the steam billow from Virginia's ears every time Quinn uttered the phrase. It had been glorious.

The thought of Nicole made her stomach drop. Between Cooper Santos throwing her for a loop, being knocked senseless by a flash bang, and running through tunnels under the streets of Washington, she hadn't responded to Nicole's wedding cake question. She had to answer before she left for India.

Meyers glanced at his watch, stood, and shot Quinn's grandfather an inquiring look. When he rested his elbows on the armrests of his chair and steepled his fingers, Meyers took the hint. "If you have any other questions, let me know."

Meyers left. Quinn, James, and her grandfather were now alone. Quinn turned to him and said, "Grandpa, you were awfully quiet during the meeting. Are you okay?"

"Yes, angel, I'm fine." After a beat, he said in a subdued tone, "Operation Blue Star was a most tragic event."

"Were you involved at all? Or Darvesh Singh? I assume he's an old spy friend of yours."

He smiled. "You're always so perceptive. Yes, we've worked together on and off for years. But no, neither of us were involved with what happened in Punjab." His smile faded. "Despite Darvesh's public condemnation of last night's events and his many years of loyal service to the Indian government, he's under suspicion. Both the Indian and US governments think he may be a part of the conspiracy."

"I can't believe it," Quinn said. She turned and looked at James. "I didn't notice him acting suspicious or anything. Did you?"

"No." James shrugged. "But if he's been an operative his entire life, he's a pro at subterfuge."

Annoyance spurted in her middle. "Are you saying he was in on this?"

"No, I'm not," James replied in a mild tone. "I'm saying if he was, we would have a hard time knowing for sure, based on his long years of experience. And to be honest,

Chapter Eleven

Quinn stood with James inside the Sri Guru Ram Dass Jee International Airport twenty minutes outside Amritsar. Named for the fourth Sikh guru and the man who established the village that would grow into the city of Amritsar, the airport—with its burnished white marble floors, chrome surfaces, and a high glass-and-steel ceiling—was a symbol of the modernization of Punjab.

Her thumb fiddled with the two gold bands on the ring finger of her left hand as she watched bags and suitcases tumble down the chute and slowly travel the long circuit of the baggage carousel. Both rings were different than the ones she'd worn during the Fitzhugh op. The wedding band was significantly wider and the diamond in the engagement ring was larger, commensurate with James's cover as a member of a successful investment firm.

James dipped his head and whispered in her ear, "Why don't you go get the key to the car while I wait for the bags?"

Her head jerked up in surprise. "Me?"

"Sure. Why not?"

"You're not afraid I'll blow this whole thing up before we even get out of the airport?"

He snorted a laugh. "No."

until we find out exactly who's behind all this, we can't dismiss the idea he might be involved somehow."

"But he was so concerned for Mrs. Sharma," Quinn said and spun back toward her grandfather. "He even took off his turban and used it to put pressure on her head wound."

"I have no doubt Darvesh came to Mrs. Sharma's aid. And I firmly believe he's not a part of the conspiracy. But James is right. Until we know more, he'll remain under suspicion."

"He did mention it was his idea to use Sikh soldiers to guard the manuscripts. He was so proud of them." Quinn dropped her head back against the back of the chair and stared up at a panel of lights in the ceiling. "Now I wonder if it was all part of the plan."

"It might have been," her grandfather said with a hint of defeat. "Hopefully you two will find out more when you get to Punjab."

Quinn's mind began to race. She had so much to do before they left that evening. Her head snapped forward. "Oh! Can you and Grandma take care of Rasputin for me?"

"We'd be happy to." His expression turned stern. "You be careful, angel." Leaning forward, he looked past her to James. A silent understanding seemed to pass between them before he spoke again. "You too, James. When it comes to Operation Blue Star, emotions can run high."

She covered his wrinkled hand with hers and gave it a gentle squeeze. "We'll be careful, Grandpa. We promise."

Side-eyed, she looked up into his face and saw no hint of doubt. James was right. Getting the car key wasn't a big deal. Still, the confidence he had in her made her feel pretty good. "Okay." She scanned the room and spotted where she needed to go. "I'll be back in a minute."

She shouldered her way through the crowd and toward the information counter. As she approached, she smiled at the middle-aged woman staffing the desk. Quinn's confidence ebbed when it was met with an almost hostile glare. Maybe the woman wasn't a morning person. After all, it was only six o'clock.

Quinn's forced smile remained plastered in place. "Good morning. I'm hoping you can help me. A friend left an envelope here for my husband and me to pick up when we arrived. I'm hoping you have it." Quinn held her breath and waited.

"What is your name?" the woman asked and pulled open a drawer.

She exhaled in relief. "Quinn Riordan." As the woman shuffled through a number of envelopes, Quinn added, "It might have my husband's name on it, James Riordan."

The woman took one from the drawer. "I must see identification before I can give this to you."

"Of course." Quinn handed her passport across the counter.

After a quick glance, the woman passed it and the envelope to Quinn.

She smiled and was about to thank the woman in rudimentary Punjabi but changed her mind. She'd studied some basic phrases during one of their various plane flights but feared she might inadvertently tell the woman to stuff a banana up her nose. Instead, she thanked the woman in English and hurried away. She'd practice her Punjabi on someone a little more receptive.

She returned just as James hauled her suitcase off the carousel.

A smile brightened his face when he saw her. "Hey! Success?" he asked and set the bag on the floor next to her.

She waved the envelope at him before she shoved it in her purse.

They waited only another minute before James's suitcase made an appearance. Reunited with their belongings, they walked out into the early-morning sunlight. Quinn squinted against the rising sun just above the eastern horizon. She took a deep breath and relished the fresh air after being in airports and airplanes over the previous twenty-four hours.

James shielded his eyes with a hand and surveyed the parking lot. "What kind of car are we looking for?"

Quinn took the envelope from her purse, slit open the top with her finger, and removed a small piece of paper. "It's a red Maruti Suzuki Alto 800. Says it's parked near a eucalyptus tree. I have the license plate number."

"We'll need it. All of these cars look the same, and half of them are red."

"Not everyone can drive a Lotus, car snob," she said and bumped him with her shoulder.

He smirked. "I've never once heard you complain about the Lotus."

"And you never will. It's the coolest car I've ever driven."

"Ah, the truth comes out," James said. He grabbed the handle of his suitcase and started for the closest eucalyptus. Quinn did the same. "You only love me because I drive a cool car."

"Yes, yes. You've found me out." Her tone was as dry as the dusty fields surrounding the airport. "It's all about the car."

"Mm-hmm. I knew it."

They passed a number of abandoned luggage carts

parked haphazardly around the parking lot and arrived at a small red car covered with a thin layer of dust. Quinn checked the string of numbers on the bumper against the ones on the paper. "This is it." She took the key from the envelope and slid it into the lock. Happily, when she turned the key, no screaming alarms blared and the hatch popped without incident. She lifted it, revealing its small trunk space. "Will the luggage fit?"

"Probably. If not, I'll have to strap you to the roof of the car."

"I'd like to see you try."

He snickered and loaded her bag. "I'll pass."

"Chicken." She watched him stow his suitcase and close the hatch with a solid thunk. After handing him the key, she settled into the passenger seat.

James folded himself into the driver's seat, closed the door, and looked over at her.

Quinn brushed her fingertips over the two-day growth of stubble on his jaw. "And for the record, it's not all about the car." She dropped her gaze to his lips, leaned in, and gave him a soft kiss. When it grew hungrier, the world dropped away. She was only aware of the heat of their kiss and her pulse thumping in her ears.

They parted reluctantly and James gave her a wistful smile. "We'd better get going before we have a security officer tapping on our window telling us to move along."

She sat back and ran her hands through her hair. "Yeah. The file I read on Indian culture said they're not big on public displays of affection."

James nodded and faced forward again. To her surprise, rather than starting the engine, he put his hand under his seat and removed a holstered pistol. He checked the magazine of the Sig Sauer P226 and slid it back into its holster. "Check under your seat," he said.

She brought out a Baby Glock in a leather ankle holster. As James had done, she checked the magazine. It was filled to capacity.

She lifted the hem of her jeans and strapped the holstered pistol around her calf. At the same time, James secured his Sig inside his waistband at his hip.

Seat belts fastened, James asked, "Are you ready for this?" The blue eyes that stared into hers were sharp and probing. "Nerves? Doubts?"

She held his gaze. "Nerves? Yeah. Doubts? Nope."

His head snapped in a nod. "Good." He turned over the engine and backed out of the parking space. "Time to solve a thirty-year-old mystery."

"After we get a little sleep?" During their flight from Dulles to Frankfurt, exhaustion had slammed her and she'd dozed some. She hadn't slept at all from Frankfurt to New Delhi, instead reading up on Indian culture and etiquette in general and Sikhism in particular. She couldn't remember the last time she'd slept more than a couple of hours in a stretch. "I could use a nap."

"Me too." He paid the parking fee at the exit plaza and followed the road toward the main highway to Amritsar. "We're not scheduled to meet with Ravi Bhatia until later today, so we'll head for the hotel and see if we can check in early."

"And if we can't?"

"We do some sightseeing and crash hard later tonight."

"Sounds like a plan." During the Fitzhugh op in London, she learned that powering through the exhaustion and staying awake until reaching a normal bedtime was the best way to adjust. Easier said than done, though. The motion of the car and the mesmerizing effect of the flat farmland rolling past her window seemed to conspire against her, as if determined to lull her to sleep.

It wasn't long before the open farmland gave way to an urban landscape. New and renovated buildings were mixed in amongst old, dilapidated ones.

A few miles later, James wheeled the car into the parking lot of an American hotel chain located outside the city center. Since James was undercover as an American businessman, it made sense they would stay in a corporate setting with corresponding comfort and amenities. Earlier, Quinn had been mildly disappointed when she'd heard they weren't slated to stay right in the middle of everything. Now, as long as the bed had clean sheets, she didn't care where they stayed.

They left their bags in the car and entered the lobby. A young man in a gray hotel uniform and black turban greeted them from behind the desk with a wide smile. The tag on his jacket informed them his name was Manveer. "Good morning. How can I help you?"

"Hello," James replied. "We're James and Quinn Riordan. We have a reservation to stay here starting tonight. We've been traveling from the States for the last twenty-four hours and could use a shower and some sleep. Is there any way we could check in early? We'd be happy to pay for an extra day."

"Certainly, Mr. Riordan. Let me see what we have available." Manveer tapped at the keyboard, paused, and typed some more. "All we have available right now is a room with twin beds." He typed some more. "We do have a suite available, although it is quite a bit more money."

"How much more?" Quinn asked.

"Six thousand rupees a night."

James looked at her. "That's less than a hundred dollars."

"That's not so bad."

James asked Manveer, "Does it have a king bed?"

"Yes."

"We'll take it," Quinn and James said at the same time.

"Excellent," Manveer said. He tapped at the keyboard with renewed vigor and completed the transaction.

At the car again, James unloaded their bags. Quinn watched with interest when he peeled back the carpet and revealed a small duffel bag stuffed in the space where the spare tire should have been. He slung it over his shoulder and flopped the covering back in place.

"James Bond's Bag of Tricks?" she asked.

"Something like that." He locked the car and looked at Quinn. "Shall we?"

"We shall," she said.

"Are you hungry?" James asked as they exited the elevator and walked toward their room. "We could get something for breakfast."

"I'm okay. I just need some sleep."

The suite was modern, clean, and thanks to the air conditioner blasting away, cool. The calendar read May, but it was already the hot summer season in Punjab. That amenity would certainly be a blessing when outside temperatures climbed. Quinn was happy to trade ambience for comfort.

"The man funk I've got going on is making my eyes water. Do you mind if I jump in the shower?"

"Go ahead." She kicked off her shoes, took her phone from her pocket, and stretched out on the bed. "I'll check my email to see what the latest wedding crisis is."

"You're a brave soul." James grabbed some clean clothes and walked into the bathroom.

She was out cold before he turned on the shower.

Chapter Twelve

"Do you have a special secret agent door knock so Ravi knows it's us?" Quinn asked as she and James approached the flat of CIA officer Ravi Bhatia.

"Nah," he said. "That's too obvious and clichéd. We'll use a coded greeting."

"Oh, and coded greetings aren't obvious and clichéd?"

"It's cutting edge."

She shot him a flat look. "Really."

"Mm-hmm. I'll say, 'What light through yonder window breaks?' and he'll answer with . . ."

"Let me guess. 'It is the east, and Juliet is the sun.'"

"See, that's what everyone would expect," he said with a glint in his eye. "That's why the answer *actually* is, 'James Bond buys his suits off the rack.'" They stopped and James knocked on the door.

He kept his gaze forward, clearly trying to keep a straight face. He failed utterly.

Holy crap. Just when she thought it was impossible for him to be any more adorable, he went and said something like that. Sadly, the door swung open before she could give him a scorching kiss.

"James! Quinn! Welcome!" a man in his late twenties

said with a friendly smile. He stepped back to allow them entrance.

Quinn and James slipped off their shoes and left them outside the door. A drool-inducing aroma surrounded them the moment they crossed the threshold. As if on cue, Quinn's empty stomach rumbled.

Their host closed the door and shook their hands. "Ravi Bhatia. Nice to meet you both."

"You too," James answered.

"Thanks for inviting us for dinner," Quinn said. "I hope it's not an imposition." Ravi wasn't particularly tall, no more than five-foot-nine. With thick black hair and dark brown eyes, he was definitely good looking.

"Not at all. I make a mean *murgh makhani*. And being here in my apartment will let us talk and not worry about being overheard." There was no hint of an Indian accent when he spoke. If anything, he sounded like a surfer dude. His loose cotton pants and gray T-shirt with "Stanford" written across the chest only reinforced that impression.

"We brought dessert," Quinn said and held up a container. *"Gulab jamun."*

"Oh! Excellent." Ravi pointed to a spot on the kitchen counter. "You can drop them right there."

Quinn did as instructed. While the three engaged in small talk, she surveyed Ravi's flat. It reminded her of her brother Monroe's place. It wasn't a mess per se. It just had a dude vibe to it. It might have been the video game controllers littering the top of the small coffee table. Or perhaps it was the wooden cricket bat propped in one corner. Whatever it was, Quinn liked it. It made her feel comfortable.

Ravi carried a steaming bowl of food from the kitchen and set it on the table.

"I don't know what *murgh makhani* is," Quinn said, "but

it looks and smells delicious." The dish might have been included in the file she read on Punjabi life and culture. But given the sheer volume of information, including lists of things in a language she didn't yet know, she couldn't recall.

"You're in for a real treat. It's goat eyeballs."

Quinn's smile remained firmly in place even as she wanted to drop to her knees and unleash a plaintive wail. Instead, she swallowed her revulsion and screwed up her courage. "I've never had those before. I look forward to trying something new."

Ravi waited a beat before a huge grin broke across his face. "I'm just messing with you. It's not goat eyeballs. *Murgh makhani* is just butter chicken." As he indicated which chairs they should sit in, he added, "And bonus points, Quinn, for not going all squeamish and freaking out when you were told you'd be eating weird food."

She heaved a massive sigh and almost wept with relief. "Thanks. But man, that was diabolical."

"I know. I'm sorry. I read your file and saw that you haven't finished your formal training yet. I thought I'd throw you a curveball and see how you did." He nodded with approval. "You passed."

"It wasn't easy." She turned to James. "Did you know it wasn't really goat eyeballs?"

"No. I was standing here wondering if I could swallow one whole, like a big pill."

Ravi chuckled while Quinn's eyes widened and she said, "Yeah. No kidding."

Their host spooned some of the shredded chicken in thick red sauce from the bowl onto their plates. Following Ravi's lead, Quinn tore off a piece of flatbread, which she did re-member was called *roti*, pinched a glob of butter chicken with it, and popped it in her mouth. The melding of the creamy butter, tomato, garlic, onion, and myriad spices with the smoky flavor of the chicken was like nothing she'd ever tasted. An involuntary hum of happiness burbled up. Embarrassed, she dipped her head and muttered, "Excuse me."

"No worries. I'm not offended, and I doubt anyone else would be by that either. People are pretty cool with Westerners. Just avoid food that has been in contact with water, you know, like fresh fruits or salads, like the plague." He picked his bottle of water and saluted them before taking a drink. "You do *not* want a case of Delhi Belly. *No bueno.*"

"Yeah, we're being careful," James said and swiped another strip of *roti* through his butter chicken.

Ravi cocked his head. "Your cover is as a married couple."

"It is," James said.

"Are you two, uh . . ." Ravi's head wobbled from side to side, and he looked at them in turn.

Quinn wasn't sure if answering Ravi's unspoken question would be detrimental to their op, so she decided to let James handle it.

"Yeah. We're together," James said.

"Cool." Ravi dumped more butter chicken onto his plate. "I thought I caught that vibe."

"What about you? Do you have a significant other?" Quinn asked.

He shrugged. "My girlfriend in California and I broke up recently."

"I'm sorry," Quinn said. She wasn't able to stop herself from asking, "You tried the long-distance thing and it didn't work out?" She hoped against hope his response would disabuse her of the notion that long-distance relationships were as horrible as everyone seemed to say they were.

"Yeah. It pretty much blows. The twelve-and-a-half-hour time difference meant we'd get about an hour a day where one of us wasn't either asleep or at work. When we did talk, it was about things and people the other didn't know." He shook his head and sopped up sauce and chicken with his *roti*. "People who say long-distance relationships can work are blowing sunshine up your ass."

Quinn felt like she'd been kicked in the gut. It wasn't the rainbows and unicorns she was hoping to hear. She peeked over at James, who wore a sympathetic look.

"Sorry, man," he said. "That sucks."

"It does." Ravi swiped a clump of flatbread over his plate and mopped up every last bit of sauce. Changing the subject, he said, "We've got an op to discuss."

James hit the ground running. "I checked in with Langley right before we left the hotel. DHS ran facial recognition on the man in the video. His name is Samir Singh. According to immigration records, he came to the US as a child with his family from a village in Punjab in 1988. They ended up in Fresno, working a peach orchard owned by relatives. He's lived in the area ever since. Or at least he did until two months ago, when he dropped off the face of the planet. The FBI is following up, interviewing friends and family there. They're crawling through his email and phone records to try and track down others who might be involved. They're also checking into his bank accounts to see if money's changed hands, and if so, where it came from."

"I'll work my contacts here to see if anyone has heard of him," Ravi said. "Maybe check out the village."

"What are your contacts saying about what happened at the Library of Congress?" Quinn asked. "Are there any radical groups here that might be connected?" Like Ravi had done, she cleaned her plate with a hunk of *roti* and stuffed it in her mouth. She made a mental note to learn how to make butter chicken.

"I'm still trying to gather intel from them. None of the usual suspects have claimed responsibility. Never heard of this Falcon character before." Ravi dipped his head toward Quinn's empty plate. "You done?"

"I am, thanks." When Ravi reached across the table to remove her plate, she stood and picked up it and James's. "Let me help."

"Sure. You want tea? Coffee?"

"I'd love some tea," Quinn said and carried the plates into the kitchen.

"Me too," James said from right behind her. He carried the empty bowl the butter chicken had been in and the plate that had held the *roti*. They set the dishes on the counter and watched Ravi fill the teakettle with water.

"He might be the leader of a Khalistan splinter group or a new one we haven't heard about yet," Ravi said. "Some of those groups have these young-buck Sikhs who revere Bhindranwale. To them, he was this mystical Kalashnikov-carrying hero who rocked an I-take-no-crap-from-anybody swagger."

Quinn crossed her arms and leaned against the counter. "How could they get Sikh soldiers in on it, though?"

"Maybe Khalistan sympathizers within the regiment knew about the conspiracy and volunteered," James offered. "Or they were recruited by higher-ups in on it and knew which soldiers would be on board. We have no idea how high this goes."

Darvesh Singh had said he'd been instrumental in getting the Sikh soldiers the gig. He could be part of the conspiracy and could have handpicked the soldiers who carried it out. For all they knew, he *was* the Falcon. A knot formed in the pit of her stomach.

Ravi put the kettle on the stove and turned toward them. "I'm sure the Indian Army is investigating."

"What about the Pakistanis?" James asked.

"I could totally see them being mixed up in this somehow. They're always looking for a way to destabilize the area. Stirring up hard feelings about Operation Blue Star could start it, even if a lot of the older people who remember what happened don't want a repeat." Ravi set three teacups on the counter.

James nodded. "What have the officials here been saying? The ambassador's kidnapping must have made the news here."

"It did, and they've responded about the way you'd expect. The SGPC and the politicians both have denounced the Sikh soldiers and claim they had nothing to do with it."

"I read about the SGPC," Quinn said. "They're the committee that oversee the upkeep of the *gurdwaras*, right? The Sikh temples?"

"Yeah."

"Do you think the SGPC is involved?" she asked.

"As a group? No. They go through the system with their grievances. An individual within the committee could go rogue, though. I haven't seen any mention of the video or demands about the Sikh Reference Library. Since no official demands have been made public, the rumors around here are the ambassador was kidnapped for ransom and the manuscripts will be fenced."

"Good. We want to keep the library angle under wraps so Quinn can ask around and not get stonewalled by people suddenly put on the defensive." James ran a hand through his hair. "So the establishment claims not to be involved, and none of the extremist groups have taken responsibility. We have no idea who the Falcon is. There may not even be a connection between Punjab and what happened at the Library of Congress. If that's the case, the whole thing was planned and executed by members of the Sikh diaspora in the US."

Quinn smiled and winked at him. "Extra points for 'diaspora,' Mr. Riordan."

James grinned and sounded like Goofy when he said, "I'm so smart."

Had they been alone, Quinn would have launched herself at him, pinned him to the wall, and kissed him senseless. But they weren't and she couldn't, so she distracted herself by asking, "Ravi, should I put the *gulab jamun* in some bowls?"

"That'd be excellent." Ravi pointed to the cupboard and handed her a serving spoon from a drawer.

Quinn set three bowls on the counter. The conversation resumed as she placed several of what looked like syrup-soaked doughnut holes into each.

"Looks like we've got our work cut out for us," Ravi said and set the tea to steep.

Quinn wasn't a waitressing pro by any stretch, but she did manage to carry all three bowls to the table without dropping them. James and Ravi followed with the fixings for their tea.

Seated again, Ravi cut one of the fried dough balls in half with his spoon and took a bite. His eyes rolled back. "Dude, these are the best."

Quinn had a similar reaction when she tried one, although she stifled her groan. "Wow." The flavor of cardamom triggered a memory of her grandmother's Swedish coffee bread.

"Our meeting with your boss is still on for tomorrow, right?" James asked Ravi after downing two of his *gulab jamun* in quick succession.

"Yeah. It's set for ten in the morning. Don't be late, but don't be surprised if you have to hang for a while before we meet with you. It's just the way it is."

"Got it."

"While you two are in your meeting, I'll go to the rebuilt Sikh Reference Library and check things out," Quinn said and sipped the tea Ravi had just poured.

"Not by yourself, you won't," James said.

"What? Why not?" Her eyebrows bunched in confusion. "I'm not gonna screw up the library part of this."

"I know you won't. That's not it," he said in a tight voice. He didn't look at her. Instead, his stare was lasered in on a spot at the center of the table. "I don't want you walking to the Golden Temple complex by yourself."

Not this again. She thought his overprotective streak had improved. Apparently, the sleeping giant had awakened. "James, I promise I'll be careful. I don't need a bodyguard."

"You don't speak Punjabi," James said, undeterred.

"If it's a bust and I can't talk to anybody, I'll bring Ravi along next time." She glanced at Ravi, who looked as if he was about to get slammed by an oncoming bus. He gave her a noncommittal shrug.

"You might get lost."

"Come on," she said, exasperated. "We both know you can always track me down with my phone, even if it's off."

"What if somebody steals your purse with your phone in it?"

"I'm sure there's somebody inside the complex who could help me contact you if that happens." She drew in a breath and fought the rising embarrassment and aggravation. For a brief moment, she thought of her mom. When Quinn's dad got all weird and tense and grumpy, her mom always defused the powder keg with patience and love.

Her hurt and anger seeped away. Quinn softened her voice and said, "Look. We both know what this is about." He was afraid history could repeat itself.

Over and over, the muscles in his jaw clenched and relaxed.

"We all know it's better for me to go in by myself. If anyone questions me, I have the perfect answer. My husband is in business meetings all day, and I want to visit the Golden Temple while he's busy. And since I'm a librarian, I pop into the library to look around." She rested her hand on his forearm. The muscles under her touch twitched. "Trust me."

Several seconds passed before he spoke again. "You can't bring your Glock with you."

She almost smiled. From his tone, she could hear his resolve beginning to crumble. "That's okay. I won't need it." She felt the tautness in his arm relax and peered into his face. The storm that had been raging a moment before had cleared. His gaze was still glued to the same point on the table, but his lips twitched with a tiny, impish smile.

"You could take the *P to Z* volume of the *Compact Edition of the Oxford English Dictionary* with you, though."

She smiled and squeezed his arm.

Clearly perplexed, Ravi frowned. "The *Compact Edition of the Oxford English Dictionary*?"

"It's kind of a long story," Quinn said. She asked James, "Is it okay if I tell him about our first date?"

"Sure, go ahead."

"Yay." She spent the next ten minutes relaying to Ravi the story of how they'd gone to dinner in Santa Monica and later walked in on two men ransacking her apartment. She explained that while James had wrestled with one of the intruders in her bedroom, she knocked the other guy out by clobbering his head with an eight-pound dictionary.

James told the next part of the tale, where Quinn had raced into the bedroom and laid out the second man with the same dictionary-cum-weapon.

"Holy smoke," Ravi said with the appropriate amount of awe when James finished. "I had no idea librarians could be so lethal."

"We can be a fearsome bunch," she said with a smile. She set her elbow on the table, rested her chin in the palm of her hand, and looked at James. "You didn't finish the story."

James's head dropped back. He expelled a long-suffering sigh and grumbled to the ceiling, "I'm never going to live that down."

Eyes dancing, she turned to Ravi and said, "So I had two unconscious home invaders bleeding all over my carpet. I wanted to call the cops, which makes total sense, right? But James told me not to. I didn't know he was a spy at the time, so I kind of freaked out. I thought he was some kind of criminal or con man or something. I took off for the front door to get away from him." There she stopped and let the ending hang.

Ravi leaned forward and waited. Finally, he blurted, "What happened?"

"He shot me in the back."

Ravi slumped back in his chair and breathed out a prolonged, "Dude. You shot her?"

James dragged a hand over his face and sat up straighter. "Only with a tranquilizer dart."

"Still, gutsy move, bro." Ravi looked over to Quinn. "And you stayed with him after that?"

"I did." She slid her hand atop James's.

"She must really be into you if she stuck around after you put a dart in her."

"What can I say?" The look James gave her nearly fried her circuits. "I'm a lucky guy."

"And this happened during a mission?"

"Mm-hmm. Me being dropped by a tranq dart was only the beginning."

Quinn tore her gaze away from James and smiled at Ravi when the latter sounded a low whistle and said, "I get the feeling this is gonna be one hell of an op."

Chapter Thirteen

James slammed on the Alto's brakes when a man on a scooter swerved in front of them. He cursed under his breath, and not for the first time since leaving the hotel. As they inched closer to the Golden Temple complex, the drive turned more nerve-wracking. The streets seemed to be congested with every form of wheeled vehicle in existence. Car, truck, and bus horns bellowed like notes belched from the pipes of a demented, off-key calliope. Bicycles, motorcycles, scooters, and mopeds dodged through stalled traffic, only making things worse. Three-wheeled auto-rickshaws called tuk-tuks added to the barely controlled chaos.

"You can just let me off here," Quinn said. "It's not far. With this traffic, it'll be faster to walk."

He frowned. "Are you sure?"

"Yes. I'll be fine."

His reluctance to let her go was obvious, but he nodded and said, "Call me if you need anything. I'll blow off the meeting and come get you."

"If I have a problem, I promise I'll call. Otherwise, I'll meet you back at the hotel. I'll take a taxi unless you're done with your meeting before then and want to pick me up." Before he could argue, she gave him a peck on the cheek and said, "See you later." She unfastened her seat belt and hopped out of the car. She closed the door and waved at him through the window. He waved back with a resigned smile.

Quinn left the Alto behind and strode down the street lined with shops and open stalls. She slowed as she passed a stall selling T-shirts, calendars, key chains, coffee mugs, and bumper stickers sporting the image of Jarnail Singh Bhindranwale. A number of boisterous young men loitered around the counter. Ravi was right. The man at the center of the storm called Operation Blue Star might be gone, but he was far from forgotten.

She arrived at the main entrance of the Golden Temple complex and copied the actions of everyone around her. She slipped off her sandals, checked them with an attendant, and covered her head with the scarf she'd purchased the day before. Then she stepped through a shallow trough of water to ceremonially wash her feet.

Two guards, both wearing long orange tunics and holding seven-foot-long spears, stood at the entrance and watched to ensure every head was appropriately covered. The spears were intimidating, but the guards were less so, especially the one who smiled when a tourist took a picture with him.

Past the guards and through a vestibule, she descended a steep set of marble stairs. At the bottom, she stepped out onto the *parikrama*, the marble walkway surrounding the square pool. Her eyes were immediately drawn to the focal point of the entire complex, the Golden Temple. It gleamed like a golden jewelry box in the bright sunlight. Around her, the devout dropped to their knees, bowed toward the Temple, and touched their foreheads to the ground.

Taking her cue from those around her, Quinn turned to the left and began to stroll along the *parikrama*. After going a short distance, she found an empty spot at the edge of the pool and sat. Some, like her, gazed at the Temple. Others read or bowed their heads in prayer.

Hundreds of pilgrims packed the causeway that stretched across the water waiting for their turn to enter the golden shrine. An endless stream of people walked along the *parikrama*. Despite the sheer number of people inside the compound, Quinn felt a sense of tranquility.

She thought back on the briefing with Sadie Morales at headquarters. During Operation Blue Star, the serenity of this place had been shattered. Quinn stared at the Akal Takht and envisioned tanks, their weight crushing the marble *parikrama* under them, pummeling the pristinely white building with mortars. She imagined the blasts of staccato automatic rifle fire echoing off the walls, rather than the melodic chant now sung over the loudspeakers.

It crushed her soul.

She was so lost in her musing she jumped when she heard a woman's voice ask, "Are you from the UK?"

Quinn craned her neck and looked up at a young woman smiling down at her.

"American, actually," Quinn replied. The woman appeared harmless enough, although Quinn felt her guard go up.

"Do you know about the Harmandir Sahib?"

"A little."

"Would you like me to tell you more about it and the way of the Sikhi?" She must have noticed the way Quinn's eyebrows rose, since she quickly added, "I am a student at Guru Nanak Dev University. I come here to practice my English and explain to people what they see and hear in this place."

That made sense, and speaking with a local couldn't be a bad thing. "That would be great," Quinn answered. "Would you like to join me?"

The woman's smile widened. She sat next to Quinn on the warm marble and adjusted the emerald green scarf covering her head. "My name is Amarjit Kaur."

"I'm Quinn Riordan."

"It is my honor to meet you, Mrs. Riordan."

Observant young woman, noticing my rings, Quinn thought. "Please, call me Quinn."

"And I am Amarjit. Are you enjoying your time here?"

"I am, although I haven't really seen much yet. I only arrived a little while ago and wanted to take it in first." Quinn looked at the Golden Temple again. "It's stunning. I've never seen anything like it."

"It is the most holy place in all of Sikhism. Harmandir Sahib means 'the Abode of God.' The beginnings of this holy shrine began when the Amrit Sarovar, the holy tank, was first dug by the fourth guru, Guru Ram Das, in 1577."

Quinn immediately recognized the name. "The airport is named after him, right?"

"Yes. *Amrit* means 'nectar' and *sar* is shortened from *sarovar*, meaning 'lake.' Amritsar means 'pool of nectar.' The Harmandir Sahib itself was built by the fifth guru, Guru Arjan Dev. It was finished in 1604."

"Was it always covered in gold?"

"No. Maharaja Ranjit Singh, the great leader of the Sikh empire, had the gold plating applied two hundred years later."

"With that long line waiting to get in, it's obviously the main draw here," Quinn said.

"Yes. They are waiting to give respect to the Guru Granth Sahib. It is where the Guru resides during the day."

"But the Guru Granth Sahib isn't a person, right?" Quinn asked. "It's a book."

"In a way. It was decreed by the tenth guru, Guru Gobind Singh, that the writings and hymns of the ten gurus would be the eleventh, final, and eternal Guru. A physical book of the Guru Granth Sahib is called a *saroop*. It is the embodiment of the living Guru."

"Is there just the one *saroop*?" Quinn asked.

"No. Like any holy scripture, there are many copies. Every *gurdwara* has a *saroop* to read from." She smiled. "You can even download the words of the Guru Granth Sahib from the Internet."

"So everyone here is reading from their copy of the Guru Granth Sahib?" Quinn asked.

"Most likely. Reading and singing from the holy scriptures guides us when we meditate on God's name and pray."

"And that's what I'm hearing over the loudspeakers?"

"Yes." Neither spoke for several moments as they listened to the recitations echoing through the complex. Quinn had no idea what was being said, but the words clearly moved Amarjit.

After a time, Amarjit said, "The Guru Granth Sahib is given greatest respect and honor. Early every morning, the *saroop* is carried on the head of a *granthi* to the Harmandir Sahib. There, it is placed on the *takht*, or throne. The *granthis* then read and sing from it throughout the day. In the evening, it is returned to its room inside the Akal Takht. The *granthis* also ensures it remains clean and well cared for."

Quinn seized on something Amarjit said. "It sounds a little like what I do, although it isn't quite as important as what a *granthi* does."

Her statement garnered a questioning look.

"I look after books, too. I'm a librarian."

Amarjit's dark eyes flashed with excitement. "You are a librarian! How wonderful. Where do you work?"

"UCLA."

"You must be a very excellent librarian to work at such

a distinguished university." Amarjit sat up straighter. "Did you know there is a library here in this complex?"

"There is?" Quinn hoped her surprise appeared genuine.

"Yes," Amarjit said with an enthusiastic nod. "It is called the Sikh Reference Library. Would you like to see it?"

"I would love to. Can you tell me where it is?"

"It would be my pleasure to take you there."

"That would be fantastic. Thank you."

They both stood and joined the crowd walking the perimeter of the pool. Amarjit pointed out various memorials and shrines along the way and explained their significance.

At another entrance to the complex directly opposite the main one Quinn had entered, Amarjit said, "The entrance to the library is outside the complex."

Once outside the compound, Quinn spotted a hand-painted sign with a red arrow and the words "Sikh Reference Library" written in English and Punjabi. After walking a short distance, they arrived at an unremarkable doorway with peeling white paint. It opened to a narrow staircase leading upward. Only the faded painted sign above the door told Quinn it was the library.

Up the stairs they went and entered the library. An older gentleman with a white beard sat at a table reading a news-paper. He reminded her of Mr. Ackerman, the widower who sat inside the Westside Library every day and did the exact same thing. The fond memory of him made her smile.

"I can see how much you love libraries from your smile," Amarjit said.

"I do love them. Libraries are more than just books. They preserve the knowledge that tells us who we are, where we've been, and how to go on from here."

"Well said. I could not agree more," said a woman as she approached Quinn and Amarjit. "I hope you do not mind my interruption. I could not help but overhear your words."

From the woman's expression, Quinn knew her presence was a great source of curiosity.

Quinn smiled to put her at ease. "No, not at all. It's always nice to meet someone who understands the importance of libraries."

"I do. It is why I am a librarian," the woman said. Her eyes were hazel, and a smattering of gray streaked her otherwise black hair.

"Me too," Quinn said and glanced around. The library wasn't fancy or ornate. The shelves were metal and utilitarian. Some were stacked with large volumes of bound newspapers; others were crammed with books from one end to the other.

Amarjit turned and pressed her palms together. She dipped her head to the other woman in a respectful bow. *"Sat Sri Akal,"* Amarjit said, reciting the Sikh greeting that roughly translated meant, "God is the ultimate Truth." "I hope you do not mind that I brought Mrs. Riordan here. As we sat together on the *parikrama*, she mentioned she is a librarian at UCLA."

Quinn noticed the woman's guard lower, and the polite smile gave way to a sincere one. "Welcome. My name is Harbir Kaur."

Quinn thanked Amarjit for spending time with her when the young woman took her leave, then introduced herself and handed Harbir one of her fake UCLA business cards. She seemed duly impressed by it. "Would you mind if I looked around?" Quinn asked.

"Please do. I am sure our library is not as large as the one you work in, but we are proud of it."

"It may not be as large, but I'm sure you have a lot of items we don't."

"That is true. We have many books and manuscripts here that are irreplaceable." Harbir lowered her voice and took a half step closer to Quinn. "I am so pleased our manuscripts are safe. I am sure you heard of the unfortunate incident at your Library of Congress several nights ago."

She wanted to know what Harbir knew, so Quinn answered, "Only a little. My husband and I have been traveling. What happened exactly?"

Harbir wrung her hands. "Soldiers in the Sikh regiment were guarding an exhibition of valuable Indian manuscripts displayed at your library. They stole them and kidnapped our ambassador to your country."

Quinn gasped. "That's terrible. Does anyone know why they did it?"

"Many think they will ransom the ambassador and sell the manuscripts," she said. A ferocious scowl twisted her features. "Such treasures should be valued for more than how much money they can fetch."

"So true," Quinn said. "Since the soldiers are Sikh, are people here concerned about backlash?"

"Some are. But we try to go about our lives. It is not the first time the rest of India has turned an angry eye toward us Sikhs."

"You mean Operation Blue Star? I learned a little about it in college."

Harbir's gaze dropped to the floor. "Yes," she said in a quiet voice. "It was a terrible time. I was young, but I know it is something I do not wish to experience again."

Quinn blinked in surprise. "You were here?"

"Yes."

"It must have been completely terrifying."

"It was. My parents, older brother, and I lived here in the complex. My father was an assistant librarian here in this very room." A shadow of sadness passed over Harbir's face. "I was only ten years old at the time. It was very hot and very loud. Explosions shook the buildings. Debris rained down on us from the ceiling. I have a memory of my father sheltering me with his body."

Quinn nodded and swallowed at the thickness in her throat. "My father would have done the same for me."

Something over Quinn's shoulder caught Harbir's attention, chasing away the shadow. Quinn turned to see a tiny, older woman walking toward them.

Quinn stood silently while the other two women spoke in rapid Punjabi. Quinn knew she was the object of conversation when Harbir showed the other woman Quinn's business card. As they talked, Quinn studied their faces. Based on their similar facial features, she had a pretty good idea who the older woman was.

Harbir turned to Quinn and spoke to her in Punjabi. When she caught her name, she realized she was being formally introduced. Harbir then switched to English and said, "Mrs. Quinn Riordan, this is my mother, Mrs. Rupinder Kaur."

Quinn pressed her palms together and bowed. *"Sat Sri Akal."*

The elder Mrs. Kaur returned Quinn's greeting, a delighted smile on her face.

"I told my mother you are also a librarian. She is quite pleased to learn of your interest in ours. This library has been a part of her life for many years."

"It's my honor to be here." Quinn paused. This was an incredible chance to get a firsthand account of what happened to the library in 1984. She didn't want to blow it, nor come off as being disrespectful or pushy. She needed to tread carefully. "I'm afraid I'm like most Americans. We don't know much about Operation Blue Star other than what we might learn in a university class. I'd like to know more. Would your mother be willing to tell me about her experience?"

Harbir and her mother held a short conversation while Quinn mentally crossed her fingers.

"She says you are the first Westerner to ask to hear her story. She would be pleased to tell you."

Quinn nodded. This wasn't only about gathering intel anymore. Looking into two of the faces of Operation Blue Star, it was now very real and very personal. It was no longer an abstract political and military event that took place before Quinn was born a half a world away. It was about real lives of real people who had lived through a terrifying and life-shattering event.

The prospect of what Quinn was about to hear filled her with awe and trepidation. From the bits Harbir had already mentioned—and what Quinn already knew of Operation Blue Star—Mrs. Kaur's story would be difficult to listen to. And yet, it was Quinn's privilege to be told the woman's account. It wouldn't be easy, but it was a story she needed to bear witness to, not so much as an officer of the CIA, but as a human being.

Quinn looked directly at Mrs. Kaur and said, "It is an honor for me to hear it."

Chapter Fourteen

The three women sat in the shade of a tree not far from the entrance to the Sikh Reference Library. The air around them was hot and dry and would only get hotter as the day wore on.

The Kaur women were settled in chairs while Quinn sat on the grass facing them. The amplified voice of a chanting *granthi* drifted over them.

When Mrs. Kaur began to speak in a strong and measured tone, her eyes were fixed on a point off in the distance, as if staring into her past.

"The army and paramilitary police had the Harmandir Sahib complex surrounded," Harbir said, translating her mother's words. "It was very tense. Early in the afternoon on the first day of June, they fired bullets into the complex, mostly at the Harmandir Sahib itself. My father and the others inside the library took cover behind steel book cabinets when some of the bullets came their way. The shooting ended that evening as suddenly as it started."

Mrs. Kaur spoke again when Harbir fell silent.

"The second of June was quiet," Harbir said a moment later. "There was no gunfire. Many pilgrims and their families traveled to Amritsar that day. They came to observe the martyrdom of Guru Arjan Dev Ji at the Harmandir Sahib the next."

"I know that name," Quinn said. "He was the one who built the Harmandir Sahib."

Mrs. Kaur glanced down at Quinn, looking rather astonished.

"Amarjit told me about him," Quinn said.

Harbir relayed Quinn's response. Mrs. Kaur nodded in approval and continued.

After another long passage, Harbir said, "It was very hot the next day, but it did not matter. Thousands of people filled the Harmandir Sahib to pay their respects to the Guru Granth Sahib and Guru Arjan Dev Ji. Men and women, old and young, entire families had come. That evening, the army imposed a curfew. No one was allowed to leave. There were still thousands of pilgrims inside."

"They wouldn't even let the women and children leave?" Quinn asked.

Harbir answered without consulting her mother. "To this day, the army insists it announced a warning to the pilgrims over the loudspeakers, telling them they should leave."

"And you didn't hear it?"

Harbir asked her mother the question and she shook her head in response. "If there had been such a warning, why would the people have stayed?"

That was a good question. Quinn tuned into the voice coming over the loudspeakers again. If they were set to the same volume that fateful day in 1984 as they were today, an announcement would have been difficult to miss.

When Quinn had no answer for Mrs. Kaur's question, the older woman picked up her narrative.

"At four in the morning on June fourth, there was a sudden and loud explosion. She thought the entire complex was going to collapse on top of us," Harbir said. "My father took my brother and me from our beds. The four of us huddled in a corner as the explosions continued around us."

As Harbir spoke, her mother stared into the distance again, obviously lost in the memory. Her folded hands rested on her lap, one thumb absently rubbing the thumbnail of the other.

"At one point, my father peeked through a window of our home into the interior of the complex. He said he saw people crawling on their bellies across the bridge away from the Harmandir Sahib. Water sprayed high into the air when shells landed in the *sarovar* and exploded."

Mrs. Kaur continued. She lifted a hand and circled it in the air.

"Helicopters flew overhead," Harbir said. "A bright spotlight shone down, marking where the bombs should go. Many young men were blown to pieces that way. It went on like this most of the day.

"The next day, the militants who had fortified the Akal Takht shot back at the soldiers trying to infiltrate the compound. The commandos had to retreat.

"The water and electricity had been cut off, so we had no food or water. We could not escape. If we went outside, we would have been shot. We all were very thirsty. As if to taunt us in our thirst, helicopters fired at the overhead water tank until it burst. All the water was lost."

The intensity and speed with which Mrs. Kaur told the next part of the story increased. Quinn found herself straining forward to catch the words Mrs. Kaur spoke even though she didn't understand them.

"That evening, there were suddenly very bright lights shining inside the complex. At first my mother and father thought they were ambulances coming to take away the many wounded and dying people. They were not. They were army tanks. They rolled down the stairs at the main entrance and drove over the *parikrama* toward the Akal Takht. All night the tanks bombarded it."

When Mrs. Kaur continued, she was subdued. "When the sun rose the next morning, we saw the Akal Takht with large holes put there by the shells. It was burning. Tanks had also invaded the complex near the hostels where many of the pilgrims had taken shelter. There were many cries of injured and wounded people. Blood and bodies littered the *parikrama*.

"By the afternoon of June sixth, the gunfire and explosions ended. The army made an announcement that we should all come outside. We were afraid to, of course. We feared we would be shot the moment we stepped out of our home. We had no choice but to do as we were told. We came out.

"The air was filled with the stench of smoke and gunpowder and death."

Harbir reached over and rested her hand atop her mother's. Quinn wanted to wrap the tiny woman in a hug but didn't want to breach etiquette. Instead, she bowed her head, stared at the blades of grass in front of her crossed legs, and blinked back the tears.

After a long moment, Mrs. Kaur resumed.

"We came out of our home," Harbir said. "My father was ordered to put his hands up. When he refused, one of the soldiers called him a terrorist and smashed him in the face with the butt of his rifle. He collapsed on the *parikrama*."

Harbir looked away from her mother and said to Quinn, "I remember the face of the soldier who hit my father. Not only because of his brutality, but because he was smoking a cigarette. I had never seen anyone smoke inside the Harmandir Sahib compound before. Tobacco is strictly forbidden." Her lips twitched with a wistful smile. "Who could have known what the lasting memories of a ten-year-old child would be."

Harbir returned her attention to her mother. When the older woman spoke again, her voice had tightened. She swiped at the tears that trickled down her cheeks with a wrinkled hand. Her agony was barely restrained.

"The man who struck my father and another soldier picked him up by the arms and dragged him away. My mother cried out for them to let him stay with us, but they did not listen to her." Harbir swallowed hard and said barely above a whisper, "That was the last time we saw him. We were told later he died in the custody of the army."

The air whooshed from Quinn's lungs like she'd been kicked in the gut. She covered her mouth with her hand. "You don't have to tell me any more if it's too painful," Quinn said when she'd regained her composure.

After Harbir told her mother what Quinn had said, the older woman responded and shook her head.

"She said if she only spoke when she felt no pain, she would be forever silent."

Quinn's throat constricted as tears filled her eyes. Unable to speak, she could only nod her understanding.

"My mother, my brother, who the army thankfully left alone because he was only twelve years old, and I joined a large group of women and children who sat in the hot sun and sweltering heat on the *parikrama*. We had no food or water. Some of the youngest and oldest did not survive.

"We were given permission to leave the complex the evening of the sixth. We walked to a local *gurdwara*. We lived like refugees. The only clothes we had were those we wore that day.

"About a week later, we were finally able to return to our

home. We were shocked and saddened to learn the library had been burned."

Mrs. Kaur scowled. Her voice was sharp as she continued.

"The army said it had caught fire when it was first invaded," Harbir said on behalf of her mother. "We knew that was not true. We would have seen the smoke and fire. It had been purposefully set some days later. For many years we believed the precious *saroops* of the Guru Granth Sahib, some handwritten by the gurus themselves, had been lost. There was a special and rare one with an inscription and the signature written in the hand of Guru Gobind Singh Ji himself. It was beautiful. Its pages were decorated with gold."

"An illuminated manuscript," Quinn said.

Harbir smiled. "Yes. My father allowed me to see it once. I was sure it was filled with magic because of the way it glowed."

"I've seen manuscripts like that, too," Quinn said, returning her smile. "Losing all of those irreplaceable manuscripts and books must have been devastating."

"Yes. These many years later, we know the army took the books out before they set fire to the library."

"Really? What makes you so sure?"

"The words of the librarian who inspected it soon after it burned. He said the bookcases had been burnt and there was ash from old newspapers. But there were no remnants of charred book covers or spines on the shelves. There was nothing on the shelves when the library was set on fire. Years later, a number of files that had been inside the library were returned. How is that possible if everything burned?"

That was exactly the same conclusion the agency had arrived at.

"The Sikh community has asked the central government to return our treasures for many years. Still we wait," Harbir said. The resigned sag of her shoulders made it clear Harbir didn't really think it would ever happen.

Quinn's charge to find the stolen books now seemed even more daunting than before. "And now you're a librarian here. That's remarkable."

"Yes. I have a deep love for this library. It helps me stay connected to my beloved father. It saddens me that my own daughters will never know their grandfather."

"How old are they?"

"They are eleven and thirteen." Her smile was one of a proud mother. "They are wonderful girls."

"I'm sure they are. They're lucky to have two very remarkable and resilient women in their lives."

Harbir tipped her head down, as if embarrassed by Quinn's comment. Mrs. Kaur had a similar reaction after Harbir told her Quinn's words.

Quinn wondered if there was more intel to gain from Harbir, but the conversation seemed to have come to a natural end. To try to pump for more information at that moment felt wrong. Not wanting to completely close the door, Quinn said, "Thank you for speaking with me today. Your stories are incredibly moving. I am so privileged you told them to me. Would it be okay if I came back with my husband in the next few days? I'd like for him to meet you and show him the library."

"Certainly," Harbir said. "Is he a librarian, too?"

"No, but he has a fondness for them," Quinn said with a smile. "We met in a library."

The dark pall of past sorrows lifted when Harbir smiled and conveyed Quinn's words to her mother. The older woman's face lit up and she spoke directly to Quinn.

"She has asked you to come eat with us at the *langar*. She wants to hear the story of how you met your husband."

"The *langar*?"

"It is a communal kitchen within every *gurdwara* where food is served to all, Sikhs and non-Sikhs, for free. Sikhism teaches that all people regardless of color, religion, gender, age, or caste are equal, and that we must share what we have with others. Our *langar* here serves thousands every day."

"It would be my honor to have lunch with you. Do you mind if I text my husband and let him know what I'm doing? I don't want him to worry."

"Of course."

Quinn scrambled to her feet and walked a few paces away, leaving Mrs. Kaur and Harbir to chat under the tree. She sent James a text, informing him she was fine and about to have lunch. She assumed he was in a meeting, so it surprised her when her phone rang.

"Hey. Glad everything is okay," James said.

"It is. This place is amazing. I met these two incredible women who lived through Operation Blue Star. I can't wait to tell you about them."

"I can't wait to hear. I also called to give you a heads-up. The big boss wants to meet you. We're having dinner with him tonight."

"Let me guess. Judge the man by the company he keeps, specifically his wife?"

"Something like that, yeah."

"Got it. I'll try to keep the dancing on the tabletop to a minimum."

"That'd be appreciated," he said without missing a beat. "And walking two steps behind me wouldn't be a bad idea, either."

She snorted. "Yeah, like that's gonna happen."

"Fine," he said with a sigh. "You can't blame a guy for trying. Let me know when you get back to the hotel, okay?"

"Okay."

"I love you."

Her insides turned to goo every time he said those three words to her. "I love you, too. Bye."

Quinn touched the screen and turned toward her lunch companions. The dopey smile brought on by his words was still plastered on her face.

Mrs. Kaur chuckled and spoke directly to Quinn as she walked toward them.

"My mother says, 'You have the face of a happily married woman.'"

She might not have been married for real, but she was happy for real. Gazing into those wise, old eyes, Quinn said, "Tell her she's absolutely right."

Chapter Fifteen

"Are you sure I'm dressed okay?" Quinn asked James as they rode the hotel elevator to the first floor. She glanced down at her cream-colored linen slacks and fingered the hem of her turquoise silk top. "Not too casual?"

"No, you look great."

"I feel like a 1950s wife hoping she doesn't screw up her husband's chance at landing that big account."

A wicked gleam flickered in James's eyes. "Just smile, look pretty, and leave the rest to me."

Her mouth flew open in surprise and she playfully slapped his arm. "I can't believe you just said that. If I didn't know you were kidding, I'd whack you harder."

"Who says I'm kidding?"

"The goofy smirk on your face kind of gives it away."

"I can't get anything past you." He looked over at her with an admiring smile. "And don't worry. Just be yourself and you'll impress. Besides, this isn't about business. This is about intel."

"Right," she said. "Intel."

The elevator bounced to a stop and the doors slid open. They headed for the entrance to the Chinese restaurant where they would be dining with Ravi and his boss, Mr.

Karnail Singh Sandhu. One of the perks of James and Quinn staying at one of the nicer hotels in Amritsar was that it was home to several high-end restaurants. Mr. Sandhu was more than happy to meet them there for dinner when he learned where they were staying.

Ravi was already waiting when James and Quinn arrived. As they chatted, Quinn noticed Ravi's accent had changed. Gone were the inflections of the California dude she and James had dined with the night before. His speech now reminded Quinn of the way Kavita Sharma spoke.

Ten minutes later, the big boss arrived. He greeted each in turn, shaking first James's hand and then Ravi's. He turned to Quinn, who launched a full charm offensive. She pressed her hands together, dipped her head, and said, *"Sat Sri Akal."*

A wide grin of approval erupted on Mr. Sandhu's face. He likewise returned her greeting and added, "I am extremely pleased to meet you, Mrs. Riordan."

"It's nice to meet you, too."

She peeked over at James. He beamed at her.

A little younger than Quinn's father, Mr. Sandhu was the same height as Ravi and solid, like he was well acquainted with physical labor. Quinn noted his beard was trimmed, unlike the long, flowing ones worn by many men at the Golden Temple. The way the tips of his mustache curled upward in a subtle handlebar was quite dashing. Dressed in black trousers, a crisp white dress shirt, and black turban, he exuded an air of affluence. Like all Sikhs, he wore a steel bracelet around his wrist.

They entered the restaurant and made their way to their table. It was slow going, though, since Mr. Sandhu stopped four different times to enthusiastically greet fellow diners and introduce James and Quinn as "important business associates from America." All were duly impressed.

As Quinn stood by and watched the man with the big smile and even bigger personality glad-hand, she saw for herself why Ravi had been inserted into Mr. Sandhu's orbit. The man knew everyone in Amritsar and everything that went on in that part of Punjab.

Once seated, Mr. Sandhu said, "It is a pity my wife could not join us this evening. Our son, Gopal, is marrying this weekend. Baldeep is busy with the final details. I am sure you understand how it is in the last few days before a wedding." His voice had a warm, rich baritone quality, which only added to his amiability.

Quinn assumed he was referring to her and James's fictitious wedding. She couldn't speak as a real bride, but she had been closely involved with enough weddings to answer with a truthful, "Yes, I know exactly what that's like. As the time until the wedding day decreases, the number of things to be taken care of increases."

"Indeed," Mr. Sandhu said. "There are a number of rituals that occur in the days leading up to a Sikh wedding, as well as after. It is a very busy time."

The conversation was put on hold when their server arrived. "If it is agreeable to everyone, I will order several dishes I know to be excellent here. We can eat as a family." When his dining companions agreed—and in that situation, dissent wasn't really an option anyway—he ordered half a dozen dishes. Quinn recognized a couple of the things he ordered and silently prayed that none of the others would contain goat eyeballs or anything that could be classified as entrails.

"Congratulations on the marriage of your son," James said once the server left.

"Thank you. We are very pleased. She is a lovely girl who comes from an excellent family." He looked to Ravi and said, "Your wedding is in the near future, is it not?"

Quinn tried to maintain a poker face in her confusion.

"I regret to say it has been called off," Ravi answered.

"I am sorry to hear this," Mr. Sandhu said. "The distance between you here in Amritsar and her in Delhi was too difficult to overcome?"

"It was," Ravi replied without elaboration.

"When you are ready, my boy, remember what I have told you before. I have plenty of Hindu friends with daughters I would be happy to introduce you to."

And there it was. Quinn's confusion vanished. Ravi had invented a fiancée in Delhi to deflect his boss. It probably wasn't a coincidence that the breakup with his real girlfriend in California coincided with his ersatz engagement coming to an end. She fought the image trying to press into her mind of James one day having a similar conversation with a boss. The only difference would be they'd be speaking Russian. The thought made her queasy.

"Thank you, sir," Ravi said.

Mr. Sandhu must have realized it was time to change the subject. He turned to Quinn. "James tells me you are a librarian."

She pushed aside the negative thoughts of what might be and focused on the here and now. "I am."

"Do you read many books?"

Quinn smiled. That was a question she got asked a lot. "As a matter of fact I do, for both business and pleasure."

"Excellent! You are just the person I want to talk to. I would like to find a new author to read. Do you have any suggestions?"

"I'm afraid my background in Punjabi fiction is lacking, but if you're interested in English, I'm sure I can come up with a few authors you can try. What kind of stories do you like?"

For the next few minutes, she conducted an impromptu reference interview. She asked who his favorite authors were and tossed out some names who wrote in the same genre. When they had settled on a handful of writers who seemed to pique his interest, Quinn took a pen from her purse and wrote the list on the back of one of her business cards. "Let me know what you think of these once you've read them. I can give you more suggestions based on who you did and didn't like."

Mr. Sandhu held the business card between his fingers and gazed at it like a treasured possession. "I feel as if I have my own personal librarian."

"It's pretty great, isn't it?" James said.

"You are a lucky man, James Riordan, to have such an intelligent and beautiful wife."

"I know. I'm very lucky." James's voice brimmed with pride.

Score one for the 1950s wife, Quinn thought with a small smile.

Mr. Sandhu's demeanor changed when he frowned and crossed his arms over his chest. "As a librarian, I am sure you have heard about the nasty business that took place at your national library."

"We did," Quinn said. "Isn't it shocking? I'm glad the library itself wasn't damaged, but the ambassador and the manuscripts disappearing has to be really distressing to people here."

"It is. I and many like me are very angry at such a reckless thing. The rash actions of a few Sikh terrorists have once again put all Sikhs under suspicion. It becomes very dangerous for us. Much of the world believes we are terrorists. We are not."

"What makes you think terrorists are behind it?" James asked. "Has anyone claimed responsibility or made demands?"

"I am not aware of any. However, it is the only thing that makes sense."

"How so?"

Mr. Sandhu stopped and shook his head. "We are here to have an enjoyable meal together. I do not wish to discuss such unpleasantries."

"Of course," James said. Quinn tried to read James's face, to see if he was as disappointed as she that Mr. Sandhu had just shut down a promising opening for more conversation. He didn't seem bothered in the slightest. He must have been confident the topic would come up again. "Quinn made a visit to the Golden Temple today, didn't you, honey?"

"I did."

Mr. Sandhu's arms uncrossed and his dour expression vanished. "Smashing! Tell me, what did you think of it?"

"It was an incredible experience. I just sat there on the *parikrama* for a while, staring at the Harmandir Sahib. I loved how it seemed to float in the middle of the *sarovar*. And of course the hymns from the Guru Granth Sahib sung by the *granthi* only added to the tranquility of it all."

Mr. Sandhu gawped at her. From across the table, Ravi stared at her, equally stunned. James, on the other hand, picked up his glass and took a sip of his drink. She knew he was covering the smile she glimpsed on his lips.

Finding his voice again, Mr. Sandhu said, "It seems you have learned quite a bit today."

"I did, especially from three wonderful women I met," Quinn said with an enthusiastic nod. "A university student I met explained to me why Sikh men have Singh in their name and women have the name Kaur."

Amusement sparkled in Mr. Sandhu's dark eyes. "And what did she tell you?"

"She said that from the start, Sikhism taught equality and rejected the caste system. Hindu last names can indicate caste, so to make everyone equal, the tenth guru said all

Sikhs should adopt or at least include the same name: Singh, meaning 'lion,' or Kaur, which is 'princess.'"

"It was explained to you very well," Mr. Sandhu said.

"Why don't you tell him about the mother and daughter you met today," James said with a subtle dip of his chin.

And there it was. He'd just steered them back on topic.

"Oh, yeah." She shot him a nearly imperceptible wink. "A lovely woman named Rupinder Kaur and her daughter Harbir told me their incredible story of perseverance and heartbreak during Operation Blue Star." Keeping her voice light and conversational, she said, "I was completely enthralled. The sad thing is, a lot of Americans know next to nothing about Operation Blue Star." She shrugged. "Or Sikhs, for that matter. I know a number of Sikh men were attacked and beaten in the United States after 9/11 simply because they had beards and wore turbans."

"Much like what happened here in the aftermath of Operation Blue Star, only much worse," Mr. Sandhu said. "Terrible retribution fell upon us Sikhs."

"I don't understand why, though. You were the ones who had your sacred shrine invaded by an army." Quinn clamped her hand over her mouth. "I'm sorry. You said you wanted to have a pleasant dinner, and I made us swerve into the subject again."

"No. Do not apologize. Perhaps you will better understand why there are those of us who are unhappy to see what those soldiers did at your library once you hear more of the story of 1984. After Operation Blue Star, most Sikhs were angry with Mrs. Gandhi for desecrating the Harmandir Sahib."

"That seems like a perfectly understandable response," James said.

"In an act of revenge, two of Mrs. Gandhi's Sikh bodyguards gunned her down outside her house in Delhi in October of 1984."

"Oh boy," Quinn breathed.

"Indeed. When the news of Mrs. Gandhi's assassination was broadcast, retaliation was swift and brutal. Anti-Sikh rioting broke out that night near the hospital where she was taken. The next day, lawless Hindu hooligans forced their way into homes in several Sikh neighborhoods in Delhi. They dragged the men out into the streets, doused them with petrol, and set them on fire. Women were killed or defiled. Homes were burned. They pulled Sikhs from buses and trains and murdered them." Mr. Sandhu's shoulders sagged under the weight of his sorrow.

"I'm so sorry," Quinn said quietly. "I had no idea. You don't have to say any more."

"The fact you have never heard these things is the reason why I must tell you," he replied. "Three thousand Sikhs were murdered in Delhi over the course of the next four days. Some say the number was many times that. I was fortunate."

"You were there? In Delhi?" Ravi asked.

"Yes. I was at university. Some of my Hindu friends hid me during the worst of the riots and killings. The violence was suppressed once the army was called in to patrol the streets."

"The police couldn't control the situation?" James asked.

"In the areas with the worst violence, they were either afraid to do anything or turned a blind eye. Since then, it has become known that political operatives within Mrs. Gandhi's party fomented much of the rioting."

"What a nightmare," Quinn said. "Things must have been tense around here for a long time after that."

"For years after, militants on both sides carried out various assassinations. Sikh militants used Operation Blue Star and the riots after Mrs. Gandhi's assassination as proof that the Hindu majority hated Sikhs. They called for the establishment of a separate Sikh homeland of Khalistan."

"Are there groups that still want that?" James asked.

Mr. Sandhu smoothed his thumb and forefinger over his mustache as he considered the question. "The militants who perpetrated acts of terrorism in the years after Operation Blue Star have been arrested and their groups disbanded. Still, there are those here in Punjab who agitate for Khalistan and protest Indian rule. Trouble usually arises at the observances of the anniversary of Operation Blue Star. Most of the support for Khalistan now is not in Punjab but comes from the Sikhs in the UK and North America. Most of us here are prosperous and happy. We live in peace with our Hindu neighbors. I even have a friend whose brother was a *jawan*, a soldier in the infantry, who was in the battle at the Harmandir Sahib. I hold no ill feelings toward him or his brother. We have moved on." Sandhu turned to Ravi. "You yourself have seen what friends Ashwin Gupta and I are."

"It is true. Mr. Gupta has come to the office many times. You always enjoy each other's company."

Quinn immediately picked up on Mr. Sandhu's offhand remark. They needed to find and talk to Ashwin Gupta's brother.

She also found the bit of information about the Sikh diaspora feeling the lingering injury of Operation Blue Star most extremely interesting. Perhaps they were the most aggrieved over the loss of the materials from the Sikh Reference Library as well. The abduction of the ambassador and the manuscripts had taken place in the United States. And the only suspect they had any information on had lived in California for over two decades.

So far, the only connection between what happened at the Library of Congress and India was the lost Sikh Reference Library. But at least they had a new lead to follow.

Their food arrived, and as they ate, the conversation turned more convivial. Quinn mentioned visiting the Sikh Reference Library in passing, to which Mr. Sandhu laughed and said, "Of course you did!" He made no further comment about it, and soon the topics of Operation Blue Star and the Sikh Reference Library were left behind for off-season cricket news and the impending release of the latest American blockbuster movie in India.

Over the course of the next three hours, they consumed an impressive amount of Chinese food.

After dessert and tea, Mr. Sandhu glanced at his watch. "It is late and I must get home."

"I hope your wife isn't annoyed with you for not helping with the wedding details this evening," Quinn said.

"Bah! She was glad to have me out of the way. My part comes when it is time to pay the bills." As if to make his point, Mr. Sandhu tossed a wad of rupees on the table to cover the check.

They exited the restaurant and stopped to say their good-byes in the same place they'd met.

"James, I will not be available to see you and Quinn on Saturday. I have the honor of attending Mr. Sandhu's son's wedding. Gopal is a friend of mine," Ravi said.

Quinn hid her confusion at his out-of-left-field statement.

"That's okay," James replied. "Quinn and I will find something to do. Maybe we'll go check out the Gobindgarh Fort."

Mr. Sandhu's eyes snapped from Ravi to James. "No. You will come to my son's wedding."

"Oh, that's very kind, but we couldn't impose," Quinn said.

"It is not an imposition. I insist you join us in celebrating my family's happiness." His eyebrows lowered and his tone was stern. "You will attend."

"We'd be honored," James said. "Thank you."

"We look forward to it," Quinn added.

"Brilliant. Now I really must be going." Mr. Sandhu shook hands with each of them, strode off down the hall, and disappeared around the corner.

"How about heading to the lounge for a drink?" James asked.

"Sounds good to me," Ravi answered.

Quinn shrugged. The first thing she wanted to find out was why she and James were suddenly going to Gopal Sandhu's wedding. "I'm game."

The ground-floor lounge was dim and sparsely occupied. They easily found three low armchairs grouped around a small table in a corner. Innocuous jazz music played softly in the background.

Ravi sipped his martini and set it on the table. Leaning back, he crossed his legs and took on an air of absolute leisure. "I hope you don't mind that I finagled an invitation for you two. The guy knows everybody. In a setting like that, I thought we might be able to sniff out any rumblings or rumors."

"It's a great idea in theory, but I don't know how it will go in practice," James said. "Quinn and I don't exactly speak Punjabi. It's hard to pick up intel when you don't understand what anyone is saying."

Quinn shot him a faux affronted look. "Speak for yourself. I know at least a dozen words."

James grinned and winked at her. "Yes, dear. You're practically a native speaker." He lifted his pint of dark porter from the table and, after downing a swallow, offered it to Quinn.

She snickered and resisted the urge to plant a kiss full on his lips. Instead, she took the glass and tasted his porter. Nodding with approval, she took a couple more swigs before returning the glass to its coaster. It was good, but she liked her chocolaty brown ale better.

"Fair point," Ravi said. "You may not be able to eavesdrop much, but I'm sure there will be some people who speak English. You might have a conversation or two that turns something up. You never know. Look what happened tonight."

"True," James replied.

"Aw, crap," Quinn said. "I just realized something. I have no idea what I should wear to a Sikh wedding. Should it be something I'd wear to a wedding back home and stick out like a sore thumb? Should I try to blend in?"

"I hate to tell you this, sweetie, but with your blond hair and blue eyes, you'll stand out no matter what you wear."

"James is right," Ravi said. "Trying to blend in is pointless. But showing respect by dressing like the other women might earn you an A for effort. You'll also appreciate the lighter-weight material in the heat."

She thought of the women she'd seen wrapped in yards of fabric. Terror gripped her very soul. "I have no idea how to wear a *sari*."

Ravi snorted and shook his head. "You don't want to. Wrap it wrong and you've got yourself a major wardrobe malfunction waiting to happen."

Quinn groaned. "So not good."

"The good news for Indo-American relations is that you don't have to wear a *sari*. You can wear a *salwar kameez*. It's loose pants and a long tunic. Most women around here wear them."

"I know what you mean. I've seen those everywhere. I can do pants," she said. When she heard James chuckling, she looked at him side-eyed. "Hush, you." At the confusion on Ravi's face, she said, "Dresses and I have a very prickly relationship."

"Ah." His face cleared. "You don't want to wear a dress anyway. You'll be sitting on the floor during the ceremony. You'll be a lot more comfortable in a *salwar kameez*."

"Sold," Quinn said. Her head dropped back against the top of her chair. She stared up at the ceiling and grumbled, "Now I have to go shopping."

"We'll go after Ravi and I get back from checking out the solar arrays Sandhu wants to show me tomorrow," James said.

Quinn lifted her head and looked at him. "You'll go with me?"

"Are you kidding?" Even in the dim light she saw his blue eyes flash with amusement. "I wouldn't miss it for the world."

"Thanks. I appreciate the backup," she said. "While you're out with Sandhu, I'll try to track down Ashwin Gupta's brother. A firsthand account from a *jawan* might shed some new light on the subject." She turned to Ravi. "Do you know his first name?"

"No. Until a little while ago, I didn't know Gupta had a brother. Ashwin's around the office and I've talked to him a couple of times, but that's it. Sandhu and I don't exactly move in the same social circles." Ravi took another sip of his drink. "If we do get a chance to talk to Gupta's brother, we need to tread lightly. It's hard to know how he'll react if we start asking about Operation Blue Star. He might be proud of his service and brag about it. He might clam up."

"His reaction is academic at this point. I have to find the guy first." As soon as the words passed her lips, her brain began to buzz with possible ways of doing just that.

James raised his glass and saluted her. "And there's that beautiful bloodhound look I've seen many times before." He glanced over at Ravi and said, "That seals it. There's no doubt in my mind. She'll find him."

Chapter Sixteen

The next morning, while James, Ravi, and Mr. Sandhu visited solar arrays, Quinn worked on tracking down Ashwin Gupta's brother. After research into exactly which infantry division was at the Golden Temple in 1984, Quinn called her grandfather and asked for his help. He could pull more strings than anyone she knew. Two hours later, he called back and informed her that Vikram Gupta, formerly of the Ninth Infantry Division of the Western Command, lived in Ludhiana, a city two hours southeast of Amritsar. Some expert social-media sleuthing then informed her he currently worked at a tire store. A quick phone call to Kapoor Tyre Emporium assured her Vikram was working that day.

As soon as James returned from his solar array tour, he and Quinn set off to the *salwar kameez* shop Mr. Sandhu had recommended. When they first entered and approached the shopkeeper, Mr. Kumar, he was clearly wary of the Americans. But once James mentioned that Quinn was in need of attire appropriate to attend Gopal Sandhu's wedding, the man became far more solicitous. Quinn also noticed a bead of sweat spring up at his temple and trickle down the side of his face. She wondered if uttering the name "K. S. Sandhu" was the Amritsari equivalent of a character in *The Godfather* saying, "Don Vito Corleone sent me." Either way, an hour later, beautiful royal blue material was chosen and measurements were taken with the promise Quinn's *salwar kameez* would be sewn and ready the next day.

Now she sat in the passenger seat of the Alto, staring at the map on her phone and directing James as they navigated through midafternoon traffic.

"I still think I should have bought you that fabulous purple *kurta*," Quinn said without looking up. "The black-and-white embroidery down the front was exquisite."

"It was. But according to Ravi *and* the woman who took your measurements, only the bridegroom and his attendants wear those long tunics. The rest of the men wear Western suits."

"Turn right at the next major street," Quinn said.

He did.

"It's up ahead on the left in a quarter of a mile." A crooked smile spread when she looked over at him. "Who says you'd be wearing it to the wedding? Maybe I just want to buy you something pretty."

"In that case, maybe we should get it." His voice turned husky when he added, "I could wear it and then, you know, *not* wear it."

She went momentarily cross-eyed. "Done."

A tenth of a mile from their destination, James pulled onto a side street and stopped. "Let's do this," he said.

They both jumped out and hurried to the back left tire. James plunged a screwdriver into the tread while Quinn pressed down on the valve stem with a key. Air hissed as the tire deflated.

Once it sat flat on the asphalt, Quinn stood and eyed the Alto. "Perfect."

James drove the last bit as fast as he dared. Even in that short distance, horns blared at them from behind. Quinn had already learned, though, that was normal on the congested roads of Punjab.

James wheeled the wounded car into the drive at the front of the shop and cut the engine.

"I hope Vikram hasn't gone home early," Quinn said. "Otherwise, we just murdered a tire for nothing."

"If that's the case, we'll stay in Ludhiana as long as it takes for us to talk to him."

They hopped out of the car and were immediately approached by a man in his late twenties, the same as them. He took one look at the car and said, "We are at your service."

Quinn smiled at the man who could not possibly be Vikram Gupta. For one thing, Vikram was in his fifties. For another, this man wore a beard and turban. He was clearly Sikh. Vikram was not.

"Thank you," James said. "Something punctured it about a mile back. We're lucky to have found a tire place so close."

The man smiled. "Then we are lucky as well."

While James and the man examined the flat and discussed tire size, Quinn surveyed Kapoor Tyre Emporium. The open repair bay sat next to a glass-fronted showroom prominently displaying assorted alloy wheel rims. Rectangular painted signs proclaiming the various American and Japanese brands sold there hung on the edifice above. A car repair shop that dealt in silencers, which she quickly realized were what Americans call mufflers, and an auto parts retailer bookended the tire store.

Through the showroom glass, Quinn spotted a man with short gray hair and a mustache sitting behind a tall counter. Vikram Gupta, she presumed.

"James, I'm melting out here. I'm going inside and hope the air is a little cooler."

"Okay, honey. I'll join you in a few minutes."

Inside, the air was only slightly cooler and heavy with the unmistakable smell of new tires.

"Good afternoon, miss." The man behind the counter stood and adjusted his glasses. The lower buttons of his light blue dress shirt strained against his paunch. One deep breath and they'd pop off and fly across the room.

"Good afternoon. My husband and I are glad we found your store so we didn't have to drive far on the rim."

"We are pleased to assist you with all your tire needs." The ring of an unseen phone drifted up from behind the counter. "One moment please." He lifted the handset and spoke. She caught the words "Kapoor Tyre Emporium" and "Gupta."

Bingo.

Quinn listened to his side of the short conversation, of which she only understood tire brand names.

He hung up the phone and said to her, "We sell many American brands here."

Quinn glanced at the stack of Bridgestones in one corner. "I can see that. We'll probably buy something that's not terribly expensive since it's just a rental."

"You do not want an inferior tire if you will be doing more driving."

"That's true. And we will be." Quinn gave him her best, most disarming smile. "My husband is here on business, so I tagged along. We'll be traveling all over." She wanted to get him talking about himself, so she asked, "Have you always worked in tires?"

"Yes, ever since I was a young man."

He didn't exactly deny being in the army, but he didn't mention it either. She needed to prod him. She wandered over to the stack of tires and poked a finger at the thick, pristine tread of the top one. "My dad is about your age. He's a Marine back home. Were you ever in the army?"

His features hardened and his left eye twitched. "No."

Crap. He was clamming up, just as Ravi had said he might. She couldn't allow him to brush her off like that. Time to rattle him, get him off balance.

"My husband and I were just in Amritsar. The Golden Temple is incredible. It's a shame about what happened to it in the 1980s with Operation Blue Star and everything."

He glared at her and said, "Excuse me, please. There is something I must take care of." Before she could say another word, he flung open the door between the showroom and the service bay and stalked out.

She followed him out and glanced to her left. James and the first man had not moved. The tire guy was in full sales-pitch mode.

At a loud, metallic clank, her head snapped to the right. She caught a glimpse of Gupta's back as he disappeared out a back door. Quinn sprinted after him.

She burst into a narrow dirt alley and spotted him to her left.

She took off after him. The distance between them closed quickly since his gait was more of a fast waddle than actual running.

"Vikram! Stop! I just want to talk!" She needed to gain another couple of yards on him and she could—

He abruptly pulled up, spun around, and brandished a

two-foot-long tire iron like a sword. "How do you know my name?"

Quinn skidded when she tried to stop, the grit slippery beneath the soles of her sandals. Her arms flailed and she fell hard on her butt. A shock wave of pain rippled up her spine.

His face filled with malice, Gupta lifted the tire iron over his head with both hands and advanced on her. "Leave me alone!"

Quinn tried to crabwalk backward. Her eyes widened as the makeshift weapon sliced through the air toward her face.

She rolled to the side.

The iron hit the dirt with a dull thud.

Gupta swung it up again, took aim, and brought it down.

She tumbled sideways the other way. The metal rod pounded the ground again, missing her by inches.

Quinn grabbed a rusted exhaust pipe from the pile of junk she'd rolled up against and bashed it on the outside of Gupta's knee with a fierce backhand.

He bellowed in pain.

She levered onto her knees and whipped the pipe around again, this time a forehand to Gupta's other leg.

He howled and dropped to his knees.

Quinn grabbed the tire iron Gupta had dropped and clambered to her feet.

James rushed up from behind. "Are you okay?"

"Yeah. I'm fine." She tossed the exhaust pipe back on the junk pile, folded her arm back, and examined her elbow. The scrape was only bleeding a little. Growing up, she'd lived a rough-and-tumble life with five older brothers. She'd had worse.

"And him?"

"He tried to bifurcate me with this," she said and pointed the tire iron at Gupta.

James hauled Gupta to his feet and pushed him against the back wall of the silencer shop. "I'm not thrilled to hear you tried to split my wife in two, Vikram."

The pain in Gupta's face morphed into fear. "Who are you? What do you want with me?"

"It doesn't matter who we are," Quinn said. She brushed the dirt from her palms, stinging from the abrasions she'd acquired while scrambling across on the ground. "We just need information from you."

"I do not know what you are talking about."

"You must. Otherwise you wouldn't have run," James said.

Gupta remained silent, his eyes darting back and forth between them.

"Let's not pussyfoot around anymore, Vikram," Quinn said. "We know you were a *jawan* in the Ninth Infantry in 1984. You were at the Golden Temple during Operation Blue Star."

Gupta looked like he was about to lose his lunch. "How do you know these things? I do not speak about my time in the army."

Quinn softened her tone. "You're afraid of reprisals, or at least resentment from Sikhs if they know you were part of Operation Blue Star, aren't you? That's why you ran. You don't want your secret getting out."

"No, I do not. When I left the army, there was still much anger. I moved here and started a new life. If asked about the army, I lied."

"And now you're afraid we'll expose you," Quinn said.

"Yes." He gulped. "What do you want with me?"

"Like she said, all we want is information," James said. "Answer our questions and you'll never see us again."

"And we'll take your secret with us," Quinn added.

Gupta nodded.

She studied his face as she asked, "Did you go inside the Harmandir Sahib complex during the attack?"

"Yes."

"Were you there in the days after the fighting was over?"

"Yes."

"Did you see what happened to the library?"

"Yes. I saw the smoke when it burned."

"During the battle?"

His left eye twitched. "Yes."

Quinn sighed. "See, Vikram? I'm disappointed in you. I thought we were having a moment, and you have to go and blow it by lying to us."

"What really happened?" James asked.

Gupta's lips stayed pressed tightly closed.

"Whatever you tell us won't come back to you, we promise," Quinn said.

James withdrew his money clip from his pocket. He flipped up five one hundred dollar bills and slid them from the wad of various currencies he carried. "Answer our questions—truthfully—and these are yours."

Gupta licked his lips and nodded.

Quinn kept her gaze pinned to his left eye. "Do you know what happened to the books in the library?"

"Yes."

"Tell us what you know."

"We were ordered to never tell anyone."

"Tell us what you know," Quinn said again.

Gupta blinked as he accessed the memories. "Many of us *jawan* who survived the battle and were not injured were ordered to go to the library and put the books in gunnysacks."

Quinn tingled with excitement. "What happened to these gunnysacks? Do you know?"

"We loaded them into trucks and drove them to a youth hostel on GT Road."

"Grand Trunk Road?" James asked.

"Yes."

"Why a youth hostel? What's the name of it?"

"I do not remember what it was called. And I do not know why we took the books there. We were only following orders."

"Did you see anyone at the hostel?"

"Yes. Several men."

"Who? Army brass?"

"No, not army. I did not know them. One man wore a Punjab Police uniform."

Quinn took a step closer. "What happened next?"

"We carried all the sacks into the hostel. Then we drove away and were told never to speak of what we had done." His gaze darted between their faces. "I am telling you the truth."

James glanced at Quinn, who nodded. He handed Gupta the bills and peeled off three one hundred euro notes. "Fix our tire as fast as humanly possible and you get these, too."

"What do we say to Gurnam? He saw me leave and you come after me."

"Tell him it was a case of mistaken identity," James said. He stuffed the euros in one pocket and returned the money clip to the other. "It's cleared up now and there's nothing else to discuss."

Vikram nodded.

Quinn brushed the dirt from the back of her slacks as they walked down the alley to the back of the tire shop.

Upon their return to the service bay, Gurnam looked at them, his face filled with apprehension. "Have we done something wrong? Is there trouble for us?"

"No, not at all," Quinn said and set the tire iron on the top of a metal tool chest. "It was just a terrible mix-up. My husband and I have apologized and everything is fine, right, Mr. Gupta?"

"Yes. Everything is fine."

"My husband and I really need to get going." She held an open palm out to James. A tiny smile formed on his lips as he dropped his money clip into her awaiting hand. She thumbed through the notes and pulled out five thousand rupees. To Gurnam, she said, "Put your best tire on our car, have it ready for us in twenty minutes, and this tip is yours."

It was ready in fifteen.

Chapter Seventeen

By the time Quinn and James returned to the hotel from their trip to Ludhiana, both were desperate for cool air and even cooler showers.

After dinner in the hotel's casual dining restaurant, they returned to their room a few minutes before the video-conference with Aldous Meyers was scheduled to begin. James had barely finished setting up his laptop on the room's coffee table and establishing a secure link when Meyers's face appeared on the screen.

"Good morning, sir," James said.

"Good evening to you," Meyers said in his usual brusque tone. "Sitrep."

Quinn spoke up first. She spent the next few minutes relaying her findings during her visit to the Sikh Reference Library the day before, her and James's invitation to the Sandhu nuptials, their encounter with Vikram Gupta, and his statement that the library books had been taken by the army to a youth hostel.

Meyers never blinked during her recitation. When she finished, he snapped a nod in approval. "Very good. I trust you'll be following up on the youth hostel angle. Do you know which one the books were taken to?"

"Not yet," Quinn answered. "My initial research found three. We'll tackle checking them out tomorrow."

"I'll be coordinating with techs in Langley to establish a cover that will allow us to visit them and ask questions," James said. There was no reason for James and Quinn Riordan to be checking out youth hostels, and they couldn't take the chance of blowing that cover. New, temporary covers complete with disguises would be put in place. "And as Quinn already mentioned, we'll be attending the wedding of Karnail Singh Sandhu's son on Saturday. Sandhu is a real mover and shaker in the region, so we're assuming there will be a lot of influential people there. We're not sure we'll uncover much, though."

"Why is that?" Meyers asked.

"It's hard to listen in on conversations spoken in Punjabi. And it seems from the people we've spoken to so far, especially those directly impacted by Operation Blue Star in some way, most want to leave the past alone," James said.

Quinn nodded. "If there's a group here that seems to harbor grievances about the past, it's the younger generation. Bhindranwale's become kind of a cult figure. He's plastered on mugs and bumper stickers and T-shirts. He's the hero that stood up to, in their view, the oppressive Hindu majority."

"An 'us versus them' mentality," Meyers said. "Attending Sandhu's son's wedding should put you right in the middle of that demographic."

Something struck Quinn. "Why haven't the men who stole the manuscripts from the Library of Congress gone public with their demands?" she asked. "Why not make a big stink about the missing Sikh library in the media and use it as a way to stir up public support?"

"I think the saying 'Don't ask a question unless you know the answer' might apply," Meyers said. "What if they go public but the government provides proof they don't have the library books? The agitators lose credibility within the community they're trying to persuade. On the other hand, if the government did have them all along and give them back, they can come out heroes for forcing their return. Until they know one way or the other, it's better for them to stay quiet about it until there's a final resolution."

"What if there isn't?" Quinn asked. "What if the government doesn't know where the books are and we come up empty, too?"

Meyers's lips pressed together. "You need to see the latest DVD the embassy received."

The screen went black. A second later Samir Singh, the same man who had been in the first video, appeared. An icy chill shot up Quinn's spine at the sinister rage darkening the man's face. His black eyes snapped with malevolence. "The Falcon is not pleased," he said in a voice brimming with vitriol. "Your silence in the face of our demands is disappointing. Do you not value the life of your ambassador? Are you so spiteful that you will not return our precious *saroops* to us, ones that were written in the gurus' own hands?

"Perhaps you do not fully understand what it is to weep over the scars left by the bullets that ripped through the *saroops* during Operation Blue Star," Samir spat.

A picture of an open Guru Granth Sahib with a slug embedded in it appeared on the screen. A second picture showed a close-up of a page where the bullet had ripped through it. The edges of the gash were singed black.

Samir's face returned and the camera zoomed out. On a stand next to him, one of the manuscripts taken from the exhibition sat propped open. Quinn wasn't 100 percent sure, but she thought she recognized it as the Bhagavad Gita she and James had viewed.

Her eyes widened in horror when Samir raised his arm

and pointed a pistol at the manuscript. Without a second's hesitation, he pulled the trigger three times in rapid succession. Bile surged up her throat at such a wanton act of destruction.

Samir sneered back at the camera. "Now you understand." His tone dripped with rancor when he said, "You should hurry. The next bullet will go into a heart, but not of a book."

The screen went black before Meyers's stern countenance reappeared.

"That guy is a big bag of pure evil," Quinn said with a snap in her voice. "I hope that doesn't get released to the public. The Sikhs I've met are nothing like him. I'd hate for them to suffer a backlash because of that weasel and his thugs."

"If it is leaked, it won't be from us," Meyers said. "Follow your leads and report back your findings."

James spoke for them both when he replied, "Yes, sir."

The transmission ended as abruptly as it started.

Quinn heaved a deep sigh and slumped back. "We're never gonna figure this out in time, if we figure it out at all."

"Let's hope Samir's tantrum was all show. He's gotta know killing their main bargaining chip is counterproductive. Otherwise, there's no reason to meet their demands and they end up with nothing."

"I hope you're right." She thought of Kavita. "If my dad had been kidnapped, I'd be a complete basket case."

"No, you wouldn't. You'd leave a trail of scorched earth as you searched for him like an avenging angel," James said. The seriousness in his tone told her he was in no way teasing her.

She tipped her chin up. "You're right. I wouldn't stop until I found him in whatever godforsaken craphole they'd stashed him in. Then I'd hunt down whoever took him. I can guaran-damn-tee you they'd be missing some parts when I got through with them." It was no accident she sounded like her dad just then.

"No doubt." He shifted and took her hand. The sincerity she saw in his face made the breath catch in her throat. "Take the passion you feel right now and harness it. Use it to help Mrs. Sharma and Kavita get their husband and father back."

He was right. She couldn't let anything, even the seemingly impossible task of finding something that had been lost since before she was born, stop her from doing everything she could to reunite the Sharma family and bring the kidnappers to justice. "I'll see if I can dig up some information on those youth hostels right now."

"While you do that, I'll do some prep work for my meeting with Sandhu tomorrow. We can watch a movie or something on TV a little later." Warm embers smoldered behind her sternum at the slow, sexy smile that spread across his face. "Even avenging angels need a little time to unwind." James's gaze lowered and settled on her lips. His smile never wavered as he leaned toward her and gave her an unhurried kiss. The tension in her body melted away as the heat in her chest slowly spread through her extremities. The kiss ended, but their lips remained only a fraction of an inch from each other's when James whispered, "Sound like a plan?"

"Mm-hmm," she hummed and went in for another kiss. A tingling sensation joined the heat and rippled through her body. "Great plan. I really like this beginning part."

He cupped her face with his hand and brushed his thumb across her cheek. "I'm a genius."

"You really are."

He smiled and pecked the tip of her nose. "You want a

bottle of water?" he asked as he rolled onto his feet and headed for the room's minibar.

"Sure." Quinn pushed her hands through her hair. She was going to miss him something fierce when he went to Moscow.

"That was a pretty massive sigh," James said.

She took the proffered water and thanked him. "Was it? I didn't even realize."

"What were you thinking about?"

She wanted to say, "I was thinking how much it's going to suck when we're apart," but refrained. Bringing it up wouldn't change anything. "I was thinking about how much I love you," she said. She stood, rose up on her tiptoes, and gave him a quick kiss. "And now I'm thinking about doing some research on youth hostels." She grabbed her laptop and flopped back on the sofa.

Getting to work, she researched the hostels on GT Road. There was little to no information on them other than their addresses. Nothing indicated if they were even around in 1984. On the flip side, there was no way of knowing if the place the books were left was still a hostel. "I'm not finding much," she told James.

"That's okay. It shouldn't take long to check them out." He stopped shuffling through the papers on his lap. A devilish gleam appeared in his eyes. "Who knows? Maybe we'll want to move out of here and stay at one."

"Yeah," Quinn answered in a dry tone. "Because staying in a luxury hotel with air-conditioning, Internet access, and an en suite bathroom is an incredible hardship."

"We'd be saving the US government money."

"Fine," she said, squinting at him. "You go ahead and stay in a three-dollar-a-night place with no privacy or A/C.

I'll stay here. The government can take the difference out of my next paycheck."

He blew out a sigh. "I'm all for saving the government money, but it would be bad form for a husband to move out on his wife over the cost of a hotel. I guess I'll just have to stay here with you." His impishness was completely adorable.

"I appreciate your sacrifice on my behalf."

His playfulness fell away. He gazed at her with an un-guarded sincerity. "Anything for you."

Before she could respond, Quinn saw a sudden flash of inspiration in his eyes. He tossed his papers on the table and leapt to his feet. "I'll be back in ten minutes," he announced and bolted from the room.

He left her staring at the door in bewilderment.

She shook off her astonishment and checked the app on her phone to see if he had taken off in the car. No, he was still in the hotel, but she didn't know exactly where. Her eyes remained glued to the blue dot. A few minutes later, it moved again and toward their suite.

She jumped, startled by an odd thumping on the door. Was he using his foot? She cautiously approached the door. "James?"

"It's me."

"What the . . ." She opened the door.

James stood in the doorway, his face incandescent with excitement. In one hand, he gripped a bottle by the neck and held two champagne flutes between his fingers.

In his other, he balanced a parfait glass filled with choco-late on a white plate. A dollop of whipped cream and a sprig of mint topped the dessert. Raspberries, blueberries, and strawberries surrounded the base of the glass.

"I got chocolate mousse from the pastry shop downstairs

for us to eat while we watch TV." He strode to the coffee table and set his load down. "It's not exactly popcorn, but I figured since we're staying at this fancy-schmancy place, we might as well take advantage of it."

"I can get behind that," she said, thrilled by this turn of events. Quinn took her place on the couch again and set her computer aside.

James plopped down next to her and uncorked the bottle with a loud pop. He filled the flutes with the effervescing wine and handed one to her. A sweet tone chimed when they clinked the glasses together.

She sipped the sweet drink, enjoying the sensation of bubbles exploding over her tongue. "Being seduced by a suave, sophisticated spy with champagne and chocolate in a hotel room? I feel like a Bond girl."

"Seduced? I'm afraid you've misread my intentions." He picked up the remote and pointed it at the TV. It flickered to life with the push of a button. "This is all about watching some quality Punjabi programming."

"Uh-huh," she deadpanned. She snuggled into James's arm curled around her shoulders and sipped her drink.

He channel-surfed until he settled on what appeared to be a Punjabi soap opera. A highly attractive man and a stunning woman shared a dramatic moment over a piece of *roti*.

James swiped a strawberry through the whipped cream and held it in front of her mouth. Quinn went to bite into it, but she stopped herself. "Ravi warned us about fresh fruit."

"It's okay. They wash all their fruits and vegetables with a special solution. Stood there and watched them do it."

"You're brilliant." Quinn bit into the strawberry. Intense flavor exploded over her tongue. "Wow, that's sweet."

"Grown here in Punjab, that's why." James ate the rest of the strawberry. "That *is* good."

"Told you." She downed the rest of her champagne and exchanged the flute for the parfait glass. She spooned a blob of mousse into her mouth. The airy texture was a perfect balance to the sweetness of the chocolate. Humming with happiness, she took another bite and watched James toss a raspberry in his mouth.

"You have a little chocolate right . . ." He pointed to the corner of his mouth.

She let his words hang in the air before finally saying, "Maybe you could get it for me."

He reached out to swipe at it with a finger.

"Nuh-uh. Think outside the box."

His eyebrow twitched. He leaned in and gently, torturously moved the tip of his tongue over the corner of her mouth. A rumble burbled up from deep in his chest. She expected him to escalate things. To her surprise, he sat back and finished off his glass of champagne. He might have been trying to affect a relaxed, blasé posture, but she knew he was up to something when she saw how his eyes twinkled.

Two could play that game.

Her movements deliberate and measured, she set the mousse on the table and refilled both flutes. After sipping more champagne, she swiped her crooked finger through the mousse, stuck it in her mouth, and closed her lips around it. Her finger lingered before she slowly slid it out through pursed lips.

James's pupils dilated.

"I don't want to hog it all." She dipped her finger into the chocolate concoction again and put it in his awaiting mouth.

He held her gaze as he sucked on her finger. Every inch of her insides quivered.

After a moment, she slipped it out, picked up a plump

strawberry, and loaded it with the dessert. She dragged it along James's neck, leaving a trail of mousse from his ear to his collarbone.

"You got a little . . ." She bit into the strawberry.

"Maybe you could get that for me."

She tossed the stem away and pressed her open mouth to his neck. In no hurry, she lingered over him, enthralled by the sweetness of the mousse and the saltiness of his skin. With each lick, each kiss, each nip, she felt his muscles grow more taut.

Already stretched to the limit, he snapped when she nibbled his earlobe. Exactly how it happened, she didn't know, but she was flat on her back with James on top of her. She stared into his eyes and awaited him with inviting, parted lips. He gazed down at her for a long moment before slowly lowering his head. Her eyelids fluttered closed at the delicious torture of his lips lightly brushing over hers.

She threaded her fingers through his hair and brought his head down, opening her mouth a little wider. Heat spread through her as their tongues and lips met in one sensual kiss after another.

James shifted, angled his head, and deepened his kiss. His hand slipped under the hem of her top and glided over her belly. She released a pleasured moan when his fingertips drifted under the fabric of her bra.

Every inch of her body throbbed in time with her pounding heart. Her tongue moved deeper while her fingers worked the button and zipper of his trousers. She slid both hands under his boxers, over his butt. She pushed him into her.

He kissed her mouth, her jaw, her throat.

She slipped a hand under the back of his shirt. He shivered when she dragged her nails over his skin. When she grabbed a handful of fabric and tugged, he rose onto his knees, tore off his shirt, and tossed it away. He gazed down at her, his eyes bright with desire.

She drank him in as he towered over her. He was so beautiful. She had to touch him. She sat up, ran her hands over his broad shoulders, and kissed his wide chest. She raised her arms when she felt the hem of her top lift. He peeled it off and flung it away.

Her arms came down and around his neck. She pulled him into a skin-on-skin embrace and kissed him, long and hard and erotic.

James leaned her back and kissed the fullness of her breast above her bra. "I'll get the mousse," he mumbled.

"I'll get the champagne and glasses." Her words were thick and sluggish as she floated in her James-induced warm, glorious haze.

He moved her bra strap down and kissed the spot where it had been. "We won't need the glasses."

An eye drifted open and she glanced down at him. When she saw that sexy smile of his, she nearly incinerated.

He rolled off the couch and onto his feet and pulled her up into his arms. After another kiss that had Quinn's legs weak and wobbly, they grabbed their dessert and drink and moved to the bedroom. Clothes were shed and bedcovers were tossed back.

They took turns smearing mousse over skin and licking it off. When they ran out of chocolate, James grabbed the champagne. Quinn expected him to take a swig directly from the bottle. He didn't.

She gasped and arched her back when he splashed a bit into her belly button, covered it with his mouth, and sucked. By the time he did this three more times, she ached for him so badly she couldn't restrain herself. She took the bottle from him, flipped him onto his back, and straddled him.

They moved together, savage and powerful, until euphoria welled up and enveloped her. She nearly blacked out from the intensity.

Afterward, Quinn squeezed James in a crushing, sweaty embrace and silently wondered if anyone would notice if she stowed away in one of his Moscow-bound suitcases.

Chapter Eighteen

James gingerly turned a page of yellowing newspaper and said quietly, "Why does it feel like I always end up sitting at a table in a library whenever I go anywhere with you?" The open hardback volume of bound newspapers was so large it covered half the metal table he and Quinn shared inside the Sikh Reference Library.

Quinn didn't even look up from the article she was reading in a similarly sized volume of a different newspaper. "You're just lucky, I guess. What do you expect, being married to a librarian?" James had taught her to work under the assumption they could always be overheard when in public, so they kept up the pretense even if their conversation was held in a volume a notch above a whisper. "We'd hit every strip club in town?"

In her peripheral vision, she saw him do a full body jerk. "I don't see you as the strip club type."

She looked up, her eyes sparkling with glee. "Stripper librarians. It could be a new thing. She starts off with her hair in a bun, glasses on a chain around her neck, and wearing a cardigan sweater. The next thing you know, she's swinging those glasses around and wearing nothing but some strategically placed colored book tape."

He started at her, dumbfounded. After a moment, he recovered and said, "You're insane."

"You love it and you know it."

He shook his head and lost the battle to fight off the grin. "Lord help me, I do love it." His features softened, and when he spoke again, his voice was deep and rumbly. "And you."

An urge to touch him, to connect with him, overcame her. She covered his hand with hers and rubbed her thumb over the back of it. "I love you, too." If her public display of affection was noticed, she hoped it would be forgiven as an American's lapse of decorum. Quinn had never really noticed how often she and James were in physical contact—held hands when they walked together, shoulder bumps, quick kisses—until she had been forced to police herself against doing those very things. Indulging herself for another brief moment, she kept her hand firmly atop his when she asked, "Have you found anything?"

"Not really. All of the articles I've read pretty much say the same things. Nothing about what we're interested in." She knew he meant any clues that might lead them to the identity of the policeman who had been present at the youth hostel when Vikram Gupta and his fellow *jawan* had unloaded the library. "How about you?"

"About the same," Quinn answered and closed the volume she'd finished looking through with a thump.

Quinn had done more research earlier that morning in hopes of uncovering a name. She'd struck out. The newspaper databases she searched had numerous stories about Operation Blue Star after the fact. The problem was those articles were for international audiences and didn't include names of locals. And many of the photographs that had been run in the papers at the time were now blocked from displaying on her computer due to copyright considerations. That didn't help her at all.

Given all those issues, Quinn had suggested they visit the library and look through the physical newspapers it had collected since its destruction. Since she'd already mentioned to Harbir Kaur, the librarian she'd spoken with a couple of days before, that she hoped to bring James to the Golden Temple complex and show him the library, Harbir hadn't seemed surprised in the least when they walked in.

When Quinn said she and James wanted to take advantage of the library to see what the newspapers had written about Operation Blue Star, Harbir didn't question it, mentioning it was a common request.

"I'm going to go get the volume of that weekly newspaper Harbir pointed out earlier," Quinn said. "Be right back."

As Quinn walked to the area where the bound newspapers were stacked flat on the shelves, Harbir hurried toward her from across the library. "Your husband is very handsome," she said in a low tone when she caught up with Quinn.

"He sure is," Quinn said.

"And so polite." Apparently James's greeting of *"Sat Sri Akal"* had earned him bonus points. "He treats you well?"

"He does." She thought of the chocolate mousse he'd surprised her with the night before. And everything after. Her scalp prickled at the memory. "He's incredibly sweet and treats me very well."

"I will tell my mother. It will please her to know this."

"Be sure and greet her for me. She's not working in the *langar* today?"

"No, she is not here today."

"That's disappointing." She really did want to show James off to Mrs. Kaur as if he was truly her husband. "We'll try to come by another time so she and James can meet."

"That would be wonderful. I look forward to it. Now I must get back to work." Harbir turned and bustled away.

Quinn returned to their table and set the volume down.

James looked up at her and smirked. "What, you didn't find a manuscript hidden behind a bunch of other books?" He was, of course, referring to the manuscript she'd found in a library in London during the Fitzhugh op.

"Nope. Sorry." She sat and opened to the first issue published after Operation Blue Star. "You've made an impression on Harbir, though."

"Really? What'd she say?"

"That you're handsome and have nice manners." Quinn shot him a crooked smile and deepened her voice. "You're quite the librarian magnet."

"You know how I like to wield my due date stamp."

She snickered. "Okay, I deserved that after the stripper librarian comments."

"I can't let you have all the fun."

"True."

They returned to studying their respective newspapers. After another twenty minutes, James said, "Hey, check out this picture. It was taken when a bunch of army and police officials toured the damage to the complex."

Quinn stood next to James and bent forward to get a better look at the grainy black-and-white photo. Five men in uniform stood as a group and stared grim-faced at something to the right of the camera. Two wore turbans and the other three military berets. She skimmed the text. "Those three guys in the front were commanders of the operation." Quinn's eyebrows shot up when she scanned the names listed under the picture. "The two guys in the back are Deputy Superintendent A. S. Dhami and Constable Kuldeep Singh." Quinn snapped a picture of the photo with her phone. "Maybe one of these two guys is the Punjabi policeman we're looking for. They seem pretty tight with the army and were clearly on scene in the aftermath." Her gut told her she was on to something. "I'll see what I can dig up on them back at the hotel."

They browsed through the newspapers for another hour and failed to uncover any new information. It was time to check out the youth hostels. They said their good-byes to Harbir and headed for the car.

Mildly cool air blew from the Alto's vents at near-gale-force winds. Despite its valiant effort, the little car's air conditioner couldn't fully overcome the face-melting heat of a Punjabi summer afternoon. Even as sweat trickled down her face, Quinn couldn't complain. At least she wasn't walking, pedaling, or riding in a tuk-tuk, fully exposed to the unrelenting heat.

A bus swerved out in front of them. James pounded the car's horn and slammed on the brakes. After some impressively aggressive driving, James stopped the car at the third and final hostel on their list. The first two had been a bust. They weren't even around in 1984. She assumed that would be the case for this one as well. Still, they had to check.

Quinn slipped off her sunglasses, pulled down the sun visor, and flinched when she checked herself in the mirror. It was like looking into the face of a stranger. She smoothed her hands over the long auburn wig and blinked at the contact lenses that changed her blue eyes to green. James assured her the contacts would become more comfortable over time. That time had not yet come.

James unfastened his seat belt and glanced at her. "Ready?"

She flipped the visor up and turned toward him. Reaching out, she brushed her fingertips over the fake goatee stuck to his chin. With his wig of shaggy brown hair, mustache, and now-brown eyes, he was as unrecognizable as she. "Ready."

They climbed out of the car, and as expected, the blast furnace–like heat almost melted her. She adjusted her sunglasses and, as they walked toward the entrance of the hostel, peeled the back of her sweat-soaked top away from her skin.

James held open one of the glass double doors. She stepped past him, slipped off her sunglasses, and surveyed the lobby. A wooden counter stood on the right side of the room. A beat-up couch with hideous orange and yellow upholstery sat against the opposite wall. The small air conditioner attached to the wall behind the counter rattled as it labored to cool the room. It was mildly successful.

James replaced his sunglasses with a pair with thick, black-rimmed frames. They approached a twenty-year-old guy in a stretched-out light blue polo shirt perched on a high stool behind the counter.

"Can I help you?"

"I very much hope so," James said in his precise British accent. "My wife and I publish a highly acclaimed travel blog. Perhaps you've read it. *Hill and Ted's Excellent Adventures.*"

Quinn dug her teeth into her lower lip to keep from laughing. The name killed her every time. The ever-thorough techs at the agency had mocked up a travel blog written by anonymous world travelers known only as Ted and Hillary. The analysts and technicians who had designed the website and written posts had really outdone themselves. Ted and Hillary's misadventure of milking a yak and the particulars of the shaggy bovines' amorous activities during their stay in a yurt on the expansive plateau of Mongolia had Quinn laughing out loud. The specificity with which the stories were told—including the smell of said yaks and the surprising sweetness of their milk—gave her reason to believe they were real-life anecdotes.

"I am sorry to say I have not read it," the young man said. At least he was honest enough to admit it. The clerks at the other two hostels hadn't been as truthful.

"Not to worry," James said. "We write for the budget-minded yet discerning traveler. Our hallmark is to not only provide readers with the cost and condition of an establishment but to give a full account of it, including its history. As for this hostel, how long has it been here? Is it fairly new, or was established many years ago? If so, when was it last renovated?" As James's voice sharpened with intensity, he leaned closer. "These are the kinds of things our readers need to know."

The young man almost fell backward off his stool attempting to keep James at a comfortable distance. "I do not have that information, sir. I have only worked here one week."

James waited a beat. When the young man made no attempt to otherwise assist them, James frowned, reached around into his back pocket, and removed a small notebook and pen. He made a show clicking the pen before flipping the notebook open and scribbling on the page. He muttered a narration as he wrote. "The hostel staff was singularly unhelpful when asked for more information regarding the age and history of renovations of the property. One must ask why."

The clerk's eyes rounded. He snatched the handset from the phone on the desk and said, "I will tell the manager you would like to speak with him. He can answer your questions." He carried on an urgent conversation in Punjabi, all the while shooting furtive glances in James's direction. "He will be here in a moment," he said as he hung up the phone.

While they waited, Quinn wandered around the lobby. She stopped in front of two framed prints hanging above the ratty couch. In both, a solemn-faced man sat cross-legged on an ornate rug and stared into the distance. Each wore an impressively long beard: one white with age, the other black with youth. She assumed they were Sikh gurus, but with no information regarding their identities given, she didn't know for sure.

She spun around when she heard footsteps. A middle aged man trotted toward them, puffing for breath and looking rather constipated. No doubt he was the manager called to answer James's questions and smooth his ruffled feathers.

While James handled their inquiries, Quinn seized the opportunity to do a little poking around. She ventured farther into the hostel and encountered a recreation room. A small TV sat on a stand against one wall. To the left of the TV was a cabinet filled with videotapes and DVDs. A Ping-Pong table stood in another corner of the room.

At its center, four women about Quinn's age sat on two couches that sported the kind of coarse fabric capable of scraping off a layer of skin. Quinn smiled and gave them an awkward wave when they glanced up at her. They smiled their acknowledgment and then returned to their conversation, which Quinn noted was in German.

Of course it was the four five-foot-tall metal bookcases set against the far wall that drew Quinn like a magnet. A sign atop one of the bookcases instructed users in a dozen different languages to "Take a book. Leave a book."

She tipped her head to one side and skimmed the titles packed tightly on the shelves. About half were in English. The rest were in an impressive array of languages. A few used scripts Quinn didn't even recognize.

A thick trade paperback embossed with golden Hebrew

letters on a cerulean blue spine caught Quinn's eye. She couldn't read the words but was pretty sure she knew the title. Her suspicions were confirmed when she pulled the book from the shelf and looked at the cover. A teenage boy with a mop of dark hair and round glasses stared at something over his shoulder. The wand in his hand pointed upward at the ready. She smiled at her find. If she'd already finished *Trip Wire*, the Edward Walker novel in her purse, she would have traded it for the Hebrew edition of *Harry Potter and the Order of the Phoenix* in a heartbeat. But she was only halfway through, and she *had* to find out how the MI6 agent would circumvent the gauntlet of laser beams crisscrossing the room and get to the safe containing the launch codes.

Sighing, she reluctantly returned the book to the shelf and continued to peruse the titles. While there were a few nonfiction titles, most were fantasy, science fiction, and thriller mass-market paperbacks.

She took a step to her right and stood in front of the last bookcase. On the bottom shelf were three old hardbacks with call number labels glued to the spines. Amongst the rows and rows of paperbacks, the library books stuck out like sore thumbs.

She squatted down, removed one of the books, and opened to the title page. Below the author's name, a stamp declared in Punjabi and English the library to which it belonged. Her heart leapt to her throat. It read, "Sikh Reference Library."

Chapter Nineteen

Quinn stared at the stamp on the title page and tried to keep from jumping to conclusions. No one could dispute the book belonged to the Sikh Reference Library, but which one? The one that had been carried off during Operation Blue Star, or the thriving library rebuilt from its ashes?

She closed the book and set it on the floor. Adrenaline flowing, she reached out, removed a second book, and opened it. The same ownership stamp graced the title page. It was the same for the third book. She thumbed through each again and found no markings to indicate the books had been weeded and discarded from the collection. Even if they had been purposefully purged, all three books had at some point been part of the Sikh Reference Library collection.

Quinn gathered the three books and stood. It took every ounce of self-control she had to keep from sprinting across the room and barreling through the door, waving the books and shouting, "Look what I found!" Instead, she willed her feet to move at a steady pace.

She returned to the lobby and found James and the manager talking on the couch. James's gaze rose from his notebook and flicked to the books she carried. His eyes then locked on hers, as if silently asking, "What have you got there?" At the same time, his crooked smile said, "Of *course* you found something."

The two men stood. James introduced her to Mr. Prasad, the hostel's manager.

"Namaste," Quinn began in a passable British accent. "I was just skimming the bookshelves in the recreation room and ran across these three books. I'm curious. Can you tell me where they came from?"

He rubbed his chin with the tips of his fingers. "Yes. As I was just explaining to your husband, the facility was renovated six months ago for the first time in many years. We removed the furniture in the recreation room and found those three books trapped between a couch and a wall. We put them with the others."

"The others? There were other books with labels like these?" She turned the books so he could see the spines and tapped the labels with her finger.

"I am sorry. I was not clear. We only found those three. I meant we put them in the bookcases with the other books."

"Oh, I understand," Quinn said. "And you didn't find any other books like this anywhere else in the hostel when you refurbished it?"

"No, we did not." Mr. Prasad's eyebrows pulled together. "Why do you ask?"

She glanced down at the book entitled *Ranjit Singh*. Thinking fast, she said, "I'm fascinated by Maharaja Ranjit Singh and the rise of Sikh Empire in the nineteenth century." What she was about to do next pained her, but it had to be done. Setting the three library books on the couch, she opened her bag and lifted out *Trip Wire*. "Would it be okay if I left this novel here and took this biography with me?"

Mr. Prasad smiled and dipped his head. "Take a book. Leave a book."

"What about the other two, honey?" James asked. "Wouldn't you like them, too?"

"I would, but I only have the one novel to trade."

The manager's brow furrowed and he cocked his head to one side. "Even the one in Punjabi?"

"Especially that one. I collect books in languages other than English." She mentally patted herself on the back. That was a pretty good lie.

James removed his fold of cash. Quinn wondered how much money it would take for them to walk out of the hostel with all three books.

He peeled off three five hundred rupee notes. Apparently the equivalent of about twenty-five dollars was a good starting price. He held the money out toward Mr. Prasad. "This should be sufficient to buy several books to replace these."

Quinn almost snorted. She doubted Mr. Prasad would use the money to buy more books.

The manager's expression remained neutral. "The books are quite old and valuable. Perhaps another thousand rupees will cover our loss."

The guy's a rare book expert all of a sudden, Quinn thought and internally rolled her eyes.

"That seems fair," James said. He slid two more five hundred rupee notes from the fold and handed the money over. Then James took another fifteen hundred rupees from his stash. "This should cover the cost of our stay here tonight. Private room, air-conditioning."

"Yes, of course." Mr. Prasad snatched the bills from James's hand. "I can give you your key now, if you like."

James shook his head. "Not necessary. We'll get it when we come back later." He returned the money to his pocket. "We appreciate how accommodating you've been, don't we, honey?"

"We do." To Mr. Prasad, she said, "Our many readers

look to us to give them advice on where they should stay when traveling. We have positive things to say about this hostel." Just in case James intended for them to actually stay at the hostel that night, she decided to give Mr. Prasad some incentive to treat them well. Her pause gave the next two words their full impact. "So far."

At the way Mr. Prasad's eyes widened just a bit, she knew she'd landed a direct hit. His Adam's apple bobbed when he gulped and said with a tentative smile, "We look forward to your stay with us tonight."

That was doubtful. A question arose in her mind when she tucked the books under her arm. "Were you aware these books belong to a library?"

"Yes."

"Why didn't you return them?"

Mr. Prasad shrugged. "It was not my responsibility to do so. I did not take them."

James must have noticed from the way Quinn's eye twitched she was seconds away from beating the man about the head and shoulders with her newly acquired books. James grabbed her free hand and hauled her toward the front door. "Thank you for your time. Good afternoon," he called over his shoulder and hustled her outside.

"Not his responsibility?" she fumed, stomping toward the car. "The hostel is ten minutes from the library."

"I know, but look at it this way. If he had returned them, you wouldn't have found them."

"You're right. I'm sorry. I get a little fanatical about library stuff sometimes."

"Sometimes?" James said, smirking at her. He laughed when she shot him a dirty look and slapped his arm. Still chuckling, he laced their fingers together. It was a pretty bold move since they were in public. "For the record, I love your passion for libraries. It's part of who you are. I would never want to squelch that fire inside you." He waited a beat and added, "Even if it means buying books in all kinds of languages everywhere we go. That's going to be a thing from now on, isn't it?"

Side-eyed, she looked up into his face. "Maybe."

"I thought so." James unlocked and opened the passenger door. A gust of hot air slammed into them. "Holy crap, it's like an oven in there," he said. "Hang on. Let me turn on the A/C for a minute before you get in." He bounded around to the driver's side and started up the car. Even with the air conditioner running full blast, it still took a couple of minutes for the temperature to lower enough for them to drive away.

Once on the road to their hotel, Quinn opened the biography of Maharaja Ranjit Singh and examined it more closely.

"What do you think?" James asked. "Those three books were part of the stolen library?"

"My gut tells me yes, but we don't have any real evidence." She turned to the verso of the title page. "This was published in 1970." A quick check of the other book in English informed her it was published in 1981. Figuring out the publication date of the Punjabi book would take a little more work. "If any of these books were published anytime after 1984, then we know for sure the answer is no. But just because they were published before 1984 doesn't necessarily prove they were part of the original library. These could be replacements purchased anytime in the last thirty years. Someone staying at the hostel could have visited the library last year and walked off with them. Then they got stuck behind that couch."

"Or they fell behind it when the entire library was brought there in 1984."

Quinn sat up straighter. "Is that possible? Was the hostel around then?"

"Mm-hmm. Prasad said the hostel opened in 1982. He's been manager for the last two years, and no one has been there longer than him. Most of the people that work there do it for free room and board. They're there for a while and then move on."

"Like the guy behind the desk when we first got there?" James nodded. "Exactly."

"So it's a no go on talking to someone who was there in 1984," she said. "It was a long shot anyway." She stared out the window and turned everything over in her mind. "You know, there might be a way for us to know for certain if these three books came from the original library. If there's a catalog of what was in the collection before it was taken, we could see if these are listed. I bet Harbir knows if such a catalog exists."

"We could do that, but how do we explain we found them in a youth hostel we haven't been staying at?" James blew out a breath. "The last thing we want to do is tip our hand to anyone that the Riordans are asking around about the long-lost library. Our cover has nothing to do with that. I think we keep this find to ourselves for now."

She gave his response some thought. "You're right." Quinn looked at him. "Do you think all the books are still hidden there? Is that why you paid for a room there for tonight, so we can hunt around for them? 'Cause I gotta tell you, I think someone would have noticed a twenty-thousand-volume library stuffed in a closet at some point over the last thirty-plus years."

"I'm sure that's true. And no, I don't want to stay there. I was greasing the wheels with Prasad in case we need to go back for more information. He'll tell us anything we want to know if he thinks I'll throw cash at him."

"That money clip of yours is like magic. Whip that thing out and people will do or say whatever you want."

The second a devilish smile came over his face, she knew she was in for it. "Go ahead," she sighed. "I threw you a hanging curveball. Knock it out of the park."

"It wounds me deeply, madam, *deeply* that you could think me so ungallant." His voice oozed with sarcasm while his mischievous smirk never wavered. "Such caddish words like, 'Will you do whatever I want if I whip something else out?' will not pass these lips."

She couldn't help but laugh. "I appreciate your chivalry."

He took her hand, kissed the back of it, and then rested their entwined hands on his thigh. "Of course. And I forgive you for thinking I could be such a lout."

The monster eye roll was accompanied by a sardonic, "Again, I thank you for your magnanimity."

He grinned and shot her a wink.

The conversation lulled. As Quinn stared out the window, her thoughts were occupied with how much she loved James and how amazing it was that she was in India in the first place. Six months ago, she was an unattached reference librarian who sated her hunger for adventure by devouring spy novels. Now she was half a world away, living the kind of grand adventure she'd always thought could only be found in the pages of a book. And she was doing so with the man she loved so much she couldn't imagine her life without his constant presence.

But she'd have to. When the specter of James going back to Moscow rose, she pushed aside the threatening melancholy by returning her thoughts to the mission at hand. "Okay, so at this point we have circumstantial evidence the books were taken from the Golden Temple complex to the hostel, but they're not there now. We don't know where they went after that, and there's no one at the hostel we can ask."

"Right," James said with a sharp nod.

"I guess the next step is to track down the two Punjabi policemen in that photo and ask them some questions. Hopefully they can help us."

"Hopefully they can. But first, put on your *salwar kameez*. We're going to a wedding."

Chapter Twenty

Quinn shielded her eyes from the morning sun with a hand and caught a glimpse of the procession slowly making its way toward them. "I guess that's the *barat*, huh?" She had actually heard the group coming before she saw them. Bagpipes seemed like an unusual choice to lead a groom and his family to the *gurdwara*, but what did she know? It was her first time at a Sikh wedding.

"That's them," Ravi said. "Probably won't see another guy riding a white horse this morning."

"Probably not." Even from a distance, she could see it was adorned with a crimson and gold blanket and sparkling golden headdress.

The groom, Gopal Sandhu, rode atop his mount resplendent in his burgundy turban, an exquisitely gold embroidered cream *kurta*, and leggings. A long scarf the same color as his turban hung round his neck. Quinn's eyes were then drawn to the kaleidoscope of vibrant colors worn by the women, many clapping and dancing, at the front of the group.

"Traditionally, the groom rides the mare from his house to where the wedding takes place," Ravi said. "That might work in small towns, but in larger cities like Amritsar, it isn't always doable. So they take a car part of the way and then walk the rest."

"That makes sense," James said.

Quinn tore her eyes away from the approaching procession and looked up at James. "I like the color of this bandana better than the one you wore at the Golden Temple yesterday," she said. She reached up and fingered the light blue fabric above his temple. "It matches your eyes. Now they really pop."

Ravi snorted. "I'm sure James's eye color was the main consideration when they chose the handkerchief color for all us non-turban-wearing guys."

"I'm sure it was," Quinn replied dryly.

After another minute, the bridegroom and his party arrived. Gopal dismounted a short distance away. He walked slowly toward the awaiting crowd with a sword sheathed in a golden scabbard clutched in both hands. Quinn spotted the familiar face of Mr. Sandhu walking next to his son.

"The next part is called the *milni*," Ravi said. "The bride's family welcomes the groom's, and then the male members of the families are formally introduced. Father meets father, uncle meets uncle, brother meets brother. You get the drift."

The *barat* stopped a few feet from the group awaiting them.

A man dressed in all white except for a royal blue scarf and dark blue turban stepped into the space separating the two groups. He took a section of his scarf, pressed it between his palms, and prayed aloud. When he finished, Mr. Sandhu and the man Quinn presumed to be the bride's father stepped into the gap. Each carried a garland of red and white flowers. After putting their palms together and bowing, the bride's father placed his garland around Mr. Sandhu's neck. He in turn did the same to his counterpart. They turned toward the photographer and together had their picture taken. Next, two older gentlemen stepped forward and repeated the actions.

As the various pairs of relatives took turns greeting each other, Quinn said to Ravi, "You seem to know a lot about Sikh weddings. I take it this isn't your first one."

"No, it's not. You know how it is when you get to be our age. It's one wedding after another."

She nodded. "I'll be in a wedding later this summer." That reminded her. Nicole had asked to video chat with her two days before. But with the time zone differences and how busy Quinn had been, she hadn't had a chance to do that yet. She tugged at the sleeve of James's suit. "Can you help me remember to chat with Nicole tonight after the reception? It'll be Saturday morning there, and I think she has the day off."

"Will do."

The delegation of male relatives was finally exhausted and the *milni* came to an end. Everyone began to file into the *gurdwara*. As Quinn approached the entrance, she tugged the royal blue *chunni*—the large shawl edged with intricate designs in silver thread matching those decorating her *salwar kameez*—up over her head. As did everyone else, she removed her shoes and stashed them away.

The coolness of the marble floor felt heavenly on the soles of Quinn's bare feet as she, James, and Ravi followed the rest of the party down the hallway to the *langar*. "Cool! A buffet," she said quietly when they entered the room.

Guests filed along either side of long tables laden with trays of food. Most of those who had already gotten their food sat shoulder to shoulder on long runners covering the tile floor. Others stood in small clusters and chatted while they ate.

"This is tea," Ravi said. "Basically, it's some Punjabi appetizers and sweets."

Quinn filed past the trays of food, figuring it best to place a bit of each on her plate even if she didn't know what it was. Once through the line, they stood together on one side of the room.

She'd just bit into a triangle-shaped fried pastry filled with savory potatoes and peas when a female voice said, "Quinn Riordan?"

Surprised to hear her name, Quinn's eyes snapped up. The young woman who had befriended her the first morning she'd visited the Golden Temple stood smiling in front of her. "Amarjit?"

"It is you. I was not sure since you are dressed in a *salwar kameez*." She gave Quinn the once-over. "You look beautiful in it."

"Thank you. You look great, too."

"I am so pleased to see you again. How did you come to be at this wedding?"

"My husband has been in business meetings with Mr. Sandhu this week. He invited us to come today." Quinn indicated James with a hand. "Amarjit Kaur, this is my husband James. James, Amarjit was my impromptu tour guide and ambassador for the Sikh religion the other morning."

"Quinn told me all about her time there. Thank you for showing her around," James said and dipped his head.

She dug her teeth into her lower lip to fight the smile. Amarjit gaped at James like he was a movie star.

"It was my pleasure," Amarjit eventually said in a dreamy tone.

"And this is our friend, Ravi Bhatia," Quinn said.

Amarjit turned her attention to Ravi and blinked. Had they been cartoon characters, Amarjit's eyes would have turned into red hearts. Quinn certainly knew the flutter of an instant crush. And to her eternal amazement, the man who had been the object of that crush stood next to her. It still blew her mind.

After they greeted each other, Quinn asked, "Are you here for the bride or groom?"

Amarjit tore her gaze away from Ravi and looked at Quinn. "I was invited by Parveen, the bride. We are friends from university."

"What a coincidence for us to be at the same wedding," Quinn said.

"Perhaps," Amarjit answered, regaining her wits. "I would agree if it was not Mr. Sandhu's son's wedding. Mr. Sandhu is very prominent in Amritsar. This is a very large wedding, and even more people will attend the reception tonight." Amarjit cocked her head. "He must think very highly of you if you were invited to witness the *Anand Karaj*."

"The *Anand Karaj*?" James asked.

"The wedding ceremony," Ravi and Amarjit said simultaneously. While Ravi chuckled, the hearts returned to Amarjit's eyes, and this time they pulsated. Quinn barely held back a snicker. The girl had it bad.

"It means 'blissful union,'" Amarjit said.

Ravi checked his watch. "Speaking of the *Anand Karaj*, we should think about getting upstairs. They want everyone to be seated before the ceremony starts."

"Quinn, would you like to sit with my friends and me? The men and women will sit on different sides of the room. You would not have to sit alone. I can explain what is going on during the ceremony if you like."

"Wow, that's really sweet of you to offer. I'd love to sit with you, but I don't want to be an imposition on your friends."

"They will not mind," Amarjit waited a beat and then added with a twinkle in her eye, "after I tell them you are married. Otherwise, I am afraid they may not have been very nice to you. With your beauty, your exotic blond hair and blue eyes, you catch the attention of men. They would not welcome the competition."

Quinn blinked in disbelief. "*I'm* exotic?" That was a word she'd never considered using to describe herself. She eyed the women around her. If it meant "different," she supposed she could be called exotic. "I guess it's all about context."

James slipped his arm around her waist and pulled her possessively to his side. "Amarjit is right, Quinn. Men have been staring at you the entire time we've been in India. Not just today."

She cut her eyes up to James's face. His serious expression told her he wasn't kidding around. Hoping to lighten his mood, she said, "I haven't noticed. The only man *I* pay attention to is you."

The corner of his mouth twitched as he considered her from under lowered eyelids. "Smooth talker."

She laughed, delighted at his response. If propriety hadn't forbidden it, she would have tugged at his necktie until he was low enough to give him a kiss. She grinned and waggled her eyebrows at him instead. She received a clandestine wink in response.

Finished with their snacks, they set their empty plates on a table and exited the *langar*. Amarjit's friends joined them as the group climbed the stairs. Along the way, Amarjit explained to them who Quinn and James were. Or at least that's what Quinn assumed, since the conversation was in Punjabi. At first, the glances sent Quinn's way were rather furtive, but as the conversation continued, the women's faces grew friendlier and more accepting. By the time they reached the top of the staircase, there were smiles all around.

They filed into a large room. A long red carpet ran down the middle, making a center aisle that led to a square stage. Quinn's eyes were immediately drawn to the shiny golden dome atop four equally burnished golden posts at the center of the stage. A raised platform sat under the dome with an ornately embroidered gold-fringed cloth draped over it. The area in front of the stage was decorated with flowers and garland-draped framed pictures of various gurus. High above it all, a canopy of rich, red cloth was suspended from the ceiling.

Unless Quinn missed her guess, a *saroop* of the Guru Granth Sahib was protected under the fringed coverlet.

As the guests entered the room, each approached the altar, bowed, then knelt and touched their foreheads to the floor. Once on their feet again, they backed up a couple of steps before turning and finding a place to sit on the floor.

"My friends and I will pay respect to the Guru Granth Sahib in its *takht*," Amarjit said. "You are not Sikh. It is not necessary for you to do so. You may go sit. We will find you."

"Okay," Quinn said. She gave James's hand a quick squeeze before they split off. While he and Ravi headed for the right side of the room, Quinn moved to the left. She sat toward the back in an area large enough to accommodate Amarjit and her friends. She hoped they didn't mind not being toward the front, but she really didn't want to call any more attention to herself than she already was by just being there. From what she had seen so far, she and James were the only non-Indians in attendance. She was at the same time honored and self-conscious. At that point, her primary goal was to make it through the day without accidentally causing offense.

While Quinn waited for Amarjit and friends, she listened to the three musicians seated to the right of the *takht*. One tapped out a complex rhythm on two drums using his fingertips, palms, and heels of his hands. The other two played harmoniums, small pump organs powered by bellows attached at the back. They worked the bellows with one hand while playing the keys with the other.

A few minutes later, Amarjit and crew sat down next to Quinn. While Amarjit's friends chatted and giggled with each other, Amarjit grilled Quinn for details on Ravi. Quinn noticed the cloud of disappointment cross Amarjit's face when her suspicions were confirmed: He wasn't Sikh.

Amarjit's interrogation ended when the bridegroom and his entourage arrived. He proceeded slowly up the aisle carrying his scabbard and a small ornamented pillow. The rest of the family members stopped at a short distance from the *takht*, and Gopal approached it alone. He placed the pillow at the front of the stage, gave respect to the Guru Granth Sahib, stepped off to the side, and sat down. Then the rest of the family bowed before the sacred text in groups of twos or threes.

Quinn sat up straighter and watched Mr. Sandhu and the woman she assumed was Mrs. Sandhu step forward. He knelt but wasn't flexible enough to fold forward and touch his forehead to the floor. Quinn suppressed a smile. Her dad wouldn't have been able to do it either. Now that she thought about it, she wasn't sure he'd even be able to sit cross-legged on the floor. In her head, she could hear him grouse that he "just didn't fold that way."

The thought of her dad triggered an unexpected wave of homesickness. As much as she loved seeing new and exciting parts of the world, she missed her parents. She silently vowed to video chat with them as soon as possible, even if it meant she had to be up in the middle of the night to do it.

Quinn corralled her wayward thoughts and watched until everyone had approached the *takht*.

The musical trio continued to sing while several women laid out a white sheet on the floor in front of the *takht*. Once it was ready, Gopal sat on the right half.

A man in a dark blue turban and a long white beard took his place behind the covered Guru Granth Sahib. He slowly waved a silver-handled animal-hair fan over it as if shooing away bugs.

After the bride's family paid their respects, Parveen stepped into the room. She was positively stunning, swathed in a long burgundy dress decorated with sparkling and flashing gold and silver beading, jewels, and sequins. Her head was covered with a shawl with a four-inch-wide band of gold and silver embroidery lining its edges. Red and gold bangles encircled her arms from her wrists to halfway to her elbows. Between the bejeweled necklaces Parveen wore and what looked like fifty pounds of clothing, Quinn wasn't sure how the bride was even able to move. Her mind flitted to Nicole and she wondered how things were going. She really needed to talk to her friend.

Parveen, flanked by her parents, slowly proceeded down the aisle. In both hands she carried flowers atop a folded piece of cloth and set them next to Gopal's pillow. Then, with the help of several dress wranglers, she sat on the white sheet beside her groom.

After another prayer, the man on the stage carefully folded back the cloth covering the Guru Granth Sahib. He proceeded to read in a melodic chant, reminiscent of what Quinn had heard over the loudspeakers the first day she visited the Golden Temple.

When he finished, Parveen's father rose and went to the bridal couple. He knelt behind them, took one end of the burgundy sash around Gopal's neck, and placed it in his daughter's hand. As he did, Parveen rested her head on her father's shoulder. The sweetness of that spur-of-the-moment gesture caught Quinn off guard. She was completely unprepared for the tears that sprang up.

While the *granthi* read from the Guru Granth Sahib again, Amarjit whispered, "There are four *Lavan*, or marriage hymns, in the Guru Granth Sahib. The couple will circle the

Guru each time a hymn is sung. When they complete the final round, they will be considered man and wife."

The *granthi* finished reading the first *Lavan* and covered the book. As the musicians sang, Gopal held one end of his scarf and slowly walked clockwise around the *takht*. Parveen followed a few steps behind him and held the other end of the scarf trailing over his shoulder. During their circumnavigation, various men near Parveen's age took turns walking beside her.

"Parveen's brothers?" Quinn whispered.

"Yes. And cousins. They are there to guide and support her."

Great, Quinn thought as her eyes burned and her nose started to itch. Now she missed her brothers, too.

"It is said that Sikh marriage is like a horse and carriage," Amarjit whispered. "Both partners have an important role. The husband is like the horse pulling it along. The wife guides it like the driver. The *palla*, the scarf, is the symbol that they are tethered together."

Quinn nodded and watched the couple slowly circle the canopied platform again. At the end of the fourth and final circuit, Gopal's two sisters walked with her.

Quinn whispered, "His sisters welcoming her into the family?"

"Yes. I had the privilege of doing that for my brother's bride a few months ago."

"That's sweet."

There was more singing, which went on for a while. Quinn noticed some in the crowd began to get fidgety, especially the younger children sitting with their mothers. They weren't really sitting, though. It was more like squirming. Those that weren't wiggly simply wandered around. As long as they didn't get too close to the front, their mothers seemed content to let them roam. Quinn couldn't blame them. Her almost five-year-old niece, Bailey, could have sat through the ceremony provided she had a notepad to draw on. On the other hand, Wyatt, Bailey's two-year-old brother and their cousin Hunter, age three, would have *maybe* made it five minutes before joining the band of roving toddlers.

And now, predictably, Quinn missed her niece and nephews.

The singing ended and everyone stood.

Quinn peeked side-eyed at the men's side of the room, curious to see how James was faring during a particularly long prayer. He, like most of the other men, stared stoically ahead with his hands clasped in front of him. Her only clue that he was getting antsy was when he shifted his weight from one foot to the other and back again.

As Quinn surveyed the room, she noted three distinct groups amongst the men in terms of head coverings and beards. The first were those who wore bandanas. The men with the bride wore shiny pink kerchiefs and those attached to the groom wore light blue. Parveen's father and male family members wore the bandanas.

The second group comprised those who, like Mr. Sandhu, wore Western clothes, turbans, and beards that were trimmed. Most, but not all, of the Sandhu clan fell into that group.

The third group wore turbans, long, untrimmed beards, and traditional clothing. They included not only the *granthi* and musicians but a number of men in the congregation as well. There were also three women standing ahead of her who wore turbans under their scarfs.

Perceived levels of devotion didn't necessarily translate to the desire for the establishment of Khalistan or any connection to the Falcon. Nor did it mean those who didn't appear to be as devout couldn't zealously agitate for a separate Sikh nation. They could be driven by a nationalistic fervor that wasn't necessarily connected to the religion itself. It was hard to argue, though, with the fact that the spokesman for the Falcon, Samir Singh, appeared to be a member of the third group. They might get a little more scrutiny from James, Quinn, and Ravi, but it was pretty clear they'd have to keep their eyes and ears open for any unusual activity.

When the prayer ended, everyone sat again. Amarjit whispered, "They will give everyone a piece of *karah prashad* to eat. It is a sacred sweet made of flour, sugar, and ghee. It can be an acquired taste, so if you do not care for it, you can hand it to me when the ceremony is over."

"Thanks for the warning," Quinn replied in a low tone.

The bride and groom were served their *karah prashad* first. Then pieces were distributed to everyone. A light brown blob of thick paste was dropped in her cupped hands. Quinn tried a small bit. It was a little gooey, but overall sweet and pretty tasty. She had no problem finishing her portion. Her only complaint was that it left a small slick of ghee, or clarified butter, on the palm of her hand. Amarjit was well prepared to handle the problem, though. She covertly opened her purse, removed two tissues, and slipped one to Quinn, who smiled her thanks as she wiped her hand.

The ceremony was now over. Guests congratulated Gopal and Parveen before heading downstairs for lunch in the *langar*.

James, Quinn, Ravi, and Amarjit sat on the floor side by side while they ate. It was the perfect time to find out if Amarjit had contact with anyone involved in the Khalistan movement.

"I was reading a biography of Maharaja Ranjit Singh last night," Quinn said, striking up a conversation. "He's a fascinating character. He must have been an incredible warrior and leader to turn the Punjab into the Sikh Empire."

"He is still known as *Sher-e-Punjab*, the Lion of Punjab.

Sadly, it was his power that held the empire together. It was no more than only ten years after his death. It only existed for fifty years."

"The pinnacle of Sikh power." Quinn cocked her head and tried to maintain a casual tone. "Are there people today that want to recapture those glory days?"

"Yes. There are those who would make a new nation called Khalistan, land of the Pure. There was a strong movement for it in the 1980s and 1990s. Today, most who are supporters are not violent. However, there are still a few militant groups who do terrible things. I do not understand how exploding trains and buses helps their cause." She scowled and her voice turned sharp with disdain. "They are nothing but terrorists."

"It's awful they keep hurting innocent people like that," Quinn said. "Are there a lot of these militant types around here? Have you ever run into people who sympathize with them?" When Amarjit's frown deepened, Quinn added hastily, "What I mean is, universities are often places where people can be radicalized. Do you see anything like that on your campus? At UCLA, there's always some group protesting something."

"Yes, I know what you mean," Amarjit said as her face relaxed into a smile. "I have heard there is a small number of radicals at the university, but I do not associate with them."

"Oh, of course not." It was a step in the right direction to know there were pockets of extremists in the area.

Not wanting to push, Quinn dropped the topic and changed it to Amarjit's studies. That was until Mr. Sandhu approached and boomed, "Ah, my favorite Americans!"

James and Quinn scrambled to their feet and greeted their host. Amarjit stood silently next to Quinn.

Grinning at Quinn, his eyes flashed with admiration. "You look smashing in your *salwar kameez*."

"Thank you," Quinn said with a pleased smile.

Mr. Sandhu's eyes cut to James. "As I said before, James, you are a lucky man." He didn't wait for a response. "Did you enjoy the wedding?"

"We did," James said. "Very much. Thank you for inviting us. It's been an amazing experience."

"I am sure it was difficult to follow along since there was no English spoken."

"That was a bit of a challenge," Quinn said. "Fortunately, my friend, Amarjit Kaur, kept me informed as the ceremony went along."

Amarjit bowed, looking more than a little intimidated.

"Are you a friend of Parveen?" Mr. Sandhu asked Amarjit.

"Yes. From Guru Nanak Dev University." Amarjit looked like she might collapse right there on the spot.

"And how did you become a friend of Mrs. Riordan?"

"I met her when she visited the Harmandir Sahib a few mornings ago. I gave her a tour and took her to visit the library there."

Approval bloomed on the older man's face. "I remember Quinn telling me of her visit. Well done. You show great initiative. Tell me, Amarjit, what is your field of study?"

"Computer science and engineering."

"Excellent." Mr. Sandhu's voice took on a businesslike tone when he said, "When you are finished with your studies, I want you to come work for me. We need people like you." He looked to Ravi. "I am sure you would agree."

"I do."

Amarjit swayed slightly and stared with glazed eyes at Mr. Sandhu. It appeared the girl's brain function was barely above life support. It was time to jump in and bail her out.

"I'm sure she'll be in touch soon, won't you, Amarjit?" Waving a hand in front of Amarjit's face to snap her out of her trance was too obvious, so Quinn gave her friend several firm pats on the shoulder.

That did the trick. Amarjit's eyes lost that hypnotized quality and she said, "I would be honored to work for you."

"I look forward to meeting with you soon." Something to the left caught his eye. He nodded and said, "My wife calls. The wedding may be over, but there is still plenty to be done. I will see you all at the reception this evening."

"We're looking forward to it," James said.

Mr. Sandhu bowed and strode off.

Amarjit's features were overcome with awe as she stared at the back of her future boss. With a reverence reserved for when one witnesses the miraculous, like childbirth or the Cubs winning the World Series, she breathed, "This is the best wedding ever."

Chapter Twenty-One

There wasn't an inch of unoccupied space on the entire dance floor. The thumping beat of Punjabi techno music blasting from giant speakers drew people to it, Quinn and James included.

Quinn wasn't the best dancer in the world, but then again neither was James. Not that it mattered to her. The way he wiggled his shoulders and his occasional hip thrust almost sent her into cardiac arrest. And it also wasn't terrible that their fellow members of the Punjabi Mosh Pit bumped and jostled her so that she constantly bashed into James and ended up in his arms. Amarjit had said it was the best wedding ever. For Quinn, the reception had it beat.

When the song came to an end, Quinn rose on her tiptoes and pulled down on James's tie until her lips were next to his ear. "I need to get a drink and cool off."

James nodded, took her hand, and threaded through the crowd to their table. He flopped down in his chair, downed the rest of his club soda, and rolled up the sleeves of his dress shirt. Like most of the men at the reception, he had discarded his suit jacket long before. His tie was loose and his collar unbuttoned as well.

Quinn finished off her bottle of water and fanned herself

with a hand. The facility where the reception was being held was modern, well-appointed, and most critically for summer, air-conditioned. But like any room with an abundance of bodies, it was hot and steamy.

Quinn brushed her fingers through her hair and unstuck the strands plastered to the back of her sweaty neck. She kind of regretted taking it out of the bun she'd had it in while wearing her *salwar kameez* and *chutti* at the wedding. Even if no one knew she was a librarian or had any knowledge of the bun-sporting stereotype, she did. So her hair went down when she'd changed her clothes while they killed the time between the wedding and reception.

"Have you seen Ravi?" James asked. "Is he still dancing with Amarjit?"

Quinn scanned the dance floor. Between the lowered house lights, flashing colored strobes, and constant movement of the partiers, it was difficult to tell. "I can't say for sure, but my guess would be yes. Other than when we went back to our hotel, she hasn't let him out of her sight. She's quite the smitten kitten."

"I noticed that, too. I'm sure he'll be able to use that to his advantage."

His words stung. "I just hope he doesn't break her heart. I like her." She knew using people to get intel was part of the program. It didn't mean she had to like it.

"I know. I like her, too. Ravi's a good guy. I'm sure he'll do his best not to hurt her."

As if using their names summoned them, Ravi and Amarjit emerged from the cluster of dancers and started toward them. They smiled and laughed, having a great time together. Or at least that was the way it appeared. Ravi could as easily be having a horrible time and as a trained operative was simply cultivating an asset.

Ravi wiped at the perspiration sprinkled across his

forehead with his sleeve and sat in the chair next to Quinn.
"You two look to have the right idea. We need a break, too."

Quinn noted both her and James's drinks were gone, and
Ravi's and Amarjit's would be soon. Thinking she would retrieve more refreshments for everyone, Quinn glanced over
at the bar to gauge how crowded it was. It wasn't, since
almost everyone either watched the revelers on the dance
floor or was on it.

At one end of the bar, two men stood with their heads
bent in deep conversation. One was Mr. Sandhu. His companion was in his mid-thirties and wore a long beard, a dark
blue turban, and white tunic. Had he sported a bandolier of
bullets, he could have been mistaken for the long-dead firebrand Jarnail Singh Bhindranwale.

Quinn had noticed him early on. He and the people he sat
with scowled with disapproval at some of the activities
taking place during the reception.

When Quinn mentioned it to Amarjit earlier, she told
Quinn they were *amritdhari*, or baptized Sikh. In addition
to wearing the five articles of faith, which included a turban
and a small dagger called a *kirpan*, they also refrained from
drinking alcohol, smoking, doing drugs, and eating meat.
Based on the alcohol alone in the room, Quinn could understand why the more devout wouldn't be happy with what
they saw.

The conversation at the bar piqued Quinn's interest. Mr.
Sandhu was an incredibly influential man. Perhaps the
man speaking with him was asking him to use his power to
push for Khalistan. Maybe he was reporting to Mr. Sandhu
on behalf of the Falcon. Maybe he *was* the Falcon. They
needed to know what the two men were talking about.

The likelihood the conversation was being carried on in
Punjabi kept Quinn in her seat. Instead, she said, "Ravi,

would you mind getting me another bottle of water from the bar?"

James pushed his chair back and said, "I can go—"

Quinn cut him off by giving his thigh a squeeze. She shot him a pointed look and tipped her head ever so slightly toward the bar.

James's face remained inscrutable, but when his eyes darted to where the men stood, she saw them flash with comprehension.

Quinn's request was not lost on Ravi. "I will be back with drinks for us all." He leapt to his feet and strode away.

Quinn kept tabs on Ravi while she, James, and Amarjit chatted about the DJ's music choices. He stood about five feet away from Mr. Sandhu and his companion. After speaking with the bartender, Ravi turned around, shoved his hands in the front pockets of his trousers and leaned back against the edge of the bar. His gaze drifted around the room, as if he was killing time while he waited.

Quinn's pulse quickened when Mr. Sandhu pulled his wallet from his pocket and opened it. He slid a wad of notes from it and handed them to the man, who took the money, pressed it between his palms, and gave Mr. Sandhu a deep bow. When he straightened, Mr. Sandhu rested his hand on the man's shoulder and spoke directly into his ear. After another bow, the man turned and hurried toward his compatriots.

Mr. Sandhu stepped over to where Ravi waited and began to speak with him.

"I'm going to go help Ravi carry drinks," James said. Quinn hoped James hadn't seen something that made him believe Ravi was being called out for eavesdropping.

Her pulse whooshed in her ears as her eyes followed James.

Mr. Sandhu smiled and vigorously shook James's hand.

Then James turned and pointed in the direction of where Quinn sat. Mr. Sandhu's face pinched as his gaze swept the area, obviously looking for her. She waved. Mr. Sandhu's face relaxed into a wide grin when he spotted her and waved back.

She would be devastated if she learned she'd just witnessed him bankrolling a pro-Khalistan terrorist cell. She truly liked the man. But then Roderick Fitzhugh had been a warm, charming, and affable snake-in-the-grass illegal arms dealer. Appearances could be deceiving.

The bartender set the drinks on the bar and Mr. Sandhu sauntered away. James and Ravi took a glass in each hand and started back toward the table. Quinn's stomach clenched as she noted them having a quick conversation. She was about to find out if Mr. Sandhu was the man she hoped he was, or the man she feared he might be.

James off-loaded his drinks, slid into his seat, and draped his arm across the back of Quinn's chair. He rested his forehead against the side of her head and said, "Nothing suspect. Ravi says the man asked Sandhu for some money to help him rebuild his aging parents' dilapidated house. Apparently the roof leaks, the kitchen is ancient, and the plumbing is dodgy."

James dipped his head so she could speak into his ear. "I'm glad. I didn't like the idea of him being involved with Sharma's kidnapping."

"We don't know for sure that he's not, but so far it doesn't seem like he is," he said. She felt him smile against her ear. "A guy going to ask for a favor from the big boss at a wedding reminds me of the beginning of *The Godfather*. Only in this case he's asking for money to help an elderly couple and not a mob hit."

Chuckling, she nodded and turned her face toward his. Their noses were only a couple of inches apart. Her gaze dropped to his smiling lips. All she wanted to do was kiss him. But she couldn't. She hadn't even seen the bride and groom kiss in public. Planting a wet one on James right then would definitely be bad form. She forced her eyes up to his. She could kiss him all she wanted later. And would she ever. The thought of it made her insides flutter.

"I thought the exact same thing when we used his name at the *salwar kameez* shop. We could call him Don Karnail Singh Sandhu." Her smile wilted. "I'll apologize to Ravi later."

James frowned. "What do you have to apologize for?"

"For sending him over to the bar and have it turn out to be nothing."

"Are you kidding? It was a great catch. You've got tremendous instincts. Don't second-guess yourself and then miss out on something because you're not sure if it's important or not." He rubbed her arm with his thumb and stared into her eyes. "Okay?"

"Okay," she said with a hesitant nod. She heaved a deep sigh and let her gaze roam his face. "Just so you know, I want to kiss you so bad right now."

She felt the smoldering desire radiating from his body. His voice was a low growl when he said, "Just so you know, I want to kiss you so bad right now, too."

Quinn jolted as if coming out from under a magic spell when Ravi said, "Hey. If you two are going to sit there and stare into each other's eyes all night, we are going back out on the dance floor. Right, Amarjit?"

"Yes." Not having to be asked twice, Amarjit leapt up from her chair. It came precariously close to tipping over backward.

"What do you say?" James asked as the crowd enveloped Ravi and Amarjit. "You want to rejoin the partying throng?"

"I guess." She was having a difficult time thinking of

anything other than hauling James into the nearest dark nook and jumping him. But they weren't there for that. They were working. She sat back to give herself some distance from him and slow her revving motor. From the corner of her eye, she noticed a man and woman from the table she'd been keeping an eye on walk toward the exit of the reception room. That wasn't remarkable. The way they furtively glanced around as they did so was.

She had no reason to believe they were actually up to no good. Perhaps they were looking for a dark place to have a clandestine rendezvous just as Quinn had been considering doing with James only a moment before. Given what she'd been told about the strict lifestyle the *amritdhari* lived, she doubted it.

Her interest in them deepened when the two stopped and made eye contact across the room with a clean-shaven man sans turban. He wore dark slacks and a pink dress shirt.

Quinn scrutinized the woman's face. She felt like she'd seen it somewhere before.

The two *amritdhari* headed for the door again when Pink Shirt Guy started to cross the room. It seemed pretty clear they were about to meet up.

She sucked in a breath when she remembered where she'd seen the woman's face. She'd been in a photo accompanying one of the online articles Quinn had recently read about pro-Khalistan protests in Amritsar. She'd made an impression on Quinn as she was the only female face amidst the sea of beards, holding an orange sign with the words "India out of Khalistan." She was also one of the few women Quinn had seen wearing a turban.

Quinn's gut told her she needed to find out what they were up to. But she'd rolled a gutter ball a few minutes before when she sent Ravi to spy on Mr. Sandhu. She wasn't about to make the same mistake. She'd go herself. If it turned out to be a complete bust, James and Ravi would be none the wiser.

Pink Shirt Guy walked past their table.

"We'll go dance some more when I get back from the ladies' room, okay?"

"I'll be here."

From sheer habit, she went in to give him a kiss before standing up but stopped when she realized what she was doing. She sighed with disappointment, stood, and followed Pink Shirt Guy out of the reception hall to the central lobby. She hoped trailing him would turn out better than when she'd followed Ben disguised as Bondarenko.

Quinn averted her eyes to keep from making eye contact when Pink Shirt Guy glanced over his shoulder. She pegged her eyes to the side and watched him turn left toward a dark hallway blocked off by a thick maroon velvet rope stretched between two brass posts.

She turned right toward the ladies' room. She walked halfway down the hall, stopped suddenly, and then groaned as if she'd forgotten something. She whirled around and backtracked her steps.

In the lobby again, a cluster of women walked right past her on their way to the ladies' room. They were so engrossed in their conversations no one gave her a second's notice.

Rather than draw attention to herself by acting skulky, she marched toward the hallway with purpose. She swung one leg over the rope and then the other. Once in the shadows, she pressed her back against the wall.

After a few seconds to gather herself, she tiptoed along the wall until she reached a closed door.

Three distinct voices pitched in a heated argument came from behind it. Unsurprisingly, all three spoke Punjabi. She slid her phone from her back pocket, started a recording app, and held the phone toward the door.

As the minutes passed, she grew apprehensive about the precarious position she'd put herself in. If any one of the three behind the door flung it open and stormed out, she'd be caught like a deer in headlights. If that occurred, her strategy was to pretend she got lost on the way to the ladies' room. If that failed, she'd hurdle the velvet rope like an Olympian, bolt out the front door, and keep running until she was halfway to Delhi.

She pushed aside that nightmare scenario and worked under the assumption she would be able to clear out just before they left the room. To do that, she needed to figure out when the conversation was coming to its conclusion. The problem was she didn't understand what they were saying. So she concentrated on the tone and volume of the voices in hopes of picking up cues that would tell her the argument had been resolved.

The voices calmed after another minute. That was her signal. Time to bail out.

A hand clamped over her mouth.

Chapter Twenty-Two

A jolt of sheer terror rocketed through Quinn when an arm shot around her waist from behind and pinned her left arm to her side. Trying to break free, she twisted and squirmed, but the arm around her tightened and lifted her feet completely off the ground. The hand clamped over her mouth pressed the back of her head against her captor's chest.

"Shhhh. It's—" a man's voice started.

She rammed the elbow of her free arm into his gut. He expelled a groan, but his grip remained tight around her.

"Quinn! It's me!" James hissed in her ear.

She stopped struggling and went limp. He set her on her feet, and when he released her, her fear swiftly morphed into adrenaline-induced ire. She spun around and pounded his chest with her fists. "Holy crap, James! You scared the living hell out of me!" she said in a furious whisper.

He gripped her wrists and stopped the pummeling. "What the hell, Quinn? What are you doing?" At the sharp edge she heard in his whispers, her anger ebbed. Her eyes snapped up to his face. Even in the dimness of the corridor, she saw the worry and confusion.

Both heads whipped toward the doorknob when it rattled

and turned. James released Quinn's wrists, caught her up in his arms, and smashed his mouth on hers. She knew the kiss was to give them cover for being in a dark hallway, but she immediately felt something underneath. It was unyielding and passionate and desperate, as if trying to convey to her the tumult roiling inside him.

Quinn gave into her own raft of emotions. She didn't care about the angry voice spewing at them in a harsh tone. She tilted her head and opened her mouth. James thrust his tongue into it, eliciting from her a guttural moan.

And then James broke off the kiss, ending it as quickly as it had begun. His head swung sluggishly toward the voice. Heavy eyelids blinked slowly over unfocused eyes. "Do you mind? My wife and I are trying to have a private moment," he slurred.

The *amritdhari* man yelled at them again in indignant Punjabi.

Quinn closed her eyes and drew in a deep breath, following James's lead to act drunk. When she opened them again, she tried to make her eyelids look as heavy as Pot Roast's when ready for a nap.

She looked at their accuser. "Hey, man. What's your damage?" Her head wobbled as if it was too heavy for her neck.

The *amritdhari* man's eyes blazed with disgust and condemnation, clearly incensed by James and Quinn's inappropriate and shocking behavior. The woman's face pinched in a deep frown. Pink Shirt Guy stood by silently with his arms crossed over his chest. Quinn noticed the barest hint of a smirk.

The woman spoke directly to the furious man. Whatever she said shut him down. He still glowered at them, but at least he wasn't verbally attacking them anymore. Quinn was even more grateful his *kirpan* had remained sheathed through it all.

Quinn had a problem. Given she and James were trying to sell the idea they were drunk and in the hallway engaged in a lusty make out session, her phone gripped in her hand seemed a bit incongruous. If James released her, they'd see it.

She slid her hand down his back and ran her fingertips over his butt. As she searched for the back pocket of his trousers, his arms tightened around her.

James listlessly wagged his head from side to side as she found the opening and slipped the phone into his pocket. "I'm sorry, but I have no idea what you're saying."

The Pink Shirt Guy said, "They say no kissing in public."

"Yeah, yeah, public. Whatever." James let go of Quinn and took her hand. "C'mon, baby. Let's not be in public." They stumbled into the room the three had just left and closed the door, plunging them into cavelike blackness.

The latch had barely clicked when Quinn pressed an ear to the door. The voices in the hallway quickly faded.

James cracked the door open and peeked through the slit. "Clear," he whispered. Quinn expected him to open the door wider so they could leave. Instead, he found the light switch on the wall and closed the door again. With a click, the darkness was overcome by harsh fluorescent light, revealing black chairs surrounding a long wooden table in the center of the room.

James stepped away from the door and faced her. He wafted his upturned palms through the air in utter bafflement. "What the hell, Quinn? You said you were going to the bathroom. But instead, I find you lurking in a dark, off-limits hallway."

"I noticed they were acting suspicious, and I recognized the woman from a photo of a pro-Khalistan protest, so I decided to follow them and check it out. They snuck into this room and started arguing. I couldn't understand what they were saying, so I recorded it for Ravi to translate later."

"Did it ever occur to you to tell me about this before-hand?"

"I'd already screwed up once this evening. I didn't want to send Ravi off on another one of my wild goose chases."

He huffed an exasperated breath and dragged his hands over his face. "You can't just go off and do stuff like this by yourself. We're partners. We should know what the other's doing, watching each other's backs. How am I sup-posed to do that if you go off and pull some crazy stunt like this?"

"You're right. I'm sorry."

"It turned out okay this time." He started to pace. "Did you at least have an exit strategy?"

She nodded vigorously. "I did. If they came out all of a sudden, I was going to claim I got lost on the way to the bathroom. Actually, I was about to leave. From the way their voices had calmed, I figured the conversation was wrapping up. You coming up behind me threw all that off."

"Don't blame this on me," he said, scowling. "If you told me what you were up to from the start, I would have handled it differently."

"You're right. I should have let you know what I was up to. It won't happen again."

He stopped pacing. "Knowing you, I doubt it," he said with a wry smile that quickly disappeared. "I'm sorry for busting your chops. I know you're new at this and still learning. But I love you, and the thought of you vanishing into thin air and me not having a clue about why or how be-cause you took off half-cocked . . ." One shoulder lifted in a slight shrug. "It freaks me out."

She went to him and took both his hands in hers. "I'm sorry, James. I really am. Now I know better. I won't do it again. I swear." Raising her eyebrows, she held his gaze. "Okay?"

His shoulders dropped. "Okay."

"Okay," she said with finality.

The tension in his body seeped away. "In case news of our little dalliance in the hallway makes its way around the reception, we should probably clear out. Are you okay with leaving?"

She turned the previous events over in her mind. "I am. There doesn't seem to be anything else for us to follow up on." Then a question dawned. "Why did you come looking for me in the first place? There wasn't any reason for you to be worried. I'd only been gone for a few minutes."

He glanced off to the side. "Our, um, *moment* in the reception hall kinda got to me. I went looking for you so we could sneak off somewhere and, uh . . ." His gaze slid back to her. "Mess around a little."

It was like a solar flare erupted in her chest. "Yeah?" She stepped closer and fiddled with the knot of his loosened tie. "That thought crossed my mind, too. As luck would have it, we've ended up in a place where we can, um . . ." She shot him a coy look. "Canoodle."

One side of his mouth pulled up in a lopsided smile. "It'd be a shame not to take advantage of it now that we're here."

"It would." She went up on her tiptoes and left a trail of soft kisses along his jawline. "And don't you think it would look kind of suspicious if we went right back to the party after giving the impression we were trying to have a 'private moment'?"

"Mmmmmm."

She smiled and nipped his earlobe. "I'll take that as a yes. We have to stay in here for a while to sell the cover."

His breathing turned shallow as she continued to kiss him down his neck and across his throat. She slowly, methodically worked her way up to his chin.

"For the cover," he whispered.

When she reached his slightly parted lips, she tantalized him by keeping hers mere millimeters from his. Their hot breath mingled as Quinn let the tension build. Heart hammering in her chest, she finally bridged the gap and pressed her lips to his.

They indulged in a long, leisurely kiss. Gradually, their breathing grew heavier as their kisses turned hungrier and more urgent. His hand slid up under the back of her blouse while hers cradled the side of his face.

Engulfed in James's embrace, his scent, his kiss, Quinn lost all sense of time and place.

James stilled his wandering hands and lessened the pressure on her lips. Feeling the change in him, she let up as well. He lifted his head and said, "We have to stop. I'm about to burst into flames."

She gusted a breathy laugh. "You and me both." They had to go. She understood that. But not before she said what was on her heart. "I love you."

His smile softened. "I love you, too." He kissed her forehead and said, "Ready to head back to the reception?"

"I am. I actually do need to make a pit stop before we go, though."

"Right." When he released her, Quinn was happy her wet-noodle legs didn't give out from under her.

James peeked out the door. He opened it wider and whispered, "Let's go."

In a hurried tiptoe, she bolted out the door and stole down the corridor with James on her heels. Once over the velvet rope and in the light of the lobby, they slowed their steps and sauntered toward the hallway leading to the bathrooms.

"Hey, how did you know I was in that corridor?" she asked. "It's in the opposite direction of the bathrooms and it was so dark, you couldn't have spotted me from the lobby. You couldn't have known I wasn't in the bathroom."

"I would have known if you'd informed me, like a partner is supposed to."

She narrowed her eyes at him. "I know, I know. I got the memo."

"Just making sure I made my point." He paused. "And to answer your question, I tracked your phone."

"Of course." She held out her hand. "Speaking of phones, can I have mine back, please?"

He took it from his pocket and placed it in her upturned palm. "Warn a guy the next time you go hunting for his pocket, would you?"

"Where's the fun in that?" She turned on the screen and stopped in her tracks. "Oh crap."

"What's wrong?"

"It's been recording this entire time." Her eyes widened at the thought of the rustling noises, moaning, and heavy breathing it had logged during the previous ten minutes. She touched the off button and put it in her pocket. "Well, that's embarrassing."

"Don't worry about it. It's not a big deal."

"Admit it," she said with a smirk. "You're a little proud, aren't you?"

From under hooded eyelids, he said, "Maybe."

"You're such a guy," she said with a laugh. "You want to wait here? I promise I'll be back in a few minutes and not go anywhere else."

"We'll see about that. And I'll be here." As she left him in the middle of the lobby, she heard him say, "Waiting." Just as she turned into the corridor, he said in a louder voice, "Patiently."

She smiled and marveled at how funny and charming and sexy he was. Pushing through the door into the ladies' room, she ignored the stares she instantly garnered and headed into the stall with the Western-style toilet. Did the other women stare at her because she was an American? Or had they heard about her and James's tryst and now she was in their minds the Debauched American? Scandalous news did tend to spread like wildfire. Unable to do anything about it now, she pushed away the thoughts and went about her business.

Mission accomplished, she exited the stall, washed her hands, and checked herself in the mirror. After drying her hands and applying sanitizer from a small bottle on the counter, she fixed her smudged lipstick and swiped a fingertip under each eye to remove bits of flaky mascara. Her hair was tousled, which wasn't necessarily a bad thing, so she let it be. Now ready to face any judgment, real or imagined, she straightened her blouse, threw open the door, and marched out.

True to his word, James hadn't moved from the spot where she'd left him. At her approach, he smiled and offered her his elbow. She returned his smile and took his arm.

Inside the reception hall again, Quinn scanned the room. The three from the hallway were nowhere in sight.

She also noted all eyes were on the performance taking place at the center of the dance floor. It was clearly something special, so leaving now would be rude. Quinn and James had no choice but to take their seats and watch.

Mr. and Mrs. Sandhu were the sole occupants of the dance floor. As a recording of a man and woman having a sung conversation played from the speakers, they circled around each other as if engaged in a kind of dance-off. Mrs. Sandhu pantomimed at her husband as the woman sang. At one point, she wagged her finger at him.

It was Mr. Sandhu's turn when the man's voice filled the room. He dropped to his knees in front of his wife and pressed his hands to his heart. Everyone in the room was completely spellbound.

Quinn leaned over to Ravi and whispered, "What's this?"

"Don't act all innocent with me, Quinn," Ravi whispered back. "You and James disappear for twenty minutes and then waltz back in like nothing happened. It doesn't take a brain surgeon to figure out you two were going at it in a supply closet."

"It was a conference room, and it's not exactly what you think."

He gave her a flat stare.

"Okay, it is what you think, but there's more to it than that. We'll explain later." She jutted her chin at the couple on the dance floor. "Seriously, what are they doing?"

Ravi squinted at her, sighed, and relented. "It's a Punjabi folk dance called *'Teri Kanak Di Rakhi.'* It's kind of a battle-of-the-sexes song. He's offering her his heart but she won't take it. When he asks her why, she answers, 'You say I can go sit by the well. And then it's, *Oh, and while you're there, you can do my laundry.*'"

Quinn giggled. "I like her. She's sassy."

"Yeah. And then she teases him by saying she can't water the fields, not because she's not strong enough, but because it will ruin her *mehndi*, the henna designs on her hands."

"The Punjabi equivalent of breaking a nail."

"Pretty much, yeah."

By the end of the song, the two danced in concert. "Looks like they got together."

"Yeah, but he's going to have his hands full," he said.

"Nothing wrong with keeping a man on his toes."

Ravi gave her a side-eyed stare. "I'm not even gonna ask."

"That's probably wise."

The crowd applauded as the Sandhus bowed and left the dance floor.

Quinn said, "Also, James and I need to get out of here."

The shift in Ravi's demeanor from laid-back to alert was subtle, but Quinn noticed it nonetheless. He turned to Amarjit. "James and Quinn must leave. I came with them in the same car, so I must go as well."

"Oh! Yes, of course," Amarjit said. They all stood and she looked at Quinn. "I have enjoyed spending the day with you."

"I have, too. Thank you for hanging out with us and being my cultural advisor."

"It was my pleasure. Will I see you again before you leave Amritsar?"

"I hope so. We'll be here for at least a few more days." In reality, she had no idea how much longer they'd be there. Quinn gave Amarjit a quick hug. "I'll keep in touch."

Amarjit gave Ravi a shy wave before moving off to sit with her friends.

They offered their thanks and farewells to the Sandhus. Mr. Sandhu's affability and Mrs. Sandhu's graciousness toward them had not changed. They'd either not heard about James and Quinn's "reckless" public display of affection, or if they had, didn't care, much to Quinn's relief.

As an added bonus, no one lobbed insults at them as they walked to the car.

Quinn considered it a win.

Chapter Twenty-Three

Quinn's phone lay on the coffee table in her and James's suite. She sat on the edge of the couch and stared at it, rubbing her sweaty palms over her thighs. What if the voices were garbled and indecipherable? What if it hadn't recorded anything at all? It would expose her incompetence and prove she had no business thinking she could ever be a covert operative. She consoled herself with the fact that if she washed out, she still had her job as a librarian.

"We'll never know what's there if we don't turn it on," James said. He glanced at Ravi and asked, "Are you ready?"

From his seat in the armchair, Ravi nodded. "Fire away."

James tapped the screen and sat down next to Quinn.

Thanks to the CIA-developed high-quality recording app, the voices coming from the phone sounded exactly as they had when Quinn heard them from the corridor. When she expelled a huge sigh, James rested his hand atop hers and gave it a squeeze.

Ravi bowed his head and stared at a spot on the floor as he listened. "'I can and I will,'" he said, translating the first man's voice on the fly. "'And don't you go all judgmental on me. The gurus' teachings are clear on this. You're the one going against them, not me.'"

The second man's voice was thunderous in his reply.

"'Do not question me. Who are you to lecture me on the teachings of gurus?'" Ravi said in a much calmer tone than the one coming from the phone. "'While you live your life of wretched Western decadence, I have dedicated my life to prayer, study, and meditation.'" The voice dripped with disdain. "'You do not even cover your head.'"

At least now she knew which voice went with which guy.

"'And you think that makes you better than me? It does not. I don't give a crap what you think of me, you asshole.'" Ravi glanced up at them. "I'm giving you the Americanized versions of a couple of those words."

The man Quinn dubbed in her head as Captain Sanctimonious exploded with a vitriolic, spleen-venting response. She could practically see him spewing spittle all over Pink Shirt Guy.

Ravi smirked. "I'm not gonna bother translating that. You get the point."

Pink Shirt Guy spoke again. Ravi said, "'If we weren't already neck deep in this, I would tell you to find someone who is pure enough to help you. But it is too late for that now. The next part of the plan is already in motion.'"

Ravi translated when the woman finally spoke up. "'Our actions might be seen as dishonorable by many of our people. But our cause is noble and right. We do this for the Khalsa. They will see it once Khalistan is a reality, not only a dream. One must do what is necessary. The gurus would approve.'"

Captain Sanctimonious apparently had gotten himself under control. He was no longer yelling. Ravi said on his behalf, "'We must report to our superior.'"

"'Yes, of course,'" Ravi said after Pink Shirt Guy spoke. "'Tell him everything—'"

His voice was drowned out by a rustling noise and a furtive "shhh." A pain-filled grunt quickly followed.

Quinn gave James a sheepish look. "Sorry."

To Ravi's unspoken question, James said, "Elbow to the gut."

"We can turn it—" Quinn started, reaching out for the phone.

"No way," Ravi said, cutting her off.

James's voice came from the recorder. "Quinn! It's me!"

A few seconds of silence ensued before a series of loud, rapid thunks kept her words from being picked up by the microphone.

James continued his narration for Ravi. "She was pounding on me."

Ravi's eyes were round when he looked at Quinn. "Remind me never to piss you off."

The thumps ended abruptly and James's voice said, "What the hell, Quinn? What are you doing?"

There was more rustling and several seconds of silence. Quinn felt the heat in her cheeks when she thought about her and James's brain-melting kiss.

Captain Sanctimonious cut loose.

Ravi winced and sucked air in through clenched teeth.

"What?" Quinn asked.

"Loosely translated, he called you a sex-crazed whore."

As if that wasn't mortifying enough, from her own traitorous phone, she heard herself release a low, pleasured moan. She slapped a hand over her face to hide her embarrassment.

Through the slits between her fingers, she saw Ravi grin and hold his fist out toward James. "Nice, dude."

James, looking thoroughly smug, bumped Ravi's fist with his.

Quinn dropped her hand and rolled her eyes. She poked James in the side with an elbow. "And what? I'm a whore while the same guy calls James a conquering hero?"

"Nope. Just said he's 'no better than a dog surrendering to his lower urges.'"

James shrugged, his smugness intact.

"Do you mind?" faux drunk James said. "My wife and I are trying to have a private moment."

Ravi ducked his head and grimaced at the flurry of furious words spewed by Captain Sanctimonious. "He suggested the only way to deal with your base desires would be to, um, castrate you."

"Dude," James exclaimed and crossed his legs as if protecting himself. "That guy is intense."

Quinn nodded. "Somebody needs to grind up some Prozac and sprinkle it over his oatmeal."

"Hey, man. What's your damage?" she heard herself ask from the phone.

It was at this point when the woman spoke. Ravi said, "She basically told the dude to lighten up. She said he's holding you two to a standard you can't possibly live up to since you don't follow the Sikh path."

More rustling and then the sound was dampened.

"I put the phone in his back pocket," Quinn explained.

James's groggy voice said, "I'm sorry, but I have no idea what you're saying."

"They say no kissing in public," Pink Shirt Guy said.

"Neither of them ever said those exact words," Ravi said. "I guess he decided to summarize."

"Yeah, yeah, public. Whatever. C'mon, baby. Let's not be in public."

Quinn gave James an amused smile. "Baby?"

"I thought I'd give it a try. You don't like it?"

"I could get used to it," she said, her smile widening.

He waggled his eyebrows at her. At the same time, his voice said from the phone, "Clear."

"And that's where we stop," Quinn said. She snatched the

phone from the table and ended the playback. "What are your thoughts on what they were talking about in the conference room?" she asked Ravi. "Do you think they're connected to the Falcon and the ambassador's kidnapping?"

"The name Falcon never came up, but that doesn't mean they aren't part of the conspiracy," Ravi said. "They talked about Khalistan and doing the wrong things for the right reasons. I think we've hit on something."

James nodded. "I agree. It sounds like something's going down soon. We need to find out what it is."

"That's more than a little terrifying," Quinn said. "It could be another kidnapping, a train or bus bombing, an assassination. It could be anything, anywhere."

James said, "First thing is to figure out who they are."

"Did you get any pictures of them?" Ravi asked.

Quinn shook her head. "Didn't get the chance. I can tell you Captain Sanctimonious was dressed like the guy Sandhu talked to at the bar. Miss Pragmatic wore a turban. I recognized her from a photo taken at a protest. It didn't identify her, though. Pink Shirt Guy was clean-shaven, no turban, and, well, wore a pink dress shirt."

Ravi stared at her with a blank expression.

James snickered and said, "Quinn likes to use descriptive names for people when she doesn't know their real ones."

"Works for me," Ravi said. "I'll work on getting their names. There weren't very many men dressed like Captain Sanctimonious at the reception and even fewer women in turbans. It shouldn't be to hard to find out who they are."

"Good. Once you do, we'll start tailing them," James said. "We might be able to figure out what they're up to based on their movements."

"And lead us to some of their associates. If we're really

lucky, even to the Falcon, assuming he's here in Punjab, that is," Quinn added.

"If we track to the Falcon, that would definitely be knocking it out of the park," James said. "We can also get Langley in on this. Maybe they can make some connections between these three and figure out what they might be up to. I don't want to play from behind on this if we can help it." James felt tense, excited energy radiating from him. "We're on to something. I can feel it."

Ravi jumped to his feet. "We haven't been gone from the reception very long. I bet it's still going. The Terrible Trio may or may not be there now, but I bet I can gather some intel on them." He strode across the floor and yanked the door open. "I'll report back in a while." And he was gone.

Quinn toed off her shoes, folded her legs up, and tucked her feet under her thighs. "What do we do now? I can't call that Punjabi policeman. I need Ravi to talk to him first in case he doesn't speak English." After a little more thought, she said, "Although, as a policeman, he probably does." She really hoped Deputy Superintendent A. S. Dhami had some helpful information, since he was the only man in the photo she could contact. Constable Kuldeep Singh had been killed in the line of duty a number of years before.

"It's a little late to call him tonight," James said.

"That's true. I guess I'll write a report for Meyers about what happened at the reception."

"Why don't I work on that while you video chat with Nicole? You asked me earlier today to remind you."

Her head dropped back and she stared at the ceiling. "I totally forgot. You don't mind?"

"Not even a little. We've been so busy, you haven't had a chance to talk to your friends and family. We have a little time now. Go for it."

"I'm not gonna argue." It was like he intuitively knew

she'd suffered sporadic pangs of homesickness throughout the day. She sent Nicole a text asking if she had time to talk. "Thank you." Quinn kissed his cheek and went to retrieve her laptop.

James moved to the desk and opened his computer. "Can I have your phone? I need to download the recording for the report."

She glanced at him from over her shoulder. "Uh, you *do* remember what's on there, right?"

"Yes, I was part of the live show," he said with a sparkle in his eye. "I'll only include what was recorded up to the point when I show up."

"That'll work." Her phone blinged, and a glance told her Nicole was ready to chat. Quinn handed her phone off to James and settled on the couch with the computer on her lap. A minute later, the call connected.

"Hey," Quinn said. Nicole's hair was a mess and her face was puffy from sleep. "You're bright eyed and bushy tailed this morning." Her friend glared at her like she was trying to cause Quinn to spontaneously combust. "Sorry I woke you, Nic. I didn't think you'd still be asleep at ten o'clock."

"It's okay." Nicole's voice was gravelly from lack of use during the night. She cleared it and wiped a hand over a rheumy eye before continuing. "Brian took me out for karaoke last night. I drank a little too much."

"Uh-oh. What's the matter?" Whenever Nicole was driven to the brink, karaoke was the one thing that never failed to bring her back. "Virginia on the warpath?"

"Nah. She's been so busy the last couple of weeks getting stats and a budget together for the next city council meeting, she's hardly ever out of her office." A series of high-pitched beeps went off in the background. "Hang on. My coffee's ready. I'll be right back."

Nicole disappeared. Quinn was left to enjoy the view of

Nicole's print of Picasso's *Blue Nude* hanging on the wall. She'd been with Nicole at the swap meet the day she'd bought it. Nicole had declared people would think she was "all cultural and crap like that" because of it. Quinn didn't know if it had worked, but it was an interesting piece nonetheless.

Nicole slid back into frame and slurped from her LA Dodgers coffee mug. "My mom is driving me batty. I swear, it'd be easier to just elope."

It wasn't the first time she'd heard Nicole say that. "What's up?"

"She's hounding me about making the wedding more Korean. She's worried our relatives will judge her if it's just a normal American wedding, which is all I want."

"What does Brian think about it?"

Nicole snorted. "He's no help. When I showed him pictures of traditional Korean wedding clothes, he got all excited. He thought they were cool. I was dumb enough to show him a *hanbok* with dragons on it."

"Dragons are cool," James said.

That perked Nicole up. "Is that James? Let me say hi."

Quinn complied by spinning the laptop and pointing the screen at him.

James twisted in his chair and gave her a wave. "Hey, Nicole."

"Don't 'Hey, Nicole' me, James," she said. The hungover lethargy from a few minutes before had disappeared. "Are you guys in a hotel room? You're in a hotel room. What are you doing in a hotel room? Oh my God! You're on your honeymoon! You two eloped!"

Quinn didn't even get a chance to be mortified at Nicole's constant obsession about her and James eloping when she realized she still wore Quinn Riordan's wedding rings. She was so used to them, it hadn't occurred to her to take them off. As a warning to James, she raised her left hand so he could see and slid the rings from her finger. Even though his eyes never moved away from the screen, he slid his left hand under his thigh.

"No, we're not on our honeymoon," he said without missing a beat. When Nicole harrumphed, he gave her a sly smile and said, "If we were, there's no way we'd be talking to you right now. We'd be busy doing other things."

"I approve of his answer," Nicole stated solemnly. "And even if you're not on your honeymoon, you're obviously in a hotel somewhere. So either way you'd better be rockin' my girl's world so hard she—"

"And now you're done talking to James," Quinn said and whirled the computer around.

"You're no fun," Nicole grumbled and pinned Quinn with an accusatory stare. "What are you two up to, anyway?"

"We're on a trip for work."

"More dusty artifacts? You looking for the Ark of the Covenant this time? You might want to check that warehouse they put it in at the end of *Raiders*."

"If we find it there, you'll be the first to know." Quinn wanted to get off the subject of where she and James were and why. "What are you going to do about the wedding? You already have your dress ordered and everything."

"I'm hoping I can talk my mom into a compromise. There's this thing called the *paebaek* ceremony. The bride and groom bow in front of the groom's parents and do some other stuff." Nicole shifted in her seat, a sure tell that something made her uncomfortable. "It's usually done after the wedding ceremony in front of the family before they go to the reception. The problem with that is everyone not at the *paebaek* is hanging out waiting for us. They'll all be drunk off their butts before we even get there." She took another sip of coffee. "What do you think about us doing the *paebaek* at the reception? I know Brian's family would be cool with it, but would it be weird for the other guests who aren't Korean?"

"Are you kidding? People will love it, and if they don't, to hell with them. It's your and Brian's wedding. You do whatever you want." Quinn squinted at her when she looked only slightly less concerned. "Why aren't you more relieved about this?"

"It would involve us both wearing *hanboks*, bowing, and pouring tea."

"Yeah, so? That doesn't sound so bad."

"And, um, at the end? The parents would throw dates and chestnuts at us."

James spun around and gave Quinn a bewildered look that matched her own.

"I hope it's more of a gentle toss than an angry pelting," Quinn said.

"They toss them, yeah. I'm supposed to catch them in my apron. Tradition says it will tell us how many kids we'll have: dates for girls and chestnuts for boys."

Quinn grinned. "I'm not gonna lie, Nic. I would pay good money to see that."

"Of course you would," she said wryly. "So what do you think? Too weird?"

"No. Not at all." Quinn wished she could share with her friend how amazing it had been to witness a Sikh wedding. "I think it's a fantastic idea. You should do it. I think it's a great way to honor your parents and share your heritage with the rest of us."

Nicole visibly relaxed and a relieved smile overcame her face. "Cool. Thanks for talking this out."

"You're welcome." Quinn's smile was crooked when she added, "You can name your firstborn date after me."

Nicole laughed and saluted Quinn with her coffee mug. "I deserved that."

"You did."

"Hey, I need your measurements for your bridesmaid's dress. I picked the purple strapless, by the way. Is there a chance you could get that done wherever the hell you are and send them to me?"

"I just had it done the other day. I'll email them to you."

"Why did you just have them done?" Nicole asked, clearly suspicious.

Quinn could have simply said she knew Nicole would need them, but where was the fun in that? "Well," she said with a wicked glint in her eye, "James and I like to play the stable boy and the baron's daughter. We thought it would be fun if—"

"Stop. Just." Nicole's eyes screwed closed in a grimace. "Stop."

Quinn laughed while James snickered and shook his head.

Nicole opened her eyes and gazed at Quinn. With a hint of sadness in her voice, she said, "I miss you."

"I miss you, too. So much." Quinn swallowed at the sudden lump in her throat. "I'm sorry I haven't been better about staying in touch. With the move and the new job and everything, it's been crazy."

"I know. Between work and wedding planning, it's been hard for me, too."

"I promise to do better."

Nicole smiled and nodded. "Me too." She glanced away from the screen to the clock Quinn knew was mounted on the kitchen wall. "I gotta go," she said and looked back at Quinn. "I need to talk to my mom. After I scrape her off the ceiling, I'll need her to help get the *paebaek* stuff going."

"Have fun. Talk to you soon."

"Bye."

Quinn clicked the icon and ended the call. She sat motionless and stared at the monitor.

James pushed back his chair and patted his thigh, inviting her to sit.

Happy to comply, she slipped her rings back on and set her computer down. Going to him, she perched on his leg and draped her arms around him. Resting her head against his, she said, "This long-distance business sucks."

"I know."

"And it's gonna suck even harder when you're in Moscow and I'm in Virginia."

"Yeah, it will." He wrapped his arms around her waist and hugged her. "We'll make it work."

She appreciated the certainty in his voice and hoped he was right. She couldn't even fathom a world where they weren't together like this all the time. "We will."

She just wished she believed it.

Chapter Twenty-Four

Quinn battled the undercurrent of terror that came with driving on the left side of the road while at the same time navigating the insane streets of Amritsar. One of those things alone would have been bad enough. Both at the same time made her palms slick. She managed, though, and once out of the city and on the highway heading south to Tarn Taran, she was able to relax a bit as the countryside rolled by. Thirty minutes later, she brought the Alto to a stop in front of the modest brick and stucco house of Deputy Superintendent A. S. Dhami, Retired, and shut off the engine.

Her phone rang. She glanced at the screen and answered it with a teasing, "You were watching me, weren't you?" The fact that James had agreed to let her go by herself to visit Deputy Superintendent Dhami was a huge deal. He'd only argued a little.

"Yes, I tracked your phone. Sue me."

Smiling, she said, "Nah. This gives me cover for whenever I track yours."

"Good point. Besides, I had to have something to do to pass the time while I'm stuck outside Captain Sanctimonious's house."

At the reception the night before, Ravi had successfully learned the identities of the Terrible Trio. Captain Sanctimonious was known as Jaswinder Singh. Sachdev Kaur was Miss Pragmatic's real name. Pink Shirt Guy was Kirpal Singh, a friend of Parveen's from university.

"No movement yet?" Quinn asked.

"Nope, not yet."

"What about Ravi?"

"He tailed Miss Pragmatic to the Golden Temple," James said. Given the number of Singhs and Kaurs they were encountering, it was easier to use the nicknames Quinn had bestowed on them.

"Hope something shakes out soon. I'll give you a call when I'm done here."

"Roger that. Good luck and stay safe."

"Will do. Talk to you soon. I love you."

"I love you, too. Bye."

Quinn touched the screen to end the call and then immediately turned on the recording app. Before returning the phone to her pocket, she tested the tiny microphone attached to the fake diamond pendant she wore around her neck, compliments of James Bond's Bag of Tricks. Since she was conducting the interview alone and wouldn't have a second pair of ears listening, she wanted a backup recording. When she was assured the phone was indeed recording, she slid it into her back pocket and ran her hands over her auburn wig. There was little chance a visit to Deputy Superintendent Dhami by Quinn Riordan would become known by the people who knew her in Amritsar. But since Quinn Riordan had no reason to be asking the kinds of questions she needed answers to, a new cover was created. She was now Elizabeth Hampshire, an American working on her doctoral thesis at Oxford.

Quinn took a deep breath, exited the Alto, and marched

up the walkway. She knocked on the front door before she could chicken out and flee to the safety of the car. The last time she'd met with an older gentleman at his house, she'd fled for her life while bullets zinged past her. Fingers crossed that wouldn't happen today.

The door swung open to reveal an older woman. She bowed and said, "*Sat Sri Akal*. Mrs. Dhami? I'm Elizabeth Hampshire."

Mrs. Dhami smiled and nodded. She stepped back and opened the door wider, inviting Quinn in. "Please."

"Thank you." Quinn stepped across the threshold and followed Mrs. Dhami to a sitting room. Deputy Superintendent Dhami rose from his armchair. He wore lightweight tan slacks and a faded blue, yellow, and white plaid short-sleeved shirt. His turban matched the blue in his shirt. Unlike Darvesh Singh, whose beard was white, the deputy superintendent's was gray. She thought him to be about ten years younger than her grandfather and his friend.

After he and Quinn greeted each other, he swept a hand toward the small sofa across from him. "Please, sit."

She gave the room a quick once-over while he settled back into his chair. Along with the requisite pictures of the gurus hanging on stark white walls, there were a number of framed photos presumably of family members as well as those of the deputy superintendent during his police days.

Her gaze fell on him. She noted his keen eyes appraising her. It was to be expected. He was a former policeman, after all. She'd have to be at her best to keep him from growing suspicious if she stumbled. Giving him a bright smile, she said, "Thank you for agreeing to meet with me on such short notice."

"Thank you for traveling here rather than speaking over the telephone. One never knows who might be listening."

"I understand completely." The chitchat seemed strained,

so Quinn decided to get to the point. "As I mentioned, I'm working on my doctoral thesis on Pakistan's Inter-Services Intelligence efforts to destabilize the Indian state of Punjab. In the course of my research, I read that you once said you hated having to fight against the young men of Punjab whose minds were being poisoned by ISI operatives. You're certain it was the ISI?"

He steepled his fingers and nodded once. "Yes. Beginning in the early 1980s, the ISI exploited the religious and nationalistic fervor of young men. They armed and trained these young men thirsting for Khalistan. These same young men then assassinated and kidnapped moderate Sikhs they believed were obstacles to their goal. Many of my fellow police officers were ambushed and killed by these pro-Khalistan militants. I myself am lucky to be alive. I was once caught in an ambush and shot in the leg."

The conversation paused when Mrs. Dhami came from the kitchen carrying a tray. She placed it on the coffee table and set out teacups and shortbread cookies scattered on a plate.

"Thank you," Quinn said and smiled when Mrs. Dhami handed her a cup of tea she'd poured. After Mrs. Dhami handed her husband his cup, she carried the empty tray back to the kitchen.

"That must have been terrible, losing men at the hands of those who were being manipulated by an outside force," Quinn said. "And for you to be shot, of course."

"Yes, it was a difficult time. The strife and conflict went on for many years."

Quinn sipped her tea. "I've read the militancy of the 1980s and 1990s has passed and the push for Khalistan is effectively over. Do you agree with that?"

He tipped his head to one side as he pondered her question. "My answer must be yes and no. Yes, the number of acts of terror has decreased. The majority of us in Punjab are content to remain a part of a united India. But no, it is not over. The ISI continues to whisper into the ears of those most susceptible: the extremists, the disaffected, the bitter. They arm and train. There is always a threat."

His words sent a chill racing up her spine. "You believe there are people here in Punjab who, for lack of a better term, you would call pro-Khalistan terrorists?"

"I do."

"Do you know who they are? What they have planned?"

"I do not. I am no longer in the police service. I do know the ISI. They will never stop."

"You believe the ISI is still pushing the idea of Khalistan even today," Quinn stated.

"Yes." He sounded as sure as if she'd asked him if he believed the sun would set later that day.

As excellent as his thoughts were on Pakistan's influence in the region, something she would discuss with James and Ravi later, Quinn needed to shift gears and find out what his experience during Operation Blue Star had been. Carefully wading into it, she asked, "Do you believe the Pakistanis were involved in Operation Blue Star?"

"By fomenting discord and extremism within the Sikh community, yes. They did not send the tanks into the Harmandir Sahib complex. That was the army and Mrs. Gandhi." The edge in his voice was palpable.

"Were you there?" She knew he had been, but she needed to get him talking about it. "Did you see what happened to the Harmandir Sahib?"

"Yes, I saw the destruction that took place," he said in a quiet voice. "The memories will haunt me until I draw my last breath."

"I'm sorry. I'm sure it was horrible." She nibbled on a cookie to give him a chance to recover before saying, "I was doing some research at the Sikh Reference Library recently and was surprised at how few periodicals they had published prior to 1984. I mentioned it to one of the librarians, and she told me a fire broke out in the library during Operation Blue Star. The army said it started during the incursion and destroyed its entire contents."

With a derisive snort, he said, "That is not what happened."

"It's not?"

"No. The army burned it purposefully, but only after all of the books had been taken away. Only a few remaining newspapers were set on fire to make it appear the library had burned."

Quinn set her cup and saucer down and slumped back, feigning shock. "Why would they do that?"

"They took the things to steal the heritage of the Sikh people, to demoralize and punish us."

"How do you know they took the books away?"

"I saw them."

She rocked forward and sat on the edge of her seat. He *was* the Punjab Police officer Vikram Gupta had seen at the hostel. "You saw the books after the fire?"

"Yes. I had been working closely with the CBI, so when I was told to go to the youth hostel on GT Road, I did not question it."

"The Central Bureau of Investigation? Sort of like the FBI?"

"Yes. The hostel had been taken over by the CBI as their base of operations. I was there when the *jawans* carried in sacks of books." He shook his head at the memory. "There were so many sacks. I remember one on a table tipped over and some of the books tumbled out onto the floor. One was a handwritten *saroop* of the Guru Granth Sahib." His voice trembled with anguish when he said, "It was on the floor."

Quinn gasped. It felt like a hand squeezed her heart. She'd witnessed only the day before at the wedding the reverence and care afforded their sacred scripture.

He straightened in his chair and raised his chin in defiance. "I could not bear to see the Guru treated in such a way. At the end of the first night, I took several of the *saroops* and a few of the books home. I hid them."

"Do you still have them?"

"No, some time after that, I contacted a member of the SGPC and gave the *saroops* and books I had taken to him."

"That's incredible," Quinn said. Something he said previously begged a question. "You said 'the first night.' Did you see the books more than once?"

"Yes. There were a number of us who were ordered to make a list of everything taken from the library."

Quinn's scalp tingled with excitement. "You mean like an inventory?"

"Yes."

"Weren't there thousands of books? That must have taken a while. Did you finish?"

"Yes. We worked very hard. We were told we must finish by September."

"Why September?"

"There was to be a convention of Sikh leaders in Amritsar. Those in charge wanted the books to be sent away before then. We put all the books into metal trunks. Then we drove them to an airfield and loaded them onto a government airplane. The CBI flew them to its headquarters in New Delhi."

"That's astonishing," Quinn said. "So they must still be in New Delhi with the CBI."

"Perhaps. It has been many years. They could have been moved again and again. I have not heard anything about them since the day I helped load them onto the airplane."

"Yes, of course," Quinn said. "You and your colleagues were busy protecting the public from terrorists."

"Indeed."

Quinn thought of the dangers her father and grandfather had faced in working to keep people safe. "Even though I'm not a citizen of Punjab, I'd like to thank you for your service."

His eyes glistened behind the lenses of his glasses, clearly touched by her words. "Thank you. It was my honor to serve."

Quinn moved her purse to her lap as a signal she was preparing to leave. "I also want to thank you again for speaking with me. This has been incredibly insightful."

"I am glad to help." He smoothed his fingers over the whiskers of his beard. "You may think me an old, conspiratorial fool, but I ask that you do not use my name in anything you write. I do not wish for my family to become targets for reprisals."

"Of course," Quinn said. "You will be known only as 'a source formerly connected to the Punjab Police.' Is that acceptable?"

He dipped his head. "It is."

"Brilliant." She stood, pressed her palms together, and bowed. "Thank you again for your time. And please thank your wife for me for the delicious tea and cookies."

He stood and said, "I will." They walked to the door together and said their good-byes.

Excited to tell James what she'd learned, she practically sprinted to the car. Once behind the wheel, she took out her phone, turned off the recorder, and called him.

"Hey, you're okay," he said. She heard him blow out a breath and pictured his entire body going slack with relief. "How'd it go?"

"Great. Have I got a story for you."

Chapter Twenty-Five

Quinn tracked James's phone to the center of Amritsar. When she caught up to him loping down the street, she stopped the Alto alongside him and rolled down the window. She ignored the horns blaring behind her and slipped into Hillary the travel blogger's British accent. "Hey, handsome. Need a ride?"

"Hey, beautiful," he said with a wide grin. He matched her accent when he replied, "No, thanks. Why don't you park in that spot up ahead and walk with me instead?"

"Will do." She maneuvered the Alto into the parking space, sprang from the car, and fell into step next to him.

She scanned the pedestrians ahead of them and spotted the back of the man she assumed to be Captain Sanctimonious. He appeared to be alone and, from his purposeful stride, had someplace to be.

"I see you're exploring a new area of the city," Quinn said, looking up at the mustache and goatee stuck to James's face. Since his assignment was to tail the very man who the night before had stared into his face and berated him, calling him an immoral horndog, a disguise was warranted.

"It's always good to experience as much as we can."

Captain Sanctimonious made a quick left into a restaurant. "I'm glad you had a successful trip to Tarn Taran. Why don't we chat over a late lunch?"

James opened the door for her, and the two stepped into a casual dining establishment. It wasn't particularly fancy. The tables were laminate, the chairs looked like rejects from a middle school cafeteria, and the walls were covered with paneling. Décor aside, the aromas filling her nose made her believe the food would be tasty.

Only a quarter of the tables were occupied, so they had no trouble locating Captain Sanctimonious. He sat at a table across from another man in a saffron turban and traditional white clothing. Captain Sanctimonious looked as thrilled to be there as a gourmand in a place called Eats.

Free to sit wherever they chose, James picked a table that gave them a clear view of the two men, but not so close as to trigger suspicion.

After a waiter handed them menus and left, Quinn took her phone from her pocket, opened the recording app, and set it atop the table.

James eyed it, picked up his menu, and skimmed it. "Need to be closer, but can't. Too weird to sit that close."

A second later, inspiration hit. She unclasped the necklace with the tiny microphone, tugged it from around her neck, and closed her hand. "I wouldn't want it to end up under the table on the floor or anything."

James glanced up and his left eyebrow twitched. Returning his attention to the menu, he said, "Yeah, that'd be a real shame."

She spotted the restrooms and pushed back from the table. "I'm going to the loo, baby. Order whatever you want for me."

His head snapped up. "Baby?"

With a crooked smile, she stood and said, "I thought I'd give it a try. You don't like it?"

"I could get used to it." He might have sounded indifferent, but from the way his eyes twinkled, she knew the truth. He loved it.

She shot him a wink. "I'll be back in a minute." She turned on the recording app and sauntered off toward the restroom. When Quinn was five steps from her target, James cut loose with a timber-rattling sneeze. The attention of everyone in the room, including Captain Sanctimonious and his dining companion, turned toward James. All they saw was a man with shaggy brown hair and glasses clamping a napkin over his face.

Distracted by James, the two men paid no attention to Quinn as she passed their table. Never altering the cadence of her steps, she tossed the pendant to the floor. It bounced to a stop next to Captain Sanctimonious's sandaled foot. Microphone now deployed, she kept her eyes fixed on her destination and continued walking.

Unlike their hotel and the opulent facility where the Sandhu wedding reception had been held, this restaurant only had a traditional Indian toilet. Quinn decided to forgo the challenge. She allowed some time to pass by cleaning her hands with a wet wipe.

Back at their table, she raised her eyebrows in silent question. His answer came in the form of his steady gaze into her eyes and the tiniest dip of his chin. The microphone on the floor was picking up voices.

"Did you order yet?" she asked and set her purse down on the empty chair next to her.

"I did. *Shahi paneer* and *thali*."

"Which is what?"

"No idea. I closed my eyes and poked at the menu."

She nodded slowly. "So we'll finally be eating goat eyeballs."

"I hate to disappoint you, but this place is vegetarian only."

"Ah, well. One of these times, our dinner will see us coming."

A pleased smile bloomed at his hearty laugh.

James took his phone from his back pocket and held it at arm's length. "Let's take a picture before our food comes." They leaned across the table, put their heads together, and smiled. They did not, however, see themselves on the screen. James had zoomed in on the unidentified man's face and clicked off several pictures. When they both sat back, James's thumbs tapped the screen. "That's going up on Facebook right now." She knew it really meant "I'm sending these pictures to the agency for facial recognition."

A few minutes later, their food arrived. The *thali* was served on a round metal plate with *roti* in the middle. Around the edge of the plate were small metal bowls filled with various condiments of different colors and textures. She guessed them to be curries and chutneys but didn't know for sure. The only thing she was sure of was the bowl filled with rice.

The large bowl of *shahi paneer* looked and smelled divine. Cubes of cheese curd were covered in a thick, rich red curry sauce similar to the butter chicken Ravi made for them earlier that week. She tore off a hunk of *roti* and dug in.

They were almost finished with their food when James's phone blinged. His eyebrows shot up in surprise. "That was fast."

"What?"

"It's about our new friend. I'll tell you later."

Movement from the two men warned Quinn they were preparing to leave. Her eyes darted to them and back to

James. She tipped forward, lowered her voice, and asked, "Do we split up and follow one each?"

He shook his head. "We let both go for now. We don't want them spotting us after seeing us here. We know where they live. We can track them down later. Plus, we have other things to tend to."

Like finding out what's on that recording, she thought.

Captain Sanctimonious stood and stalked away.

"That guy's a real ray of sunshine," Quinn said.

James nodded and let the conversation lull while they waited for the older man to leave. The man checked his phone and, after another minute, pushed back from the table and headed for the exit.

A few minutes later, James asked, "Are you ready to go?"

"I am." She pressed her fingertips to her throat. "Oh, dear. I've lost my necklace. I'm certain it was still on when we sat down. I knew I should have had that dodgy clasp repaired."

James made a show of peering under the table while Quinn stood and brushed at the front of her clothes as if trying to dislodge it from a fold.

"I don't see it," James said.

"Maybe it fell on my way to the loo." She kept her head down as she slowly retraced her steps.

Several of the diners glanced at her. Finding her search less than compelling, went back to their food.

"Here it is," she said in a relieved voice. She picked up the necklace from under the table. "Now I'm ready to go."

Quinn sat on the sofa in Ravi's apartment with a yellow legal pad resting on her lap. Several of its pages were covered with the notes she'd scrawled while Ravi translated the recording of Captain Sanctimonious and friend. It was all so much to take in. She skimmed the pages again to get it straight in her mind.

"Okay, so according to facial recognition from the agency, the man at the restaurant with Captain Sanctimonious is Gurbachan Singh Gill," she said, "a big shot in a political organization based here in Amritsar called the Khalsa Federation."

"Right," James said. "And to no one's surprise, the group's primary stated goal is the establishment of the sovereign state of Khalistan."

Ravi chimed in. "He's been in the local news lately because he's running for office."

"Which explains why he popped up so quickly when the agency ran facial recognition on him," James said, nodding.

"That group has never been linked to any terrorist acts, though," Ravi said. "It's always called for Khalistan to be established by working from within the political system."

"From what we're seeing and hearing, it sounds like Mr. Gill and friends are impatient with that philosophy and have decided to work outside the system," Quinn said. "That's not surprising considering he was formerly a member of the SGPC but quit because they were too moderate." She glanced down at her notes. "From Gill and Captain Sanctimonious's lunch conversation, we now know the Terrible Trio were talking about getting ready to receive some kind of shipment tomorrow night. What do you think it is?"

"If they're going full terrorist mode, my guess is arms or explosives," James said. "Captain Sanctimonious mentioned there were many people ready to use its contents. They must have a pretty wide network ready to go."

"If the shipment is weapons, I wonder if Pakistan's ISI is behind it," she said. "That's exactly the kind of thing Deputy Superintendent Dhami said they did. It could absolutely destabilize the area. It wouldn't surprise me if Pink Shirt Guy is ISI."

"That's a great observation. You might be right," James said. He sat back and crossed his arms over his chest. "The deeper we go, the more complicated this gets. Now we might have a Pakistani connection. If there is one, that opens up a whole new can of worms the size of boa constrictors."

Ravi shook his head. "Yeah, no kidding. And we're still no closer to finding Ambassador Sharma. I gotta say, with the way Gill kept telling Captain Sanctimonious to be patient, that the operations in the UK and Canada were about to begin and the one already under way in the US was going exactly according to plan, this thing looks to be huge. We'll have a whole new group of terrorists to deal with."

"More kidnappings. More assassinations. More bombings. More senseless deaths." It made the contents of Quinn's stomach lurch up her esophagus. She took several sips of water to combat the foul taste that invaded her mouth. "We have to stop them."

James held her gaze. In his eyes she saw the confidence and determination that always settled her. "We will."

They turned their attention to Ravi when he said, "Captain Sanctimonious never called Gill the Falcon." His eyes darted back and forth between James to Quinn. "Do you think he is?"

James spoke first. "Obviously we can't know for sure until we have some concrete evidence, but based on what we saw today, I'm thinking he might be."

Quinn nodded. "I agree, although we can't rule out the scenario where Gill is a lieutenant here in Punjab and the Falcon is based in the US." She paused before adding, "Or anywhere in the world." She tossed the legal pad onto the coffee table and sat forward. Closing her eyes, she rubbed her forehead with her fingertips. "So what do we do now?" she asked before opening them again.

"First off, we fill Meyers in on Gill and the shipment," James said. "Quinn, you also need to advise him what Dhami said about the CBI flying the library books to New Delhi."

"Right," she said. "The next step is to try and find out what happened to the books after that. To be honest, I don't see me getting very far. No one there is ever going to talk to some random American nosing around. Unless I get the name of a specific person I can talk to at the CBI, I think kicking it to the State Department and letting them handle it is the way to go."

"Yeah," Ravi said. "And you're right about not getting far in New Delhi. It's a giant bureaucracy. Even if by some miracle you did find someone who knew exactly what happened to those books, they're not going to tell you."

"Crap," she grumbled. She lowered her head and stared at the floor. Acute disappointment stabbed at her. "I really thought we'd find them."

"Hey, don't." James scooted closer and slipped his arm around her shoulders. "The library books still might get tracked down. And if it is, it'll be because of what you uncovered. You, Quinn Ellington, might have hit a roadblock. It just means now you hand off the investigation to people who can hopefully get around that roadblock and keep going."

"I know. You're right. It still sucks."

He hugged her to his side. "Yeah, it does. Just don't give up."

"All right, before you two bust out in a rousing chorus of 'You Raise Me Up,' we need a plan."

"Hey!" Quinn said, her snickers chasing her disappointment away. "That's an epic song."

"It is epic." Ravi's smile turned rascally. "And I promise

to perform my interpretive dance routine to that epic song for you someday, after we figure out what we do now."

"I don't know about you, Quinn, but the promise of seeing Ravi's interpretive dance is all the motivation I need."

She cocked her head. "Works for me."

"Here's the deal," Ravi said, turning serious again. "One of our top priorities is intel on Sharma's location. If Gill is the Falcon, he knows where Sharma's being held. If he's not but is high up the food chain like we think he is, he'll still know."

"Are you saying we snatch and interrogate him?" Quinn asked.

"No," Ravi answered quickly. "Not yet, anyway. Not when there's an easier way to get a ton of intel from him without him knowing it."

"Sure, monitor his communication: phones, texts, emails, messenger pigeons, semaphore," Quinn said. "The agency will get on that the minute we tell Meyers about Gill."

James spoke up. "It won't do much good. This bunch is too careful. The agency has been combing through all of that for the guy in the DVDs, Samir Singh, and they haven't turned up anything." He stared hard at Ravi. Quinn practically saw the wheels turning in James's brain. "You're saying we should get up close and personal. Plant bugs in his house."

"Break in?" Quinn asked.

Ravi nodded. "Yeah. And while you're there, load a virus onto his computer so we can hack in and see everything on it. Check around for evidence of where Sharma might be or what they plan to do with the shipment, and what the operations are in the UK and the US. Anything. Everything."

"Gill did mention he has some kind of campaign event

going on tomorrow night, the same night the shipment moves," James said.

"Giving him an alibi?" Quinn asked.

He shrugged. "Probably."

Ravi said, "I'd suggest Quinn and I break into Gill's house and bug it, but I'm not sure you'd be on board for that, James."

Stone-faced, James stared at Ravi like he'd just heard the least funny thing ever.

Undeterred, Ravi shot Quinn a mischievous smile before continuing. "But since I value my life and would like to retain the ability to someday father children, you and Quinn break into Gill's house. While you do that, I follow Captain Sanctimonious to the handoff of the shipment. With a tactical backup team called in from somewhere in the region, we take them down. We stop a shipment of some nefarious cargo and catch I Might Be a Pakistani Spy Pink Shirt Guy and Captain Sanctimonious in the act."

"Getting the Indian government's approval for that, of course," James said.

"Of course. Nobody wants an international incident. Let the alphabet soup agencies in DC navigate the diplomatic land mines." Ravi lifted his computer from the coffee table and set it on his lap. "Let's get Meyers on the line and hash this out with him."

Quinn's gaze fell on the cricket bat in the corner of the room. "What if this nefarious shipment turns out to be nothing more than soccer balls and cricket equipment for a bunch of boys' and girls' clubs? It could really hit the fan."

"If it does, you'll always be a librarian and I can go into private security or something. And of course Ravi will be okay," James said. "He has his interpretive dance career to fall back on."

Chapter Twenty-Six

James and Quinn sat in the Alto a block over from Gurbachan Singh Gill's two-story villa located in a modern subdivision twenty minutes outside Amritsar. Across the open field between them and the house, James had observed through high-powered night vision binoculars when Gill and his wife left more than an hour before. The wooden gate in the high stucco wall surrounding the property had opened. The driver in the sleek black Mercedes-Benz carrying the Gills had guided the car through the gap and onto the street. Since then, the two operatives had waited as the evening sky turned from twilight to dusk to darkness.

James kept the binoculars trained on the house as he spoke. "So far I count two wireless security cameras. I'm sure there are more."

"What do we do about them?"

"Wireless cameras means there's a WiFi signal." He handed her the binoculars, twisted around, and snagged his laptop from the black canvas backpack sitting on the backseat. He opened it, established a link, and began to type. "We disable the signal, no pesky recordings. With how few houses there are out here, it shouldn't be too hard to figure out which access point is his." The glow of the screen

bathed James's face in a soft light. "That was easy. There
are two. The one with the strong signal is probably that
house right there." He pointed down the street from where
they were parked.

"Which means the weaker signal is Gill's."

"That's the assumption." His fingers flew over the keyboard as he spoke. "The AP has a password, of course.
Fortunately we work for an agency that can help us with
that."

"There's an app for that?"

"Pretty much, yeah. I'm running an algorithm that should
give us the password in a few minutes."

"Five bucks says it's his birthday."

"If it is, that's just sad."

Quinn stared at Gill's house through the car window.
"Does it seem like all this security is overkill? Like he's
protecting something super valuable?"

"Maybe, although I don't think having security cameras
installed is all that excessive. All these houses out here are
huge and probably targets for thieves. If Gill's place is
booby-trapped like the temple at the beginning of *Raiders
of the Lost Ark*, then you might be on to something."

"Let's hope it's not. I really don't feel like dodging poisoned darts tonight."

"Where's your sense of adventure?" he teased.

"Breaking and entering is plenty adventurous for me
right now, thank you very much. I'll save being impaled in
the ass by a deadly projectile for another time." Devil horns
practically sprouted from James's head. "Don't even start."

"Who? Me? All I was going to say was, 'I bet my
projectile—'" His computer beeped, cutting him off. "And
the password is . . . a string of numbers that looks suspiciously like a birthday." He looked at her side-eyed. "Don't
look so smug."

"Who? Me?"

"Yeah, you." After some more tapping at the keyboard, he said, "WiFi is off, so cameras are off. We don't want to draw attention, so we'll go around to the back of the property and climb over the wall. Let's hope we won't have to tranq a guard dog."

"Fingers crossed."

James closed the laptop and set it on the floorboard behind Quinn's seat. "How are you? Are you ready?"

"Now that we're about to break into someone's house, I'm a little nervous." Her palms were damp and her heart thumped.

"Understandable." He took her hand and didn't even recoil at how clammy it was. "We've got this."

Her smile might have been a bit feeble, but she tried.

His smile in return was confident and relaxed. She hoped someday she'd be as unperturbed about breaking into someone's house as James was. He leaned across the center console, gave her a kiss, and said, "Gear up. It's go time."

Her entire body was awash with tingles. To combat the gremlins whispering for her to stay in the car, she concentrated on her last-minute preparations. She pulled the black balaclava on over her head and stuffed the tail of her French braid up the back of it. It covered everything but her eyes. Now dressed in black from head to toe, she said, "I feel like a ninja."

"A ninja librarian. I like it."

"We can be very stealthy." She unzipped the backpack at her feet, removed a pair of night vision goggles, and strapped them on. The world turned black and green when she powered them up. Finally, she tugged on her black leather gloves and gripped the straps of the backpack. "Ready."

James finished adjusting his goggles, reached up, and flicked a switch next to the light in the ceiling of the car.

When he opened the door, the interior remained dark. Likewise, Quinn opened her door, climbed out, and closed it with a stealthy thunk. She hunkered down next to the back fender. James duckwalked around the back of the car and joined her.

They hoisted on their backpacks. "We'll cross the field and head for the northeast corner. You go first. I'm right behind you," James said.

Quinn sucked in a deep breath, gusted it out, and spun out from their hiding place. Hunched, she ran across the road and into the open field. She watched for uneven ground in front of her. Any hazards like rocks or holes could send her sprawling.

She wasn't exactly sprinting, but with the exertion, the awkwardness of the goggles, and stress, it felt like perspiration seeped from every pore. And how was it possible that it felt as if no matter how far she ran, she seemed to never get closer to the far edge of the field?

Her sole comfort as her lungs burned was hearing James's breath puffing behind her.

She stumbled when a terrible thought hit her. What if there were snakes? Did they have cobras in Punjab? What if she stepped on a cobra? Her thoughts catapulted forward like she'd pressed the red button and her turbos kicked in.

Even with the cumbersome night vision goggles and backpack weighing her down, she'd never run faster in her life. She finally reached the edge of the field, sprinted across the street in front of Gill's house, and slammed into the stucco wall. Legs trembling, she leaned against it, pulled the balaclava away from her mouth, and greedily gulped down mouthfuls of air.

James pulled up next to her. "Are you okay? Halfway across you took off like a bat outta hell."

"Snakes," she said between gasps.

"You saw one?" His voice cracked like a whip.

"No." She sucked in half the oxygen in Punjab through her nose and gusted it out through pursed lips. "I hate snakes. The thought of stepping on a cobra turned me into the Road Runner."

He relaxed, but only a little. He was still on high alert as he scanned the area. "Hate snakes. Good to know." Looking at her again, he asked, "Ready to move?"

It felt like her muscles had been reduced to jelly, but she was still vertical, so that was a good sign. She pushed herself away from the wall, yanked the balaclava over her mouth, and readjusted her backpack. "Yeah."

"I'll take point." He crept along the wall toward the back of the property with Quinn on his six.

At the end of the wall, James stopped and peered around the corner. "Clear." They turned left and kept moving.

Halfway along the back wall, James stopped again, shrugged off his backpack, and dropped to his knees. He unzipped the bag and removed a chain ladder. Standing again, he chucked one end of it over the top of the eight-foot wall and slowly retracted it until the hooks latched on. After tugging on the ladder to make sure it was secure, he climbed it, swung over the top of the wall, and disappeared. Quinn heard him land lightly on the other side. There were no blaring sirens, no pack of snarling dogs.

"You're good to go," she heard him say.

She grabbed a rung, put the toe of her black boot on a lower one, and hoisted herself up. As she moved her way up the ladder, she was glad to be wearing gloves. The rough stucco would have turned her knuckles into raw hamburger.

Once at the top, she straddled the wall and gathered up the ladder. She handed it down to James, who dropped it to the ground. Then he lifted his hands toward her. She whipped her other leg over and slid off. James caught her and lowered her to the grass.

As James stowed the ladder, Quinn surveyed the house. All the interior lights were out. She guessed they'd never heard of leaving a light on in the house to discourage burglars. Like James and her.

They crept across the grass to a back door leading into the house. James examined it and then checked a large window to their left. Returning to the door, he lowered to his knees, took out his pick set, and went to work on the lock. "The sensors on the windows and doors are wireless. With the WiFi disabled, the alarm won't go off."

A minute later, they were inside the house. They moved through the first floor and began to hide their tiny listening devices. Quinn noted the furniture was elegant and high-end. Gill was doing very well for himself.

"I'm going to go look for an office and Gill's computer. You go upstairs and bug the bedrooms and bathrooms," James said.

"Roger that." As she climbed the stairs, she thought about the poor analysts who would be stuck listening to the feeds from those bugs. They were sure to be serenaded by some really awkward and embarrassing noises.

She went to the master bedroom first. After stashing a couple of bugs, she slid open the drawer in one of the nightstands. It held a couple of paperback novels, a tube of hand lotion, scissors, and a pair of glasses. Not finding anything interesting there, she hurried around to the other nightstand. The pistol was interesting, but given Gill's penchant for security and the fact they suspected him as the Falcon, it wasn't surprising. The rest of the contents of the drawer were unremarkable: a wristwatch, a flashlight, several batteries, and an old transistor radio. There was a better than even chance her dad's nightstand contained similar items. She could have spent an hour searching through the dresser drawers and closet, but she didn't have an hour. Getting the listening devices deployed was her primary objective.

Next, she headed into the master bathroom. A quick perusal of it told her both Gill and his wife took various prescription medications. Once again, she found nothing out of the ordinary. She blew a sigh and hoped James was having better luck than she in uncovering evidence that linked Gill to the Falcon.

She left the master suite and moved down the hall to another bedroom. She placed a bug and moved on to the last room at the end of the hall.

She stopped into the doorway and looked at the low platform in the center of the otherwise empty room. There was a wide, flat object completely covered by an ornately embroidered swath of material. It was pretty clear to her that a copy of the Guru Granth Sahib was under that coverlet. She had no idea if it was common to have one in a personal residence or not. If not, perhaps Gill had some kind of special dispensation as a former member of the SGPC.

Indecision kept her frozen in place. The curious bibliophile in her wanted her to uncover it and take a peek but didn't know if it would be considered disrespectful. After convincing herself that as a librarian, she would never do anything to harm a book, she crept into the room and knelt next to the platform.

Not wanting to examine the pages through night vision goggles, she swung the backpack off her shoulders and removed a mini flashlight. When she lifted off the goggles, she was pleased to find moonlight helped illuminate the room.

Pulse galloping, she carefully rolled the coverlet back

to reveal the bottom half of the open book. A shimmering golden glow radiated from the pages. Not in a weird, paranormal way, but in a "this is why they call them illuminated manuscripts" kind of way.

She uncovered the book completely and turned her flashlight on the manuscript. Borders of intricate geometric designs in gold, blue, green, and red surrounded the thick, black handwritten Gurmukhi script at the center of the pages. It reminded her of the manuscripts she and James saw at the Library of Congress. The exquisite one she examined now could have easily been included in the exhibition.

As she bent closer to examine its golden paint, the words of librarian Harbir Kaur rang in her ears. Harbir had said as a child she'd seen a manuscript of the Guru Granth Sahib and thought it was "filled with magic because of the way it glowed."

The air around her felt suddenly charged with electricity. Could the manuscript Quinn looked at now be the same one Harbir remembered seeing as a little girl?

No. It couldn't be.

There had to be hundreds of illuminated copies of the Guru Granth Sahib in the world. There was no reason to assume this was the very one Harbir had seen.

There was one way to be sure. Harbir had mentioned an inscription written in the hand of Guru Gobind Singh. The problem was she wouldn't recognize his signature if she saw it. It wouldn't exactly be written in English. That wasn't going to stop her from checking to see if anything was there, though.

Since inscriptions are usually written on the flyleaf, she moved a bit of the coverlet over the corner of the page to use as a bookmark. Then she used both hands to close the book before opening the front cover.

"Whoa," she breathed when she saw the inscription. The

handwriting was different from the text of the book itself. While that writing was tight and cramped, the handwriting on the flyleaf was grand and free. Many of the characters had long, swooping tails.

She couldn't trot around the bases yet. She needed to know what the writing said. She grabbed her phone and snapped a picture. Knowing at the moment Ravi had his hands full dealing with whatever the shipment was, she had to get help from another source. It took all of two seconds to come up with the perfect person. She tapped out a high-priority email to Patricia and asked for a translation.

She put her phone away and returned the book and coverlet back the way she'd found it. In all the excitement, she almost forgot to bug the room. She slid one of the devices under the platform and cleared out.

Night vision goggles on again, she hustled down the stairs in search of James. She spotted him walking toward a closed door in the far corner of the living room. It seemed like a strange place to put a closet or bathroom.

"Hey," she said when she caught up to him in front of the door. "How's it going?"

"Good. I uploaded the virus onto his computer. He really needs to think about using more than one password." The doorknob didn't turn.

"Find anything that links him to being the Falcon? Schematics for the Library of Congress? Emails to Samir Singh? Feed from a video camera trained on Ambassador Sharma?"

"Nope. Nothing. From the few English things I glanced at, he's all about raising money for his run for office." He unzipped his pick case and said, "I should have you work this for practice, but I get the feeling now is not the best time."

She snorted. "You think?"

He slid the implements in the keyhole. "This is a pretty

serious lock. Whatever is behind this door, he wants to keep it secure."

"Weapons stash?"

"That's my guess." He moved one of the picks back and forth. When the lock didn't do what he wanted, he mumbled a curse under his breath, rolled his shoulders, and started again. "How about you? Anything interesting upstairs?"

"As a matter of fact, there's a Guru Granth Sahib that's suspiciously similar to the one Harbir told me she saw at the Sikh Reference Library when she was a kid."

"That's weird. How could Gill have ended up with it?"

"Good question. You know how Deputy Superintendent Dhami gave the things he swiped from the youth hostel to a guy from the SGPC? Maybe Gill *is* the SGPC guy."

"Booyah." James turned the knob and cracked open the door. "Either way, why wouldn't he have given the stuff back to the library?"

"Another really good question. It may not even be the same manuscript. If it's not, then all of these questions are irrelevant. I've got Patricia looking into it for me."

"She's a crack librarian." James stood and stowed the pick set. "She'll have an answer in no time." He swung the door open wider to reveal a staircase leading down.

James bounded down the steps.

"How cool would it be if we found Ambassador Sharma being held prisoner down here and saved him?" Quinn asked, following right behind him.

"Very." He came to an abrupt stop on the bottom step. "Not gonna happen, though."

Quinn squeezed past him and looked around. The unexpectedly large concrete bunker was packed with metal trunks stacked two or three high.

"There's gotta be a hundred trunks in here," James said.

"Gill's got enough weapons here to outfit an army. Is he

seriously thinking about an armed insurgency? That's crazy. The response from New Delhi would make Operation Blue Star look like a paintball battle in my parents' backyard."

"Whatever he's got planned, this isn't good." He dropped his backpack to the floor, took his flashlight from his pocket, and removed his goggles and gloves. Quinn did the same. He shined a circle of light on the closest container. "Let's see what kind of weapons he's got squirreled away."

James unfastened the metal clasps while Quinn checked her phone, which had just vibrated. "Patricia says the inscription is called the *Mul Mantar*. It's kind of a mantra from the Guru Granth Sahib. And the signature underneath is Guru Gobind Singh's." She shook her head in disbelief. "I think it's the same manuscript."

James lifted the lid of the trunk and peered in. "Uh, Quinn?"

She took a step forward and stared at the contents. The container wasn't crammed with automatic rifles, rocket propelled grenades, boxes of ammunition or plastic explosives. It was packed to the brim with books.

Her mind could barely process what she saw. "What the . . ." She picked up a book and noted the label on the spine. "This is a library book."

James flipped up a dozen books and checked the spines. "They all have spine labels."

Quinn opened to the title page. There was a stamp of ownership. She'd seen it before. It was the same stamp as on the books she found at the youth hostel. "It says Sikh Reference Library." Dumbfounded, she stared at James. "I don't understand," she said. "Is this it? Did we find it? Is this the library?"

James opened another container. And another. And another. All were packed with books. He checked several books in each. "They're all stamped Sikh Reference Library."

Her gaze swept the room. "I don't get it. Why would Gill as the Falcon insist the books be returned if he has them here all along?"

Quinn's internal organs liquefied when she felt hard metal press against the back of her skull. The voice directly behind her spoke in words she didn't understand. She took them to mean "Don't move."

Chapter Twenty-Seven

James whirled around, and in a split second, Quinn watched an array of emotions crash over his face: shock, fear, anger, inspiration, desperation, and finally surrender. She knew he wanted to fight but couldn't chance it. One wrong move from either of them and Quinn's gray matter would end up splattered all over the trunks filled with the books of the lost but not forgotten Sikh Reference Library.

From behind her, a hand stretched out toward James, palm up. James placed the flashlight in the hand and raised his in the air.

The pressure of the gun muzzle on the back of Quinn's head was unrelenting. In a stern tone, their captor said something in Punjabi and pointed the beam of the flashlight up the stairs. James slowly and deliberately began the climb up.

Quinn followed James, her hands up in surrender. The gun threatening to turn her brain into Swiss cheese finally relented. Her level of fear went from almost passing out to only almost throwing up.

She made it up the stairs despite terror rippling through her. They shuffled to the center of the living room now awash with light and came to a stop at the bark from behind.

Their captor stepped around and stood before them. Quinn sucked in a quick breath. It was Miss Pragmatic. Quinn noted the exact second surprise registered on Miss Pragmatic's face when she looked into their eyes. Both sets staring back were blue.

Nostrils flaring with indignation, she stepped in front of Quinn and ripped the balaclava off her head. Her recognition of Quinn was instantaneous. She flung Quinn's mask to the floor, grabbed James's covering, and snapped it off.

Miss Pragmatic stepped back, clearly shocked to find a couple of Westerners burgling Gill's house. Her astonishment transformed to aggravation as she considered them, obviously trying to work out what she should do next.

James tensed, like a tiger ready to pounce. Miss Pragmatic shrewdly recognized it. She stared him down, extended her arm, and trained her Beretta at Quinn's forehead. He stood down.

Miss Pragmatic's dark, blazing eyes never left James as she held the gun to Quinn's head with one hand and patted her down with the other. All Quinn could do was close her eyes and concentrate on not blacking out. Miss Pragmatic took Quinn's phone and tossed it onto a nearby armchair. She then crouched, ran her hand over Quinn's thighs and calves, and relieved Quinn of her Baby Glock.

Quinn opened her eyes. Miss Pragmatic pointed the Glock at James while the Beretta remained on her.

Miss Pragmatic barked at him, presumably telling him to divest himself of his weapons. Her tone grew more menacing when he didn't move. She cocked the hammer of the Beretta.

Quinn didn't move, barely daring to breathe. A bead of sweat sprang from her temple and raced past her ear. The situation had grown so volatile it was like a room filled with hydrogen. One tiny spark and the whole thing would explode into a roiling ball of fire.

"You don't need to do that," James said in a conciliatory tone. He gingerly lifted the hem of his shirt to reveal his Sig.

That set Miss Pragmatic off on a screaming jag. Quinn squeezed her eyes shut and hoped the pistol didn't have a hair trigger.

James spoke in a soft, singsong voice. "Relax. I'm not going to do anything crazy. I'm taking my gun out with two fingers and setting it on the floor. See? Now quit pointing the cocked Beretta at her chest."

Quinn peeked through cracked eyelids when Miss Pragmatic spat another order at James. The Beretta hadn't moved, and she waved the Glock in the direction of James's calves. He removed the tranq pistol strapped to his ankle. Then he pulled up the bottom of his other pant leg to prove it was free of weapons.

Miss Pragmatic kicked away James's weapons and jerked her head toward the dining room. She picked up the balaclavas and clamped them between her arm and rib cage. Quinn and James marched to two wooden chairs and sat. Miss Pragmatic pointed at their boots and spoke in an insistent tone. When Quinn raised her eyebrows in question, the woman gestured at the laces.

"I think she wants us to untie our boots," Quinn said.

"She's going to use the laces to tie us up." James tugged at the lace on his right boot. "Do what she wants. No telling what she might do when she's so hopped up on adrenaline."

Miss Pragmatic scowled at them and ordered them to be quiet. That's what Quinn assumed, anyway. Regardless, they silently pulled out the laces and tossed them to the floor at Miss Pragmatic's feet.

The constricting tightness in Quinn's chest gave way, at least a little, when Miss Pragmatic finally decocked the pistol Quinn had been staring down the barrel of for the past five minutes. Miss Pragmatic set the Glock on the floor and tossed a balaclava onto each of their laps. After some miming, they figured out she wanted them to hood themselves by putting the headgear on backward to completely cover their faces.

"Don't worry, baby. We'll get out of this," James said and pulled the mask on over his head.

Quinn was plunged into darkness when she brought the balaclava down over her face. Her eyes strained to try to see any light or shapes. It was hopeless. The material was too thick. She was effectively blind.

Quinn heard noises two feet to her right. No doubt Miss Pragmatic was tying up James. Knowing their captor was occupied, ideas of escape crackled through Quinn's mind. She pictured where Miss Pragmatic had set the Baby Glock on the floor a few feet in front of her. Could she rip off the balaclava, snatch the pistol, and fire off a round? What if she hit James by accident? What if Miss Pragmatic put a couple of rounds in her before she even reached the Glock? What if she'd picked up the Glock and it wasn't even on the floor anymore?

There were too many what-ifs. At the exact moment she realized she had no choice but to stay put, James said in a low tone, "No, Quinn. Don't." He knew exactly what she'd been thinking.

A minute later it was her turn. Miss Pragmatic yanked Quinn's hands behind her, wrapped the bootlace tight around her wrists, and secured it with a knot. The lace dug into her skin, and her fingers began to throb.

Miss Pragmatic slid Quinn's laceless boots off her feet. Quinn heard two clunks a short distance away, just as she had a moment before. In her mind, she pictured four boots piled against a wall. She felt the lace wrap firmly around her ankles.

When Miss Pragmatic spoke again, Quinn wasn't sure if she was addressing them or not. After listening for a minute, Quinn realized she was having a phone conversation. It might have been a call to the police, but she doubted it. The last thing you want is the police poking around when a stolen library is in your basement. The more likely scenario was Miss Pragmatic receiving instructions from Gill about what to do next.

Quinn had to get her hands free. Thanks to the good people at the CIA, she had a plan for doing exactly that.

Quinn couldn't see anything, but still she closed her eyes to concentrate on her first task. She had to get her wedding rings off. With the thumb and forefinger of her right hand, she gripped the diamond engagement ring and went to slide it off. It wouldn't budge. Her fingers had plumped up like bratwursts.

Tendrils of panic slithered up her spine. What if she couldn't get the ring off? She beat back the whispering fear by tapping into her innate tenacity. Her dad called it being pigheaded, but whatever. Never giving up until she discovered the answer to a question was one of the things that made her a good reference librarian. Now she'd call on that pigheadedness to get her and James out of the jam they were in.

She flexed and wiggled her fingers to get the blood circulating, then tugged at the ring again. It moved. She almost blurted an "Oorah!"

It took a little time and a lot of twisting, wiggling, pushing, and tugging, but she successfully worked the ring over her knuckle and onto the pinkie of her right hand. Thankfully, the wedding band removal was less of an ordeal. Still, by the time it was off, she dripped with sweat, her shoulders ached, and she struggled to breathe through the thick material of the balaclava.

She ran the tip of her index finger along the inside of the wedding band and over the ridge where a two-inch-long, eight-inch-wide stainless steel saw was embedded. She dug her fingernail under the strip and pried it from its hiding place. It was extremely thin and its flexibility would be a detriment. She was nevertheless confident the saw's razor-sharp teeth would cut through the bootlace. Eventually. She hoped time would be on her side.

With her wrists tied and her hands crossed behind her, her brain had a hard time figuring out which finger the rings should be returned to. Nevertheless, she worked it out and successfully slid the wedding band back on. The transfer of the engagement ring didn't go as smoothly. She dropped the saw.

She swallowed a curse and jammed the ring on her finger. She was trussed up like a Thanksgiving turkey and had let the one thing that might save her and James slip from her fingers. Hot tears burned her eyes. A toxic sludge of panic, doubt, exhaustion, and frustration churned in her gut and threatened to defeat her.

She gritted her teeth and forced herself to concentrate. She and James were in a serious predicament. And damned if she'd allow the man she loved to end up buried in a shallow grave in a suburban backyard like Bailey's dead goldfish. She'd destroy anyone, including herself, to save him.

With a renewed sense of purpose, she focused on the task of reacquiring the saw. Knocking it to the floor would be a disaster, so she lightly brushed the tips of her fingers over the wood of the seat. She touched the thin piece of metal and carefully pinched it between her thumb and forefinger.

Once the saw was secured, she expelled a slow, silent breath in relief.

Fixing all of her mental energy on her fingers, she put the Tiniest Saw Ever to work. Her hands were in an awkward position, but she managed to get the teeth to gnaw at the restraint. She just needed time and persistence. While she had an abundance of the latter, she was running out of the former.

She was so engrossed in working the tiny blade it startled her when she heard a man's voice. The balaclava was abruptly snatched off Quinn's head.

She clamped her eyes shut against the sudden light. After a few seconds, she peered through slits at Mr. Gurbachan Singh Gill. From his thunderous countenance and the way his dark eyes glowered at them from under thick eyebrows, it was clear he was incensed by their high crime.

"Who are you?" Gill barked.

Quinn stared at him with a flat expression and kept sawing.

He stepped in front of Quinn and scowled at her. He was wiry, with spindly limbs and long, bony fingers. Still, he by no means looked frail. To her, he looked scrappy. "Who are you?" he asked again. His voice grew more sinister as his fury deepened. "You will answer me." He drew a hand back and slapped Quinn hard across the face.

"No!" James shouted.

The force of the slap snapped her head to the right. Her cheek flamed hot and prickled like the stings of a thousand bees. Indignation blazing in her chest, she slowly turned her head and glared at Gill. "I'm a librarian. I'm here to recover some overdue library books."

Gill's thin lips turned white and he trembled with rage. He cocked his arm and smacked her other cheek with a backhand. It sent her careening to her left.

"You son of a bitch!" James yelled. "I'm gonna kill you!"

"Silence!" Gill roared.

Quinn righted herself again. The coppery taste of blood invaded her mouth. Through the blurriness of her watering eyes, she saw James straining against his restraints. And still, she sawed. Another thread gave way. She needed a little more time.

She narrowed her eyes at Gill. "Did you know when a library does an inventory of its materials, they find that at least four percent of their collection is missing? We're not just talking about things people check out and never return. These are things that were just flat-out stolen. Can you believe people steal library books? That's just low."

"Is that why you have broken into my home? To steal my books?"

"Your books?" Quinn said with a derisive laugh. "The books stashed downstairs were taken from the Sikh Reference Library during Operation Blue Star."

His chin jerked up in surprise.

Quinn kept at him. "You know what? You should really give those books back. Especially that nice *saroop* of the Guru Granth Sahib you've got upstairs."

That earned her the hardest slap of all.

"I'm gonna kill you! I'm gonna kill you, you son of a bitch!" James raged.

Quinn glanced over at her partner. His eyes were wild with fury and the veins in his neck bulged. She looked up at Gill again. "You're making my husband mad." She turned her head and spat a glob of blood onto the Persian rug. It felt good. "You better knock that off, Mr. Gill. Or should we call you the Falcon?"

Gill frowned. "The Falcon? I do not know what that means."

"Don't play dumb with us. You had the ambassador

kidnapped. You called for the library to be returned. And since you already have it tucked away in your house, you know the books won't be. It keeps the Sikh people distrustful of the central government. You want to lead the charge for Khalistan. You want to be the big kahuna if it's ever established. That's it, isn't it?"

"You are not in a position to ask me questions."

"Oh, come on, Mr. Gill. Don't you read? This is the part where the villain reveals his whole nefarious plan."

The force of the slap knocked her from her chair. She hit the floor with a grunt. She rolled onto her back in time to see James go into full Hulk mode.

With a primal roar, his arms jerked up and broke free. He launched from his chair and rammed his shoulder into Gill's gut. His momentum drove them both into Miss Pragmatic. The Beretta fell from her hand when they all smashed against the wall.

With every ounce of strength she had, Quinn strained at the compromised bootlace around her wrists. It snapped.

Quinn stretched for the Beretta. It was beyond her reach. She needed to get to it before Miss Pragmatic, but her ankles were still tied. She pushed up onto her hands and knees and inchwormed toward the gun.

Miss Pragmatic untangled from the two men and made a break for the Beretta. The two women reached for it at the same time. Miss Pragmatic grabbed it. Quinn gripped the other woman's wrist and beat her hand against the wall. She pounded away until the pistol clunked to the floor. Quinn went to snatch it but was jerked back when Miss Pragmatic yanked Quinn's braid.

"Ow! No hair pulling, you bitch!" Quinn yelled. She grabbed the belt around Miss Pragmatic's waist with both hands. With her full weight, Quinn hauled at Miss Pragmatic and toppled her backward. Quinn lunged for the Beretta and grabbed it by the top slide. She spun around, drew her arm back, and threw a right cross. Fist connected with jaw. The added weight of the pistol made the punch so powerful, Miss Pragmatic was knocked out before she landed face-down on the rug.

Quinn heard grunting and scrabbling on the floor behind her. She spun around. "James!"

Gill had James pinned. The sharp point of Gill's un-sheathed *kirpan* hovered an inch from James's face. His grip on Gill's wrist was all that kept the dagger from plunging into his eye socket.

Quinn aimed at Gill and was about to pull the trigger when James threw Gill off.

A shout from behind drew Quinn's attention. A big man armed with a semiauto rifle charged at them. She leveled the Beretta at him and squeezed the trigger three times in quick succession. He crashed to the floor.

Quinn turned back toward James and Gill. Their positions had reversed. James pressed the edge of the dagger against Gill's throat. "Where's Sharma?"

"I do not know." Gill's bravado was gone, and the tremble in his voice told Quinn he was absolutely petrified.

"You had him kidnapped," James growled. "Where is he?"

"I did not. I do not know anything about that. I swear." Gill sounded like he was on the brink of tears.

James's nose was inches from Gill's. "What about the shipment of guns going down tonight?"

"The shipment is not guns. It is heroin. I will use it to buy votes."

"To get elected and agitate for Khalistan?"

"I do not care about Khalistan. I only say those things to make angry Sikhs in the UK and US and Canada send money to the Khalsa Federation."

"Is that why you kept the library books downstairs? To keep people bitter and angry?"

"Yes." Gill heaved to catch his breath. "Please do not kill me."

"How did you get the library books without anyone else knowing about it?"

"A man from the CBI contacted me when I was a member of the SGPC. The books were in a warehouse in New Delhi. He was told to contact us to have them returned under the condition we admit Bhindranwale ordered them hidden for safekeeping, a secret kept even from us. The location was lost when the Sant and his men were killed. I was to say I discovered them in a warehouse in Amritsar."

"And you hatched this plan to not tell anyone the truth so Sikhs would stay angry and send you money?"

"Yes. By that time I had learned bitterness is very lucrative."

"You're a real miserable piece of shit, you know that?" James snarled.

Quinn spoke up. "So when government officials said the materials had been returned, it was true. But because the government didn't want to admit they ever had them, they denied everything and continue to stick with the story that the books burned when the library caught on fire."

"Yes. The books were delivered to a warehouse in Amritsar to support what they wanted Sikhs to believe. I told the CBI I would reveal my discovery when the time was right. When I moved into this house, I had the basement added to keep them here." His voice was pleading when he croaked, "I have answered your questions. Please do not kill me."

"He really is a miserable piece of shit," Quinn said to James. She felt no regret when she spat blood on the rug again. "You can kill him now."

"With pleasure." James lifted the knife from Gill's neck and dropped it to the floor. He slapped Gill four times hard across the face. "That's for Quinn." Then he clenched his hand into a fist and, before smashing it into Gill's face, said, "And this is for everyone else."

Chapter Twenty-Eight

Quinn sat on the floor of Gill's dining room and stared dully at the glob of blood she'd spat on the rug earlier. She yearned to flop on her back, spread out her arms like an eagle, and contemplate the ceiling for the rest of the night. But she couldn't. She was surrounded by chaos. Miss Pragmatic was still unconscious. Gill was curled in the fetal position with his hands clamped over his face, slowly rocking back and forth. The big guy with a gunshot wound or three called out. And the basement was filled with thousands of purloined library books. Her retreat into a blissful, catatonic state would have to wait.

James picked up the *kirpan* and sliced through the bootlace around his ankles, then the one around Quinn's. He scooted next to her, held her chin between his thumb and forefinger, and turned her head one way and then the other. "The son of a bitch turned both of your cheeks bright red. When he slapped you over and over like that, I really did want to kill him."

"I know."

"How's your mouth? Still bleeding?"

She probed the inside of her cheeks with her tongue. "I think it's stopped. There's a pretty big gash on one side."

He nodded. "You pissed him off pretty good."

"That first slap pissed me off pretty good. I get snarky when I'm mad. Plus, needling him gave me time to keep sawing through the bootlace."

"I used my saw, too." He smiled at her. "Getting the ring off wasn't easy, was it? My fingers were so slippery and sweaty, I almost dropped it."

"I actually dropped my saw." When his eyes widened, she added, "But luckily it landed on the seat of the chair."

"I was almost all the way through when he knocked you out of your chair. It snapped with that boost of adrenaline."

"Same thing happened to me when you tackled Gill."

He gave her a soft kiss on the lips. "I'd love nothing more than to sit here with you, but we have a pretty colossal mess to deal with. The first thing we need to do is make sure no one else is lurking around. I'll go check the perimeter. Can you check on Mr. GSW over there?"

"Nice descriptive name," she said with a smile. "I'm so proud."

He winked, clambered to his feet, and offered her his hand. She took it and he hauled her up. "There are some plastic handcuffs in my backpack. Secure Gill and Miss Pragmatic, would you? I'll be back in a few minutes." He slid his feet into his boots and clomped to where Miss Pragmatic had left his Sig and tranq pistol. He returned the latter to its holster around his ankle while the former stayed gripped in his hand.

James disappeared out a side door and Quinn got to work. She found her Baby Glock on the table where Miss Pragmatic had set it when she tied them up. She exchanged the Beretta for the Glock and returned her firearm to its holster. Next, she picked up Gill's *kirpan* from the floor and removed Miss Pragmatic's from her belt. Those went next to the Beretta on the table. Finally, she retrieved the rifle

Mr. GSW had dropped and lined it up with the rest of the weapons.

Mr. GSW groaned in pain. She went and stood over him. His blood-drenched hands clutched his right thigh. He was pale but alive.

"I gotta go handcuff your friends first," she said. "In the meantime, I don't want you getting any ideas." She knelt next to him, removed his *kirpan,* and patted him down. He carried no other weapons.

"I'll be right back."

She hustled across the living room and ran down the stairs to the basement. The books called to her like a Siren's song, enticing her to open their crates and gaze at them. "Later," she promised.

She gathered up her and James's backpacks and bounded up the steps, taking them two at a time. By the time she returned to the dining room, Miss Pragmatic had managed to sit up. She still looked dazed and confused.

"Hello, sunshine," Quinn said and set the backpacks on the table. She rummaged through James's until she located the plastic cuffs. In less than a minute, they were cinched tight around Miss Pragmatic's wrists. "It's not as much fun when you're the one tied up, is it?"

Quinn moved over to Gill. He released a long, tortured moan when she pulled his hands away from his face.

"Suck it up, dude," Quinn said.

Now that neither could cause any more trouble, she returned to Mr. GSW. Even in his debilitated state, he glowered at her and muttered in a tone that made her glad she didn't understand what he said.

"Yeah, well, you work for a really bad man," she said.

She knelt next to him again with the intent of examining his wound. When she tried to move his hands, he resisted. "The only way I can help you is if you let me look at it."

He squinted at her, and when she arched an eyebrow in

response, he capitulated. "There's no blood spurting, so that's good news." Dark red blood seeped up from the wound. "A doctor will take a look at it, but if he thinks taking the bullet out will hurt you more than help, you've got yourself a nice new souvenir. Good luck going through security at airports." She stood. "We do need to make sure the bleeding stops, though. I'll be right back."

She went to the kitchen and opened drawers until she found some towels. She grabbed several, then ran to the living room and gathered up three sofa cushions. Mr. GSW hissed in pain when she lifted his leg and set it atop the stack of cushions.

"It needs to be elevated." She put the towel over the hole in his leg, grabbed his hand, and placed it on top of the towel. Pressing her hand atop his, she said, "Keep pressure on it." To make her point, she put more weight on her hand. "Pressure."

He nodded and the anger in his eyes receded.

"Here, this will make you a little more comfortable." She lifted his head with one hand and slid two towels under it. After gently lowering it, she patted his shoulder.

James returned. "There's no one else around, although Gill's wife is unaccounted for. There could be more trouble if and when she shows up."

"Hold that thought." She left a puzzled James, pounded up the stairs, and yanked the bedspread off the guest bed. She bounded down again and said as she covered the wounded man, "He's looking a little shocky."

The thought that unexpectedly hit her made her grimace like she'd sniffed one of Monroe's dirty gym socks. "What if Mrs. Gill planned on staying in town all night and Miss Pragmatic came here to hook up with Gill while she was gone? That would explain why she showed up while the Gills were out. And why Mrs. Gill isn't here now. He's old enough to be her father. That's just. Ew."

"Isn't adultery a big no-no?"

"Yeah, but I gotta believe stealing libraries and trading drugs for votes isn't exactly gonna win you Sikh of the Year, either."

"That's true. What's more likely is that she came here to wait for word on how the deal went down with Captain Sanctimonious and Pink Shirt Guy. And us being here meant Mrs. Gill needed to stay somewhere else."

"I like that better. Not quite so scalding shower–worthy." Just the thought of it made her shiver. "Speaking of our two favorite drug runners, have you heard anything from Ravi?"

"Yeah. The deal went down just this side of the India-Pakistan border. And it was exactly what Gill said. Heroin, most likely from Afghanistan."

"It's sure looking more and more like Pink Shirt Guy is ISI, doing whatever he can to destabilize Punjab, just like Deputy Superintendent Dhami said." She crossed her arms. "What do we do with these three?"

"Ravi already contacted our station in New Delhi. There's a helicopter in the air to pick up the people he has in custody. These three will catch a ride to a rendezvous point where the helicopter will pick them up."

Quinn looked over at the older man lying on the floor. "Do you think Gill is the Falcon?"

"I don't know," he said and ran his hand through his hair. "We haven't found a shred of evidence that links him to Sharma or the stolen Hindu manuscripts."

"I guess our people in New Delhi will find out if he's the Falcon or not. In the meantime, what do we do with the library books? I don't want them out of my sight."

"I don't either. We need them secure while the higher-ups use them to negotiate with the Falcon or whatever else they want us to do with them."

"I hope they don't want us to give them to any of the groups around here. I don't trust them. I'd rather drive the books to the library and put them on the shelves myself. We could load up the Alto. It would take a million trips, but it would be worth it."

"I agree." He stared right through her and rubbed the stubble on his cheek in contemplation. A half minute later, she practically saw the lightbulb blink on over his head. "I have an idea for getting them out of here."

"How are we going to manage that? There are dozens of crates, and they're way too heavy for me to help carry."

"We get a little help." He took out his phone and placed a call. "Ravi, what's the ETA on the helicopter?" He paused. "After you hand them off, can you round up a couple of big moving trucks?" He listened and said, "I know it's late. Get them here as soon as you can. We can wait. And bring your friends. We need some muscle. We've got a library to move."

It was four o'clock in the morning when two large moving trucks rumbled down Gill's street and disappeared into the compound behind the high walls. Gill's penchant for blocking prying eyes worked in their favor.

By the time they arrived, Gill, Miss Pragmatic, and Mr. GSW had already been trundled into a large SUV. It never ceased to amaze Quinn how those black, tinted-windowed vehicles could show up anywhere, any time. She pictured one rolling across a sun-kissed beach on a remote tropical island and gliding to a stop in front of some unsuspecting bad guy resplendent in an unfortunate Speedo who believed he was beyond their reach.

The only redeeming quality of Gill's was his wish to shield his wife from any repercussions stemming from his illegal activities. Gill had informed James and Quinn that when Miss Pragmatic called him and said two people had broken into his house, he hastily arranged for his wife to spend the night with their daughter, who lived in town. Of course, he only relayed those details after they pointed out the authorities would assume his wife knew about his activities and consider her an accessory. Mrs. Gill would certainly be questioned, as would a lot of other people, but that wasn't James and Quinn's concern.

While they'd waited for the moving trucks to arrive, Quinn had taken pictures and videos of the books to document where they had been found. She had also managed to get in a couple of hours of sleep. Meanwhile, James had scoured through Gill's computer looking for any evidence of him being the Falcon before handing it off to the men in the SUV. There was plenty to prove he was up to his eyeballs in all kinds of shenanigans to rake in piles of money not only in Punjab, but from the US, Canada, and the UK. He found nothing that connected him to the Falcon or Ambassador Sharma.

Quinn and James exited the house and watched the trucks come to a stop. Ravi and a US Army Special Forces soldier climbed down from one of the cabs while two more hopped down from the other. The trailer doors opened and nine more soldiers jumped out.

An officer stepped forward and offered a handshake. "Captain Logan. I hear you need help moving some books."

Captain Logan was in his early thirties with closely cropped brown hair under his beret and penetrating green eyes. With his clipped speech and intense, no-nonsense expression, he gave the impression he was a man who got things done.

"I'm James and this is Quinn." They took turns shaking the captain's hand. "And yes, we do need some help. We appreciate it."

"Glad to be of assistance. What have we got?"

Quinn waited outside with Ravi while James took Captain Logan to inspect the contents of the basement. A few minutes later, they returned and the captain started giving orders to his team. "We've got at least a hundred metal trunks to move. We'll work in two teams of six. Two stack crates inside the trailer while the other four haul them upstairs. Two men per trunk. Let's move."

"Ravi and I will carry, too," James said.

Four men broke for the backs of the trucks while the other ten tromped into the house. Quinn trailed behind them and felt a little awkward with nothing to do. She could catalog a trunk full of books, but she couldn't help carry one.

With nothing else to do, she spectated. Watching ten handsome, burly men carry heavy things back and forth in front of her was in no way a hardship. Only Nicole joining her with a bowl of popcorn would have made it better.

It didn't take long for the teams to fall into a rhythm. The moment one pair of men emerged from the basement with a crate, another would scamper down the stairs to haul up the next. And so it went until the basement was empty and the trucks were loaded.

Only a few hours before, it appeared moving all those trunks was an impossible task. And now in short order, the task was complete. She found it ironic and somehow fitting that the United States Army finished the job the Indian Army began over thirty years before. She was proud to be a part of it.

"You'll take it the rest of the way?" Captain Logan asked.

"We will," James answered. "Thank you again for your help."

"You're welcome." He snapped a nod toward Quinn. "Ma'am." To his team, he said, "Saddle up. Our ride's incoming."

Thirty seconds later, Quinn heard the faint sound of helicopter rotors chopping the air. The Special Forces team assembled behind the gate as it flew closer.

In the graying morning light, a Chinook helicopter approached. The gate flew open and the team moved out. The Chinook landed in the open field across the street. The entire team piled into the helicopter and lifted off. Its wheels had been on Punjabi soil for a total of sixty seconds.

"Well, that was impressively efficient," Quinn said as the Chinook disappeared from sight.

"You should have seen them when we took those guys down during the rendezvous last night," Ravi said. "Captain Sanctimonious and Pink Shirt Guy and their men had just started transferring the boxes when Logan and his team had them surrounded. I'm pretty sure a couple of Captain Sanctimonious's guys wet themselves."

Quinn chuckled. "It's all fun and games until the rifles are pointed at you."

"Yup."

"Let's get out of here," James said. "I gotta think a helicopter landing in the middle of a subdivision might get the neighbor's attention. My guess is the police will be here soon."

"I need to get one more thing before we go," Quinn said. She ran into the house and raced up the stairs. She sprinted down the hall and skidded to stop at the room with the Guru Granth Sahib. After rolling the coverlet off, she closed the giant book and covered it again. With it resting on her outstretched forearms, she carried it down the stairs. "The Guru calls shotgun."

Chapter Twenty-Nine

Quinn bounced when the truck hit a pothole, causing her finger to miss the icon on her phone to end the call. She successfully stabbed the screen on her second attempt and slid it under her thigh. "Meyers said once we get back to the hotel, we're to hold tight while the powers that be figure out what to do next."

"Roger that," James said. "What did he say when you told him we found the library?"

She snorted. "He already knew. It seems our overnight shenanigans had the NESA desk hopping. Still, he was his usual effusive and ebullient self," she said sarcastically. "We got a 'well done.'"

"That sounds about right."

Within a minute, the truck's rocking put Quinn to sleep. She woke twenty minutes later when they rumbled into the hotel parking lot. Her eyes were dry and gritty, and her nap had in no way been long enough. But it was better than nothing.

Ravi went home to shower and change his clothes while the wheels of diplomacy ground away. Quinn and James went to their suite and did the same. Ravi returned a short time later, and the three celebrated the recovery of the library by enjoying breakfast at the hotel. Despite the gash on the inside of Quinn's mouth and her underlying worry their orders from on high would be something other than returning the books to the Golden Temple, she demolished her breakfast.

They went back to the suite and waited another agonizing hour before Meyers called. "Quinn, James, and Ravi are here on speaker," she said. A knot of nerves twisted in her stomach.

"Our State Department and various Indian ministries have been discussing the disposition of the library books," Meyers said. "As you would expect, there were a variety of opinions on exactly what that should be. The Indian central government demanded the books be turned over to them in order to secure Ambassador Sharma's release."

That made Quinn grimace. Of course she wanted the ambassador to be freed. She just didn't trust the government to actually follow through on returning the books. She wouldn't put it past them to stash the books in the same New Delhi warehouse they'd languished in following Operation Blue Star.

"Given their history with the library, State was not about to agree to that. Let's just say that caused a bit of tension."

She heaved a sigh in relief.

"In the end, it was Kavita Sharma who ended the stalemate."

"Not that I'm surprised, but how did she do that?" Quinn asked.

"She pointed out that one, the books never belonged to the Indian government in the first place, and two, if they were the ones who returned the library, their decades-long stance that it had burned would be exposed as a lie."

"So what happened?" Ravi asked.

"Mr. Gill's story provides a way for the books to be

returned immediately and the central government to save face. The books are to be brought to the Golden Temple anonymously, saying Bhindranwale had them moved to a warehouse in Amritsar where they were recently discovered."

"I'm glad the books will be going back where they belong," Quinn said. "But there are plenty of people who will know the part about Bhindranwale hiding the books is a flat-out lie."

"The hope is the return of the library will overwhelm that detail," Meyers said.

Quinn shrugged, mostly to herself. It rankled, but she couldn't see a better solution.

"You are to get the books back to the Golden Temple as soon as possible," Meyers said. "I'll let you three plan how best to achieve your objective. Keep me apprised." The call ended.

"I don't like the idea of calling in an anonymous tip to some random person at the Golden Temple and telling them where we parked the trucks," Quinn said. "What if someone responds the same way Gill did when the CBI called him?"

James nodded. "You're right. We need to make sure the handoff is public."

"While keeping our involvement in all this quiet," Quinn said. "I can't call Harbir Kaur and say, 'Guess what I found?'"

"No, but Ravi could call her with an anonymous tip and tell her where the trucks are."

"I could write a note spelling out the Bhindranwale/ warehouse angle," Ravi said. "Leave it with the books."

"That should do it," James said. "Tell her to look for the trucks outside the Golden Temple in an hour. That should give us plenty of time to get there."

"Done."

Quinn retrieved Harbir's business card with the library's phone number and handed it to Ravi.

He placed the call and, after a brief exchange, muted his phone. "Harbir's not there today. Should I give them the tip anyway?"

"Do you have another number for her?" James asked Quinn.

"No." She frowned, not thrilled with the idea of giving the information to someone she didn't know and trust. She rocked forward as sudden inspiration hit. "Hang up. I've got an idea."

Quinn followed the two trucks in the Alto as their caravan unceremoniously crawled through traffic toward the Golden Temple. Unfortunately, the exquisite Guru Granth Sahib on the seat next to her carried no magical properties that could clear a path in the road ahead.

Even so, the traffic didn't bother her. The library would soon be back where it belonged.

They drove to the library side of the Golden Temple complex. She spotted Amarjit Kaur standing on the sidewalk exactly where she had asked her to wait. The trucks drove a short distance beyond Amarjit and pulled over. Quinn stopped the Alto in front of her friend. She shut off the engine, leaned across the center console, and shoved the door open.

"Hi," Quinn said. "Hop in." To free up the seat, she hefted the thick book and set it on her lap.

Amarjit slid in and faced Quinn. "I am so pleased to see you again. I—" Her smile dropped away when she noticed the book in Quinn's lap. "Is that a *saroop* of the Guru Granth Sahib?"

"Yes. Let me—"

"You should not be holding it that way." Amarjit flipped her scarf up over her head. "It is terribly disrespectful." It was clear she wasn't happy with Quinn at the moment. "You should not be holding it at all."

"I know and I'm sorry. I have no other choice. Please just hear me out. I need your help."

"I will not help you sell a stolen *saroop*." Amarjit grabbed the door handle and yanked on it.

Amarjit already had a foot out the door when Quinn said, "No. Please. Wait. It's not like that at all. This *saroop* was part . . . *is* part of the Sikh Reference Library taken away during Operation Blue Star." Quinn shoved the driver's seat all the way back, laid the book flat on her lap and opened the front cover. "Read the inscription."

Amarjit twisted around and glanced at the page. "Is that really written in the hand of Guru Gobind Singh Ji?"

"We think so." Quinn opened to a random page to show Amarjit the illuminations.

"Where did it come from?" Suspicion still colored her tone.

"Look, Amarjit. I need you to trust me on this. I can't get into all the details of why or how, but we found the library. It's in those two trucks parked up ahead. We're here to return it. I need your help to do that."

Amarjit's jaw dropped. Her gaze alternated between Quinn and the trucks. "You are sure they are the same books?"

"We are." Quinn handed Amarjit Ravi's letter. "Read this."

As Amarjit's eyes darted back and forth across the page, Quinn watched her astonishment grow. When she finished, she shook her head and asked, "Why do you need my help?

Why not tell the leaders this yourself? Or tell Harbir Kaur
in the library? She should know first."

"I tried contacting Harbir, but she's not at the library
today. And I can't go up to there because we don't want to
draw any attention to ourselves. You can't tell anyone about
James and me being involved in this. At all." She gave
Amarjit a pointed look. "Ever."

Amarjit considered her for a long moment. "I understand." She sounded guarded when she asked, "Is Ravi a
part of this, too?"

"Yes and no," Quinn said. "When we found the books,
we called him to help us, just like I called you. He got
the trucks and helped us move the crates. And he wrote the
letter in Punjabi for us." Everything she said was true.
She just wouldn't add the part about him being a covert CIA
operative.

"What if they ask how I came to find these things?"

"Tell them a stranger handed you the letter and told you
where to find the *saroop* and the trucks."

Amarjit's jaw set with resolve. "I will help you. What do
you want me to do?"

"Take the *saroop* and the letter into the complex. Find
someone you trust, a *granthi* or whoever, and give them to
him. Do it in public if you can. And then have him come out
here to look through the crates in the trucks. Bring as many
people from inside the complex as you can. The more people
who know about this, the better. We don't want anyone
else swiping the library and using it for political or financial gain."

"No, we do not want that." Amarjit eyed the book in
Quinn's lap. "I hope I am forgiven for not following the
protocols for carrying the Guru."

"I think they might let it slide this time." She closed the
book, set it on Amarjit's lap, and laid the coverlet atop it.

"We'll be watching from a distance. Good luck, and thank you for helping us."

"It is my honor to do so." She looked into Quinn's face. "Will I see you again?"

"I hope so. I'm not sure how much longer James and I will be here. We'll try to see you again before we leave. If not, we'll definitely stay in touch. I promise."

Amarjit smiled. "Yes, I would like that." She exited the car and set the book on her head. "Good-bye."

Unexpected emotion constricted Quinn's throat. Her voice was hoarse when she said, "Bye."

Amarjit turned and walked toward the entrance to the complex.

Ten minutes later, Amarjit and a cluster of men re-emerged. James and Ravi jumped down from the cabs of their respective trucks, removed the padlocks from the backs, and sprinted toward the Alto. James climbed into the passenger seat while Ravi dove into the back.

Quinn had parked far enough away to remain unnoticed but close enough to see everything. "From the way they're practically sprinting toward the trucks, I get the feeling Amarjit was successful in convincing them," Quinn said.

James used his phone to record the scene. "I'm sure showing up with a priceless *saroop* didn't hurt."

One of the younger men rolled up the back door, clambered up into the cargo space, and lifted the lid of one of the metal trunks. He stood stock-still and stared at the contents. Time seemed to freeze as everyone looked up at him. Quinn found herself holding her breath as she watched and waited.

He raised his hands and lifted his face to the sky. Then he took a book from the container and held it up for all to see. He handed it off when one of the men below reached for it. Several more were distributed for inspection. They showed each other the stamp of ownership on the inside covers. Tears pricked Quinn's eyes when she watched two older men, who she guessed were survivors of Operation Blue Star, bury their faces in their hands. Their shoulders shook as they wept.

The back door of the other truck was opened and more crates were inspected. The ever-growing crowd meant news of the delivery was spreading like wildfire. A number of phones were held in the air to record the event.

Quinn noted when two people shot out the door that led to the library and ran for the trucks. "I'm bummed Harbir is missing this."

"Check it out," Ravi said from the backseat. "'Sikh Reference Library' is trending on Twitter. And someone is streaming this on Facebook."

"Good," James said. "We won't have to work very hard to get the word out."

Quinn took several sips from her water bottle. The day was beginning to heat up. "Hopefully they'll release Ambassador Sharma soon. I mean, Khalistan hasn't happened and probably won't, but maybe they'll give up on that point. The library is back. That should count for something."

Over the course of the next half hour, they watched the crowd organize and begin to unload the trucks.

Quinn noticed a tiny woman join the crowd. "There's Mrs. Kaur, Harbir's mother." Happiness bubbled up. "I'm so glad she gets to see this. Her husband worked in the library, and the whole family was caught in the middle of Operation Blue Star." Her joy was blunted when she watched Mrs. Kaur swipe at her cheeks. "It must be bittersweet for her. It's great to get the library back, but I'm sure it reminds her of her husband." The memory of the pain in Mrs. Kaur's face the day they spoke was like a knife stab in the heart.

"Do you want to go talk to her?" James asked. "You

deserve a chance to enjoy this moment with her, even if she can't know you were involved."

"I'm supposed to stay out of sight."

"It's okay. The crowd is big enough, and she's standing behind all the cameras. And you two are short. No one will even see you."

Quinn huffed a laugh and slapped his arm with the back of her hand. "I'm not short. I'm vertically challenged."

James's immediate response of, "Yes, dear. Whatever you say," elicited a snicker from the backseat.

"And yes, I would love to talk to her, but she doesn't speak English."

"I can go with you," Ravi said.

James nodded and scrutinized the crowd. "All three of us should go. We can tell her you and I are leaving soon and wanted to visit the Golden Temple one last time."

"And while we were here, we heard about the library and wanted to check it out," Quinn finished for him.

"Sounds good," Ravi said.

They exited the car, circled around, and came up on the crowd as if arriving from inside the complex. They stopped and watched the proceedings a short distance from Mrs. Kaur. Quinn wore her best surprised face when she approached the older woman and said, "Mrs. Kaur?"

A smile of recognition grew. After Mrs. Kaur spoke excitedly to Quinn, Ravi stepped forward and said, "She said she's very happy to see you again."

Quinn pressed her hands together and bowed. "I'm happy to see her again, too."

Through Ravi, Quinn introduced the two men. The sheer delight glowing on Mrs. Kaur's face when James greeted her told Quinn she heartily approved.

After Quinn conveyed the story of how they came to be at the Golden Temple that morning, Mrs. Kaur replied through

Ravi. "She says she was serving in the *langar* when she heard about the commotion at the library. She had to find out what it was all about."

"You must be thrilled that after all these years the library has finally been returned," Quinn said.

"She says she is. She only wishes Harbir was here to see it," Ravi said.

"I'm sorry she's missing it, too," Quinn said. The concern on Mrs. Kaur's face had Quinn asking, "Is everything okay?"

Mrs. Kaur wrung her hands as she spoke.

"Harbir called her three days ago and said she had some business to attend to and asked her to take care of her two daughters. She hasn't seen or heard from her since she dropped the girls off."

"Mrs. Kaur doesn't live with Harbir?" James asked.

"No," Ravi said. "She lives with Harbir's older brother."

Mrs. Kaur related more information. "Harbir and her husband have been estranged for about a year," Ravi said. "He became addicted to drugs and disappeared. She's afraid he contacted Harbir and asked for money or something. She's concerned Harbir might be in trouble."

"Has she contacted the police?" James asked.

Ravi asked Mrs. Kaur James's question. "She did. They told her unless there's a body, there's nothing they can do."

Ravi asked her a question of his own. "I asked her if she knew where the husband is. She said she has no idea. It's been six months since Harbir heard from him. They think he's homeless and likely lives in squalor with other drug addicts."

Quinn wanted to go to wherever the CIA had stashed Gill and kick him in the head. Instead of trying to find a way to stop the rampant drug use in the area and heal the people caught in its web, he exploited it for his own financial and political gain. The guy was lower than a parasite in a scummy pond.

"Would she like for us to see if we can find out where Harbir went?" James asked. "That might ease her mind."

As Ravi translated James's question, relief and gratitude overcame the worried expression on Mrs. Kaur's face. She waved a hand toward the southwest and then the northeast as she replied.

"Harbir's flat is that way," Ravi said with a tip of his head. "She's asked us to go look around. She left her grand-daughters helping in the *langar* and needs to get back."

"We'll do whatever we can to help," Quinn said.

Ravi and Mrs. Kaur had a conversation with more gesticulating toward the neighborhood to the south. It ended suddenly when Mrs. Kaur hurried off toward the door to the library.

"What's up?" James asked.

"She'll be back in a couple of minutes. She went to get the extra key Harbir keeps in her desk. Apparently, her daughters lock themselves out of their flat on a regular basis."

She returned and handed Ravi the key. After bowing their farewells, they crossed the street.

"Harbir's place is within walking distance," Ravi said. He led the way as they shouldered through the crowded street. They walked past open-air stalls selling bright swaths of fabric. The number of people dropped considerably when they pushed past the bazaar and turned onto an alley.

They walked halfway down the block, past residences marked by front doors next to wooden garage doors.

Ravi stopped at one such residence and unlocked the door. They filed inside and tromped up a set of stairs. At the top, they stepped into a family room with a sofa and a couple of chairs pointed at a television. It was all modest and tidy. But with the curtains drawn and stale air surrounding them, the room felt stagnant and oppressive.

"Would it be okay if I opened the balcony's glass door?" Quinn asked.

"I don't see why not," James said.

Quinn opened the drapes and slid back the door. She wasn't sure the warm air laden with the stench of diesel fumes and rotting garbage was much of an improvement.

"I'll go check the bedrooms," James said and disappeared down a hallway.

Ravi sat down at a computer atop a wooden desk in one corner of the room and switched it on.

Quinn, of course, was instantly drawn to the built-in bookshelves covering a section of wall. While many of the titles were Punjabi, a good number were in English. The majority of books were on Sikhism, Sikh history, the Punjab, and Operation Blue Star. Those subjects weren't a surprise to Quinn. She did wonder about the numerous books on Hinduism, though.

Quinn moved away from the bookshelves and searched the family room for any clues as to Harbir's whereabouts. There were no scraps of paper left out on the coffee table, no blank page on the top of a notepad to rub a pencil over to reveal an impression.

She picked up and studied a framed photograph of Harbir and her family. It had to be at least a year old, given Harbir's husband sat next to her. She adjusted her estimate of the photo to being at least three years old when she noted Harbir's adorable daughters appeared to be around eight and ten years old. Quinn hoped the husband and father would get clean and reunite with them.

She returned the photo to the table and looked around.

Framed pictures on a wall caught her attention. She moved closer and examined the two larger prints first. One consisted of small portraits of the ten gurus. The other featured a lone guru, ramrod straight astride a black horse. He was magnificent in swaths of rich pink and purple fabric. A plume of white feathers was attached to the front of his golden turban by a large jewel. A white bird of prey with wings outstretched sat on his gloved fist.

Another family photo, its colors faded with age, hung below the gurus. The family consisted of five members: husband, wife, two boys, and a girl.

Quinn studied it for a moment and then realized the woman in the photo was a much younger Mrs. Rupinder Kaur. That meant the young girl sitting next to her, approximately age eight, was Harbir. The man on the other side of Mrs. Kaur must have been Harbir's beloved father. Quinn's brow furrowed when she noted there were two boys, both older than Harbir, standing behind the other three. She distinctly remembered Harbir mentioning she had an older brother, but not two. Maybe Quinn had misheard.

Her thoughts were interrupted when Ravi asked, "Quinn, can you look through the drawers in this desk? Maybe find a phone number or address or something. I'm still wading through the files on the computer."

"Sure. I can read whatever's in English anyway." She stepped over to the desk and opened the top left drawer. She rummaged through it and found nothing other than a stapler, a box of paper clips, and other assorted office supplies. The next drawer down contained a stack of loose papers and several manila folders. She removed the entire pile and carried it to the kitchen table.

She shuffled through the top papers first. They were various bills and statements. She slid those off to the side and opened the top folder. Inside, a snapshot lay atop several pages printed from a computer. The photo was of two males. Dark peach fuzz on the upper lip and cheeks of the younger put him at about fifteen or sixteen years of age. Quinn recognized him as the oldest boy from the family photo on the wall. In this photo, though, he was older and stared defiantly into the camera with a Kalashnikov rifle cradled in his arms. Her breath caught the instant she looked at the man next to him. He was in his mid-thirties and wore a blue turban and a bandolier of cartridges across his chest.

"Bhindranwale," Quinn said. The golden domes of the Harmandir Sahib gleamed behind them. They were on the roof of one of the buildings inside the complex. The sandbags stacked against the wall directly behind them filled Quinn with foreboding. She flipped the picture over and checked for a date. The hairs on her arms stood straight up. March 1984. It appeared Harbir's oldest brother had fought, and likely died, alongside Bhindranwale during Operation Blue Star.

She set the snapshot to the side and glanced through the papers. Each of the four pages featured a printout of a different black-and-white photo. The first was of a number of men in army uniforms standing inside the Golden Temple complex. Based on the damaged Akal Takht behind them, it had been taken soon after the assault ended. She spread the other three papers out on the table and pored over them. Then she saw it. The same soldier, who appeared to be an officer, was in all four pictures. In one, smoke curled up from a cigarette held between his fingers.

"Holy crap," she whispered. Harbir's words rushed into her mind. A soldier who smoked a cigarette inside the complex had beaten her father in front of her and then dragged him away. Could that soldier and the one in the photo be one and the same?

Quinn stared at the soldier's face and couldn't shake the

weird feeling she knew it. "Holy crap," she said again, and jumped to her feet. Her chair tipped backward and crashed to the floor.

"You okay in there?" Ravi asked.

She scooped up the pages and ran to show Ravi. Heart pounding, she laid the four pages across the keyboard. "The same army officer appears in all four pictures. Do you recognize him?"

Ravi bent over and examined each. "I don't think . . ." He paused and stared up at Quinn, his eyes wide with shock. "Dude. That's Ambassador Sharma."

"That's what I think, too," Quinn said. "He's a lot younger, obviously. But it's definitely him. I think Sharma is the soldier who took Harbir's father away. I wonder if Harbir knows that man is the ambassador."

"I think I can answer that. Listen to what she wrote in a document I found. 'Amongst his many titles, Guru Gobind Singh Ji was called the Keeper of the White Falcon. He is often pictured with one. When the army desecrated the Harmandir Sahib, a white *baaj* circled over it and then perched on a branch.' *Baaj* is Sanskrit for 'falcon,'" Ravi interjected. "'I and many others like me trapped inside and facing death saw it. It was the Guru telling us he was with us. It comforted us then. Now it is his fierce avenger. I am the Guru's bird of prey. I am his falcon.'"

"There's a picture of a guru with the falcon on the wall over there." Quinn's legs almost gave out from under her when all the pieces fell into place. "Her brother, her father, Sharma, the library, the falcon. It's all tied to her and Operation Blue Star. Harbir is the Falcon."

James's voice called out from another part of the flat. "Hey, guys? You'll wanna come see this."

Ravi sprang from his chair, and the two bolted past two bedrooms to the end of the hall. Quinn stopped and stared into the room. Against one wall was a low workbench covered with spools of wire, a soldering iron, alligator clips, batteries of various sizes, and boxes of ammunition. She eyed what was left of a rectangular block wrapped in black plastic sitting atop the workbench. "Please tell me that's a block of cheese," Quinn said.

"I wish," James said. "It's C-4. Harbir made a bomb."

Chapter Thirty

"Now what? Based on when she dropped her daughters off with her mother, Harbir has a two-day head start," Quinn said. "How in the world are we going to find her?"

"We crawl over every inch of this apartment until we find something," James said.

Ravi was already striding down the hallway. "I'll go back on her computer."

"I'll finish looking through the files," Quinn said, trailing behind him.

"I'll get on the phone with Meyers and get him up to speed," James said. "The Indian authorities need to be brought in the loop and be on the lookout for her."

Quinn snagged the printouts from the desk and walked back to the kitchen. After righting the chair, she sat down and flipped open the next file in the stack.

Ravi returned to his place in front of the computer, the keys clacking as he worked. A moment later he said, "Classic rookie terrorist mistake. Harbir never cleared her browser search history."

"Despite the fact she's had an ambassador kidnapped and valuable manuscripts swiped, and fashioned a homemade

bomb, I think she's still more librarian than terrorist,"
Quinn said.

Ravi snorted. "You librarians really stick up for each
other, don't you?"

"That sounds exactly like something James would say."

James walked into the room with his phone to his ear.
Apparently on hold, he swung the mouthpiece down and
asked, "I would say what now?" After Quinn told him, he
smiled and nodded. "Yeah, I'd totally say that because it's
true. You librarians have some kind of secret society—" His
head snapped up. "Yes, I'm still here," he said into the
phone and headed down the hallway again.

"She went to anarchist websites that tell how to make
bombs," Ravi said. "She also did a ton of research on
Sharma, not just his background, but also a calendar of the
events he'd be attending. No big surprise that she also
looked at sites about the exhibition at the Library of Congress." He paused. "This is weird. She looked at some
websites about the *sapta puri.*"

"What's that?" Quinn asked. The folder she'd just examined was a bust. She closed it and pushed it off to the side.

"Hinduism's seven holy cities of pilgrimage."

Quinn sat up straighter. "Wait a second. Harbir has a
bunch of books on Hinduism." She went over to the book-
shelf and scanned the titles. She slid one on Hinduism off
the shelf, flipped to the index, and skimmed it for the
words *sapta puri.* "Here we go." She turned to a map of
India that indicated each holy city with a star. Most were in
northeastern India. "The closest one to Punjab is Haridwar."

"She went to a bunch of sites specifically about Varanasi."

Quinn turned a couple of pages to a glossy picture of
buildings crowded along the banks of a river. She read,
"'Varanasi in Uttar Pradesh is one of the oldest cities in
the world. Built along the Ganges River, it is the holiest
of the *sapta puri.* It is the equivalent of Jerusalem for

Christians and Jews, Mecca for Muslims'"—she looked over at Ravi—"'or Amritsar for Sikhs.'"

"You think she went to Varanasi?" he asked.

"Think about what happened during Operation Blue Star. Her father was taken away from her. She kidnaps Sharma, the man who hauled him off. The Indian Army took the Sikh Reference Library. She steals priceless Hindu manuscripts. The holiest city in Sikhism was invaded and its sacred shrine desecrated."

"She goes to do the same to a temple in the holiest city in Hinduism," Ravi finished for her.

"I bet this was never about Khalistan for her. Just like Gill, she used it to get Samir Singh and the soldiers at the Library of Congress on board. For them it's about Khalistan. For her, it's revenge."

James reentered the room. "Revenge?"

Quinn filled him in on what she and Ravi deduced.

Ravi rubbed his hand over his face in frustration. "The problem is if Harbir is going to go desecrate a temple, which one? I bet there are a thousand in Varanasi."

Quinn crossed the room, sat down on the couch, and set the open book on her lap. "It's got to be meaningful. It has to connect back to Operation Blue Star somehow."

"I'll dig deeper into her browser history," Ravi said, turning back to the computer.

Quinn skimmed the page about Varanasi's long history and turned to the next. When she read two words, a sense of dread flooded her. "I think I know where she's headed," Quinn said in a quiet voice. "There's a temple called the Kashi Vishwanath. Some consider it the most important temple in Varanasi because it houses a sacred artifact of Shiva."

Ravi stopped typing and looked at Quinn over his shoulder. "I've heard of that temple."

"You think she's going after that temple because of that object?" James asked.

"No. The spires of the temple are covered in gold donated by Maharaja Ranjit Singh. He's the same guy that gilded the Harmandir Sahib." She paused. "The Kashi Vishwanath is also called the Golden Temple."

The words had barely passed Quinn's lips before James was on the phone with Meyers again.

Ravi spun around again and pounded at the keyboard. "From here to Varanasi is about twelve hundred kilometers."

Quinn did a quick conversion in her head. "About seven hundred fifty miles. If Harbir drove or took public transportation of some sort, it would take a couple of days. She might be just getting there now. It'll take too long for us to drive."

James ended his call. "We won't drive. By the time we get to the airport, the agency will have a plane gassed up and ready to go."

From the time they left Harbir's flat to when James landed the Cessna TTx at the Varanasi airport, only five hours had elapsed.

The last couple of miles of their cab ride from the airport to the temple were the slowest and most maddening part of the trip. As advertised, Varanasi was incredibly old, and as such, the streets were narrow and congested.

The taxi dropped them off as close as they could get. They would have to walk the rest of the way to the temple itself. Apparently, the Indian government had taken their warning to heart, since the area was crawling with armed soldiers. The temple itself remained open, along with its long-established security checkpoints.

As they pushed through the crowd toward the alleyway

that led into the temple, Quinn couldn't help but notice the stark differences between the two Golden Temples. The one in Amritsar was straight lines and right angles. The shrine was set off by itself with space around it. It was the center of everything and could not be ignored. The buildings around it were spotless and bright and orderly.

The Kashi Vishwanath temple and the area around it was the opposite. It was loud and dirty and chaotic. The temple itself was almost hidden by the buildings around it, wooden signs attached to walls, and multiple lines of telephone wires strung every which direction. In Varanasi, the exterior of the Golden Temple featured spires that were tall, round, and pointed. She wondered if it was as crowded and smelly and overwhelming inside of the temple as it was outside. It wasn't that she thought one group was more or less devout than the other. To an outside observer like herself, it was just the aesthetics were very different.

Quinn's eyes never stopped moving as she scanned faces outside the entrance in hopes of spotting Harbir. "I don't know how she thinks she's going to get inside with all this security," Quinn said. "It's not like they won't see what she's got in her bag."

"Unless she found a tunnel or something to get in some other way," Ravi replied.

"Let's hope that's not a thing," she said.

Ravi surreptitiously handed his nine millimeter to Quinn and said in her ear, "I'm going inside the temple and check things out. You and James can't get in because you're not Hindu. If I don't see Harbir, I'll stay in there as long as I can on the chance she gets through security."

Quinn slipped the pistol into her bag. "You won't be armed."

"That's okay. If I spot her, I'll find someone who is and

have them arrest her." He turned and disappeared into the crowd.

James and Quinn patrolled the area for an hour, continuously searching the crowds that flowed around them. She felt like a salmon swimming upstream.

The oppressive heat and the noise and the stench and the mass of humanity pushing in on Quinn wore her down. Dripping with perspiration, she said, "I was wrong. Coming here wasn't Harbir's plan at all. This soul sucking humidity is gonna kill us while we wait for someone who's not even gonna show up. She's about to do something terrible somewhere, and it's my fault we're not in the right place."

"It's not your fault." James's eyes never stopped moving even as he responded. "If Ravi, Meyers, the agency, or the Indian government thought you were wrong, don't you think one of them would have spoken up? I don't think you're wrong. There are a lot of reasons nothing has happened. Maybe she changed her mind. Or she's waiting for something or she had travel delays." He rubbed a circle on her back with his hand. "This could take some time. We just have to be pa—"

The sound of rapid gunshots from an automatic weapon filled the air. Quinn ducked and looked around for the shooter. Pandemonium erupted as people screamed and scattered for safety.

James grabbed Quinn's hand and ran for cover. They plastered themselves against a wall.

There was no spray of dust coming up from bullets hitting the ground. No victims fell prostrate, wounded and bleeding. And yet the noise of the gunshots continued.

James and Quinn peeked around the end of the wall toward where the sound originated. A rifle barrel poked out from a window of the uppermost floor of a building across the street from the temple's spires. It wasn't aimed at the people in the street below. The rifle put round after round directly into the gilded pinnacles of the Hindu Golden Temple.

The boots of soldiers armed with rifles pounded the ground as they ran past James and Quinn and toward the building.

"Bullets into the temple," Quinn shouted at James and pointed up at the window. "Just like the beginning of Operation Blue Star."

He nodded, his face grim.

Soldiers sprinted toward the entrance of the building. They were driven back by a second rifle firing at them through another window.

"She's not alone," James said.

"I've got to talk to her." Quinn bolted from their shelter and ran for where the soldiers were hunkered down.

"Damn it, Quinn! No!" James shouted and raced after her. "Are you trying to get yourself killed?"

They joined the line of soldiers. Quinn headed toward the man in charge. "No, but I have to talk to her. She might listen to me."

The second they reached the commander, a bullet whizzed past and embedded in the plaster of the wall behind them. He scowled at them. "You should not be here. Go back to safety."

"But I know one of the people up there. I need to talk to her. She'll listen to me."

"No!" the commander shouted. "It is not safe. Go!"

Quinn started to push past the commander. Her plan to run for the building was thwarted when James's arms shot around her waist. He pinned her firmly to him and said, "Oh no, you don't."

"But I have to talk to her." Quinn's voice was strained and desperate.

"Then yell at her from here." His arms cinched tighter.

She dropped her head back against his chest and sighed in defeat. "Fine." She cupped her hands around her mouth and shouted, "Harbir! It's Quinn Riordan. Please stop shooting and come out. You don't need to do this. The library was returned to the Harmandir Sahib this morning. You got what you wanted. Tell us where Sharma is and give yourself up before anyone gets hurt or killed."

A man's voice yelled at them from above. "The Falcon is not here."

"Harbir!" Quinn hollered. "Please!"

"I have told you already," the voice said. "The Falcon is not here. She has sent us to inflict wounds on the Hindus' holiest temple. They will know our pain. We will continue until we are out from under Hindu oppression and live in a free Khalistan."

The rifle pointed at the temple disappeared from the window. It was immediately replaced by something the size and shape of an angular bowling pin.

"RPG!" James shouted.

The rocket-propelled grenade launched and hit one of the spires with an earsplitting explosion. Fire and thick black smoke boiled up. Then six rapid *fwoomps* sounded. One after the other, six grenades detonated and blew the other spire to smithereens. Chunks of debris hurtled through the air.

Flying rubble rained down. Quinn's hand flew up to the top of her head when it felt like someone drove a spike through her skull. She felt something warm and sticky, and looked at her hand. Blood.

Chapter Thirty-One

"Quinn! You're bleeding!"

"I'm okay." Pinpricks of light sparkled in her vision. "Although I think I'm literally seeing stars."

James scooped her up and started walking. "I'm getting you out of here. You can't help Harbir now. After the stunt they just pulled, the army will use deadly force to take out whoever's up there."

Bleeding and woozy, she was in no position to argue. She closed her eyes and rested her head on James's shoulder.

She opened her eyes again when he lowered her to the ground and leaned her against the side of an ambulance. The vehicle seemed to be momentarily abandoned. Given the commotion, that wasn't really a big surprise. James opened the back doors and climbed in. Thirty seconds later he hopped out with a bottle of hydrogen peroxide and a wad of gauze. He knelt down next to her. "How are you feeling?"

"Like Wile E. Coyote when one of his contraptions back-fires and an anvil drops on his head."

"Do you know where you are?" He poured some of the liquid onto a piece of gauze and dabbed the gash. She sucked in air through gritted teeth.

Despite her stinging scalp, she cut her eyes up at him. "I

do. Why? Did you get clunked on the head, too? Amnesia is so clichéd."

He heaved a long-suffering sigh. "Humor me."

"We're in Varanasi outside the Kashi Vishwanath temple." She looked over at its entrance. People streamed out. Many were covered in dust. Some were hurt and helped out by others. "Ravi. He was inside." She struggled to get up.

James kept her down with a hand on her shoulder. "You're not going anywhere. I'll go check on him after I get you cleaned up."

"I'm okay. I'll just have a gargantuan headache later. Please go find Ravi. He might be hurt a lot worse than me."

He helped her stand and walked her to a more protected area. "We don't want anyone finding you and asking how you know Harbir." He pinned her with a penetrating stare. "You'd better be right here when we get back. No rushing into burning buildings, no tackling terrorists, and no shoot-outs at the OK Corral. Got it?"

"Got it." She sat on the ground and gave him a three-fingered salute. "Scout's honor."

He took her raised hand and put a piece of clean gauze in her palm. "Hold this," he said and guided her hand and dressing to the laceration. "Right there. I'll be back in a few."

She watched him speed off toward the temple.

From her position, she could see the action at the building where the attacks had been launched. Gray smoke billowed from the upper windows. Tear gas, she presumed. A couple of minutes later, two Sikh men were frog-marched from the building by a cadre of soldiers in gas masks. There was no sign of Harbir.

James returned with Ravi ten minutes later. His clothes and hair were dusted gray with fine, powdery grit. Other than a cut on the bridge of his nose, he appeared unhurt.

"Glad you're okay," Quinn said. "How's it inside the temple?"

James and Ravi sat on the ground on either side of her. Ravi took the sterile pad she offered him and gingerly blotted the cut on his nose. "It's a pretty big mess. There are some serious injuries, but no fatalities. Not yet, anyway. There's a pile of rubble they have to sift through."

"That doesn't sound good," she said.

"It's not," James said, his voice grim. "Anything happen while I was gone?"

"They took two Sikhs into custody."

"Was Harbir one of them?"

"No. Unless they left her dead inside the building, the guy was telling the truth. I don't think she was up there."

"Crap," James grumbled. "That means she's still running around India with a bomb. What's her plan for it?"

Quinn said, "She's been carrying out precise revenge for specific elements of Operation Blue Star and how it affected her. She's already taken revenge for the books and manuscripts, her father, and the Golden Temple. The only thing she hasn't done yet is set fire to a Hindu library." The second the words left her mouth, three sets of eyes widened to the size of dinner plates.

"Do you think she's going to burn down a library?" Ravi asked.

"I wouldn't put it past her," James said. "Like Quinn said, it's the one thing she hasn't done yet. Which library? Is there one connected with this temple?"

Quinn pondered the question. "If there is, I think she would have been here to watch it burn." Her eyebrows bunched in thought. "Maybe she went to blow up the equivalent of the Library of Congress?" She pulled out her phone and did a quick search. "The National Library is in Kolkata."

Ravi's face scrunched and he shook his head. "No. Like you said, she's after a specifically Hindu library. We're in the most sacred city in Hinduism. What about libraries here in Varanasi?"

Quinn pulled up a list. "There's one at a public university called Mahatma Gandhi Kashi Vidyapith," she said, scrolling through the list. "Oh boy."

James stiffened. "What?"

"Banaras Hindu University. It's only a few kilometers south of here."

"It's got 'Hindu' right there in the name," Ravi said.

Quinn skimmed the information on the university. "Among other things, they study the Hindu Shastras and Sanskrit literature. The problem is, they have a whole bunch of small departmental libraries in addition to a main one. Which one will she go to?"

"I'll call the university and tell them they need to evacuate all of them," Ravi said.

"We need to get there." James surveyed the area. Not far from them sat an unmanned police car. He stood and offered his hands to Quinn and Ravi. "Our ride awaits."

Chapter Thirty-Two

They piled into the police car. James sat behind the steering wheel, Ravi rode shotgun, and Quinn was firmly ensconced in the backseat. With Ravi's help, James entered Banaras Hindu University into the police car's satellite navigation system. James studied the map on the screen, then put the car in gear and raced off.

While James careened through the narrow, winding streets with lights flashing and siren blaring, Ravi called the university's security office. At first, his tone as he spoke in Hindi was calm, yet urgent. It wasn't long before it escalated into a shouting match. He yelled. He shrugged. He pounded the dashboard with a clenched fist. After an extended tirade, he yanked the phone away from his ear and jabbed at the screen with his finger.

"Sounds like that didn't go well," Quinn said.

Ravi cut loose with a rant in Hindi that could peel the paint off a wall. He switched to English and spat, "Those idiots won't evacuate the libraries. They won't act until they're sure it's a credible threat."

"I assume you told them about what happened at the temple," James said.

"I did. The guy's response was, 'We are not a temple.'"
He glowered out the window and muttered, "Moron."

James glanced in the rearview mirror. "I hope things are going better for you, Quinn. Figure out which library Harbir might go to?"

"I'm working on it." She scrutinized the main library's website. "Cool. They have a library school."

"You're such a library nerd."

"You love it and you know it."

"I do." James paused a beat before asking, "Okay, Miss Library Nerd, let's start with the central library. Can anyone just walk in, or is there some kind of process you have to go through to get a pass?"

Quinn skimmed the access rules. "It's pretty strict. You can only get in with a university ID. Without that, you have to pay twenty rupees and need a letter of introduction from a department head."

"Theoretically, then, if Harbir got a letter, or forged one, she could get inside."

"Yes. Absolutely."

"Wouldn't getting into a faculty or departmental library be even more restrictive?" Ravi asked.

"That's my feeling," Quinn said.

"So we start at the central library," James said. "Get us there."

"Okay. It's called the Sayaji Rao Gaekwad Library. Ravi, if you see any signs that point us to it, give a shout," Quinn said and opened a map on her phone.

"Roger that."

"We're almost to the campus," she said. "The roads are laid out in semicircles with spokes. We need to get on Semi Circle Road Number Two. Then turn right on Radial Road Eight. The library will be on the right."

James used the police car to full advantage and sped

through the campus. Quinn went almost horizontal during the violent right turn onto Radial Road Eight.

The car screeched to a stop in front of the library. They jumped out and sprinted for the entrance. Terrified students and faculty rushed from the building.

"Looks like we guessed right," Quinn shouted and dodged a flailing backpack.

They pushed against the stream of people racing out the doors, hurdled the turnstile, and ran into the central rotunda. Tables and study carrels were littered with books and papers left behind.

Bookshelves surrounded the central study area. Above, a second floor of shelving circled the rotunda. There were a million places Harbir could be hiding.

"Where is she?" Quinn shouted.

Ravi spoke with one of the librarians helping evacuate the last remaining students. She pointed toward a specific section of shelves.

"A student saw a woman messing with a bomb in the reference section a few minutes ago," Ravi said. "She's in the *Q*s. Religion."

Quinn looked at the librarian. "*Q?* Religion is *B*."

"That is the Library of Congress Classification," the woman answered in English. "We use Colon Classification."

"Interesting. I'd love to learn—"

James grabbed her hand and jerked her along. "You can nerd out later."

"Right. Sorry."

They weaved their way through tables and chairs to the reference section. They spotted Harbir at the end of a book stack, hunched over a black canvas bag. They stopped several yards away.

Quinn kept her voice calm and conversational when she

said, "Hi, Harbir. It's me. Quinn Riordan. You remember me, right?"

Her head snapped up. When Harbir looked directly at her, Quinn felt the blood drain from her face. The kindness, the intelligence, the humor that had once shone in Harbir's eyes was gone. Now they were dull, hollow, and lifeless. Haunted by the sins of others, she was driven by the demons of revenge, bitterness, and resentment to commit sins of her own.

"Please don't do this. The books from the Sikh Reference Library were found and returned just this morning. Please don't burn this library. It had nothing to do with what happened in 1984."

Harbir stood. "No, I must. They must feel the pain and loss I have lived with my entire life."

"But doing this won't lessen your pain and loss," Quinn said. "Disarm the bomb and give up. Think of your daughters. They need you. Their father is already lost to them. They shouldn't lose their mother, too. Don't let Operation Blue Star destroy any more lives."

Harbir's certainty appeared to be wavering. She glanced down at the bomb. Her face turned to stone when she looked at Quinn again. "I am the Guru's Falcon. I—"

The earsplitting crack of a gunshot made Quinn jump. A dark, round mark appeared on Harbir's forehead. She crumpled to the floor.

"No!" Quinn screamed. She lunged forward, but James held her back. She struggled to free herself and go to her friend. "No!"

James didn't let go. "She's gone."

"She can't be. She has daughters who need her. The library needs her." Quinn stopped struggling and stared at the lifeless body through blurred vision.

A soldier cautiously stepped into view two aisles over. His rifle remained trained on Harbir.

"I know, baby. I'm sorry." James gently pulled her to him and wrapped her in his arms. She buried her face in his chest and sobbed.

After a minute, James whispered, "I'm sorry, but we need to clear out."

She nodded, knowing they couldn't risk being exposed. She lifted her head from his chest, drew in a hiccuppy breath, and wiped her wet cheeks with her fingers. "Let's go."

She was completely numb as they walked through the library and out the door. Eyes to the ground, she never made eye contact with the soldiers, police, and bomb squad swarming the building.

Quinn, James, and Ravi left the police car behind and walked to the edge of the campus. There, Ravi hailed a tuk-tuk and ordered it to take them to the nicest hotel in Varanasi.

Between their dirty, sweaty clothes, Quinn's bloody and matted hair, and the gash on Ravi's nose, they looked like they'd barely survived a zombie apocalypse. It was no wonder, then, that everyone gaped at them as they traveled to the hotel. Quinn was beyond caring. To say it had been a long day was a magnificent understatement.

Once checked into a room, Quinn showered and rinsed the blood from her hair, careful not to have the water spray directly on the wound. Now clean and swathed in a thick hotel bathrobe, she picked up her dirty clothes and considered tossing them onto one of the funeral pyres floating on the nearby Ganges. She stuffed them in a bag for the hotel to launder instead.

She sat on the edge of the bed while James inspected her scalp. "It doesn't need stitches." He stepped back and considered her. "When was the last time you ate?"

She gave him a blank stare. "I have no idea." She thought back over the events of the previous twenty-four hours. "Before going to the Golden Temple this morning, I think? You haven't eaten either."

"That's why I'm calling room service."

"What about Ravi?"

"We talked while you were in the shower. I'll order for him and he'll come over when the food gets here."

James called and placed their order. Then he hiked his thumb toward the bathroom and said, "I'm gonna go take a quick shower."

"Okay." She crawled across the mattress and settled back against a pile of pillows.

James disappeared into the bathroom. Seconds later, she heard the spray of water.

She grabbed the remote and turned on the TV. Video played of the cratered and burning golden spires of the Kashi Vishwanath temple. A sharp sob escaped when a picture of Harbir appeared. She covered her mouth with a hand, her chin quivering as grief welled up. She clicked off the TV and stared at the blank screen.

It wasn't supposed to be like this. Her heart wasn't supposed to break for the person who had caused so much terror and mayhem and destruction. The bad guys they went after were supposed to be evil and soulless and faceless, not someone she knew personally and liked and considered a friend. Who was a mother and wife and daughter.

Overall, her first assignment as a covert operative had been a success. They had recovered irreplaceable items of a long-lost library, busted open a drugs-for-votes conspiracy, intercepted a heroin shipment, and stopped the destruction of a university library. The mystery, the intrigue, the thrill of discovery, the immersion into a different culture had been as exhilarating as she always believed it would be.

But it came with a price she never expected: anguish over the devastated lives left in vengeance's wake, anger over the wanton destruction of precious cultural artifacts, sorrow for failing to save a bitter and broken soul, grief that her actions indirectly led to the death of a friend.

The bathroom door opened. James stepped out wearing only a white towel around his waist. The second he looked at her, he said, "Quinn? Baby, what's the matter?" He was at her side in an instant and gathered her in his arms.

She laid her head on his chest and wept, her hot tears dripping onto his cool skin. When the flood of emotion ebbed, she croaked, "I couldn't save her."

"You tried," he said softly. "It's not your fault."

She sniffed and nodded against his chest. "There was a moment in the library when I thought . . ." She couldn't bring herself to finish the sentence.

"I know. I saw it, too." His arms squeezed her tighter. "You're not responsible for what happened to her. She made choices. Her actions had consequences. Things would be different if she hadn't had the ambassador kidnapped and the manuscripts stolen. She was the one who built a bomb and was about to blow up a library."

"Is that how you deal with knowing your actions led to someone's death? Or inaction?"

"It's even harder when you're the one who ends a life," he said quietly. "You have to remind yourself over and over again that decisions were made and actions were taken by others to put you in that position of life and death."

"Have you, um . . ."

He didn't make her finish her question. "Yeah, I have. Twice. I did what I had to do." His thumb brushed her cheek. "Feel any better? Did what I said help?"

"I do and it did. Thanks." Quinn did honestly feel better.

But she also knew that she was forever changed by what had happened that day.

"You're welcome." He kissed the side of her head. "Any time." He glanced at the clothes they'd bought in the hotel's boutique neatly folded at the foot of the bed. "I should get dressed before the food comes."

"Don't do it for my sake, although my guess is Ravi would appreciate it if you wore pants."

He chuckled and said, "Accurate." James picked up his ringing phone from the nightstand. "Anderson."

She lifted her head and looked at him.

"It's Meyers," he whispered.

She nodded and returned her head to his chest.

After a stint of listening, James said, "That's great. I'll let them know." He paused. "We'll be flying back to Amritsar first thing tomorrow. Our clothes and gear are still there, and Ravi needs to get back to work." He ended the call with, "Roger that."

He dropped the phone on the mattress. "The tech guys got access to Harbir's computer and did their thing. They figured out Samir Singh and his thieving army buddies had Ambassador Sharma holed up in a house in Anacostia."

"No wonder they dropped off the map so fast. That's only a couple of miles from the Jefferson Building. They probably had him stashed before we even realized he'd been taken." She tilted her face up toward his. "Please tell me they got him out safe. I mean, the guy was a massive son of a bitch to Harbir's father, but hopefully he's changed since then. Besides, Kavita and her mom want him back."

"They did. And before you ask, they secured the stolen manuscripts, too."

"Good. And there's no connection to Darvesh Singh?"

"No. The army officer in charge of putting the security team together for the Library of Congress detail has been taken into custody. He's apparently a relative of one of the guys who shot up the Kashi Vishwanath today. He knew which soldiers were pro-Khalistan and recruited them to steal the manuscripts and kidnap Sharma."

"I'm glad Mr. Singh has been cleared. I'm sure Grandpa is, too."

"Mm-hmm. Meyers also told me to tell you job well done and it's time to come home." James kissed her forehead and then bounced off the bed. "But first, we feast."

Quinn watched him gather his clothes with a sense of melancholy. Not only would it take time for her to fully process the events of the past couple of weeks, the bliss of constantly being in James's presence was coming to an end. Again.

The realization their spontaneous op to India had allowed them to stay together longer than expected cheered her. At that very moment, James was supposed to be in Moscow, not dropping his towel in front of her. She hoped another international library emergency would arise before he returned to Russia, requiring them to jet off on another adventure together. If not, she would savor every moment with him until he left. It was all she could do.

She was in love with a spy.

Chapter Thirty-Three

Quinn hiked the front of her strapless violet bridesmaid dress up with both hands and was thankful she'd made it through Brian and Nicole's wedding without a wardrobe malfunction. Now she just had to make it through the rest of the reception and she'd be home free. Her shoes were killing her, and her sweats called to her from her hotel room upstairs. She ignored the urge to flee the reception and pressed on.

She spied Nicole still in her traditional Korean clothes after the *paebaek* and sidled up next to her. "You should be an outfielder for the Dodgers. You can catch anything in that apron of yours. Two chestnuts and three dates? I can't wait to see you with five kids."

"Yeah, don't hold your breath, Q," Nicole said. "My mother rigged it somehow."

"Sure she did."

"That's my story and I'm sticking to it. Besides, I'm not going to let fruits and nuts control how many kids we have."

"That's probably wise."

Nicole glanced around the room. "Where's James?"

"He went to the men's room. He'll be back in a minute."

"How's it going with you two? I haven't even had a chance to ask."

Quinn snorted. "You've been a little busy, being the bride at this shindig."

"True. So how's it going?"

"Good." She was lying. It wasn't good. Only two weeks after she and James had returned home from India, he'd left for Moscow. They'd valiantly tried to stay in touch, and at first they did. But in the intervening three months, things got in the way. The time difference between Virginia and Moscow, his work, and her work and training meant the gaps between those moments when they managed to talk grew longer and longer. What she had suspected all along was true. Long-distance relationships sucked.

"That sounds marginal." Nicole zeroed in on her. "Spill."

Her friend could always see right through her. "He's been traveling constantly for work, so this is the first I've seen him in a while." She couldn't exactly tell Nicole he was stationed in Moscow, so she fudged that part of the story. What she said next was the truth. "He flew in so late last night, we haven't really had a chance to spend much time together yet." The few minutes they'd eked out right before the ceremony had been surprisingly weird and strained. He'd seemed nervous and jumpy.

"Yeah," Nicole said. "I was bummed he wasn't at the rehearsal dinner last night."

Brian, once again in his tuxedo, joined them and took his bride's hand. "I'm sorry to interrupt, but you need to change before we cut the cake." He smiled. "Or is it unpeel the cupcakes?"

"I'll go do that right now." To Quinn, she said, "I gotta go, but I want to talk more about this later. Okay?"

Quinn plastered on a happy face and took Nicole's other

hand in both of hers. "Don't worry about it. It'll be fine. You go change. I want one of those cupcakes."

Nicole grinned and squeezed Quinn's hand before walking off with her groom.

Quinn's smile dropped away and she huffed a discouraged breath. She scanned the room and was about to go hang out at the librarians' table when she felt a hand on the small of her back. Without even looking up, she knew it was James. His familiar scent told her. How much she'd missed it, missed him—it made her physically ache.

"Can you leave for a few minutes and take a walk with me?" he asked.

At the strain she heard in his voice, she looked up into his face. The seriousness she saw filled her with dread. *This is it*, she thought. *He's going to break up with me.* The distance was just too much. Or worse, he'd met someone in Moscow and it was time for him to move on. She put on a brave face and said, "Sure."

He laced their fingers together and led her out of the hall and into the warm summer night. When they reached the edge of the beach at the back of the hotel, she kicked off her shoes and carried them as they walked across the sand toward the surf.

They stopped where the water rolled up the wet sand and almost touched their feet. Quinn turned her head and gazed past the Santa Monica Pier to the park where she and James had sat on a bench during their first date. It was an elegant irony their end would come so near the place of their beginning.

She turned away and stared out at the breaking waves.

James faced the vast darkness before them. When he finally spoke, his voice was soft. "I can't do this anymore. It's too hard."

As much as she'd tried to prepare herself, it didn't help. Tears pooled in her eyes.

She kept them forward, even when he looked at her and said, "I keep thinking about how it was in India, spending every moment of every day with you. It was perfect. And then boom, it's over and I'm shipped off to Moscow. And now with our schedules, we can't even find time to talk. I miss you so much. I'm miserable and I gotta think you are, too." He stopped, took a breath, and blew it out. "Something has to change."

Trying to speak was useless. She couldn't even swallow.

"Because I can't live like this anymore. All I think about is you. I think about how I want to make love to you and have you fall asleep with your head on my chest and wake up the next morning with you in my arms. Always. Forever."

"Wha—, um, what?"

"But it's not just about that," he said, his words now tumbling out in a rush. "I want to sleep and eat and do laundry and watch TV and go on ops and hunt down bad guys with you. I want to do everything and nothing at all. Whatever. Always. With you. I love you. I want to marry you."

Speechless, she blinked at him.

He took a small red box from his pocket and popped up the lid. Nestled in white velvet was a diamond ring flashing in the moonlight. He looked into her eyes. "Quinn, will you marry me?"

She stared at him, trying to comprehend what he'd just said. In an instant, her mind cleared. He was asking her to spend the rest of her life with him. A life where she would wake up and see his face every morning regardless of the continent they were on. A life where they might go to the grocery store together one day and dodge bullets the next. A life where the only thing that truly mattered was that he would forever be by her side, and she by his. Of course there was only one answer. "Yes." She smiled up at him. "Yes."

His grin lit up his face. He took the ring from the box and slipped it on her finger. Then he pulled her into a long, tender kiss.

The kiss ended, but James kept her firmly in his embrace. His slow, sexy smile nearly had her clawing at his clothes. "I hope you don't mind if your ring doesn't shoot pepper spray, have a saw hidden in the band or function as a secret decoder."

She smiled and kissed him. Some time passed before she finally answered, "I don't mind at all." She rested her left hand flat on his chest and admired the ring. *Her* ring. A *real* engagement ring. "It's beautiful. I love it." She glanced up at him. "And I love you." Gazing at her hand again, she said, "To be honest, I've missed not having rings on that finger." She rolled her hand a little. The moonlight caught the facets, causing the diamond to sparkle like a star in the dark sky above.

"From now on that finger will never be naked again. As for the rest of you . . ."

She laughed when he waggled his eyebrows.

Her smile dimmed. "You have to go back to Moscow."

"I know. I just couldn't face being stuck there without a light at the end of the tunnel, you know? I think we can handle the separation better as long as we know we'll be getting married."

"I think so, too. And I have my training to finish up."

"Exactly. Once you're done and we get married, who knows where we might end up. The agency likes using real-life husband-and-wife teams in the field. And they already know how great we are together."

She was about to explode with excitement. "Traveling the world with my handsome spy husband? I can't wait."

"Neither can I." He kissed her again and then looked down at her with a wistful smile. "And as much as I like it out here, making plans with you and kissing you in the moonlight, we have a reception to get back to. We don't want to antagonize the bride."

"No, we don't." She looked down at her ring. "Should we tell Nicole now or do we wait? I don't want to step on her and Brian's big day."

James chuckled. "Are you kidding? She'll want to know why you didn't text her while I was proposing. You wait and tell her later we got engaged at *her* reception? She'll throttle you."

"Oh, man. You're right. We'll take her aside and tell her in private right after they do the cake. If she wants us to announce it tonight, great. If not, we can spread the news tomorrow." She cocked her head. "There *is* someone I'd like to tell first even if it is late. Do you have your phone? This dress has an appalling lack of pockets."

"The number is already programmed in," he said, handing it to her.

"Of course you know who I'm going to call. Smartypants." She touched the screen and put the phone to her ear.

"Hello?" the voice said.

"Hi, Grandpa. Guess what?"

Can't get enough of Quinn and James?

Look for more adventures in

AN UNCOMMON HONEYMOON,

coming soon from
Zebra Shout.

And keep reading for
a sneak peek!

The bottom of Quinn Ellington's unbuttoned white lab coat fluttered behind her like a superhero's cape as she strode along the corridor inside a Frankfurt pharmaceutical research facility. James Anderson kept pace beside her, his matching lab coat equally billowy. The aluminum briefcase hanging from his hand sporadically brushed against her thigh.

Dr. Dieter Ziegler and his assistant had joined a meeting in the conference room at the end of the hallway a moment before. That meant she and James had thirty minutes to slip into Ziegler's office, steal the vials from his safe, and sneak out without being noticed.

No problem.

Quinn dipped her chin and adjusted her black-rimmed glasses, shielding her face from the woman passing them from the other direction.

"You want to do something next weekend?" James asked when the woman was out of earshot.

She smiled at his attempt to keep her loose during her first mission as a full-fledged CIA undercover operative. "I can't."

"Why not?"

"I've got a wedding to go to."

"Blow it off."

"I can't. I kinda have to be there."

"Why?"

"I'm the bride." Their pace slowed as they neared Dr. Ziegler's office.

"You know, now that you mention it, I have a wedding to be at, too."

"Yeah? That's weird. I wonder if it's the same one."

James held the ID badge he'd liberated from an unsuspecting senior scientist in front of the electronic lock. When the red light turned green, he pushed in the door and held it open. Quinn swept past him into a small front office.

A brass nameplate placed at the front edge of the desk informed them Sabine Müller was the name of Ziegler's assistant.

"Maybe I'll see you there," Quinn said. She tried the knob on the door leading to the inner office. Locked. She slipped the lock pick set from the pocket of her lab coat and zipped open the case. She took two implements and slid the wiry ends into the lock.

"How about you meet me at the front of the sanctuary, say 4:15 or so?" James asked.

"I can do that. I hope you don't mind, but my dad will be with me. Fair warning. He'll be armed."

"No need for a shotgun. I'll be there of my own free will."

One of the tumblers in the lock gave way. "Nah, it'll just be his sidearm under his tux jacket. You know how Marines are."

"I do," he said. "I'll be armed, too, by the way."

"Me too. I picked up a pretty thigh holster for the occasion. It's white and lacy. You'll like it."

She smiled at his rumbling growl.

"All right, you two. That's enough," she heard the long-suffering Darius Sampson say through the communication device in her ear. "You keep it up and I'm gonna hurl all over this van full of expensive surveillance equipment. I'll tell Meyers to send you the bill."

"Okay, okay. We don't want any hurling," James said.

"What are you two doing anyway, going on an op so close to your wedding? Sounds crazy to me."

"The wedding has totally consumed my life the last two months. I needed a break before someone tossed me in a rubber room and threw away the key," Quinn said.

"Hard to argue with that, I guess," Darius replied.

"I'm sorry I wasn't able to help you more with all the planning," James said. "Living in Moscow made it difficult."

"It's okay. My mom was a huge help. I'm glad your stint there is over."

The lock gave way and she cracked open the door.

"We're in," Quinn said as she and James stepped into Ziegler's office. The door clicked closed behind them.

"Roger that," Darius said. "Ziegler and his assistant are still in the meeting."

Quinn took a quick survey of the room. The large office was well appointed with its massive wooden desk, leather couch, and bar with bottles of various types of liquor on the shelves behind it. One of the perks of being the company's chief research officer, she supposed. Ziegler might have occupied a corner office, but its location didn't mean it was meticulously kept. The desk was cluttered with stacks of scientific journals, papers, and files. Not one more book could have been wedged into the overstuffed bookcases. As much as the librarian in Quinn was drawn to examine and straighten those books, she resisted. She wasn't there for that.

James handed her the metal briefcase and headed for the desk. He inserted a flash drive into Ziegler's computer and began to type.

Quinn went straight for the painting of a tranquil lake setting located on the wall above the sofa. She set the briefcase on one cushion and stepped up onto the other. Reaching out, she slid the painting mounted on rails to one side to reveal a wall safe.

From her lab coat pocket, she removed her smartphone and a thin cable. She plugged one end of the cable into her phone and the other into a port next to the keypad on the face of the safe. With a tap on the screen, she launched the CIA-developed app that would provide her with the digital key.

While the app ran, she took a small, flat plastic box with Ziegler's fingerprint on a thin piece of latex from her other pocket and opened it. She placed the latex on the pad of her thumb and breathed on it several times to moisten it.

Her phone chimed and displayed the six-digit passcode. She pressed her thumb to the biometric scanner and punched the code into the keypad.

The safe started to beep.

Crap.

Was it supposed to do that?

"Babe? I might have set off—" The beeps ceased and she heard a soft click. She released a relieved breath. "Never mind. We're good," she said and swung the safe's door open.

Inside, a half dozen glass vials of emerald-colored liquid were precisely arranged on a shelf. "Why is the evil stuff always green?"

"That mandate is clearly stated in Section 37 of the

League of Evil Scientists Handbook," James replied, his eyes never leaving the computer screen. "I'm sure Ziegler checked to make sure the color of his psychotropic agent was regulation."

Quinn grinned as she lifted one of the vials from the safe and carefully secured it in the slot cut out in the gray foam lining the briefcase. "I bet he did. He wouldn't want to get kicked out of the League of Evil Scientists for such a heinous violation." She repeated her actions and secured another vial. "Almost done?"

"Yeah. I uploaded the Trojan horse onto his system already. I only need a couple more minutes to finish copying the restricted data files."

"Uh, guys?" Darius said. The tightness in his voice snapped Quinn to attention. "You may not have a couple of minutes. Ziegler and his assistant just left the conference room."

"What?" she said with a frown. "He's not supposed to be out of there for at least another twenty minutes."

"I dunno. No one else has left. Even the CEO is still there. Hang on. Maybe they're not . . ." After a pause, Darius said, "They are on their way to you."

"Copy." Under his breath, James grumbled, "Dammit."

Adrenaline flooded Quinn's system. Moving quickly, she snatched the last two vials in each hand and jammed them into the foam. She slapped the briefcase shut and snapped the fasteners.

Quinn closed the safe, removed the phone cable, and slid the painting back in place. She leaped from the couch, grabbed the briefcase's handle, and looked at James. His blue eyes were slightly wild as he urged on the computer. "Come on, come on, come on."

"Forget it. We gotta go."

"Done!" James yanked out the flash drive and sprang to his feet.

The urgency in Darius's voice sliced through her. "Too late. They'll see you if you come out now."

"Maybe we can chance it and tell them we were waiting for him but decided to leave," Quinn said.

James shook his head. "This is a restricted floor. We're not even supposed to be here."

"Crap. You're right." She looked at the bar and then at James. "Do we hide or shoot our way out?"

"Make a decision, guys," Darius said. "They're almost there."

James grabbed Quinn's hand and pulled her behind the bar. "We hide. Let's hope they came back to get something for the meeting and will leave again right away. If not, we tranq them and take off." Crouched behind the bar, they balanced on the balls of their feet, removed their tranquilizer pistols from their ankle holsters, and held them at the ready.

"They're about to open the outer door," Darius said.

Quinn strained to hear clues as to exactly where Ziegler and Sabine were. She heard their muffled voices through the wall between the two offices. If James was right and they had come back for something related to the meeting, was it inside Ziegler's office? If so, he would go to unlock the door any second. She hoped she hadn't left any evidence informing Ziegler the lock had been picked. Otherwise, trouble would come their way fast. She swallowed and tightened her grip on her pistol.

She flinched when she heard what sounded like a body slamming against the door. The knob rattled, but the door remained closed. There was another loud thump.

James glanced at Quinn in confusion. She shrugged in response.

The doorknob turned and the door flew open. Ziegler

murmured in a low tone, prompting a giggle from Sabine. Heavy breathing punctuated throaty moans.

Oh.

God.

No.

No, no, no.

Quinn's blue eyes rounded and she looked at James. He wrinkled his nose in reply.

She heard two clunks on the floor, which she assumed was Sabine kicking off her shoes. A white lab coat arced through the air and draped over the bar.

Ziegler spoke in an urgent growl.

Sabine's response was breathy and pleading.

For a fleeting moment, Quinn considered turning the tranquilizer gun on herself.

Air gusted from the couch cushions with a *fwoomp*, the telltale sound indicating the amorous couple had crashed onto the leather sofa.

It sounded like a wrestling match had broken out.

Quinn winced when Sabine expelled a prolonged, guttural groan.

At the unmistakable clap of a hand slapping flesh, Ziegler blurted, *"Ach! Ja!"* With each smack, the level of his lusty enthusiasm rose.

Quinn bit her lip and struggled to keep the giggles at bay.

James's face relaxed into a grin.

The movements on the couch turned rhythmic.

A boisterous duet of ardent and sustained ecstasy filled the room.

Quinn grimaced and squeezed her eyes shut.

When the exclamations subsided and all she heard was ragged breathing, Quinn dared to open her eyes and peek at James.

He winked and shot her a crooked smile, which quickly faded. The eyes boring into hers turned intense and probing.

She held his gaze and gave him a sharp nod. Time to focus.

Quinn concentrated on the sounds coming from Ziegler and Sabine. Neither spoke as they rose from the sofa. Clothes were straightened and the lab coat disappeared from atop the bar.

One sound Quinn hoped not to hear was Ziegler settling in behind his desk. If that happened, they could be stuck behind the bar for who knew how long. Would they have to tranquilize him and his assistant to escape after all?

As Ziegler and Sabine moved about the room, Quinn kept her stare zeroed in on the open end of the bar. If either came around to pour drinks, she would drop them.

To her great relief, Ziegler didn't take a seat at his desk, nor did either step behind the bar. The door between offices opened and shut. Quinn blew out a long, slow breath.

"They're on their way back to the conference room," Darius said after the outer door closed with a clunk. "You two okay?"

"Yeah, we're fine," James said.

"What happened? I couldn't hear anything through your comms."

"We were witness to what would best be described as a quickie," Quinn said.

Darius snickered. "I wondered. They looked pretty happy coming out of that office."

James and Quinn stood and hurried out from behind the bar. "Get us out of here and we'll describe every awkward detail for you later," James said.

"Nah. I'm good." After a beat, Darius said, "The hall is clear. You're good to go."

"Copy," James said, holstering his pistol. Quinn did the same.

Seconds later they were through the front office and out the door. Once in the hallway, they turned and retraced their steps.

They were halfway to the elevator when Darius said, "Security guard incoming from the corridor up ahead."

"Is there a bathroom or janitor's closet we can duck into?" Quinn asked.

"Nothing close enough," Darius said. "If you hurry, you can get into the stairwell next to the elevator before he turns the corner. Try not to look too obvious, though. You don't want to catch the eye of the security people watching these feeds."

Quinn practically jogged to keep pace with James when his stride lengthened. He arrived at the door first and shoved it open. Quinn caught a flash of a gray uniform as she swept past James and started down the stairs.

The sound of their pounding feet echoed off the concrete walls of the cavernous stairwell. They descended one floor and had three more to go when they heard the metal door bang closed.

"He's after you. Step on it," Darius said.

"Halt!" a voice boomed from above.

When James leapt over the steps two at a time, so did she.

Being short, it wasn't an easy feat. "I feel like a mountain goat," she said between panted breaths.

They tore past the door with a "1" painted on it.

"One more floor," James said. "Darius, we need the van out front."

"On it."

"Halt! Jetzt!" the voice shouted.

Quinn launched over the last three steps and stuck her landing next to the door that exited to the ground floor.

She stooped, took her tranquilizer pistol from its holster, and slipped it into her lab coat pocket. James did the same.

Shoulder against the door, she held the handle and looked at James. "Ready?"

"Ready."

Quinn yanked open the door. They left the stairwell and kept their steps measured as they walked down the short corridor and into the lobby.

Her eyes darted about, surveying the area. Two security guards stationed on either side of the exit scanned faces as people left the building.

Quinn slipped her hand into her pocket and wrapped her fingers around the pistol's grip. She looked through the glass doors. No sign of the van. "Darius?"

"Almost there," Darius said. She heard the blast of a car horn. "Move it, ya jerk!"

James glanced around. "Hurry up, buddy."

"Halt!"

Quinn looked over her shoulder. The guard from the stairwell sprinted toward them, pistol in hand. He did not look happy.

She withdrew her pistol, whirled around, and fired.

At the sound of the gunshot, shrieks broke out. People dove for cover.

The security guard stumbled forward, his face registering shock. He dropped to his knees and collapsed facedown on the marble floor.

Next to her, James fired off two shots. She spun around and watched the two guards by the exit drop.

Quinn and James sprinted past the unconscious men and burst through the front doors, leaving chaos in their wake.

To their left, a black van took a turn at an impressive clip. Two of its tires nearly lifted off the ground.

They darted across the cement courtyard and arrived at the edge of the parking lot at the same time the van screeched to a stop.

James jerked open the back door. Quinn flung the briefcase into the back of the van and dove in after it. James hauled himself up behind her. "Go!" he shouted and slammed the door.

The van's violent acceleration sent Quinn tumbling backward. She crashed into James, pinning him against the back. He wrapped her in his arms and kissed the side of her head.

Trembling from the river of adrenaline coursing through her veins, she had no intention of moving. "Well, that was exciting."

"It was," he replied. "If we can handle that, our wedding will be a breeze."